HAPPY HOUR ™

PETER MILLIGAN

MICHAEL MONTENAT

FELIPE SOBREIRO

ROB STEEN

AHOY COMICS

COMICSAHOY.COM   🐦 @ AHOYCOMICMAGS

HART SEELY - PUBLISHER
TOM PEYER - EDITOR-IN-CHIEF
FRANK CAMMUSO - CHIEF CREATIVE OFFICER
STUART MOORE - OPS
SARAH LITT - EDITOR-AT-LARGE

DAVID HYDE - PUBLICITY
DERON BENNETT - PRODUCTION COORDINATOR
KIT CAOAGAS - MARKETING ASSOCIATE
LILLIAN LASERSON - LEGAL
RUSSELL NATHERSON SR. - BUSINESS

PRINTED IN THE U.S.A. - FIRST PRINTING - AUGUST 2021 - ISBN: 978-1-952090-05-9

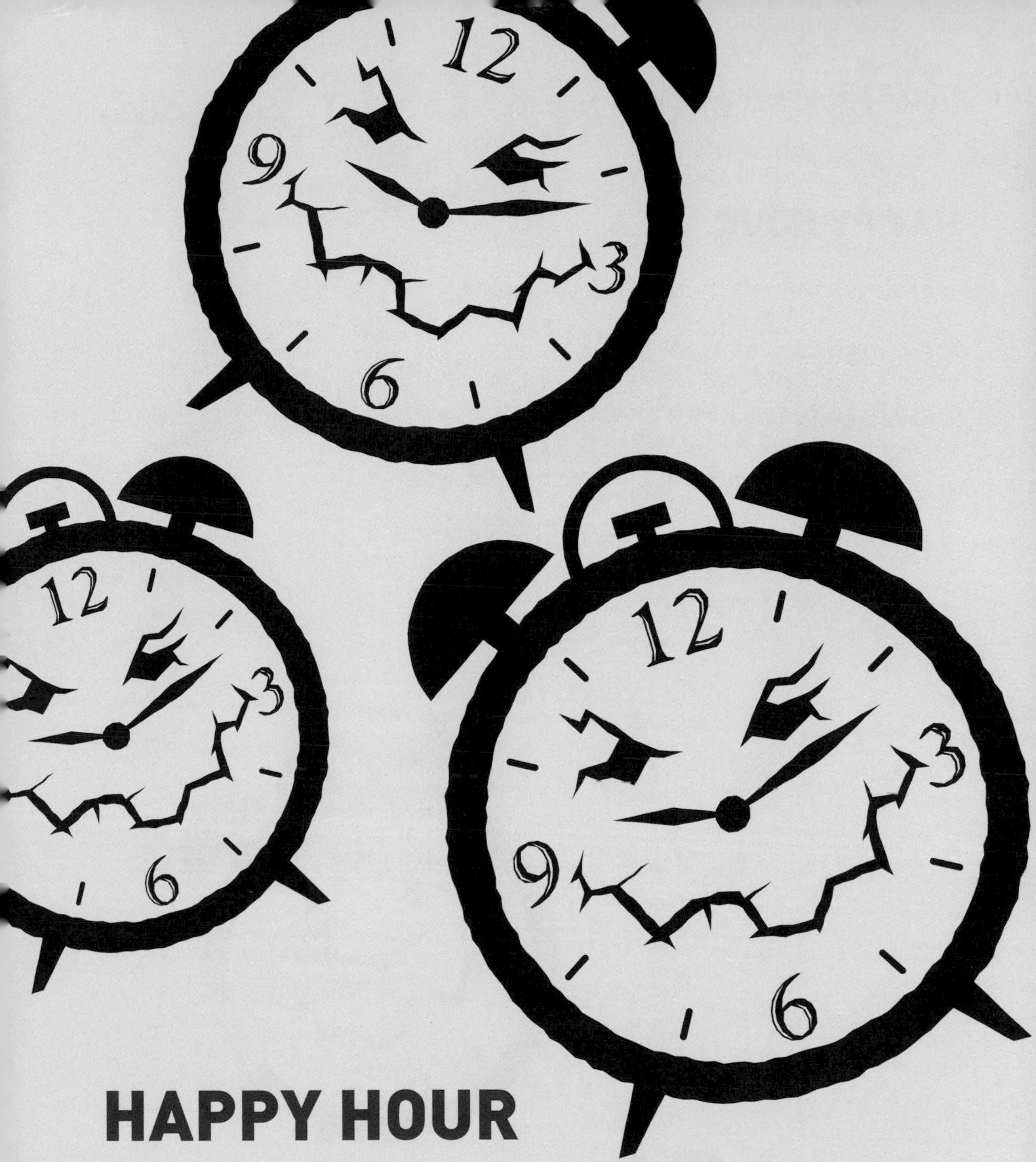

HAPPY HOUR

PETER MILLIGAN WRITER
MICHAEL MONTENAT ARTIST
FELIPE SOBREIRO COLOR
ROB STEEN LETTERS

MICHAEL MONTENAT COVER
TODD KLEIN LOGO
JOHN J. HILL DESIGN
DERON BENNETT ASSOCIATE EDITOR
TOM PEYER EDITOR
CORY SEDLMEIER COLLECTION EDITOR

CREATED BY PETER MILLIGAN AND MICHAEL MONTENAT

C O N T E N T S

HAPPY HOUR

INTRODUCTION

[This is a two-part transcript of remarks delivered by U.S. Rep. H. Corn Broderick III (R-[REDACTED]) from the floor of the U.S. House of Representatives.]

I.

Madame Speaker, colleagues, friends, and especially my good neighbors in the 57th District of the great state of [REDACTED].

Benjamin Franklin's tripartite promise for this majestic land is enshrined in his *Federalist Papers:*

1. Life
2. Liberty
3. And the pursuit of happiness.

We living Americans, plus our ancestors, plus their descendants, totally own the first two, starting with the sanctity of *life*. We thus close our eyes and sway to the music of our protectors: the crackle of crisp commands from the police loudspeaker, the relaxing hum of the military drone above. Life, in those precious moments, is affirmed.

And it could not soberly be said that the United States of America does not own *liberty*. Despite relentless attacks—from Bidenites and Neo-Bidenites alike—liberty is preserved and cherished from sea to shining sea by vigilant citizens' groups as diverse as the Daughters of the American Revolution and the Sons of the American Revolution.

But whither *the pursuit of happiness?* One searches in vain. It seems that every time our country stands tall and takes action—on anything at all, from *regime change* to *qualified immunity*—the arch-complainers swarm toward the light like filthy cockroaches, bringing with them the neo-bellyachers, crypto-whiners, lonely wallflowers, faithless clergy, regretful newlyweds, and tragic, tuberculin street hustlers that comprise the great, unworthy majority of American voters.

These shameless bottom-feeders tear through life's Golden Corral buffet and stupidly heap their plates with the foodstuffs of woe. Which would be God's own justice if these vermin only poisoned themselves. Instead, they splash 1,000 little gobs of toxicity onto their neighbors' plates through "protest," "Twitter," and other wanton exhibitions of wickedness. Their festering rot infects the very lifeblood of our Republic.

There ought to be a law.

And there *is* one, if only in this visionary picture-book for small children and the young-at-heart, *HAPPY HOUR*, which you (and I) are about to read for the very first time. A Yahoo search asserts that author Peter Milligan isn't American, which has the ring of falsehood and slander. His gallant crusade to encode into law the deviltry of discontent, which I am told is outlined here in his ambitious work, could only have sprouted in the free, unmasked air of Texas, Florida, Maricopa County, or Staten Island (an uncorrupted sliver of New York City that has long deserved statehood).

I ask for a recess so that you, the esteemed members, my staff, and I may read *HAPPY HOUR* in full. I will return to summarize once we have fully absorbed its wisdom. Thank you.

II.

Okay…okay…first of all, it's ***not for children***, right? I thought because of the pictures…the pictures! Lord, scrape them from my sight with your sword! The pictures! They made it so real. So real. And the colors…

I think we can now agree with Yahoo that Peter Milligan is not American. You'd have to be…foreign. Because this…this stack of pages filled with I-don't-know-what…is anything but a plan to make America great. It's…a satire.

A *satire!!*

You know what satire is, don't you, friends? It's a joke where they take out the humor and replace it with hate! And they punch up! To bruise! The more powerful! Mockingly! Don't do that, friends! Don't do that! It's wrong to punch up!

Look at this! Who is this artist? Michael Montenat. Where did he come from? What does he want? How does he get up every day, put his coat and tie on, sit at his desk, and draw pictures like this? Where is that part again…Here. What is he doing with her toes? (Swallows hard.)

Friends, you know me. You know that I have given my all to this nation as a U.S. representative, a state legislator, Commissioner of Sewers, churchman, barbershop quartet baritone, beauty contest judge, and car wash entrepreneur. In the wake of the bloody violence *HAPPY HOUR* has done to my own happiness, I declare I have now given my country…enough. More than enough.

Effective immediately, I resign from the U.S. House of Representatives.

H. Corn Broderick III
April 2021

H. Corn Broderick III is the former U.S. Representative from the 57th District of the state of [REDACTED].

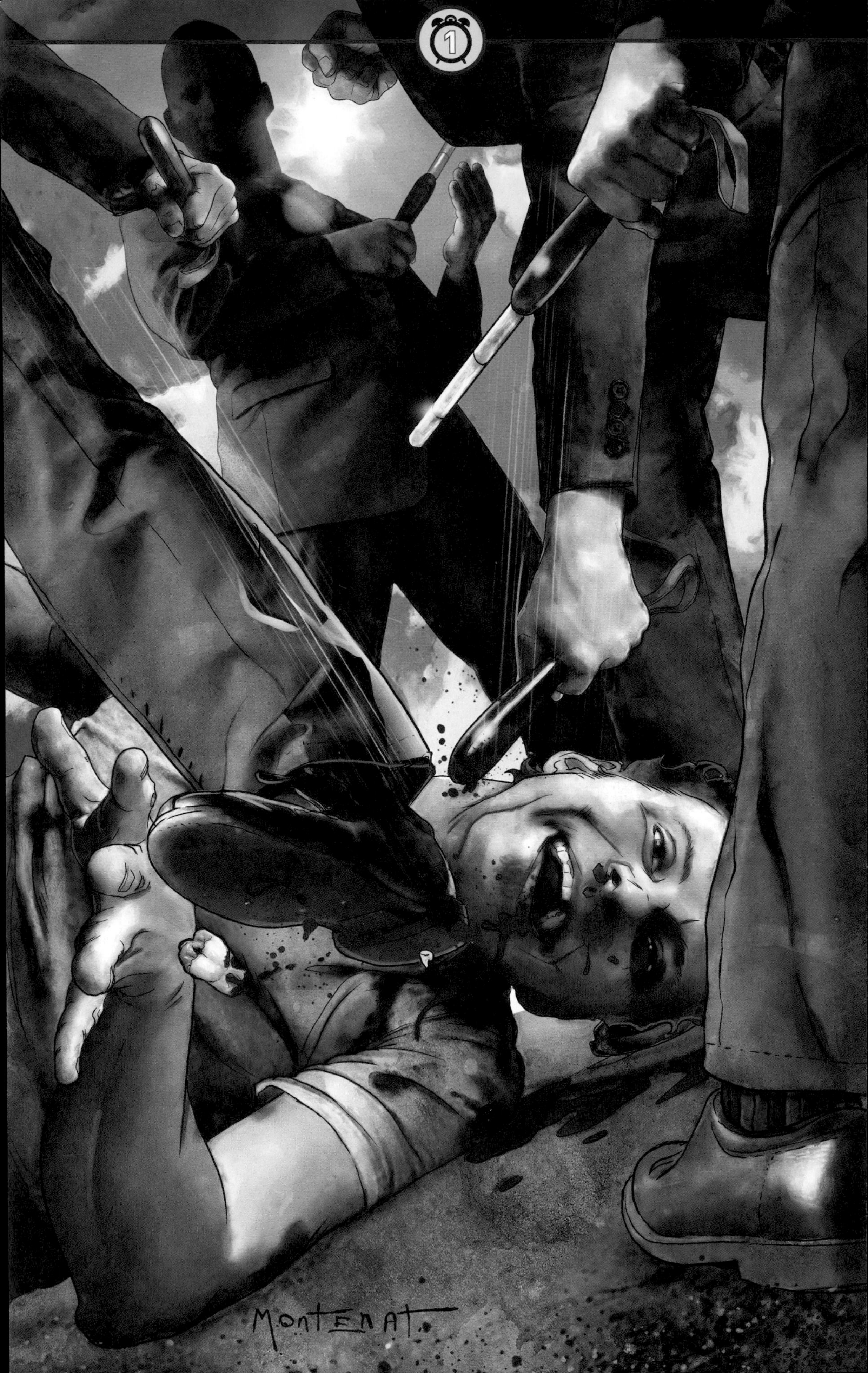
1
MONTENAT.

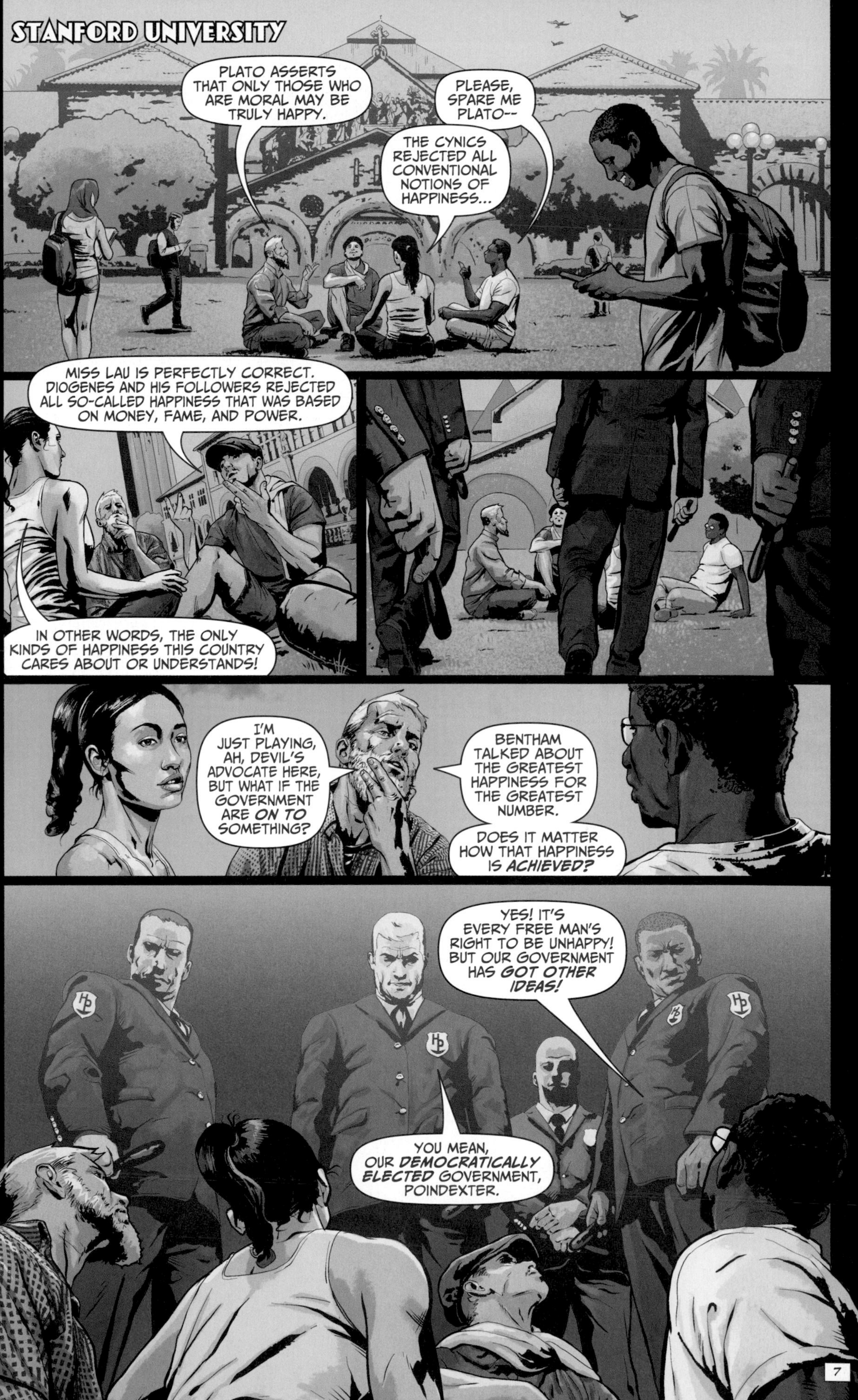
STANFORD UNIVERSITY
PLATO ASSERTS THAT ONLY THOSE WHO ARE MORAL MAY BE TRULY HAPPY.
PLEASE, SPARE ME PLATO--
THE CYNICS REJECTED ALL CONVENTIONAL NOTIONS OF HAPPINESS...
MISS LAU IS PERFECTLY CORRECT. DIOGENES AND HIS FOLLOWERS REJECTED ALL SO-CALLED HAPPINESS THAT WAS BASED ON MONEY, FAME, AND POWER.
IN OTHER WORDS, THE ONLY KINDS OF HAPPINESS THIS COUNTRY CARES ABOUT OR UNDERSTANDS!
I'M JUST PLAYING, AH, DEVIL'S ADVOCATE HERE, BUT WHAT IF THE GOVERNMENT ARE *ON TO* SOMETHING?
BENTHAM TALKED ABOUT THE GREATEST HAPPINESS FOR THE GREATEST NUMBER.
DOES IT MATTER HOW THAT HAPPINESS IS *ACHIEVED?*
YES! IT'S EVERY FREE MAN'S RIGHT TO BE UNHAPPY! BUT OUR GOVERNMENT HAS *GOT OTHER IDEAS!*
YOU MEAN, OUR *DEMOCRATICALLY ELECTED* GOVERNMENT, POINDEXTER.

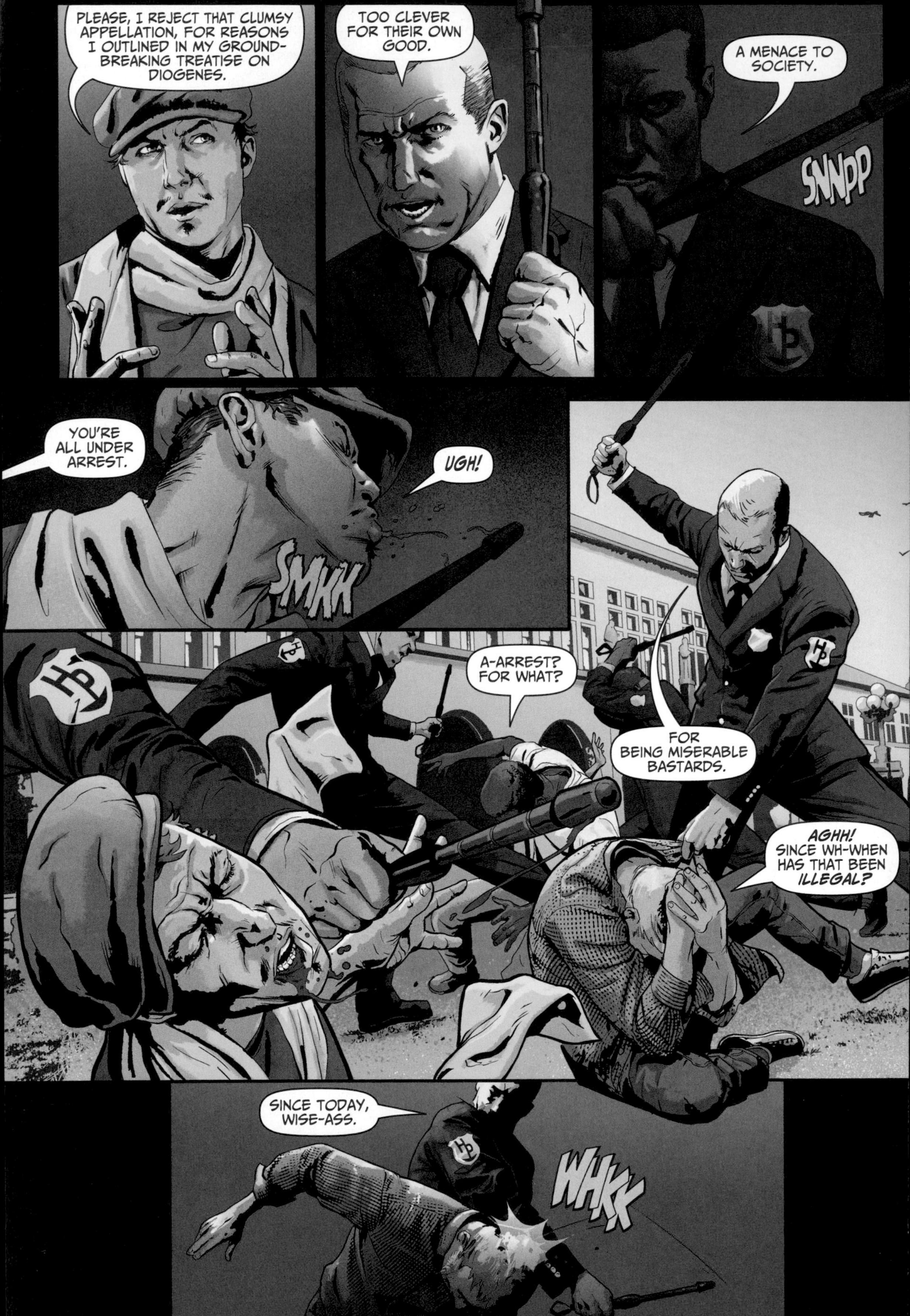
PLEASE, I REJECT THAT CLUMSY APPELLATION, FOR REASONS I OUTLINED IN MY GROUND-BREAKING TREATISE ON DIOGENES.
TOO CLEVER FOR THEIR OWN GOOD.
A MENACE TO SOCIETY.
SNNPP
YOU'RE ALL UNDER ARREST.
UGH!
SMKK
A-ARREST? FOR WHAT?
FOR BEING MISERABLE BASTARDS.
AGHH! SINCE WH-WHEN HAS THAT BEEN ILLEGAL?
SINCE TODAY, WISE-ASS.
WHKK

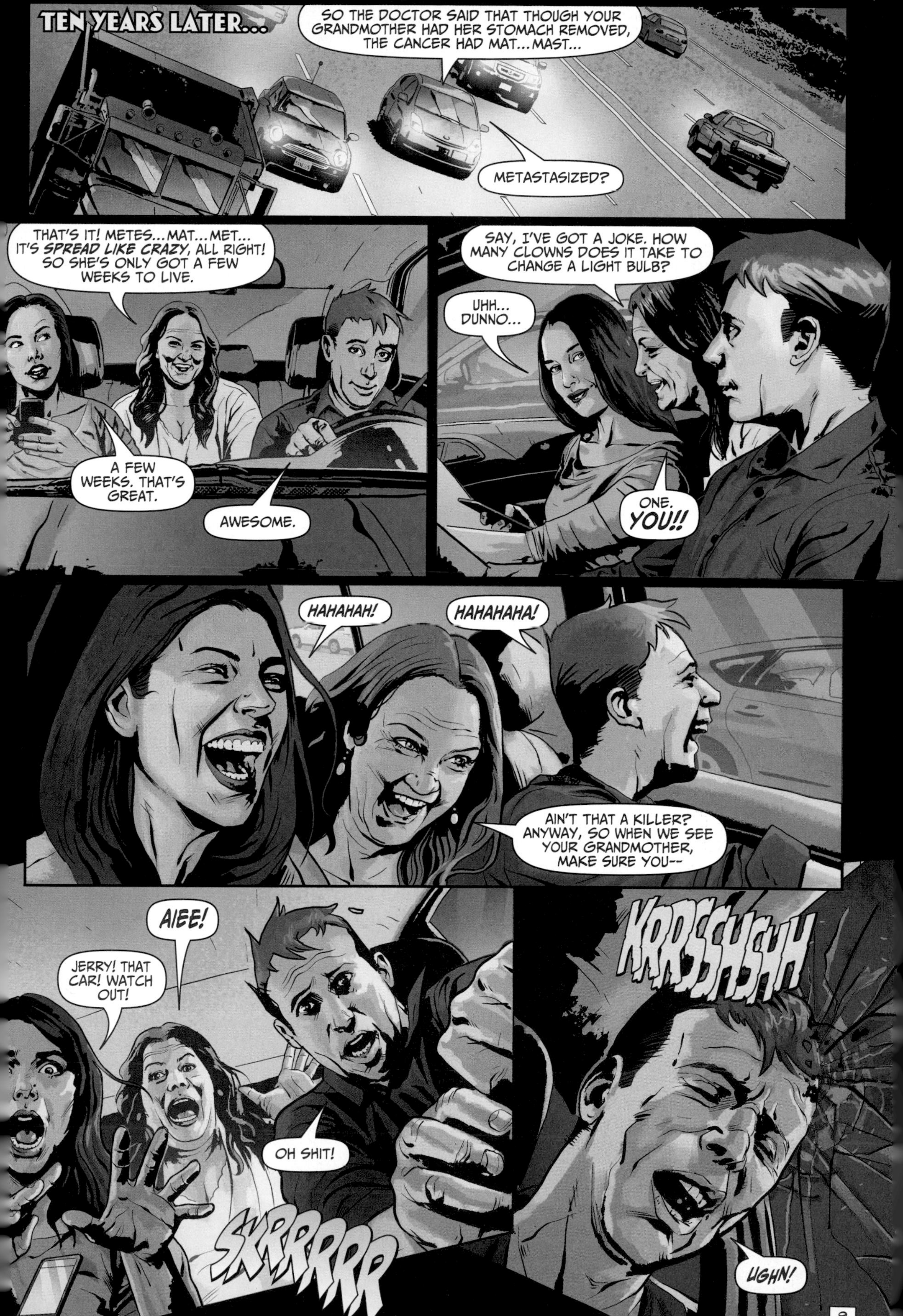
TEN YEARS LATER...
SO THE DOCTOR SAID THAT THOUGH YOUR GRANDMOTHER HAD HER STOMACH REMOVED, THE CANCER HAD MAT... MAST...
METASTASIZED?
THAT'S IT! METES... MAT... MET... IT'S SPREAD LIKE CRAZY, ALL RIGHT! SO SHE'S ONLY GOT A FEW WEEKS TO LIVE.
A FEW WEEKS. THAT'S GREAT.
AWESOME.
SAY, I'VE GOT A JOKE. HOW MANY CLOWNS DOES IT TAKE TO CHANGE A LIGHT BULB?
UHH... DUNNO...
ONE. YOU!!
HAHAHAH!
HAHAHAHA!
AIN'T THAT A KILLER? ANYWAY, SO WHEN WE SEE YOUR GRANDMOTHER, MAKE SURE YOU--
AIEE!
JERRY! THAT CAR! WATCH OUT!
OH SHIT!
SKRRRRR
KRRSSHSHH
UGHN!

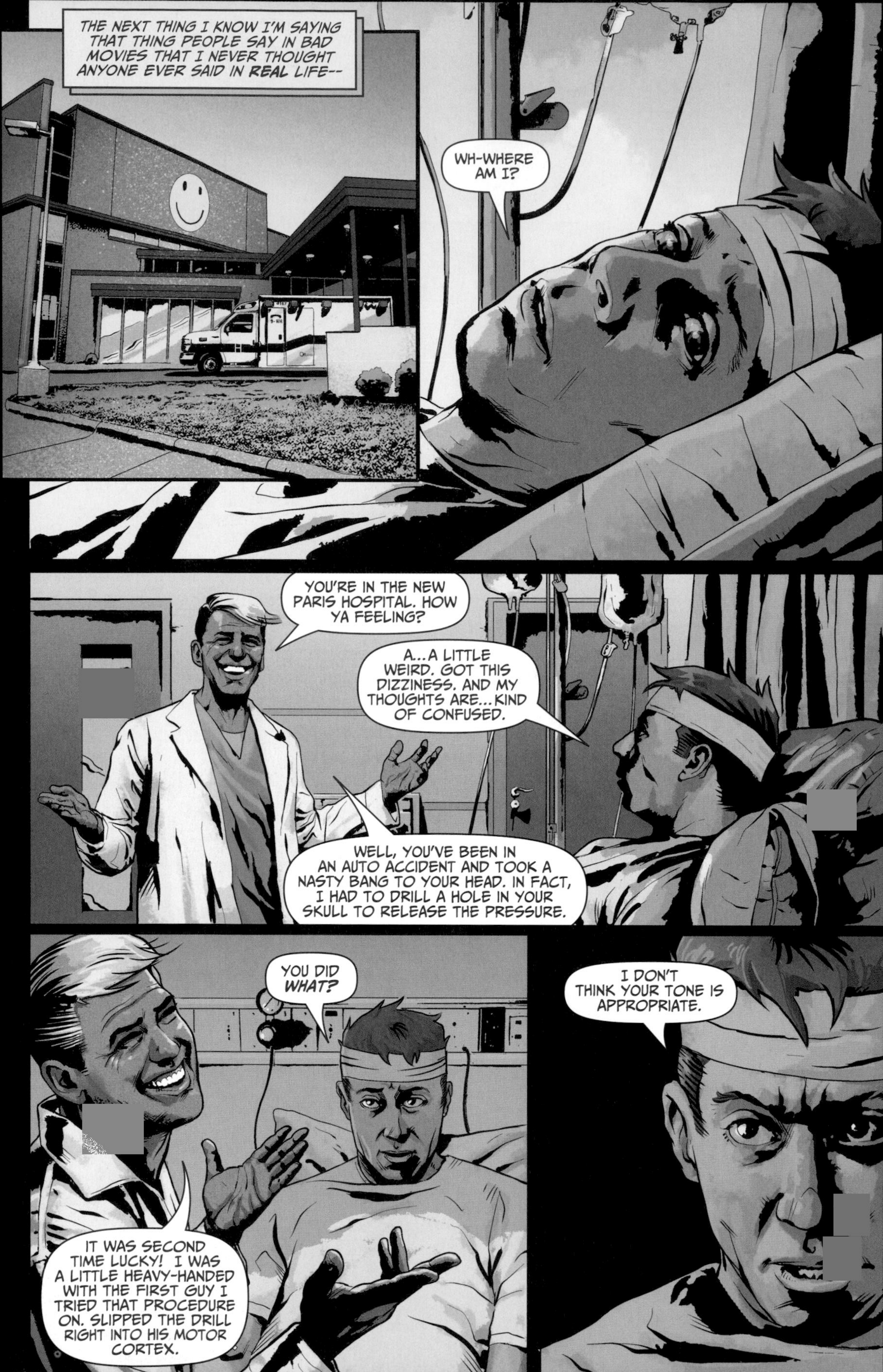
THE NEXT THING I KNOW I'M SAYING THAT THING PEOPLE SAY IN BAD MOVIES THAT I NEVER THOUGHT ANYONE EVER SAID IN REAL LIFE--
WH-WHERE AM I?
YOU'RE IN THE NEW PARIS HOSPITAL. HOW YA FEELING?
A...A LITTLE WEIRD. GOT THIS DIZZINESS. AND MY THOUGHTS ARE...KIND OF CONFUSED.
WELL, YOU'VE BEEN IN AN AUTO ACCIDENT AND TOOK A NASTY BANG TO YOUR HEAD. IN FACT, I HAD TO DRILL A HOLE IN YOUR SKULL TO RELEASE THE PRESSURE.
YOU DID WHAT?
IT WAS SECOND TIME LUCKY! I WAS A LITTLE HEAVY-HANDED WITH THE FIRST GUY I TRIED THAT PROCEDURE ON. SLIPPED THE DRILL RIGHT INTO HIS MOTOR CORTEX.
I DON'T THINK YOUR TONE IS APPROPRIATE.

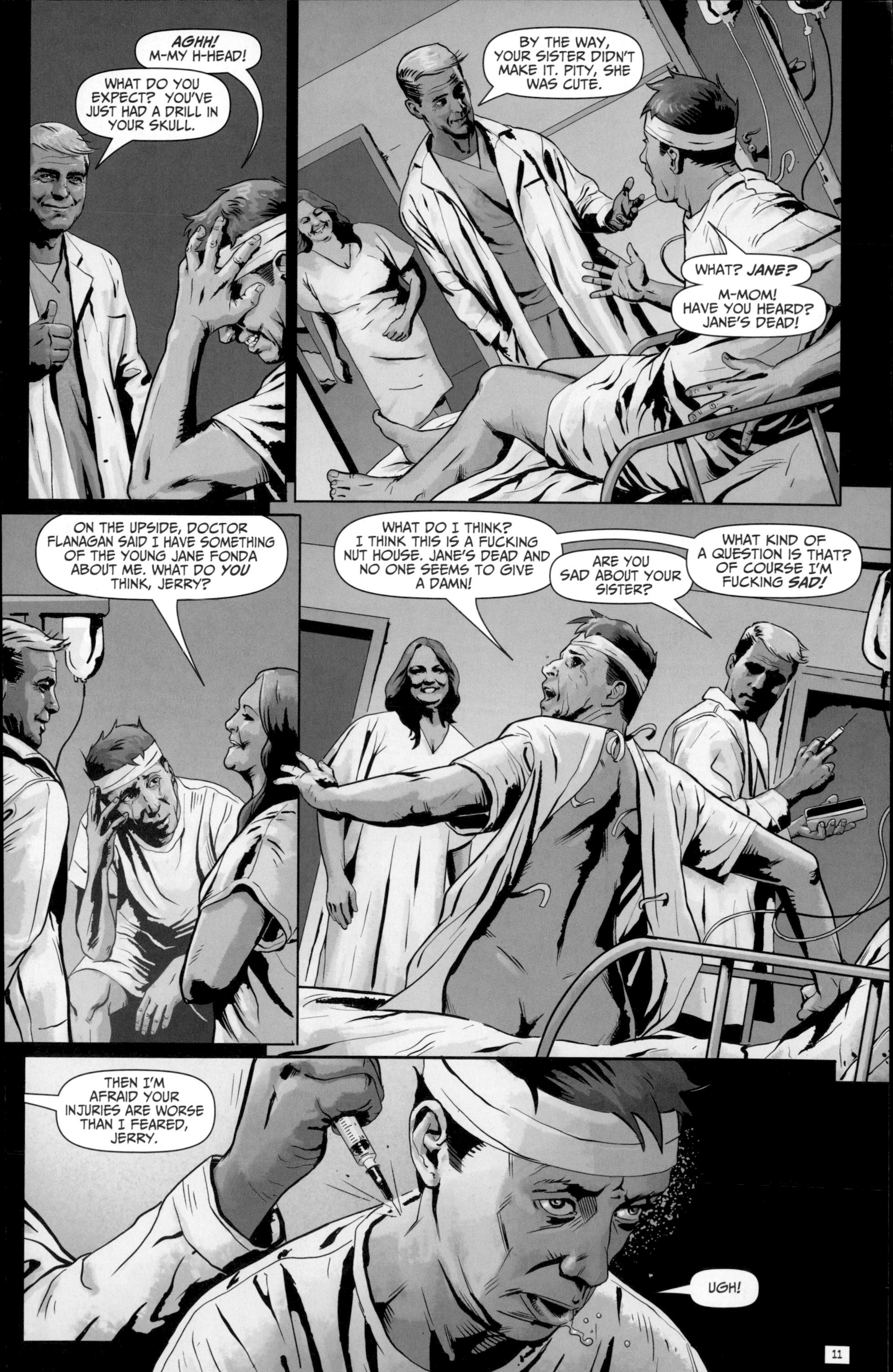
AGHH! M-MY H-HEAD!
WHAT DO YOU EXPECT? YOU'VE JUST HAD A DRILL IN YOUR SKULL.
BY THE WAY, YOUR SISTER DIDN'T MAKE IT. PITY, SHE WAS CUTE.
WHAT? JANE?
M-MOM! HAVE YOU HEARD? JANE'S DEAD!
ON THE UPSIDE, DOCTOR FLANAGAN SAID I HAVE SOMETHING OF THE YOUNG JANE FONDA ABOUT ME. WHAT DO YOU THINK, JERRY?
WHAT DO I THINK? I THINK THIS IS A FUCKING NUT HOUSE. JANE'S DEAD AND NO ONE SEEMS TO GIVE A DAMN!
ARE YOU SAD ABOUT YOUR SISTER?
WHAT KIND OF A QUESTION IS THAT? OF COURSE I'M FUCKING SAD!
THEN I'M AFRAID YOUR INJURIES ARE WORSE THAN I FEARED, JERRY.
UGH!

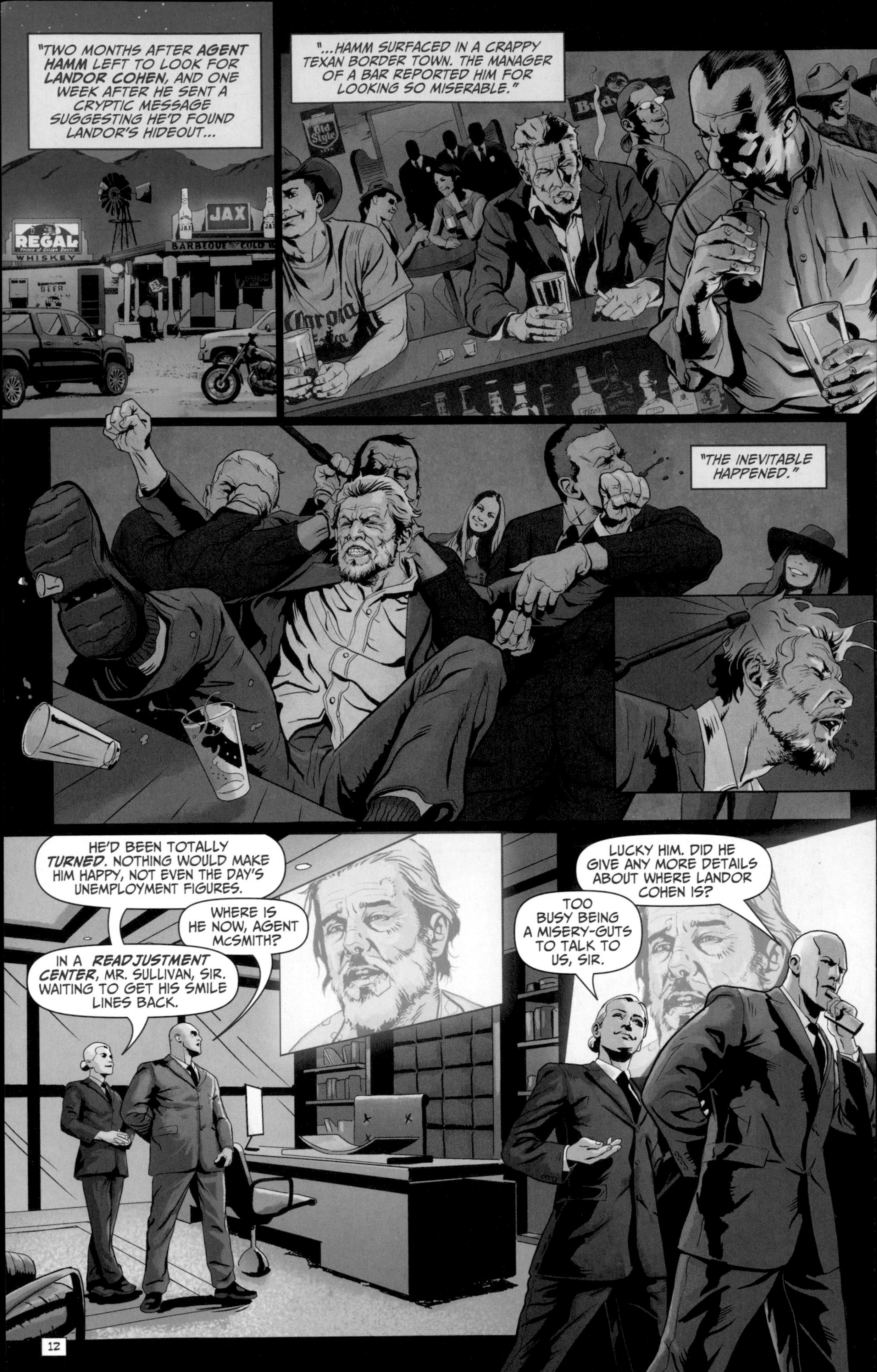
"TWO MONTHS AFTER AGENT HAMM LEFT TO LOOK FOR LANDOR COHEN, AND ONE WEEK AFTER HE SENT A CRYPTIC MESSAGE SUGGESTING HE'D FOUND LANDOR'S HIDEOUT...
REGAL
WHISKEY
JAX
BARBEQUE
BEER
"...HAMM SURFACED IN A CRAPPY TEXAN BORDER TOWN. THE MANAGER OF A BAR REPORTED HIM FOR LOOKING SO MISERABLE."
Old Style
"THE INEVITABLE HAPPENED."
HE'D BEEN TOTALLY TURNED. NOTHING WOULD MAKE HIM HAPPY, NOT EVEN THE DAY'S UNEMPLOYMENT FIGURES.
WHERE IS HE NOW, AGENT McSMITH?
IN A READJUSTMENT CENTER, MR. SULLIVAN, SIR. WAITING TO GET HIS SMILE LINES BACK.
LUCKY HIM. DID HE GIVE ANY MORE DETAILS ABOUT WHERE LANDOR COHEN IS?
TOO BUSY BEING A MISERY-GUTS TO TALK TO US, SIR.

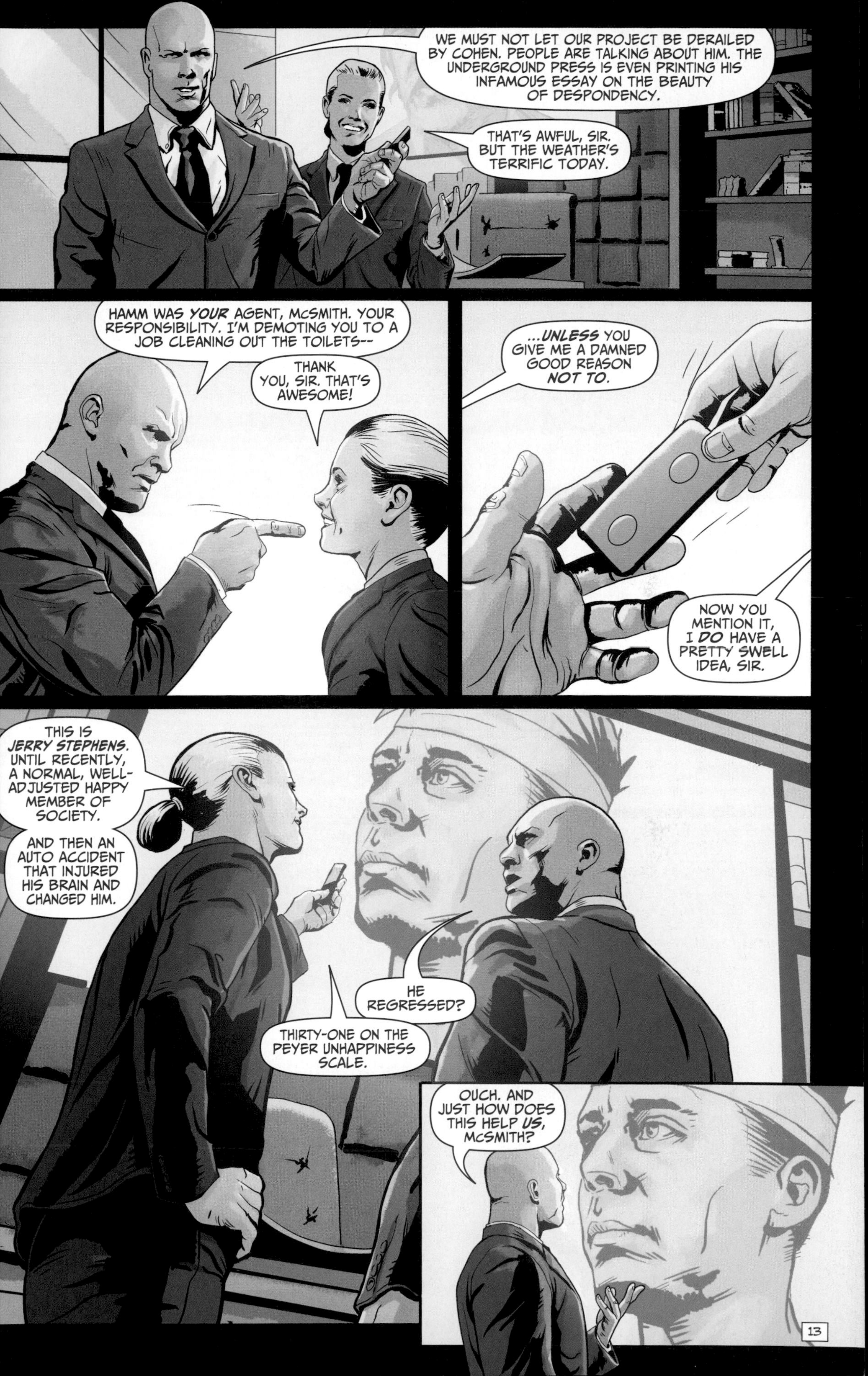

WE MUST NOT LET OUR PROJECT BE DERAILED BY COHEN. PEOPLE ARE TALKING ABOUT HIM. THE UNDERGROUND PRESS IS EVEN PRINTING HIS INFAMOUS ESSAY ON THE BEAUTY OF DESPONDENCY.
THAT'S AWFUL, SIR. BUT THE WEATHER'S TERRIFIC TODAY.
HAMM WAS *YOUR* AGENT, McSMITH. YOUR RESPONSIBILITY. I'M DEMOTING YOU TO A JOB CLEANING OUT THE TOILETS--
THANK YOU, SIR. THAT'S AWESOME!
...*UNLESS* YOU GIVE ME A DAMNED GOOD REASON *NOT TO*.
NOW YOU MENTION IT, I *DO* HAVE A PRETTY SWELL IDEA, SIR.
THIS IS *JERRY STEPHENS*. UNTIL RECENTLY, A NORMAL, WELL-ADJUSTED HAPPY MEMBER OF SOCIETY.
AND THEN AN AUTO ACCIDENT THAT INJURED HIS BRAIN AND CHANGED HIM.
HE REGRESSED?
THIRTY-ONE ON THE PEYER UNHAPPINESS SCALE.
OUCH. AND JUST HOW DOES THIS HELP *US*, McSMITH?

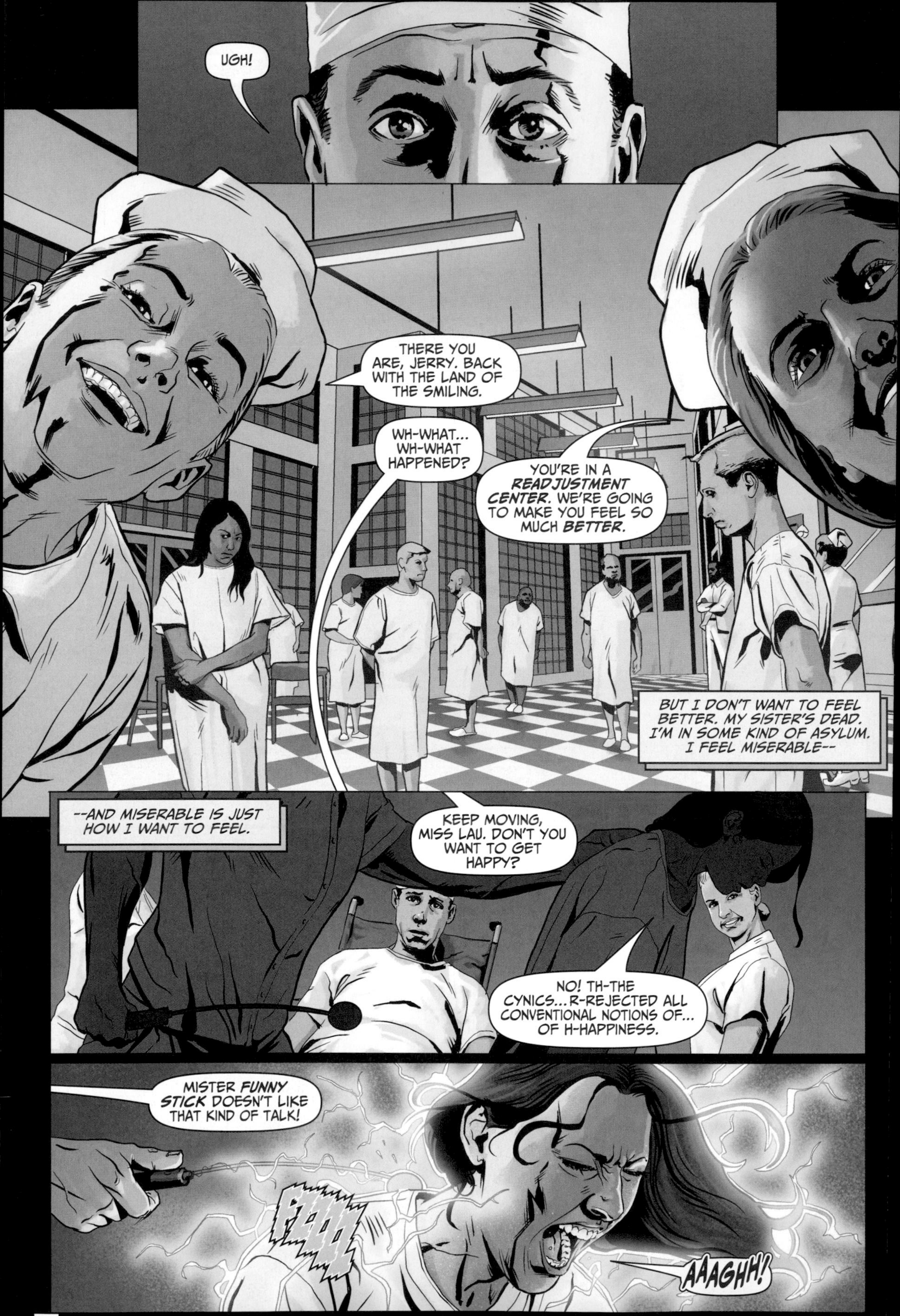
UGH!
THERE YOU ARE, JERRY. BACK WITH THE LAND OF THE SMILING.
WH-WHAT... WH-WHAT HAPPENED?
YOU'RE IN A *READJUSTMENT CENTER*. WE'RE GOING TO MAKE YOU FEEL SO MUCH *BETTER*.
BUT I DON'T WANT TO FEEL BETTER. MY SISTER'S DEAD. I'M IN SOME KIND OF ASYLUM. I FEEL MISERABLE--
--AND *MISERABLE* IS JUST HOW I WANT TO FEEL.
KEEP MOVING, MISS LAU. DON'T YOU WANT TO GET HAPPY?
NO! TH-THE CYNICS... R-REJECTED ALL CONVENTIONAL NOTIONS OF... OF H-HAPPINESS.
MISTER *FUNNY STICK* DOESN'T LIKE THAT KIND OF TALK!
FZZZ
AAAGHH!

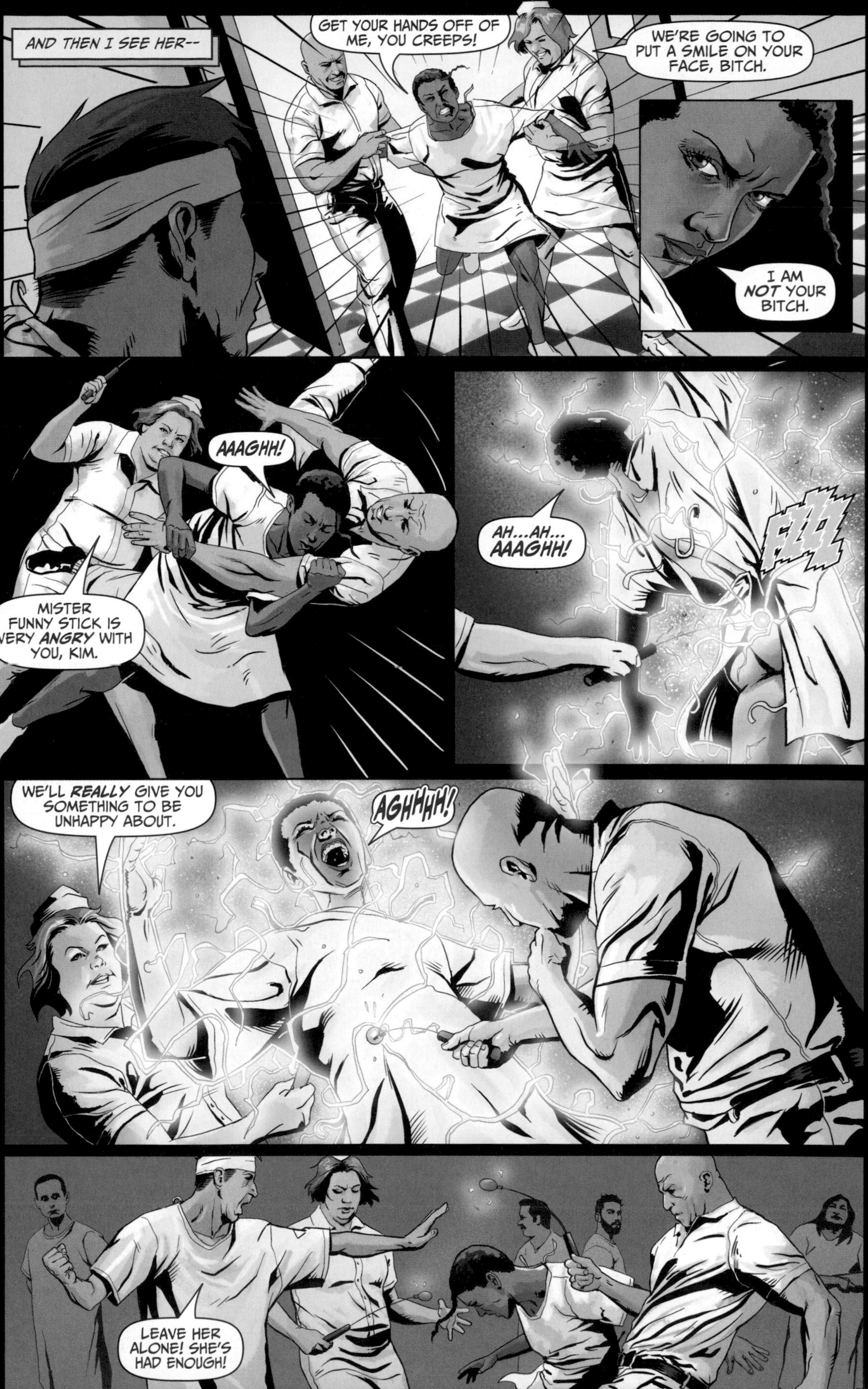
AND THEN I SEE HER--
GET YOUR HANDS OFF OF ME, YOU CREEPS!
WE'RE GOING TO PUT A SMILE ON YOUR FACE, BITCH.
I AM NOT YOUR BITCH.
AAAGHH!
MISTER FUNNY STICK IS VERY ANGRY WITH YOU, KIM.
AH...AH... AAAGHH!
FZZZ
WE'LL REALLY GIVE YOU SOMETHING TO BE UNHAPPY ABOUT.
AGHHHH!
LEAVE HER ALONE! SHE'S HAD ENOUGH!

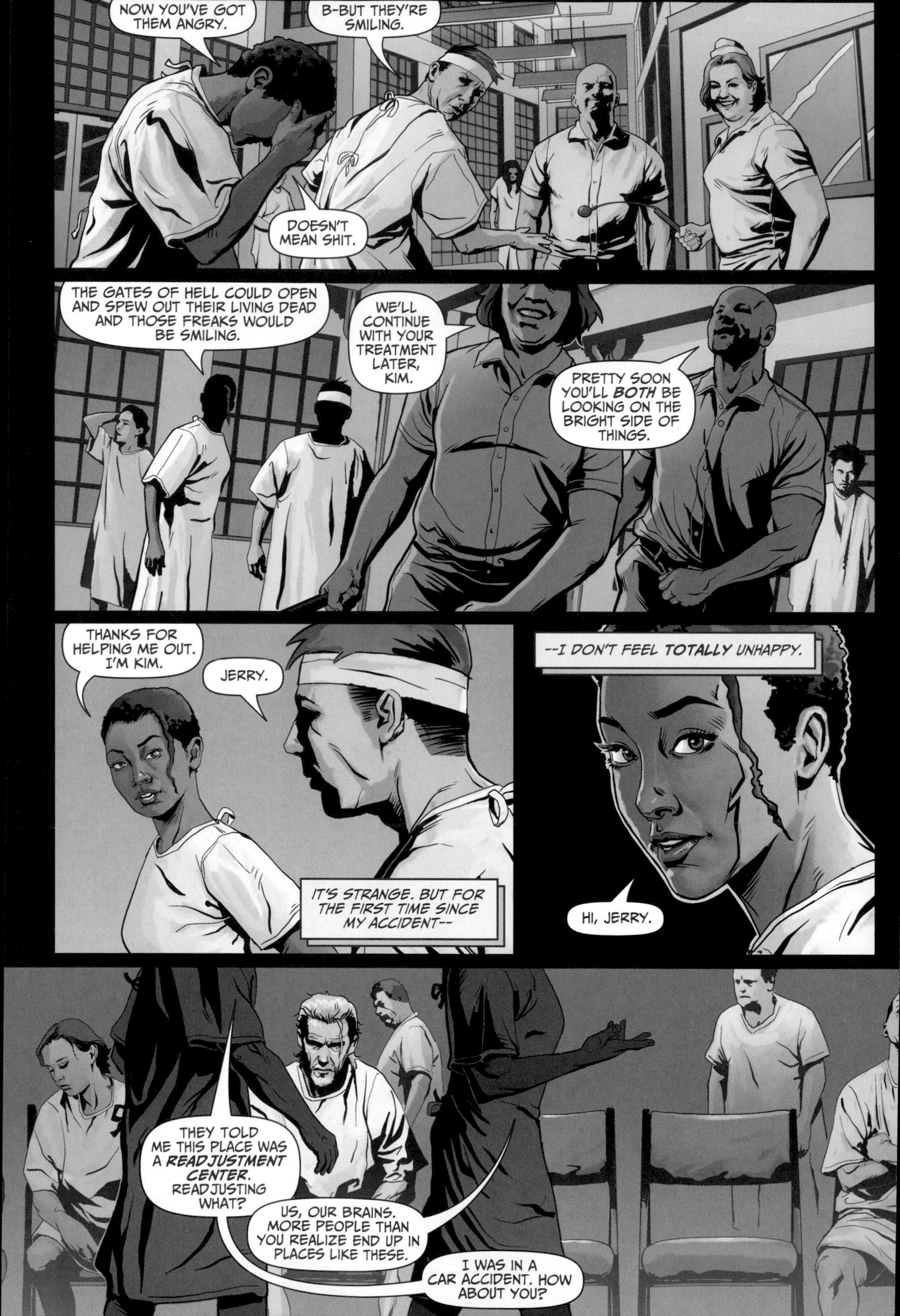
NOW YOU'VE GOT THEM ANGRY.
B-BUT THEY'RE SMILING.
DOESN'T MEAN SHIT.
THE GATES OF HELL COULD OPEN AND SPEW OUT THEIR LIVING DEAD AND THOSE FREAKS WOULD BE SMILING.
WE'LL CONTINUE WITH YOUR TREATMENT LATER, KIM.
PRETTY SOON YOU'LL BOTH BE LOOKING ON THE BRIGHT SIDE OF THINGS.
THANKS FOR HELPING ME OUT. I'M KIM.
JERRY.
IT'S STRANGE. BUT FOR THE FIRST TIME SINCE MY ACCIDENT--
--I DON'T FEEL TOTALLY UNHAPPY.
HI, JERRY.
THEY TOLD ME THIS PLACE WAS A READJUSTMENT CENTER. READJUSTING WHAT?
US, OUR BRAINS. MORE PEOPLE THAN YOU REALIZE END UP IN PLACES LIKE THESE.
I WAS IN A CAR ACCIDENT. HOW ABOUT YOU?

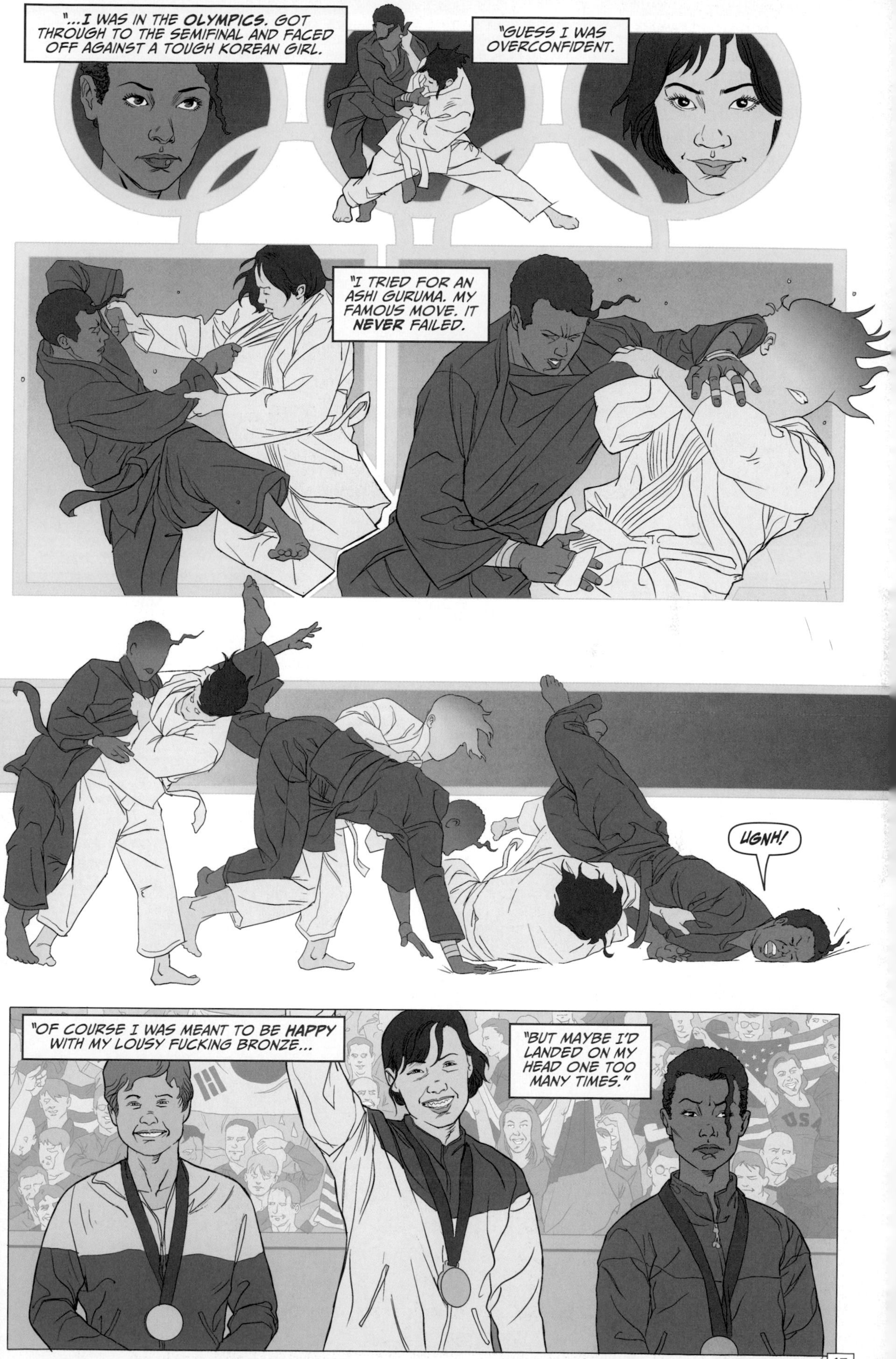
"...I WAS IN THE OLYMPICS. GOT THROUGH TO THE SEMIFINAL AND FACED OFF AGAINST A TOUGH KOREAN GIRL.
"GUESS I WAS OVERCONFIDENT.
"I TRIED FOR AN ASHI GURUMA. MY FAMOUS MOVE. IT NEVER FAILED.
UGNH!
"OF COURSE I WAS MEANT TO BE HAPPY WITH MY LOUSY FUCKING BRONZE...
"BUT MAYBE I'D LANDED ON MY HEAD ONE TOO MANY TIMES."
USA

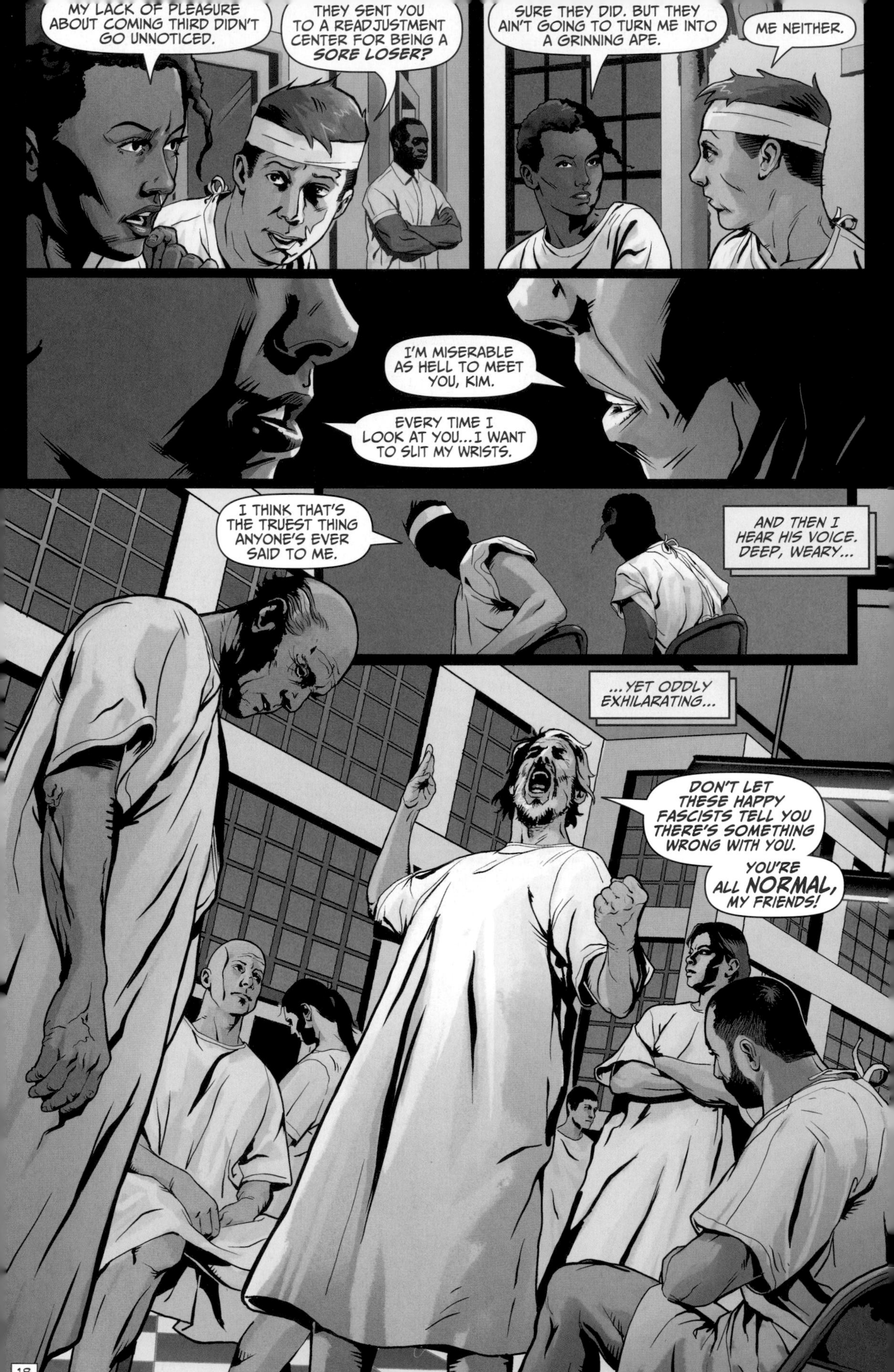
MY LACK OF PLEASURE ABOUT COMING THIRD DIDN'T GO UNNOTICED.
THEY SENT YOU TO A READJUSTMENT CENTER FOR BEING A SORE LOSER?
SURE THEY DID. BUT THEY AIN'T GOING TO TURN ME INTO A GRINNING APE.
ME NEITHER.
I'M MISERABLE AS HELL TO MEET YOU, KIM.
EVERY TIME I LOOK AT YOU...I WANT TO SLIT MY WRISTS.
I THINK THAT'S THE TRUEST THING ANYONE'S EVER SAID TO ME.
AND THEN I HEAR HIS VOICE. DEEP, WEARY...
...YET ODDLY EXHILARATING...
DON'T LET THESE HAPPY FASCISTS TELL YOU THERE'S SOMETHING WRONG WITH YOU.
YOU'RE ALL NORMAL, MY FRIENDS!

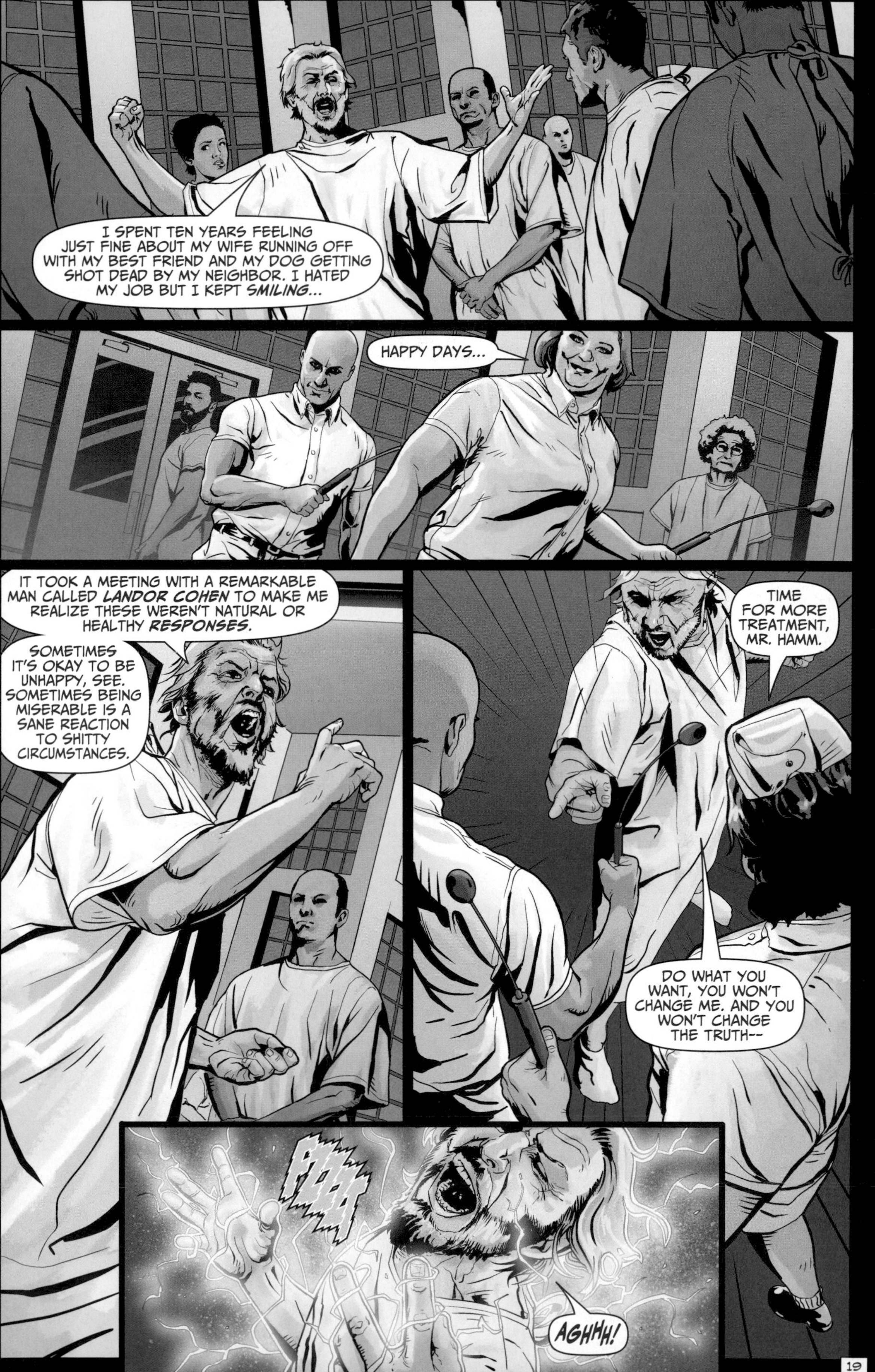
I SPENT TEN YEARS FEELING JUST FINE ABOUT MY WIFE RUNNING OFF WITH MY BEST FRIEND AND MY DOG GETTING SHOT DEAD BY MY NEIGHBOR. I HATED MY JOB BUT I KEPT *SMILING*...
HAPPY DAYS...
IT TOOK A MEETING WITH A REMARKABLE MAN CALLED *LANDOR COHEN* TO MAKE ME REALIZE THESE WEREN'T NATURAL OR HEALTHY *RESPONSES.*
SOMETIMES IT'S OKAY TO BE UNHAPPY, SEE. SOMETIMES BEING MISERABLE IS A SANE REACTION TO SHITTY CIRCUMSTANCES.
TIME FOR MORE TREATMENT, MR. HAMM.
DO WHAT YOU WANT, YOU WON'T CHANGE ME. AND YOU WON'T CHANGE THE TRUTH--
FZZZT
AGHHH!

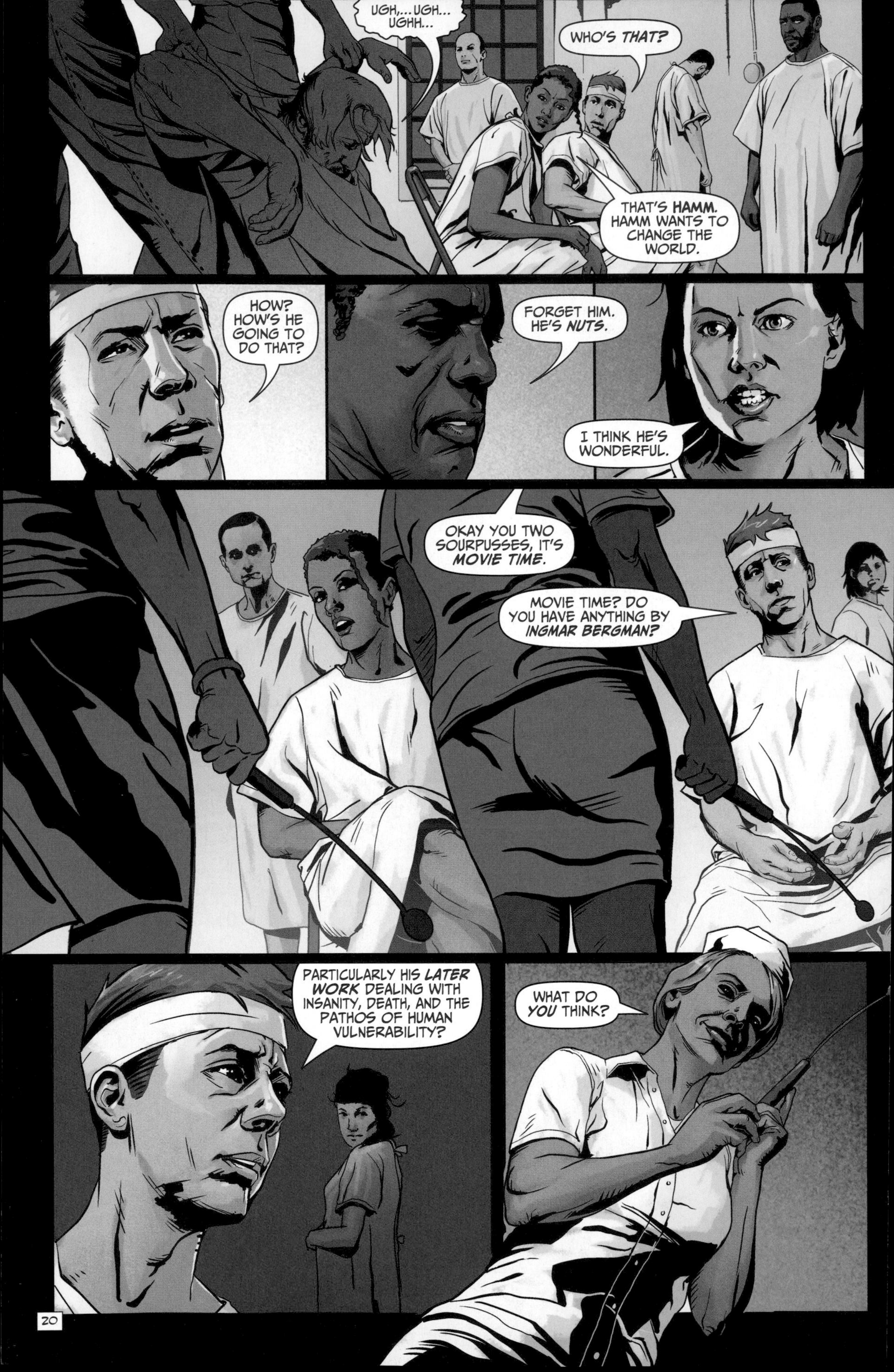
UGH,...UGH... UGHH...
WHO'S THAT?
THAT'S HAMM. HAMM WANTS TO CHANGE THE WORLD.
HOW? HOW'S HE GOING TO DO THAT?
FORGET HIM. HE'S NUTS.
I THINK HE'S WONDERFUL.
OKAY YOU TWO SOURPUSSES, IT'S MOVIE TIME.
MOVIE TIME? DO YOU HAVE ANYTHING BY INGMAR BERGMAN?
PARTICULARLY HIS LATER WORK DEALING WITH INSANITY, DEATH, AND THE PATHOS OF HUMAN VULNERABILITY?
WHAT DO YOU THINK?

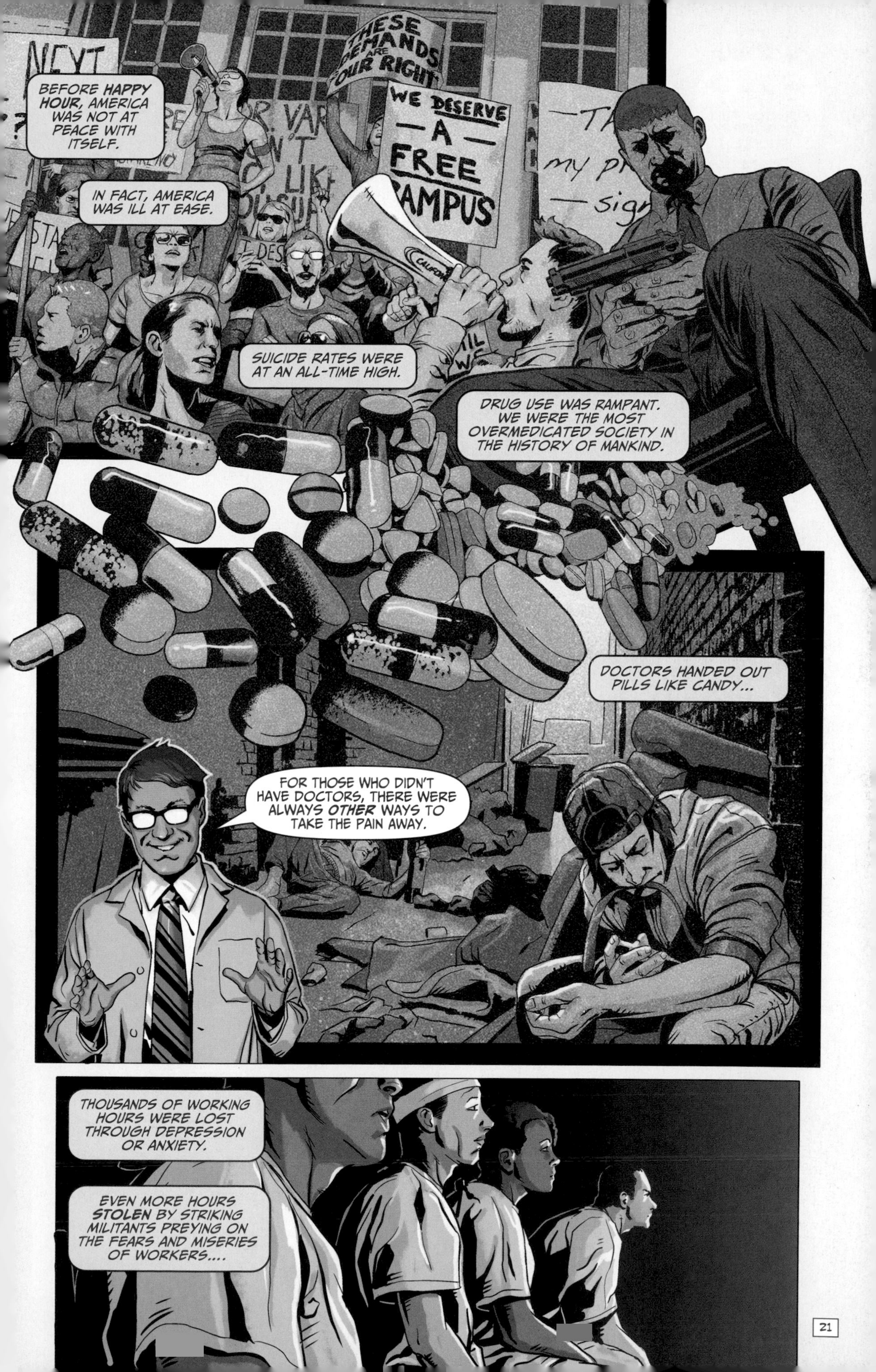
THESE DEMANDS ARE OUR RIGHT
WE DESERVE A FREE
BEFORE HAPPY HOUR, AMERICA WAS NOT AT PEACE WITH ITSELF.
IN FACT, AMERICA WAS ILL AT EASE.
SUICIDE RATES WERE AT AN ALL-TIME HIGH.
DRUG USE WAS RAMPANT. WE WERE THE MOST OVERMEDICATED SOCIETY IN THE HISTORY OF MANKIND.
DOCTORS HANDED OUT PILLS LIKE CANDY...
FOR THOSE WHO DIDN'T HAVE DOCTORS, THERE WERE ALWAYS OTHER WAYS TO TAKE THE PAIN AWAY.
THOUSANDS OF WORKING HOURS WERE LOST THROUGH DEPRESSION OR ANXIETY.
EVEN MORE HOURS STOLEN BY STRIKING MILITANTS PREYING ON THE FEARS AND MISERIES OF WORKERS....

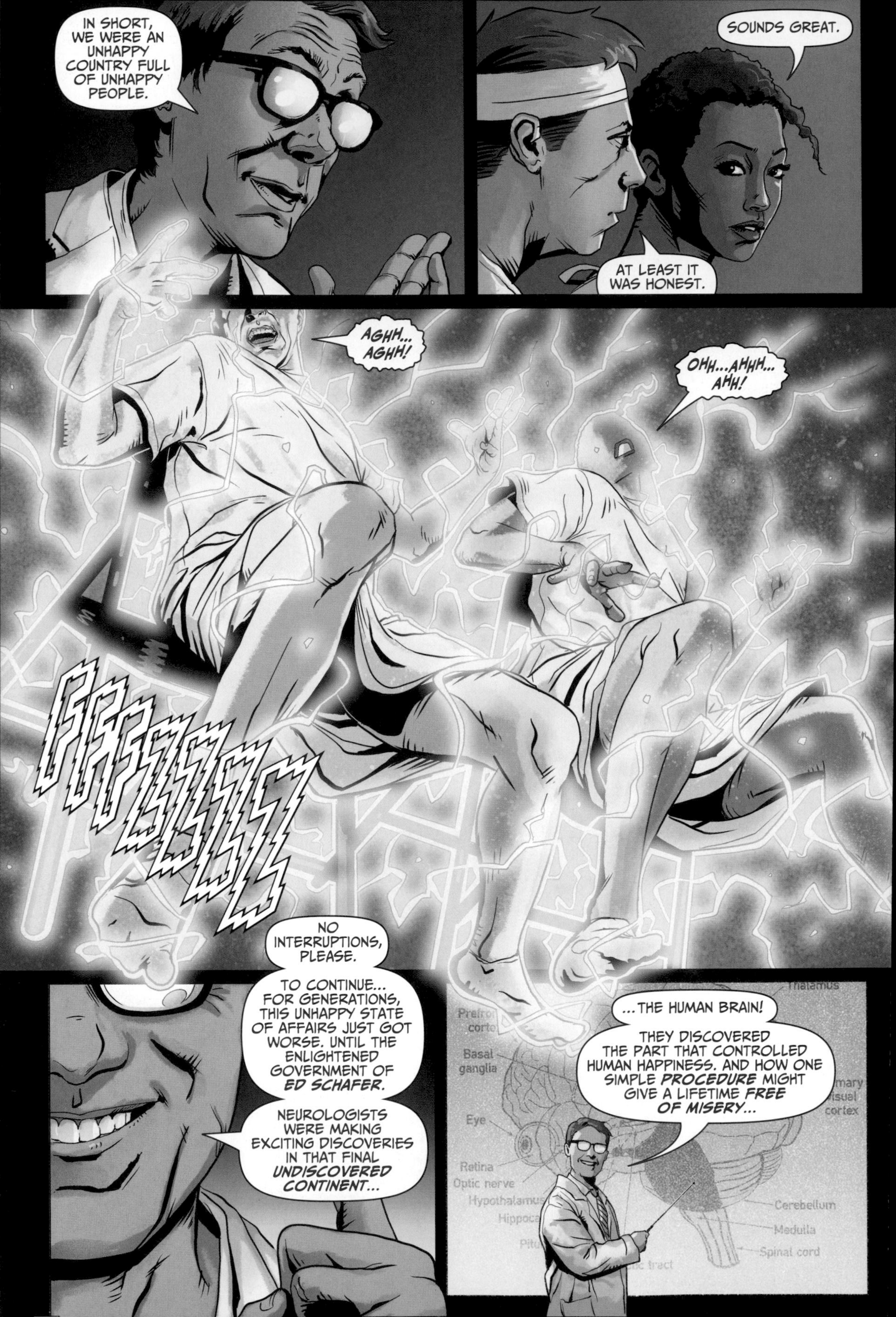
IN SHORT, WE WERE AN UNHAPPY COUNTRY FULL OF UNHAPPY PEOPLE.
SOUNDS GREAT.
AT LEAST IT WAS HONEST.
AGHH... AGHH!
OHH...AHHH... AHH!
NO INTERRUPTIONS, PLEASE.
TO CONTINUE... FOR GENERATIONS, THIS UNHAPPY STATE OF AFFAIRS JUST GOT WORSE. UNTIL THE ENLIGHTENED GOVERNMENT OF ED SCHAFER.
NEUROLOGISTS WERE MAKING EXCITING DISCOVERIES IN THAT FINAL UNDISCOVERED CONTINENT...
...THE HUMAN BRAIN!
THEY DISCOVERED THE PART THAT CONTROLLED HUMAN HAPPINESS. AND HOW ONE SIMPLE PROCEDURE MIGHT GIVE A LIFETIME FREE OF MISERY...
Basal ganglia
Eye
Retina
Optic nerve
Hypothalamus
Cerebellum
Medulla
Spinal cord

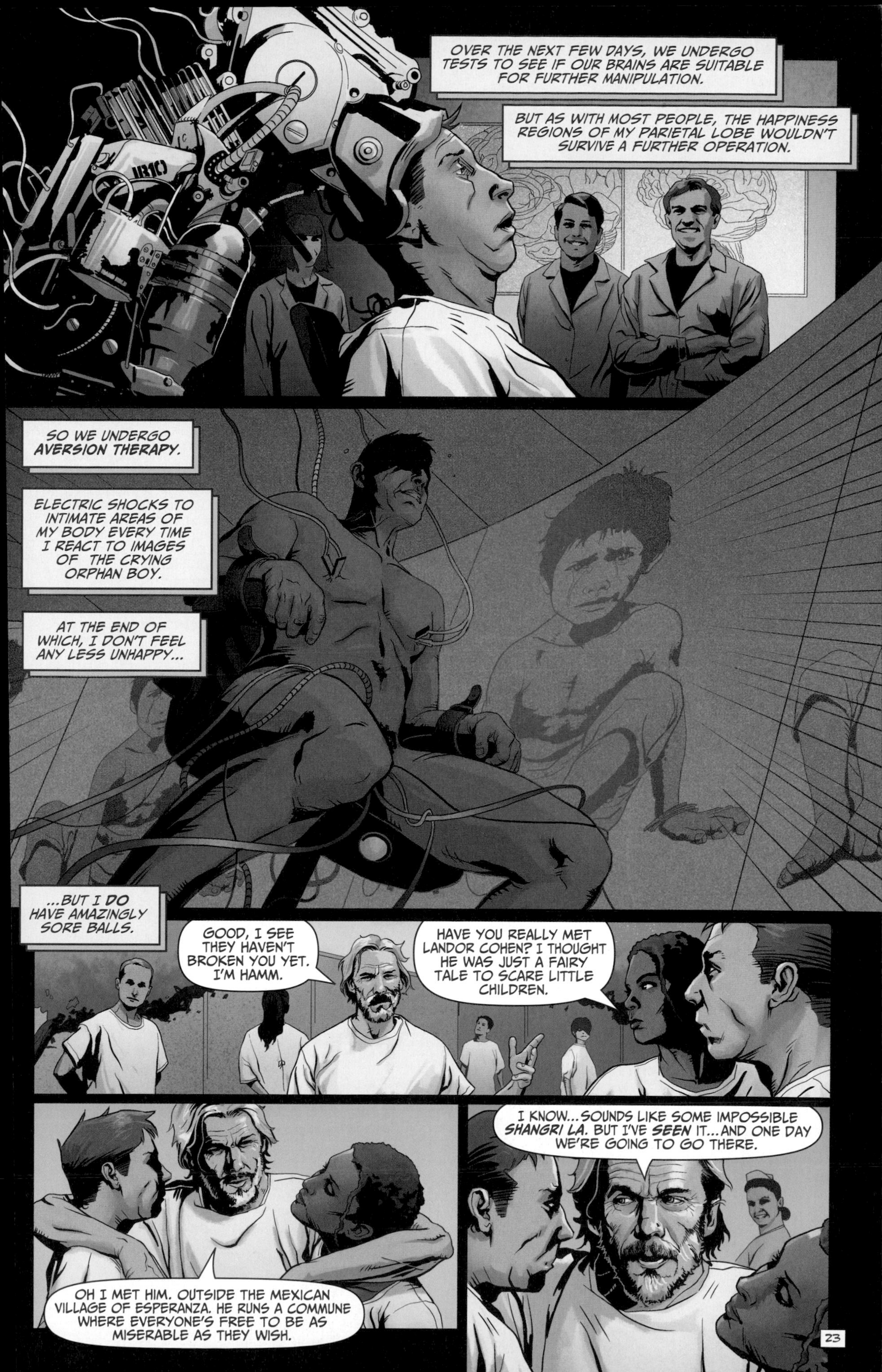
OVER THE NEXT FEW DAYS, WE UNDERGO TESTS TO SEE IF OUR BRAINS ARE SUITABLE FOR FURTHER MANIPULATION.
BUT AS WITH MOST PEOPLE, THE HAPPINESS REGIONS OF MY PARIETAL LOBE WOULDN'T SURVIVE A FURTHER OPERATION.
IB10
SO WE UNDERGO AVERSION THERAPY.
ELECTRIC SHOCKS TO INTIMATE AREAS OF MY BODY EVERY TIME I REACT TO IMAGES OF THE CRYING ORPHAN BOY.
AT THE END OF WHICH, I DON'T FEEL ANY LESS UNHAPPY...
...BUT I DO HAVE AMAZINGLY SORE BALLS.
GOOD, I SEE THEY HAVEN'T BROKEN YOU YET. I'M HAMM.
HAVE YOU REALLY MET LANDOR COHEN? I THOUGHT HE WAS JUST A FAIRY TALE TO SCARE LITTLE CHILDREN.
OH I MET HIM. OUTSIDE THE MEXICAN VILLAGE OF ESPERANZA. HE RUNS A COMMUNE WHERE EVERYONE'S FREE TO BE AS MISERABLE AS THEY WISH.
I KNOW...SOUNDS LIKE SOME IMPOSSIBLE SHANGRI LA. BUT I'VE SEEN IT...AND ONE DAY WE'RE GOING TO GO THERE.

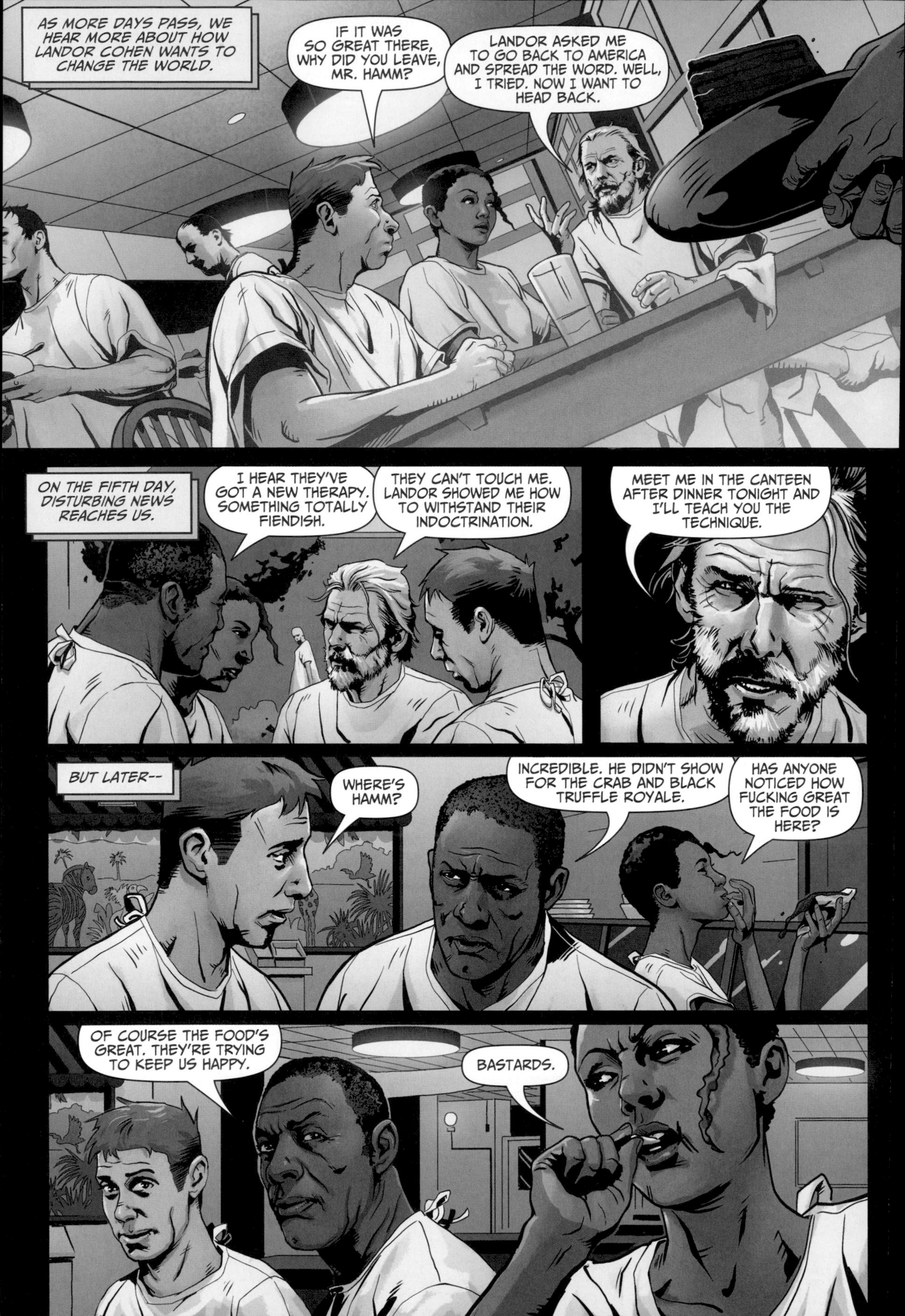

AS MORE DAYS PASS, WE HEAR MORE ABOUT HOW LANDOR COHEN WANTS TO CHANGE THE WORLD.
IF IT WAS SO GREAT THERE, WHY DID YOU LEAVE, MR. HAMM?
LANDOR ASKED ME TO GO BACK TO AMERICA AND SPREAD THE WORD. WELL, I TRIED. NOW I WANT TO HEAD BACK.
ON THE FIFTH DAY, DISTURBING NEWS REACHES US.
I HEAR THEY'VE GOT A NEW THERAPY. SOMETHING TOTALLY FIENDISH.
THEY CAN'T TOUCH ME. LANDOR SHOWED ME HOW TO WITHSTAND THEIR INDOCTRINATION.
MEET ME IN THE CANTEEN AFTER DINNER TONIGHT AND I'LL TEACH YOU THE TECHNIQUE.
BUT LATER--
WHERE'S HAMM?
INCREDIBLE. HE DIDN'T SHOW FOR THE CRAB AND BLACK TRUFFLE ROYALE.
HAS ANYONE NOTICED HOW FUCKING GREAT THE FOOD IS HERE?
OF COURSE THE FOOD'S GREAT. THEY'RE TRYING TO KEEP US HAPPY.
BASTARDS.

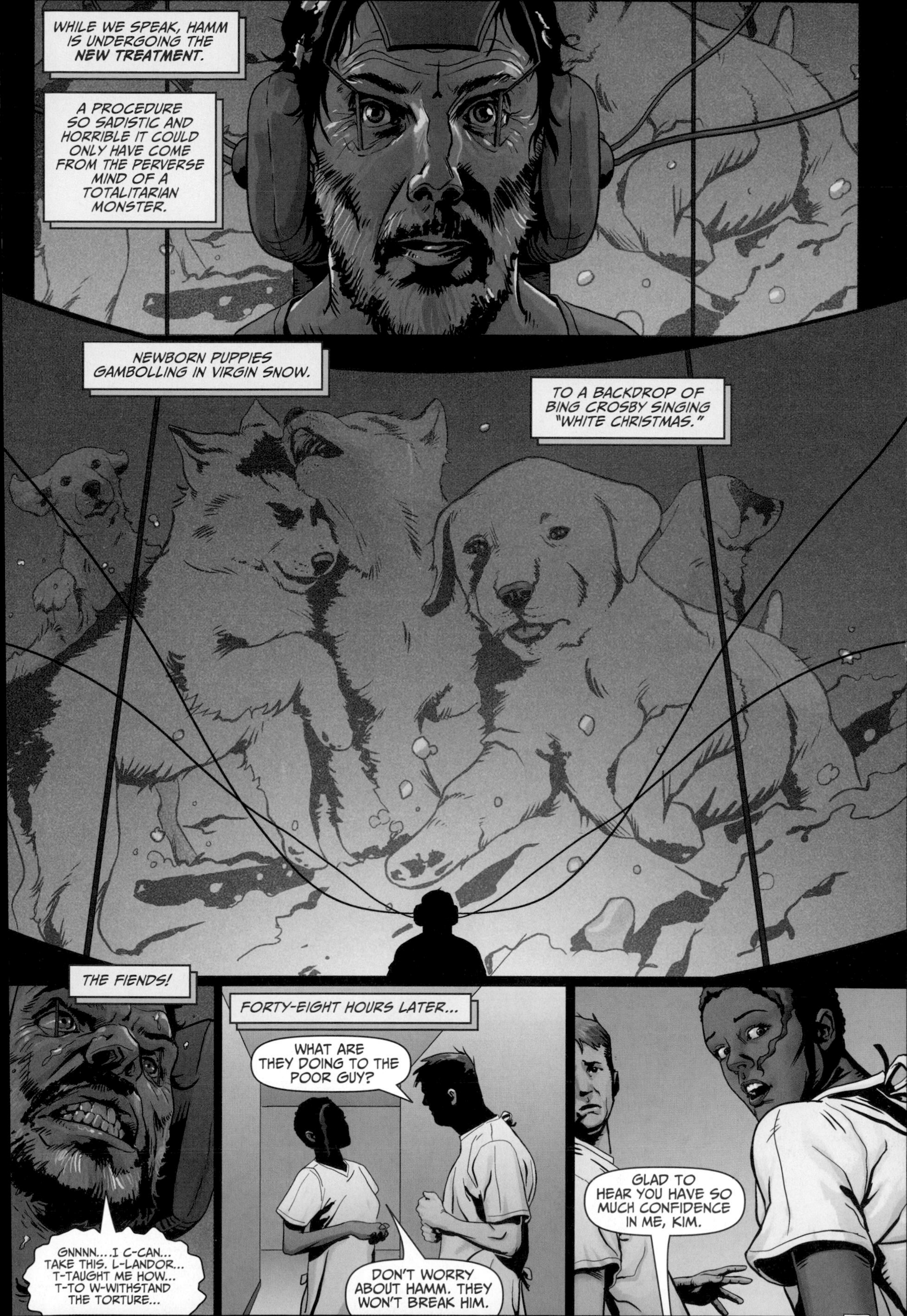

WHILE WE SPEAK, HAMM IS UNDERGOING THE NEW TREATMENT.
A PROCEDURE SO SADISTIC AND HORRIBLE IT COULD ONLY HAVE COME FROM THE PERVERSE MIND OF A TOTALITARIAN MONSTER.
NEWBORN PUPPIES GAMBOLLING IN VIRGIN SNOW.
TO A BACKDROP OF BING CROSBY SINGING "WHITE CHRISTMAS."
THE FIENDS!
GNNNN... I C-CAN... TAKE THIS. L-LANDOR... T-TAUGHT ME HOW... T-TO W-WITHSTAND THE TORTURE...
FORTY-EIGHT HOURS LATER...
WHAT ARE THEY DOING TO THE POOR GUY?
DON'T WORRY ABOUT HAMM. THEY WON'T BREAK HIM.
GLAD TO HEAR YOU HAVE SO MUCH CONFIDENCE IN ME, KIM.

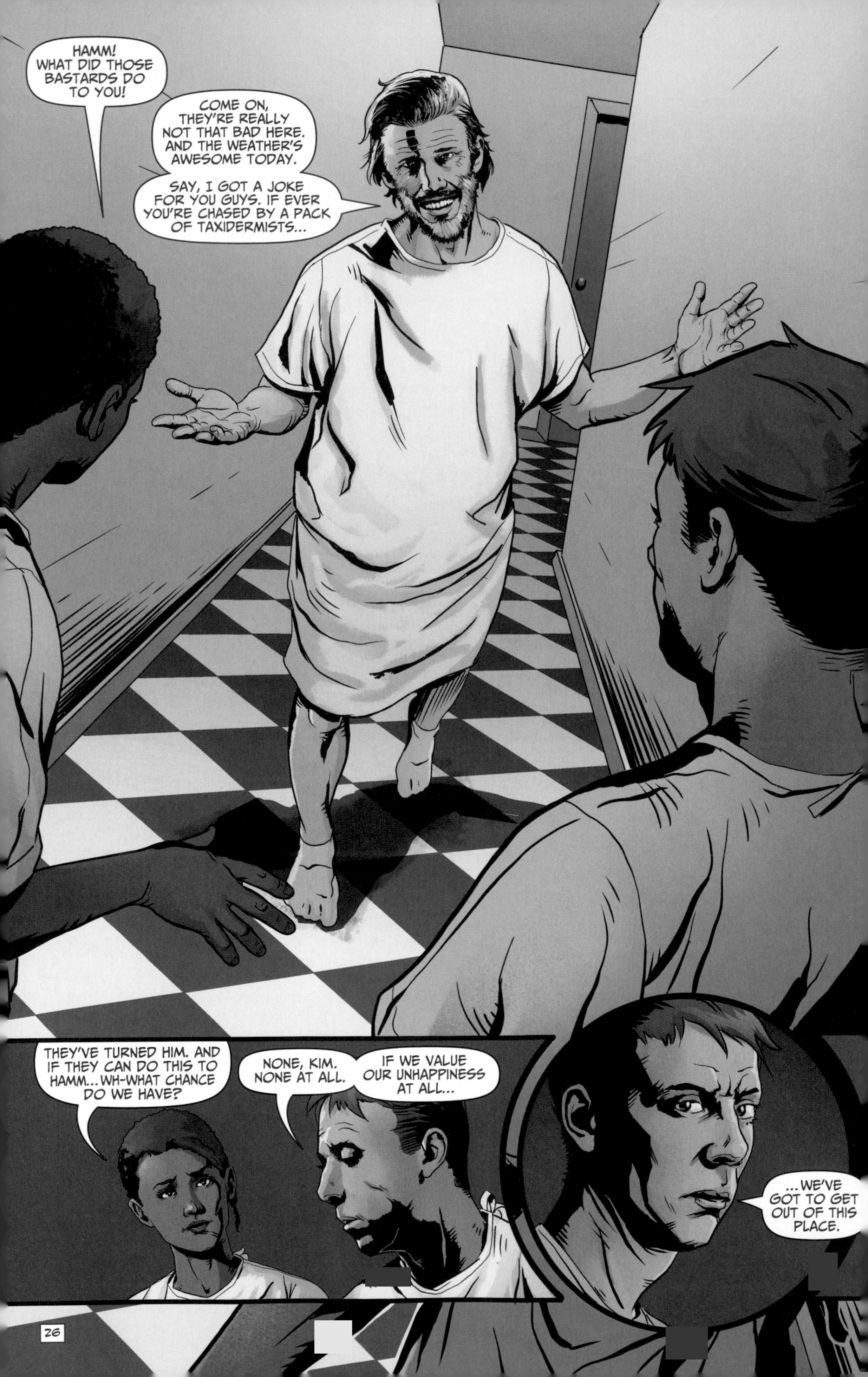
HAMM! WHAT DID THOSE BASTARDS DO TO YOU!
COME ON, THEY'RE REALLY NOT THAT BAD HERE. AND THE WEATHER'S AWESOME TODAY.
SAY, I GOT A JOKE FOR YOU GUYS. IF EVER YOU'RE CHASED BY A PACK OF TAXIDERMISTS...
THEY'VE TURNED HIM. AND IF THEY CAN DO THIS TO HAMM... WH-WHAT CHANCE DO WE HAVE?
NONE, KIM. NONE AT ALL.
IF WE VALUE OUR UNHAPPINESS AT ALL...
...WE'VE GOT TO GET OUT OF THIS PLACE.

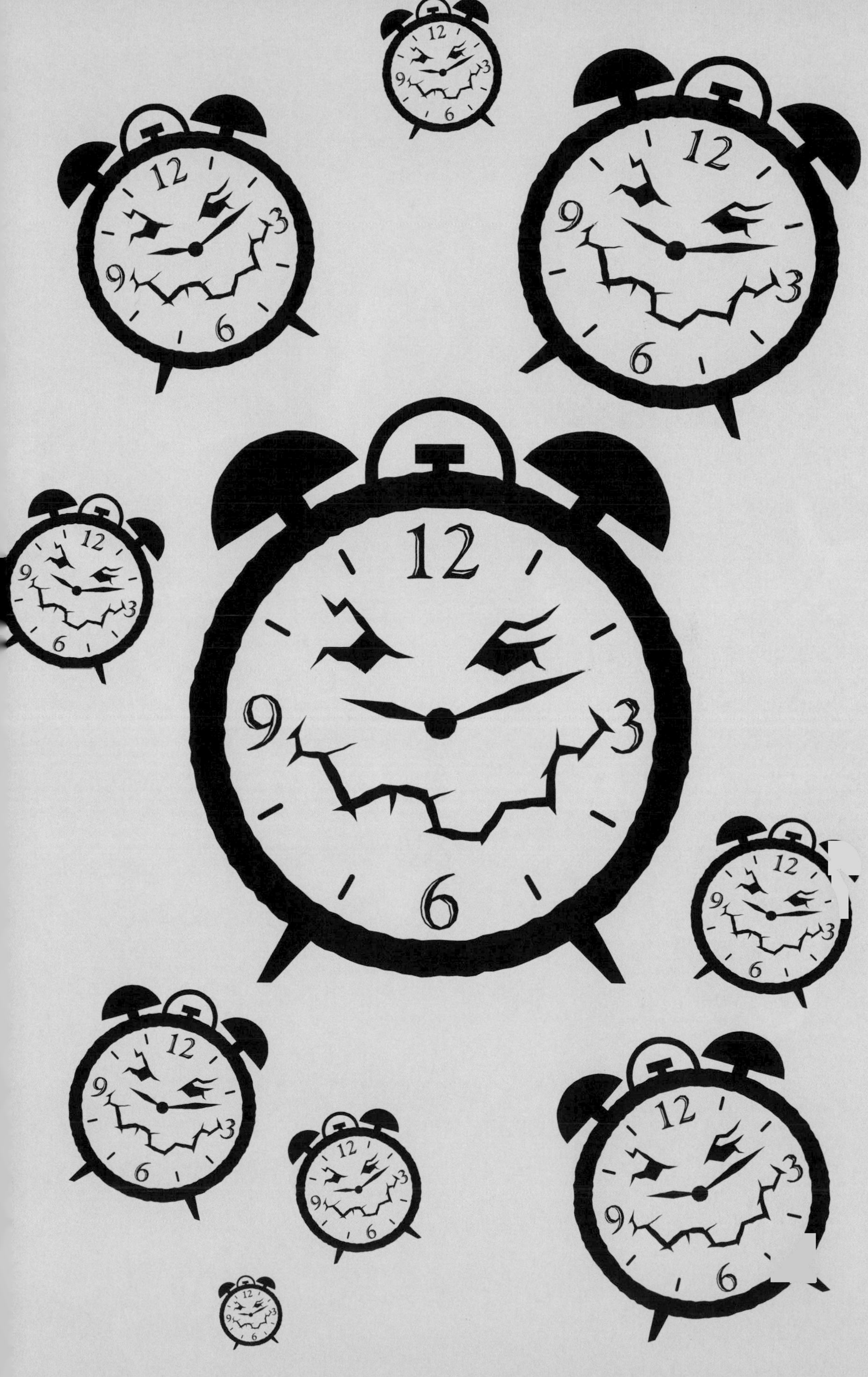

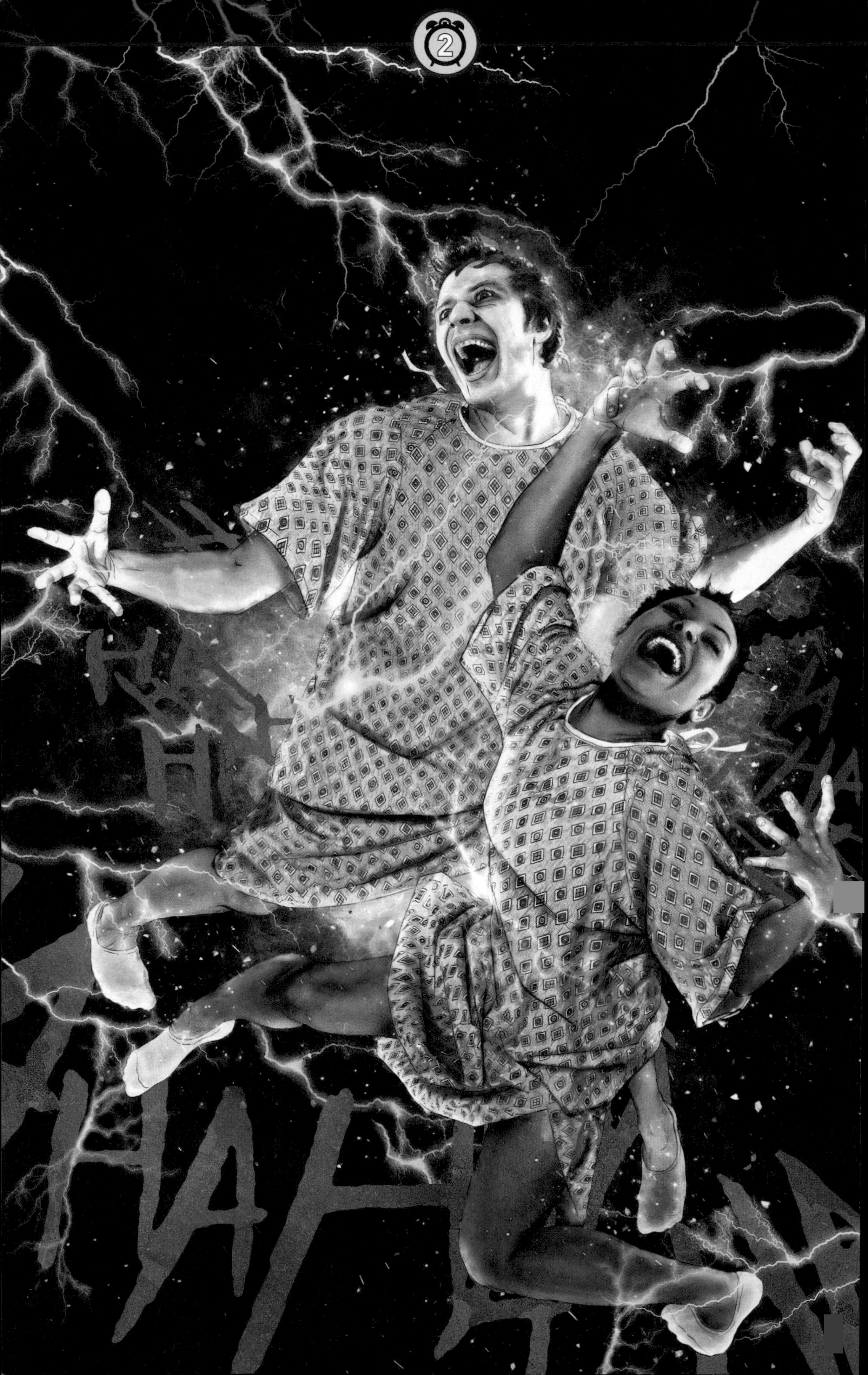
2
HA
HA
HA
HA

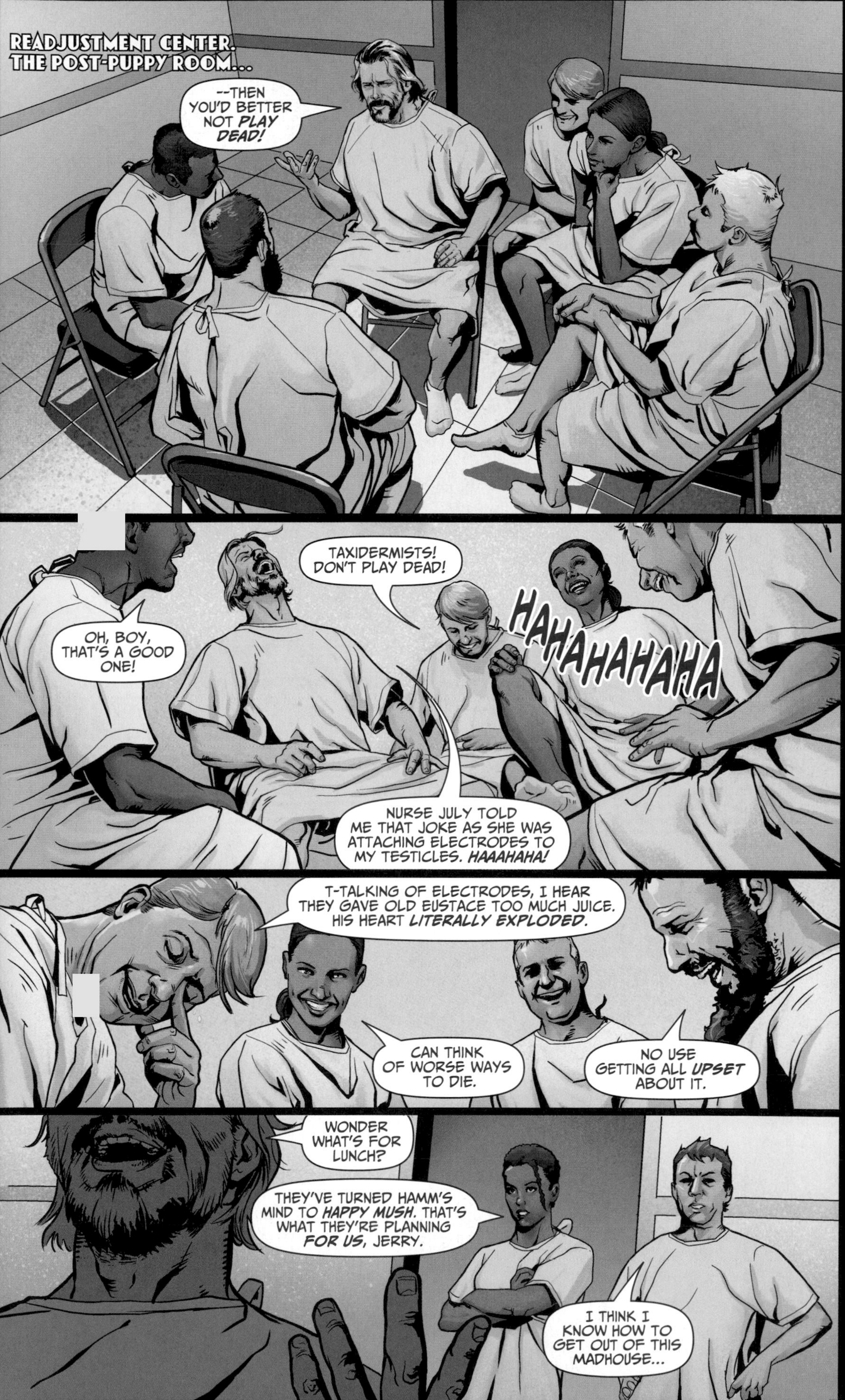
READJUSTMENT CENTER. THE POST-PUPPY ROOM...
--THEN YOU'D BETTER NOT PLAY DEAD!
TAXIDERMISTS! DON'T PLAY DEAD!
OH, BOY, THAT'S A GOOD ONE!
HAHAHAHAHA
NURSE JULY TOLD ME THAT JOKE AS SHE WAS ATTACHING ELECTRODES TO MY TESTICLES. HAAAHAHA!
T-TALKING OF ELECTRODES, I HEAR THEY GAVE OLD EUSTACE TOO MUCH JUICE. HIS HEART LITERALLY EXPLODED.
CAN THINK OF WORSE WAYS TO DIE.
NO USE GETTING ALL UPSET ABOUT IT.
WONDER WHAT'S FOR LUNCH?
THEY'VE TURNED HAMM'S MIND TO HAPPY MUSH. THAT'S WHAT THEY'RE PLANNING FOR US, JERRY.
I THINK I KNOW HOW TO GET OUT OF THIS MADHOUSE...

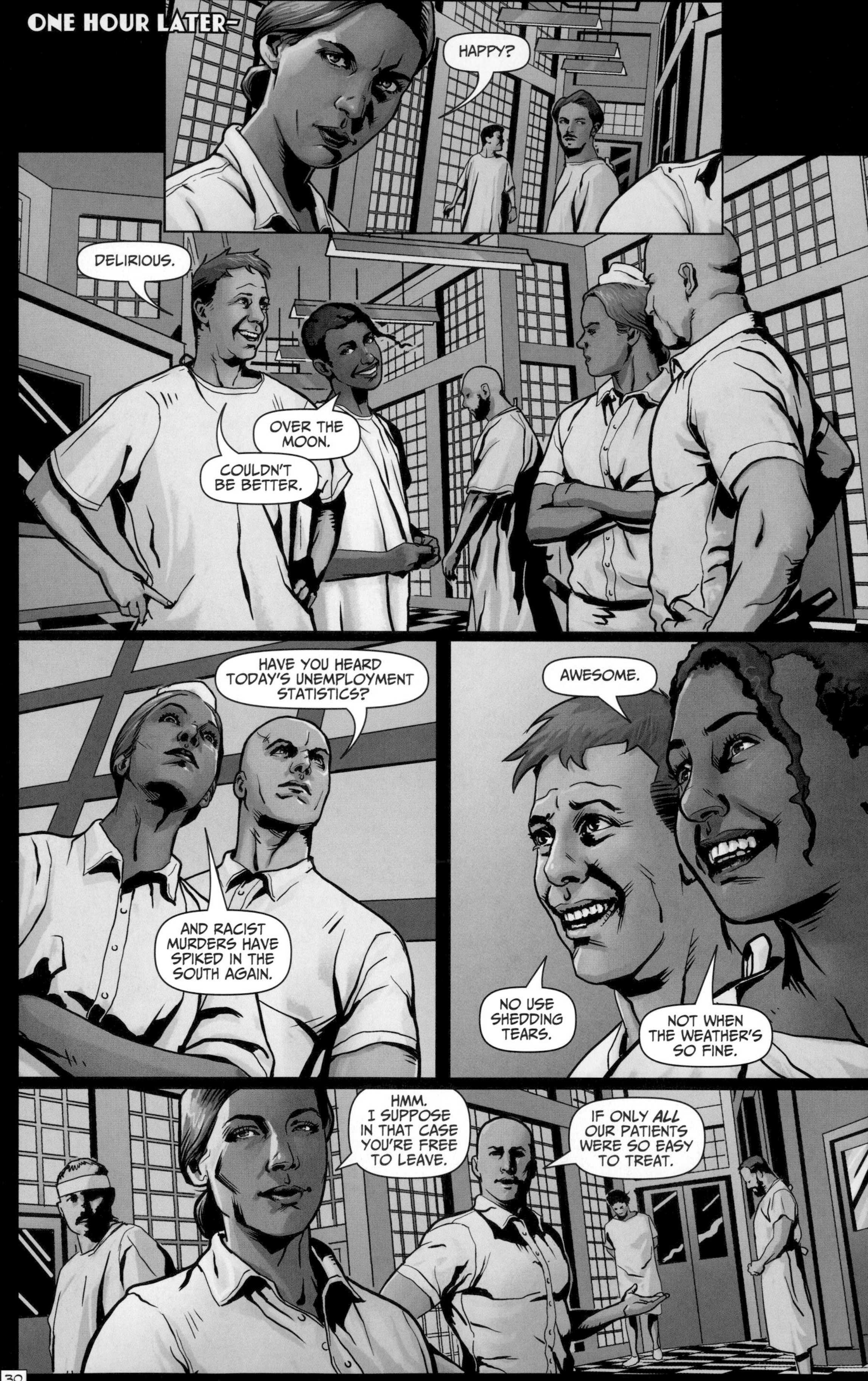
ONE HOUR LATER–
HAPPY?
DELIRIOUS.
OVER THE MOON.
COULDN'T BE BETTER.
HAVE YOU HEARD TODAY'S UNEMPLOYMENT STATISTICS?
AND RACIST MURDERS HAVE SPIKED IN THE SOUTH AGAIN.
AWESOME.
NO USE SHEDDING TEARS.
NOT WHEN THE WEATHER'S SO FINE.
HMM. I SUPPOSE IN THAT CASE YOU'RE FREE TO LEAVE.
IF ONLY *ALL* OUR PATIENTS WERE SO EASY TO TREAT.

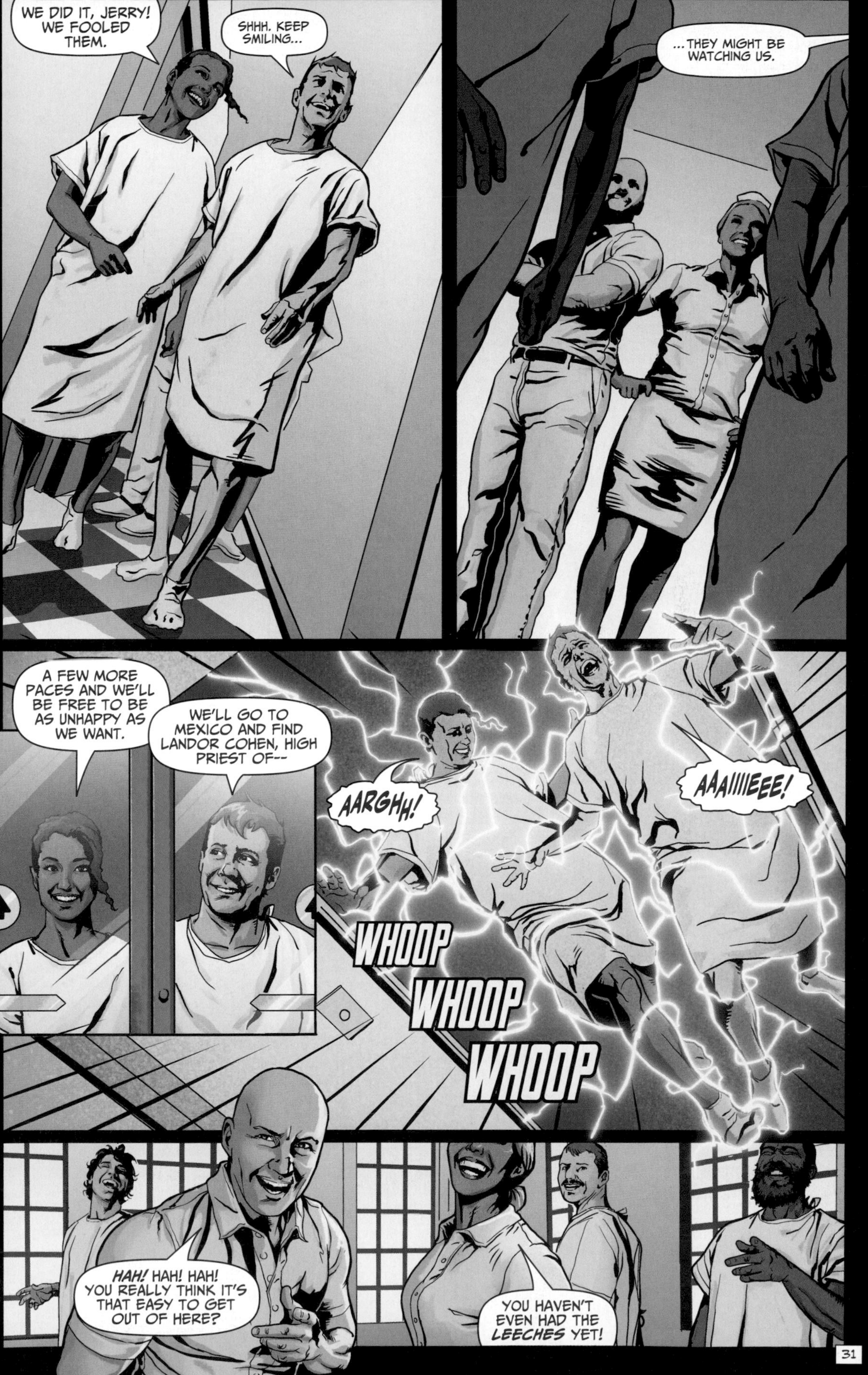
WE DID IT, JERRY! WE FOOLED THEM.
SHHH. KEEP SMILING...
...THEY MIGHT BE WATCHING US.
A FEW MORE PACES AND WE'LL BE FREE TO BE AS UNHAPPY AS WE WANT.
WE'LL GO TO MEXICO AND FIND LANDOR COHEN, HIGH PRIEST OF--
AARGHH!
AAAIIIIEEE!
WHOOP
WHOOP
WHOOP
HAH! HAH! HAH! YOU REALLY THINK IT'S THAT EASY TO GET OUT OF HERE?
YOU HAVEN'T EVEN HAD THE LEECHES YET!

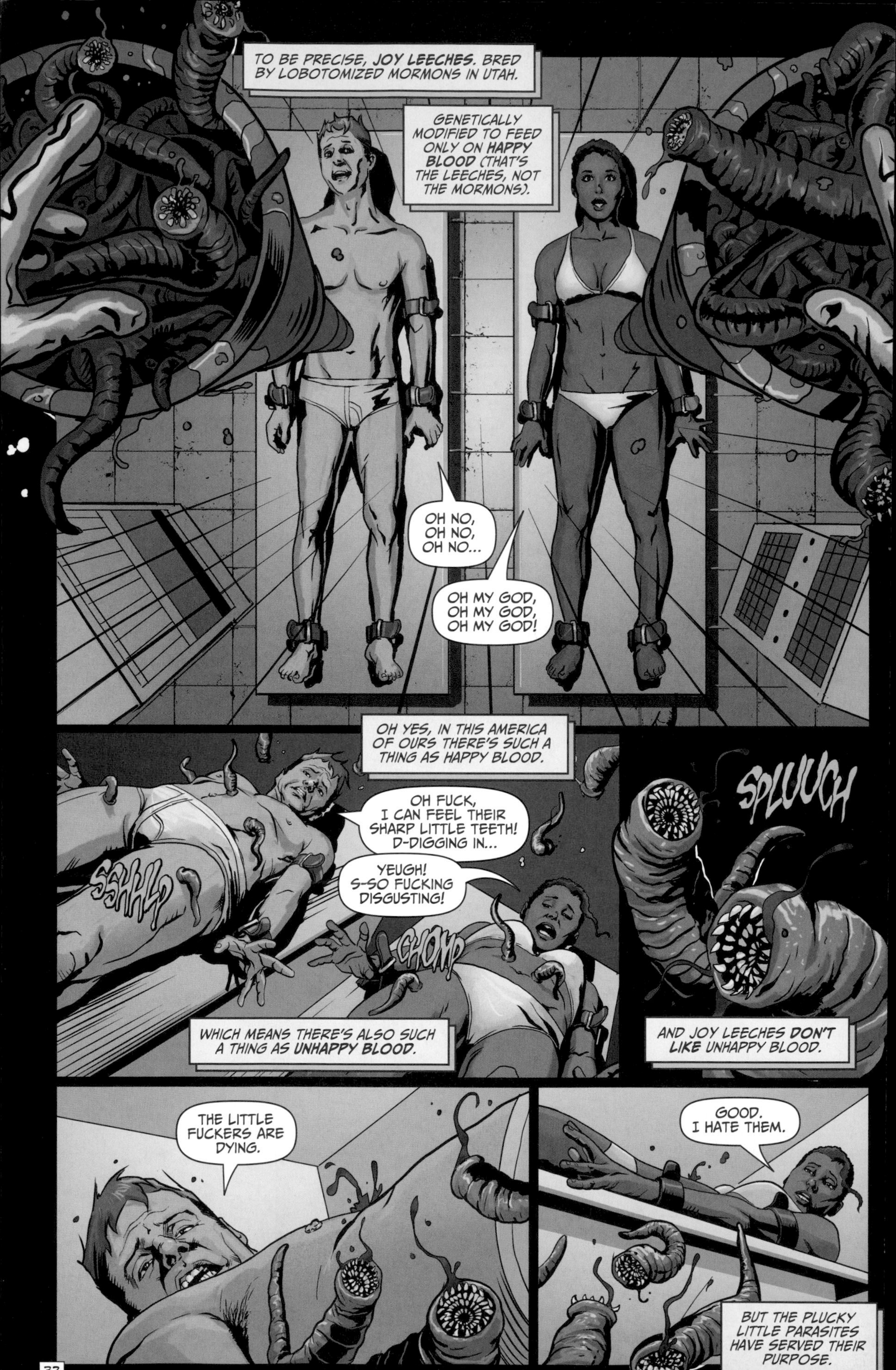

TO BE PRECISE, JOY LEECHES. BRED BY LOBOTOMIZED MORMONS IN UTAH.
GENETICALLY MODIFIED TO FEED ONLY ON HAPPY BLOOD (THAT'S THE LEECHES, NOT THE MORMONS).
OH NO, OH NO, OH NO...
OH MY GOD, OH MY GOD, OH MY GOD!
OH YES, IN THIS AMERICA OF OURS THERE'S SUCH A THING AS HAPPY BLOOD.
OH FUCK, I CAN FEEL THEIR SHARP LITTLE TEETH! D-DIGGING IN...
SSHHLP
YEUGH! S-SO FUCKING DISGUSTING!
CHOMP
WHICH MEANS THERE'S ALSO SUCH A THING AS UNHAPPY BLOOD.
SPLUUCH
AND JOY LEECHES DON'T LIKE UNHAPPY BLOOD.
THE LITTLE FUCKERS ARE DYING.
GOOD. I HATE THEM.
BUT THE PLUCKY LITTLE PARASITES HAVE SERVED THEIR PURPOSE.

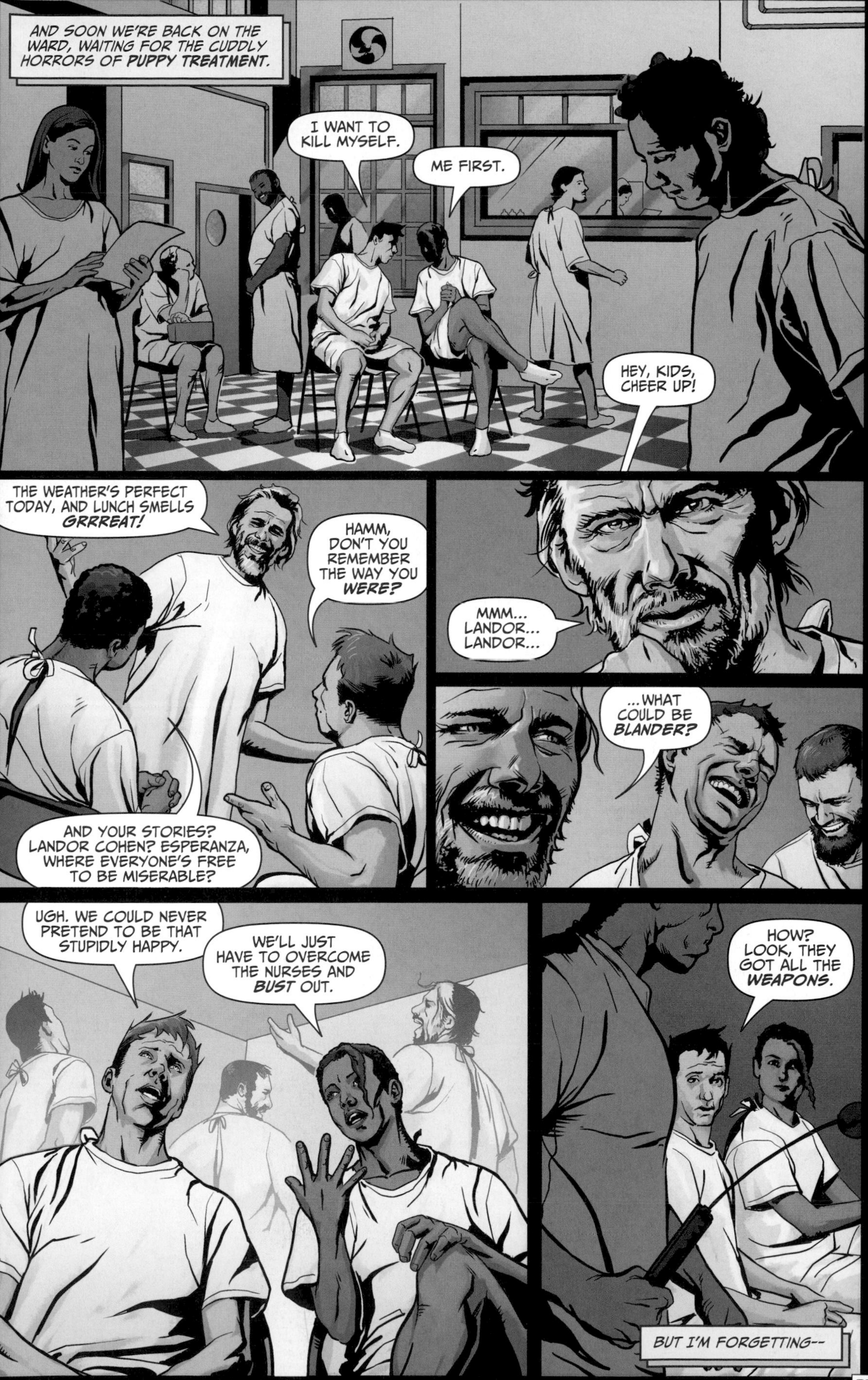
AND SOON WE'RE BACK ON THE WARD, WAITING FOR THE CUDDLY HORRORS OF PUPPY TREATMENT.
I WANT TO KILL MYSELF.
ME FIRST.
HEY, KIDS, CHEER UP!
THE WEATHER'S PERFECT TODAY, AND LUNCH SMELLS GRRREAT!
HAMM, DON'T YOU REMEMBER THE WAY YOU WERE?
AND YOUR STORIES? LANDOR COHEN? ESPERANZA, WHERE EVERYONE'S FREE TO BE MISERABLE?
MMM... LANDOR... LANDOR...
...WHAT COULD BE BLANDER?
UGH. WE COULD NEVER PRETEND TO BE THAT STUPIDLY HAPPY.
WE'LL JUST HAVE TO OVERCOME THE NURSES AND BUST OUT.
HOW? LOOK, THEY GOT ALL THE WEAPONS.
BUT I'M FORGETTING--

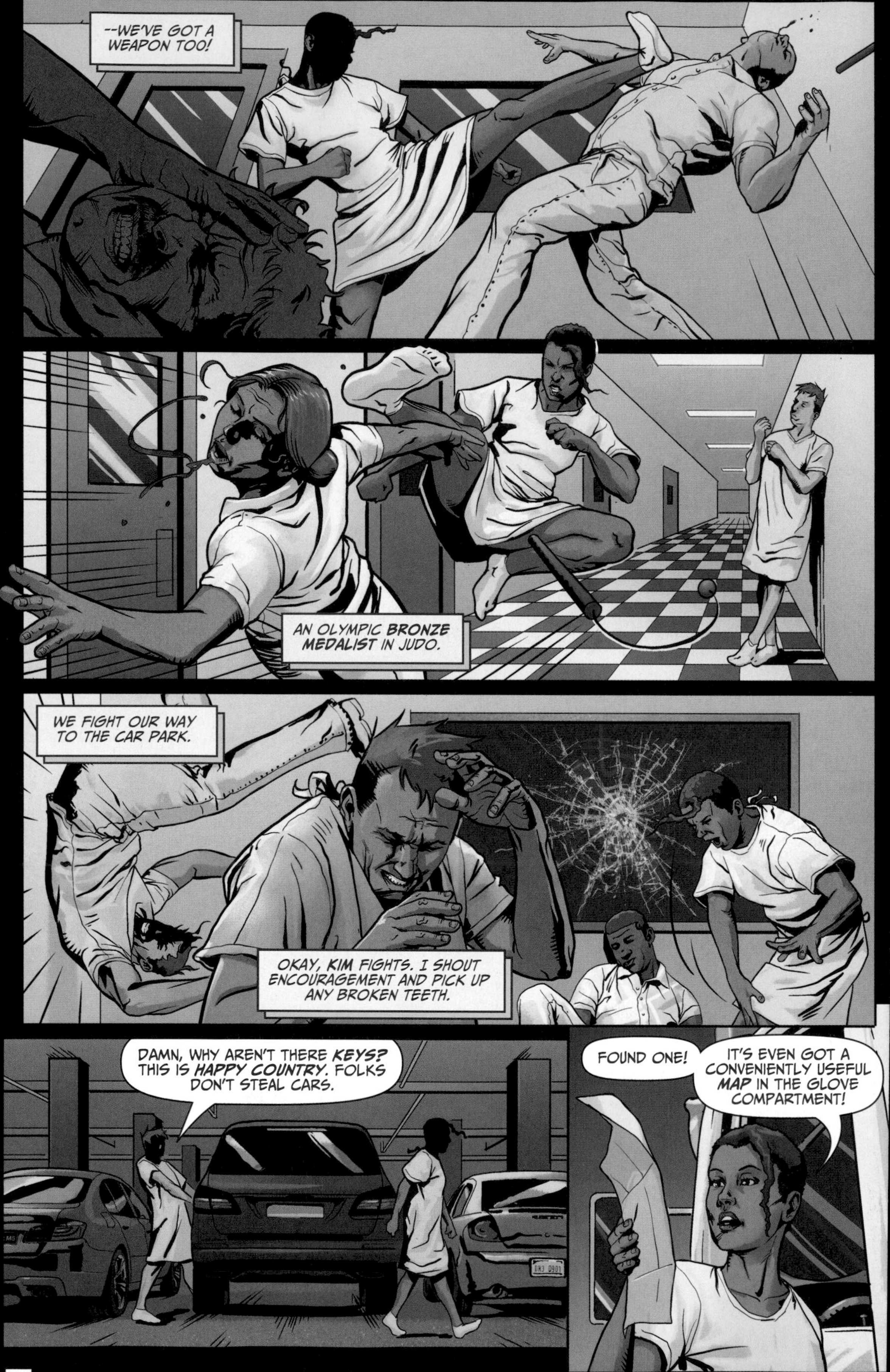
--WE'VE GOT A WEAPON TOO!
AN OLYMPIC BRONZE MEDALIST IN JUDO.
WE FIGHT OUR WAY TO THE CAR PARK.
OKAY, KIM FIGHTS. I SHOUT ENCOURAGEMENT AND PICK UP ANY BROKEN TEETH.
DAMN, WHY AREN'T THERE KEYS? THIS IS HAPPY COUNTRY. FOLKS DON'T STEAL CARS.
FOUND ONE!
IT'S EVEN GOT A CONVENIENTLY USEFUL MAP IN THE GLOVE COMPARTMENT!

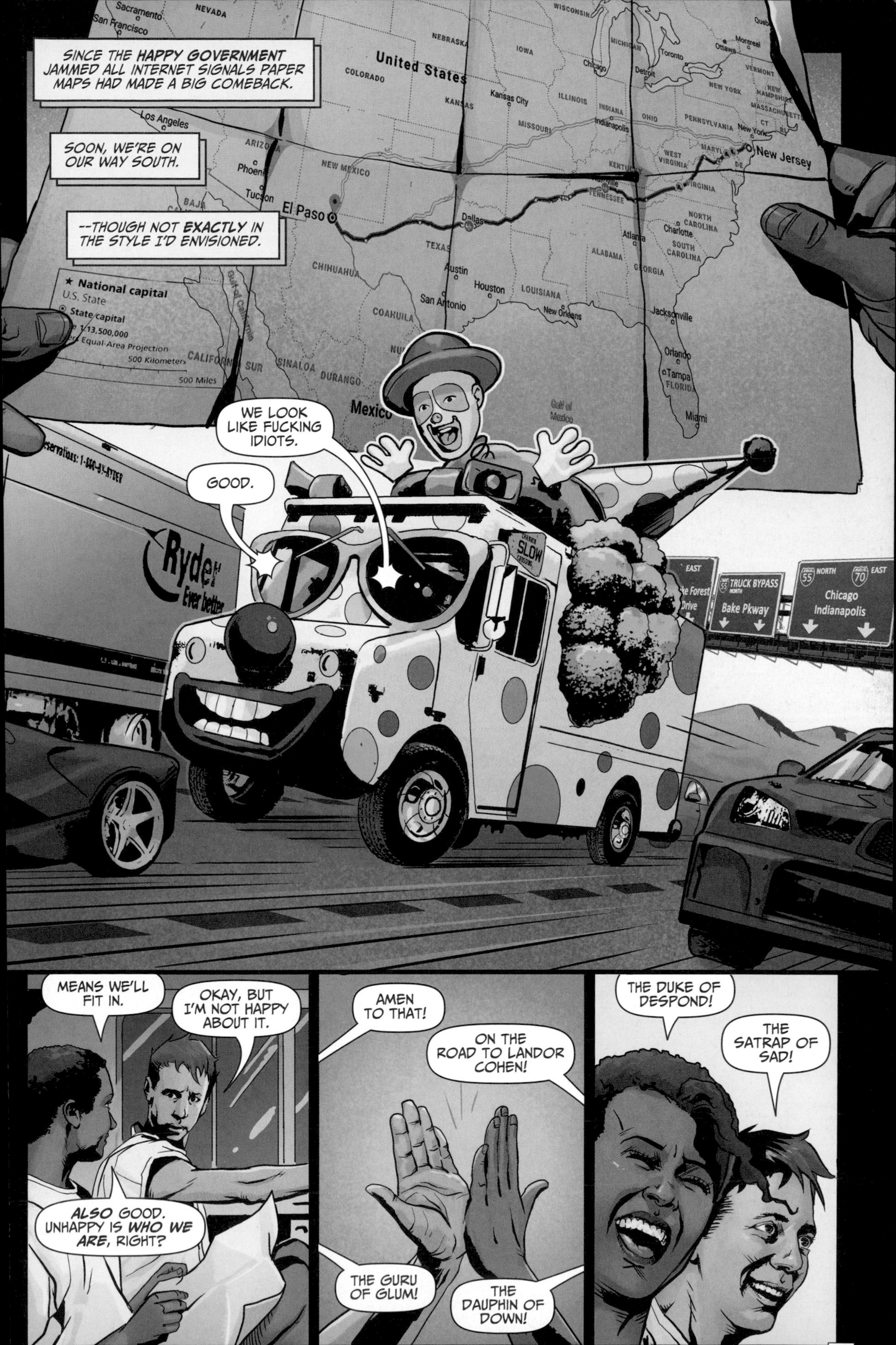
SINCE THE HAPPY GOVERNMENT JAMMED ALL INTERNET SIGNALS PAPER MAPS HAD MADE A BIG COMEBACK.
SOON, WE'RE ON OUR WAY SOUTH.
--THOUGH NOT EXACTLY IN THE STYLE I'D ENVISIONED.
WE LOOK LIKE FUCKING IDIOTS.
GOOD.
SLOW
Ryder Ever better
TRUCK BYPASS
Bake Pkwy
NORTH
EAST
Chicago
Indianapolis
MEANS WE'LL FIT IN.
OKAY, BUT I'M NOT HAPPY ABOUT IT.
ALSO GOOD. UNHAPPY IS WHO WE ARE, RIGHT?
AMEN TO THAT!
ON THE ROAD TO LANDOR COHEN!
THE GURU OF GLUM!
THE DAUPHIN OF DOWN!
THE DUKE OF DESPOND!
THE SATRAP OF SAD!

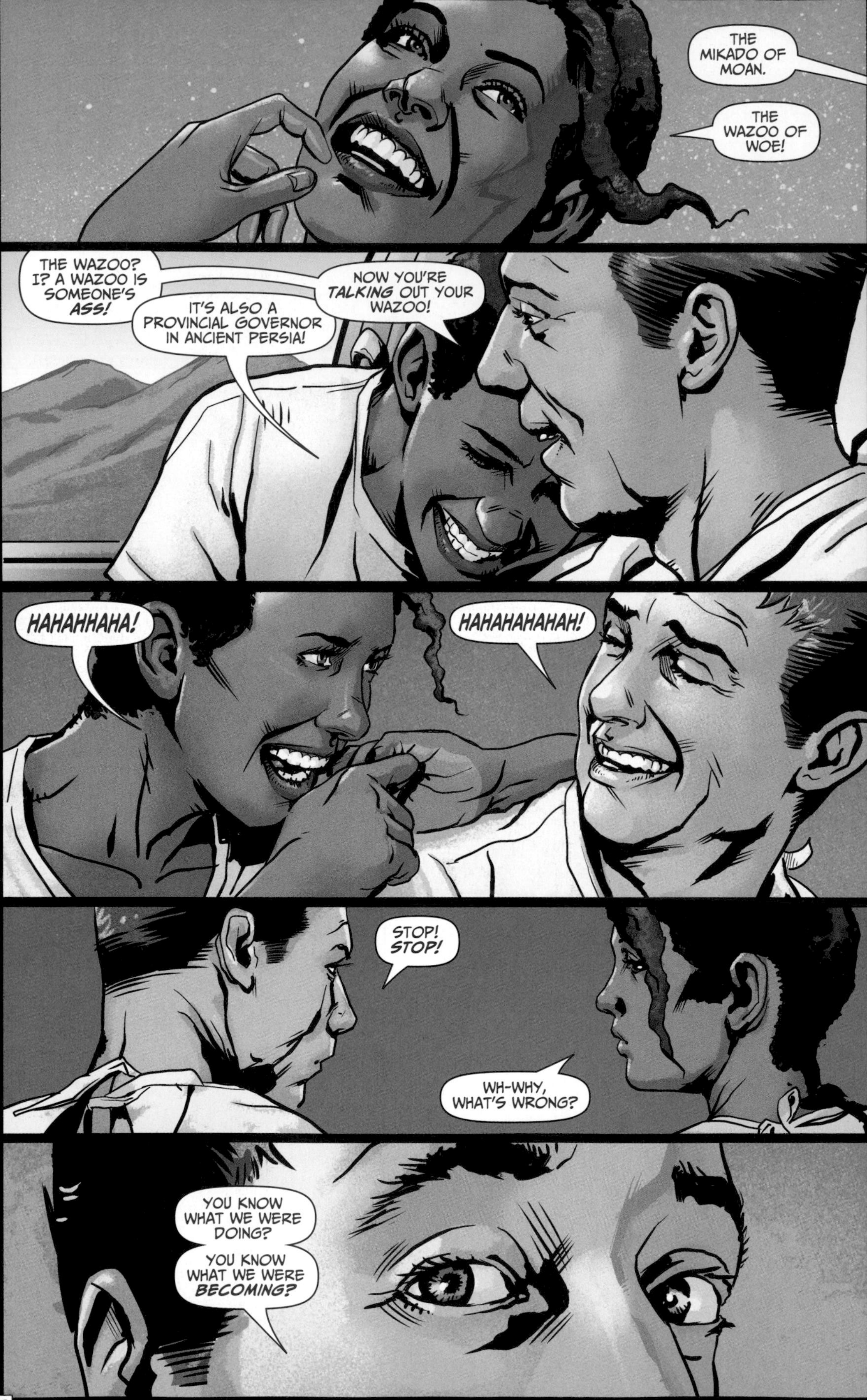
THE MIKADO OF MOAN.
THE WAZOO OF WOE!
THE WAZOO? I? A WAZOO IS SOMEONE'S ASS!
IT'S ALSO A PROVINCIAL GOVERNOR IN ANCIENT PERSIA!
NOW YOU'RE TALKING OUT YOUR WAZOO!
HAHAHHAHA!
HAHAHAHAHAH!
STOP! STOP!
WH-WHY, WHAT'S WRONG?
YOU KNOW WHAT WE WERE DOING?
YOU KNOW WHAT WE WERE BECOMING?

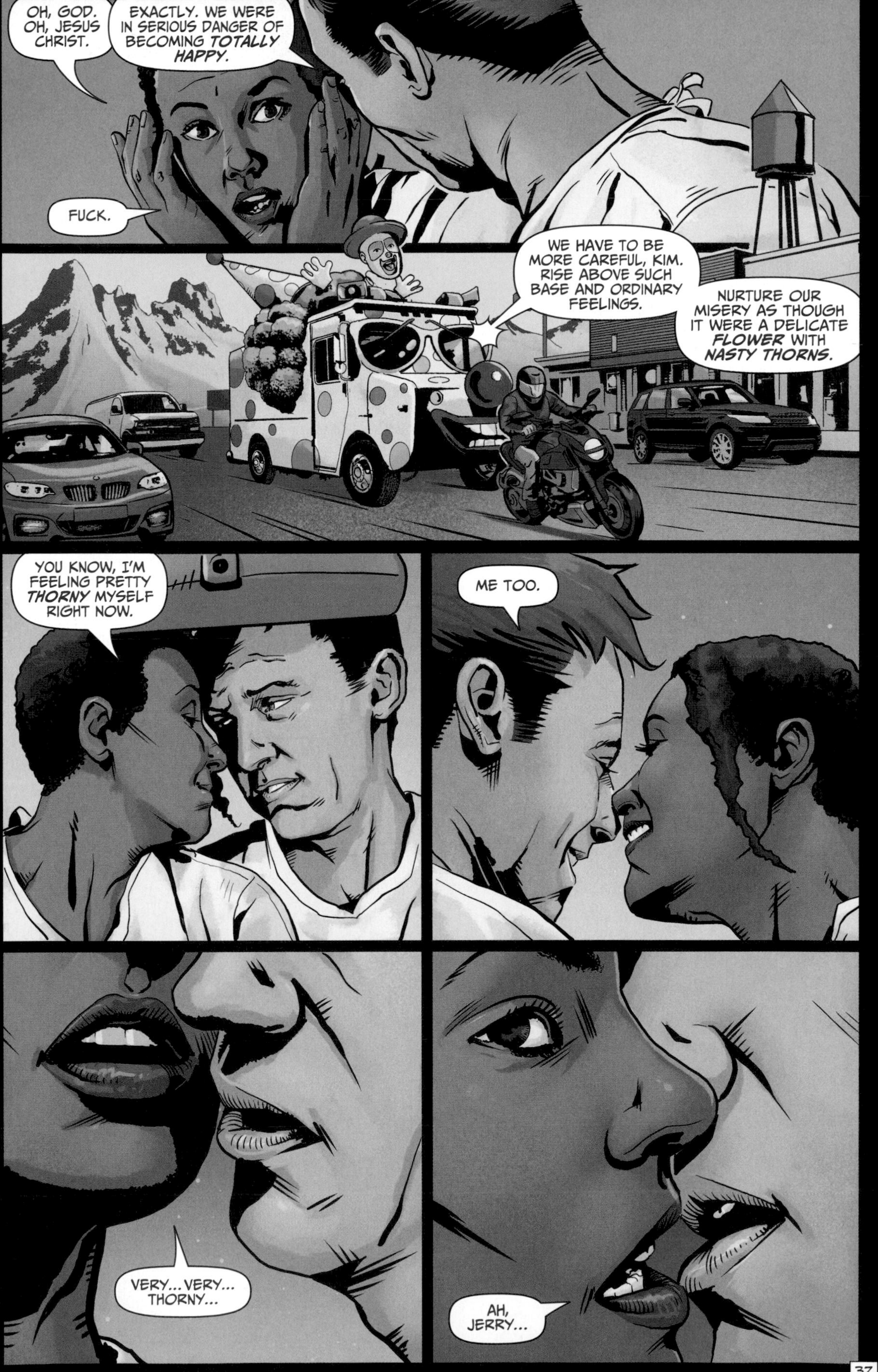
OH, GOD. OH, JESUS CHRIST.
EXACTLY. WE WERE IN SERIOUS DANGER OF BECOMING *TOTALLY HAPPY.*
FUCK.
WE HAVE TO BE MORE CAREFUL, KIM. RISE ABOVE SUCH BASE AND ORDINARY FEELINGS.
NURTURE OUR MISERY AS THOUGH IT WERE A DELICATE *FLOWER* WITH *NASTY THORNS.*
YOU KNOW, I'M FEELING PRETTY *THORNY* MYSELF RIGHT NOW.
ME TOO.
VERY...VERY... THORNY...
AH, JERRY...

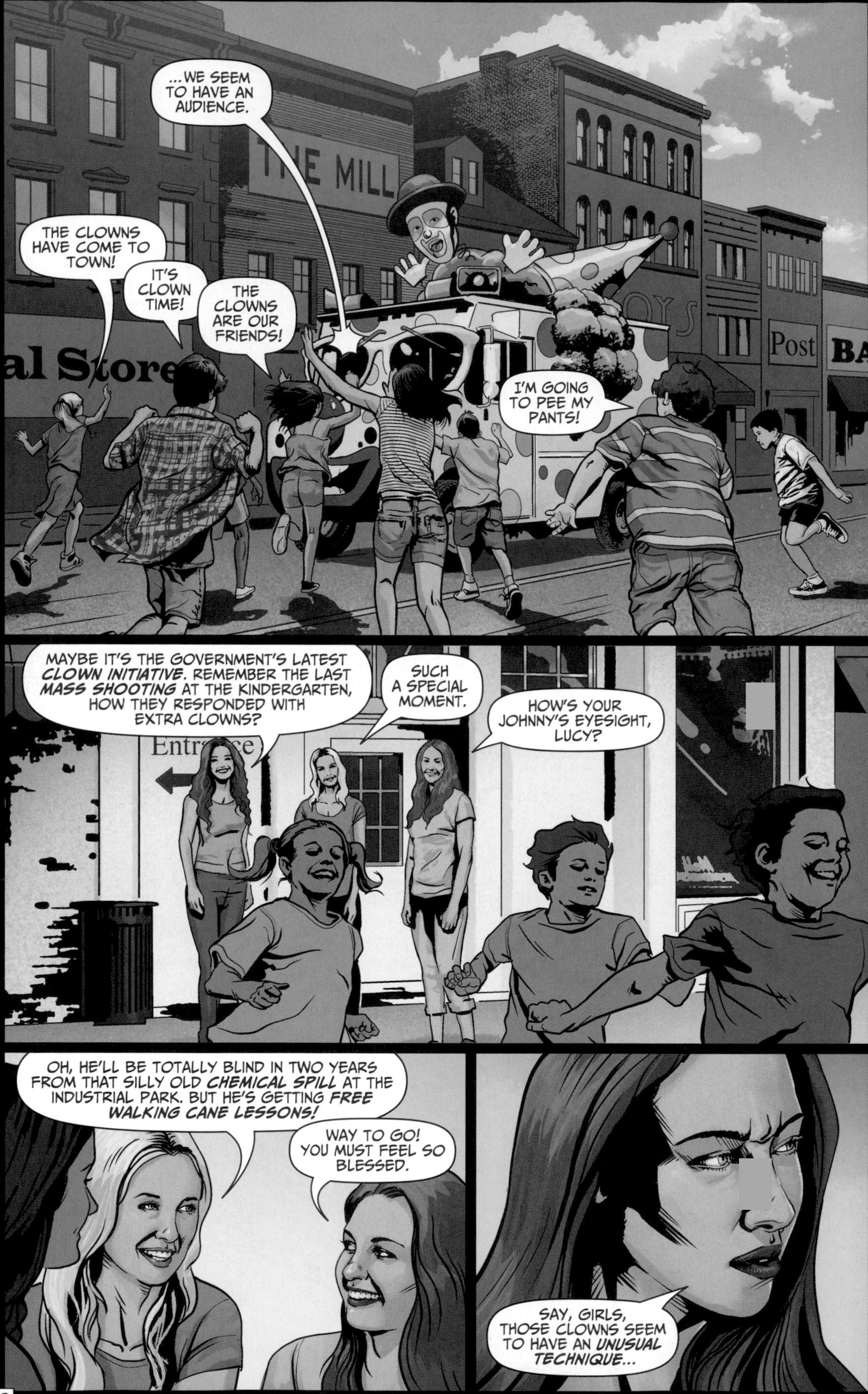
THE MILL
...WE SEEM TO HAVE AN AUDIENCE.
THE CLOWNS HAVE COME TO TOWN!
IT'S CLOWN TIME!
THE CLOWNS ARE OUR FRIENDS!
Post
I'M GOING TO PEE MY PANTS!
MAYBE IT'S THE GOVERNMENT'S LATEST *CLOWN INITIATIVE*. REMEMBER THE LAST *MASS SHOOTING* AT THE KINDERGARTEN, HOW THEY RESPONDED WITH EXTRA CLOWNS?
SUCH A SPECIAL MOMENT.
HOW'S YOUR JOHNNY'S EYESIGHT, LUCY?
OH, HE'LL BE TOTALLY BLIND IN TWO YEARS FROM THAT SILLY OLD *CHEMICAL SPILL* AT THE INDUSTRIAL PARK. BUT HE'S GETTING *FREE WALKING CANE LESSONS!*
WAY TO GO! YOU MUST FEEL SO BLESSED.
SAY, GIRLS, THOSE CLOWNS SEEM TO HAVE AN *UNUSUAL TECHNIQUE*...

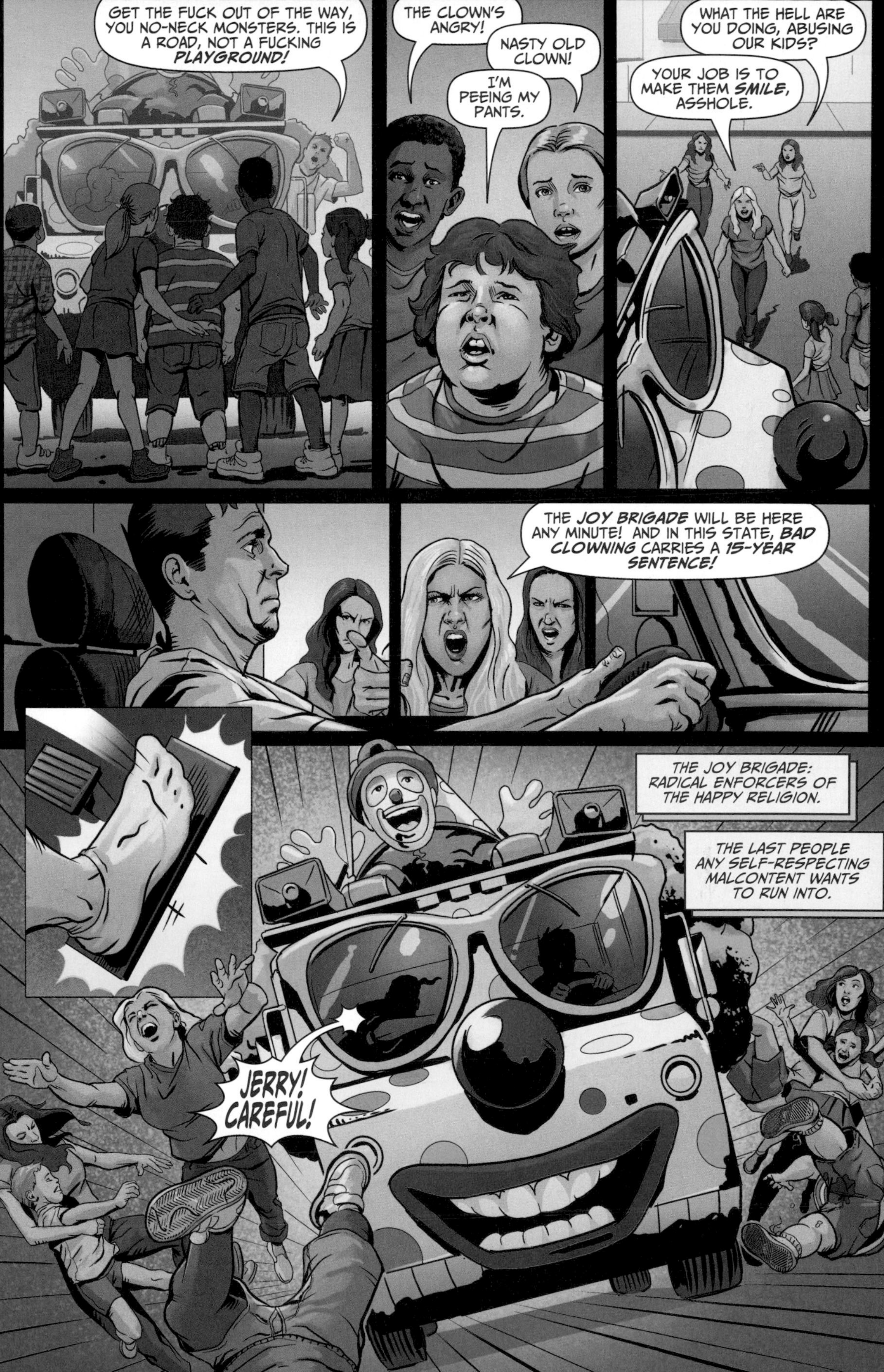
GET THE FUCK OUT OF THE WAY, YOU NO-NECK MONSTERS. THIS IS A ROAD, NOT A FUCKING PLAYGROUND!
THE CLOWN'S ANGRY!
NASTY OLD CLOWN!
I'M PEEING MY PANTS.
WHAT THE HELL ARE YOU DOING, ABUSING OUR KIDS?
YOUR JOB IS TO MAKE THEM SMILE, ASSHOLE.
THE JOY BRIGADE WILL BE HERE ANY MINUTE! AND IN THIS STATE, BAD CLOWNING CARRIES A 15-YEAR SENTENCE!
THE JOY BRIGADE: RADICAL ENFORCERS OF THE HAPPY RELIGION.
THE LAST PEOPLE ANY SELF-RESPECTING MALCONTENT WANTS TO RUN INTO.
JERRY! CAREFUL!

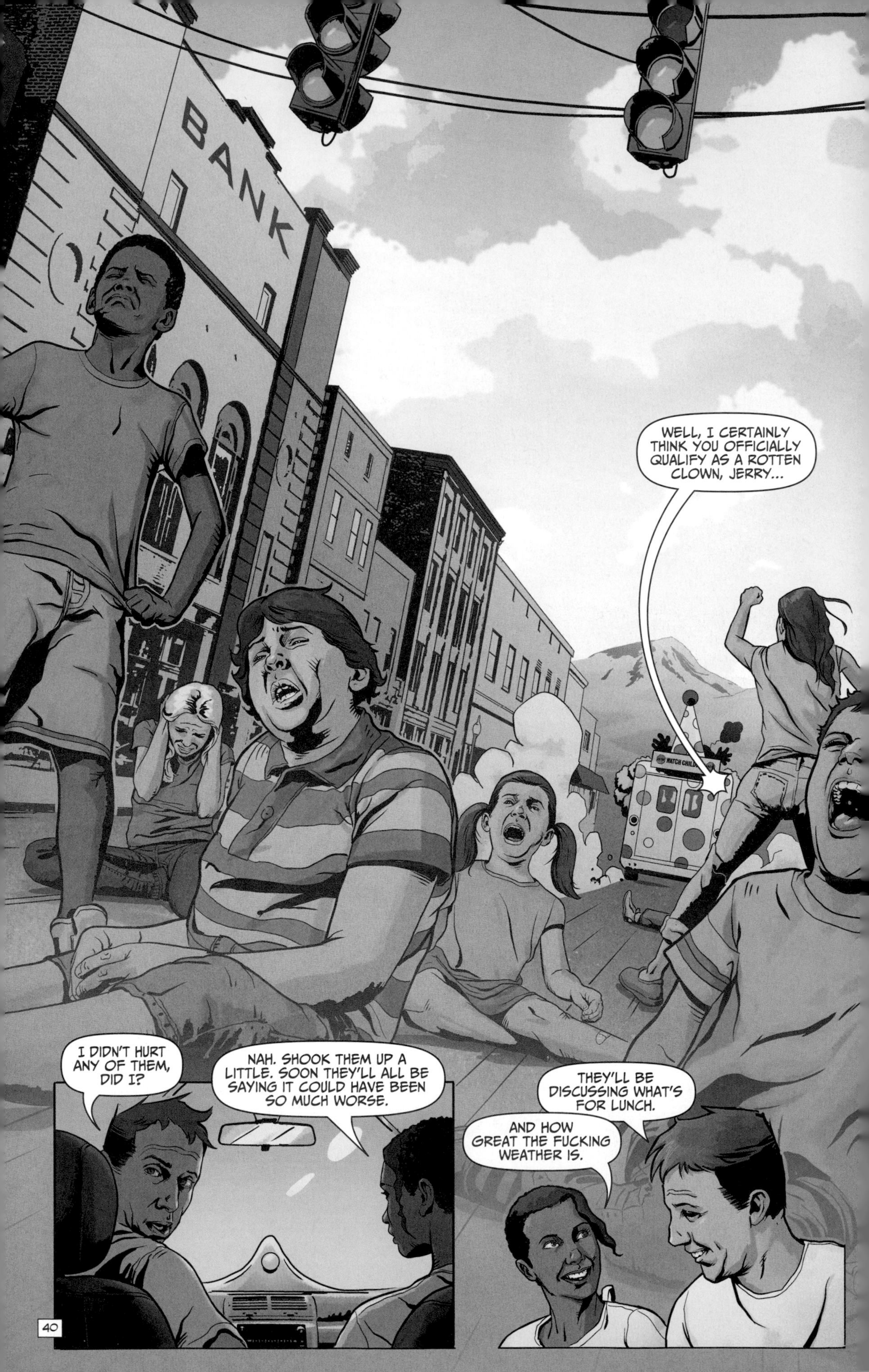
BANK
WELL, I CERTAINLY THINK YOU OFFICIALLY QUALIFY AS A ROTTEN CLOWN, JERRY...
I DIDN'T HURT ANY OF THEM, DID I?
NAH. SHOOK THEM UP A LITTLE. SOON THEY'LL ALL BE SAYING IT COULD HAVE BEEN SO MUCH WORSE.
THEY'LL BE DISCUSSING WHAT'S FOR LUNCH.
AND HOW GREAT THE FUCKING WEATHER IS.

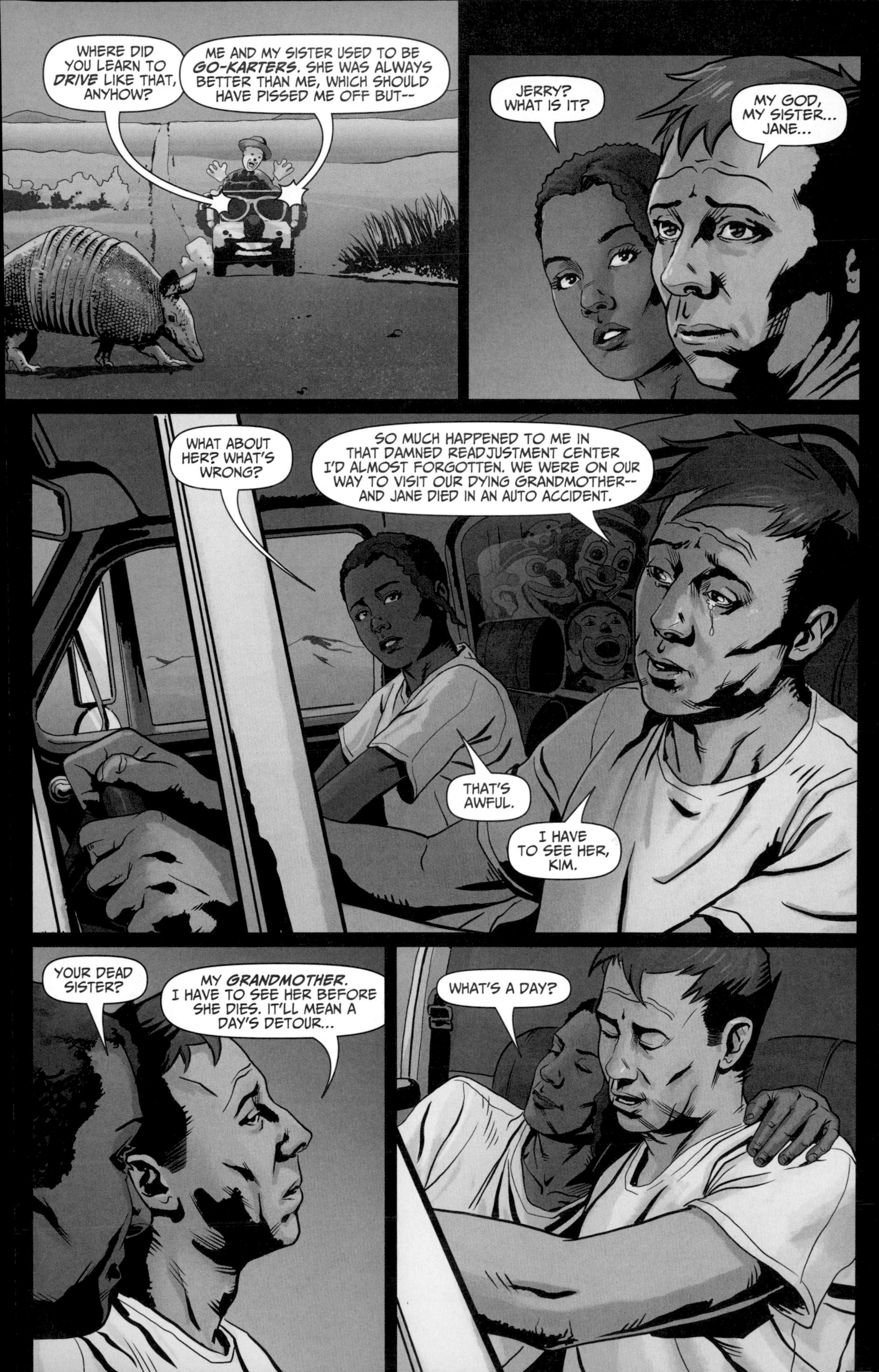
WHERE DID YOU LEARN TO DRIVE LIKE THAT, ANYHOW?
ME AND MY SISTER USED TO BE GO-KARTERS. SHE WAS ALWAYS BETTER THAN ME, WHICH SHOULD HAVE PISSED ME OFF BUT--
JERRY? WHAT IS IT?
MY GOD, MY SISTER... JANE...
WHAT ABOUT HER? WHAT'S WRONG?
SO MUCH HAPPENED TO ME IN THAT DAMNED READJUSTMENT CENTER I'D ALMOST FORGOTTEN. WE WERE ON OUR WAY TO VISIT OUR DYING GRANDMOTHER-- AND JANE DIED IN AN AUTO ACCIDENT.
THAT'S AWFUL.
I HAVE TO SEE HER, KIM.
YOUR DEAD SISTER?
MY GRANDMOTHER. I HAVE TO SEE HER BEFORE SHE DIES. IT'LL MEAN A DAY'S DETOUR...
WHAT'S A DAY?

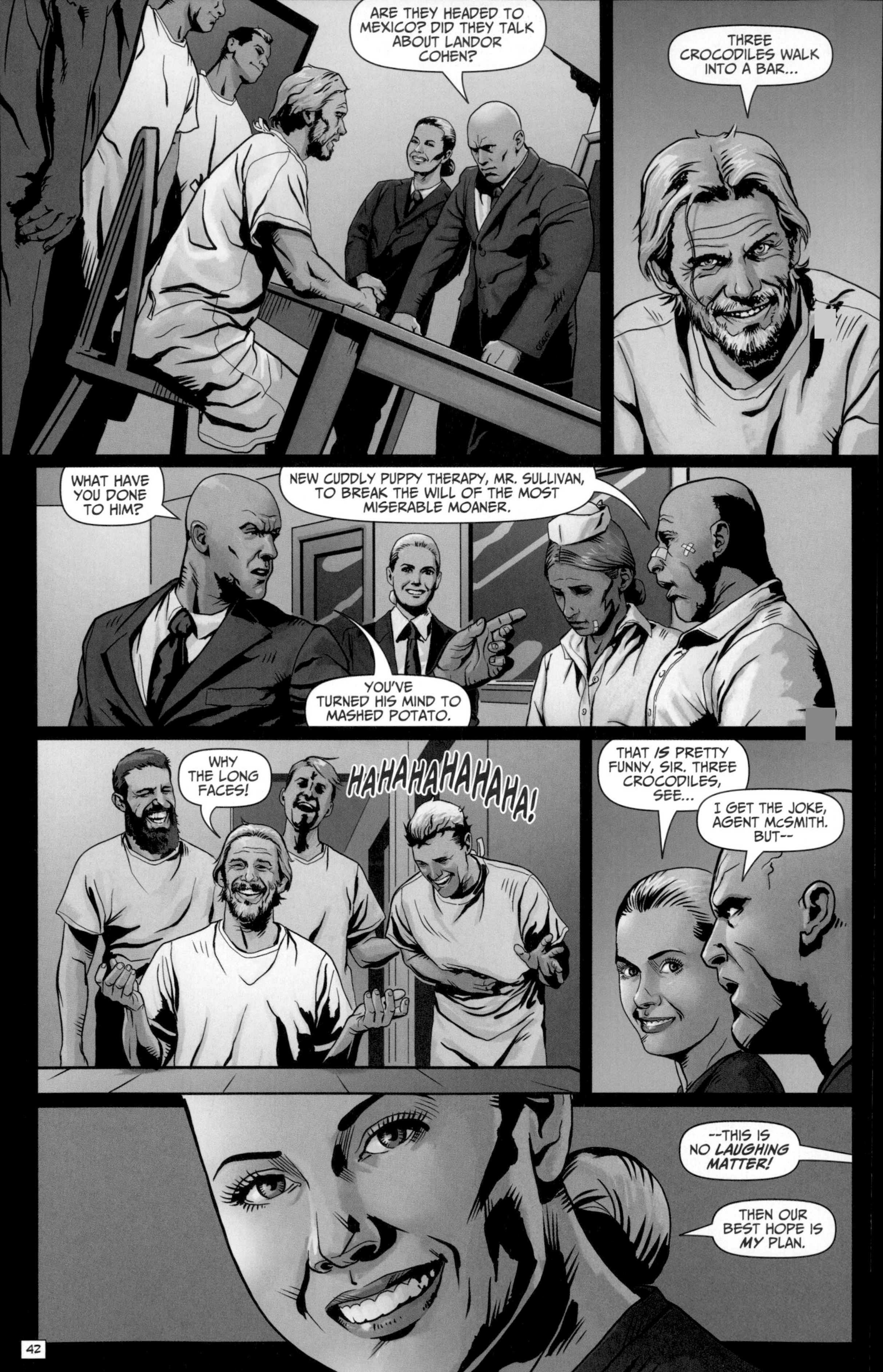

ARE THEY HEADED TO MEXICO? DID THEY TALK ABOUT LANDOR COHEN?
THREE CROCODILES WALK INTO A BAR...
WHAT HAVE YOU DONE TO HIM?
NEW CUDDLY PUPPY THERAPY, MR. SULLIVAN, TO BREAK THE WILL OF THE MOST MISERABLE MOANER.
YOU'VE TURNED HIS MIND TO MASHED POTATO.
WHY THE LONG FACES!
HAHAHAHAHAHAHA!
THAT IS PRETTY FUNNY, SIR. THREE CROCODILES, SEE...
I GET THE JOKE, AGENT McSMITH. BUT--
--THIS IS NO LAUGHING MATTER!
THEN OUR BEST HOPE IS MY PLAN.

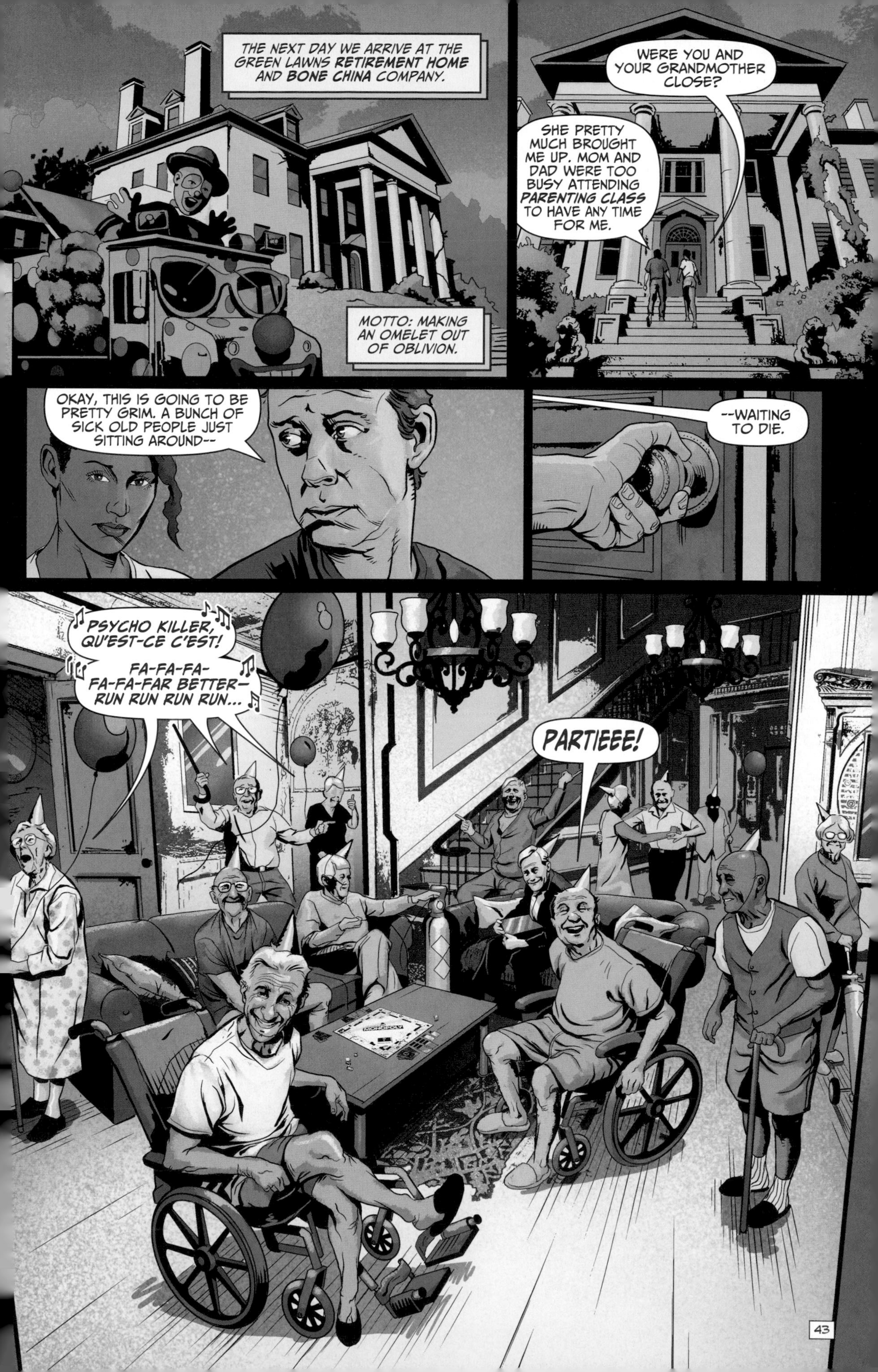

THE NEXT DAY WE ARRIVE AT THE GREEN LAWNS RETIREMENT HOME AND BONE CHINA COMPANY.
MOTTO: MAKING AN OMELET OUT OF OBLIVION.
WERE YOU AND YOUR GRANDMOTHER CLOSE?
SHE PRETTY MUCH BROUGHT ME UP. MOM AND DAD WERE TOO BUSY ATTENDING PARENTING CLASS TO HAVE ANY TIME FOR ME.
OKAY, THIS IS GOING TO BE PRETTY GRIM. A BUNCH OF SICK OLD PEOPLE JUST SITTING AROUND--
--WAITING TO DIE.
PSYCHO KILLER, QU'EST-CE C'EST!
FA-FA-FA-FA-FA-FAR BETTER– RUN RUN RUN RUN...
PARTIEEE!

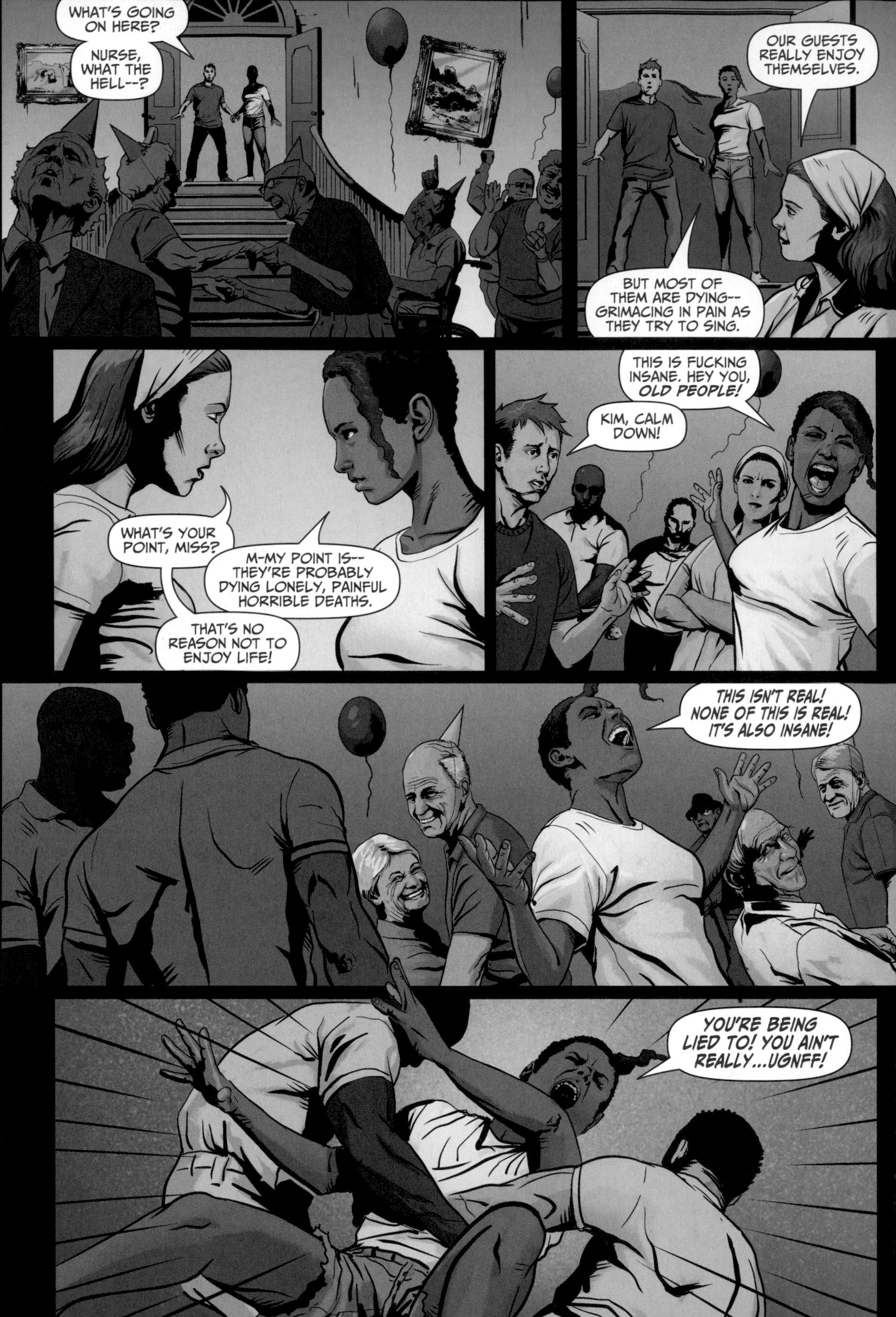
WHAT'S GOING ON HERE?
NURSE, WHAT THE HELL--?
OUR GUESTS REALLY ENJOY THEMSELVES.
BUT MOST OF THEM ARE DYING-- GRIMACING IN PAIN AS THEY TRY TO SING.
WHAT'S YOUR POINT, MISS?
M-MY POINT IS-- THEY'RE PROBABLY DYING LONELY, PAINFUL HORRIBLE DEATHS.
THAT'S NO REASON NOT TO ENJOY LIFE!
THIS IS FUCKING INSANE. HEY YOU, *OLD PEOPLE!*
KIM, CALM DOWN!
THIS ISN'T REAL! NONE OF THIS IS REAL! IT'S ALSO INSANE!
YOU'RE BEING LIED TO! YOU AIN'T REALLY...UGNFF!

UGNH!

ARE YOU WITH THAT DISRUPTIVE YOUNG WOMAN?

N—NO, I HARDLY KNOW HER. I'M HERE TO SEE MY GRANDMOTHER. *GLADYS STEPHENS*.

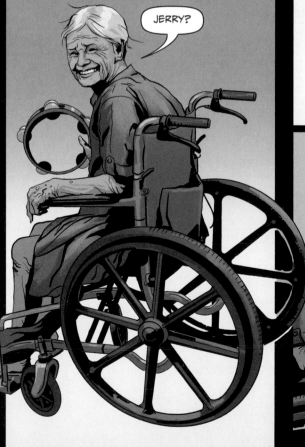

JERRY?

GRANDMA.

I PRAYED I'D SEE YOU AGAIN.

I—I'D HAVE COME SOONER, BUT THINGS GOT... COMPLICATED.

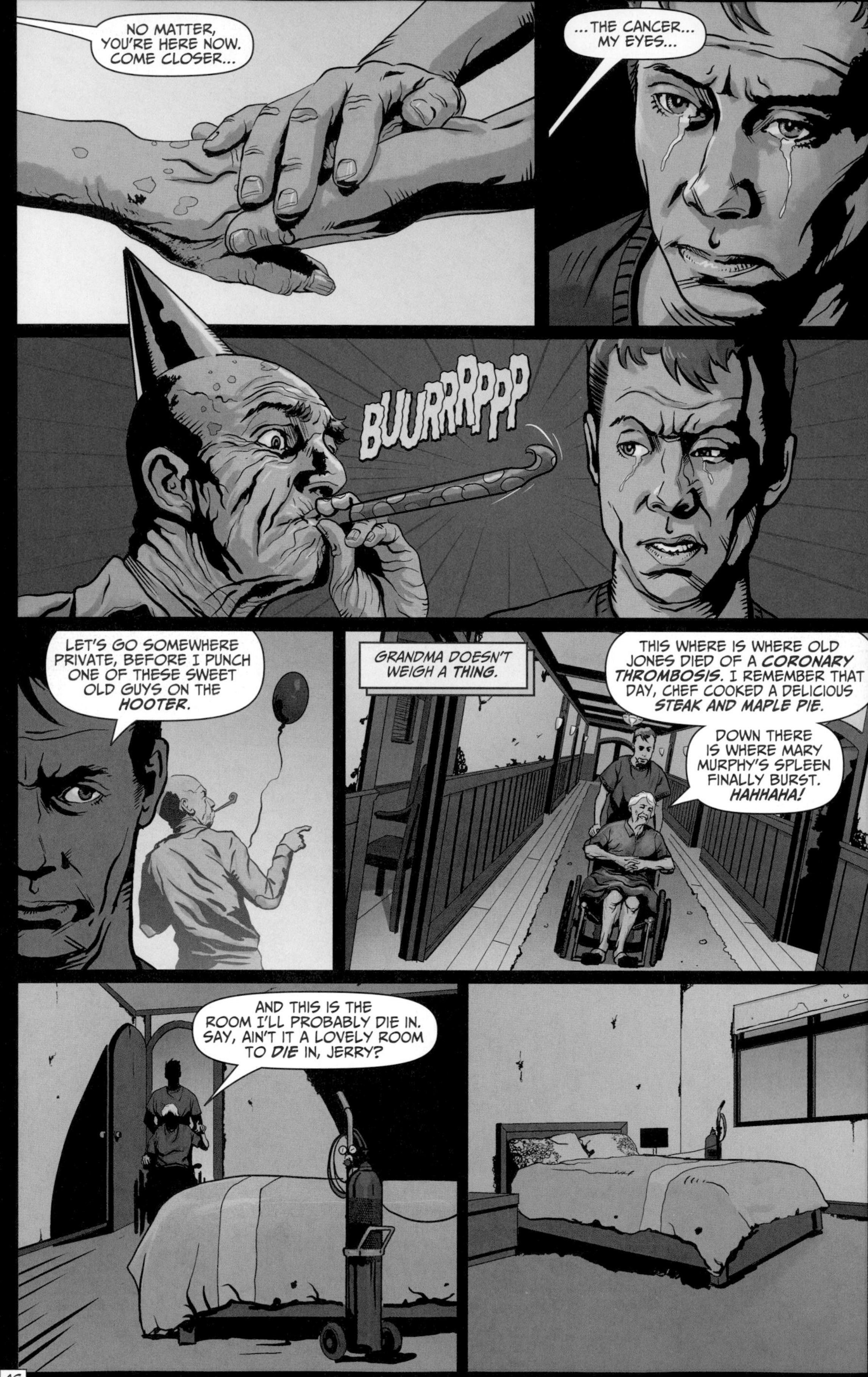
NO MATTER, YOU'RE HERE NOW. COME CLOSER...
...THE CANCER... MY EYES...
BUURRRPPP
LET'S GO SOMEWHERE PRIVATE, BEFORE I PUNCH ONE OF THESE SWEET OLD GUYS ON THE *HOOTER*.
GRANDMA DOESN'T WEIGH A *THING*.
THIS WHERE IS WHERE OLD JONES DIED OF A *CORONARY THROMBOSIS*. I REMEMBER THAT DAY, CHEF COOKED A DELICIOUS *STEAK AND MAPLE PIE*.
DOWN THERE IS WHERE MARY MURPHY'S SPLEEN FINALLY BURST. *HAHHAHA!*
AND THIS IS THE ROOM I'LL PROBABLY DIE IN. SAY, AIN'T IT A LOVELY ROOM TO *DIE* IN, JERRY?

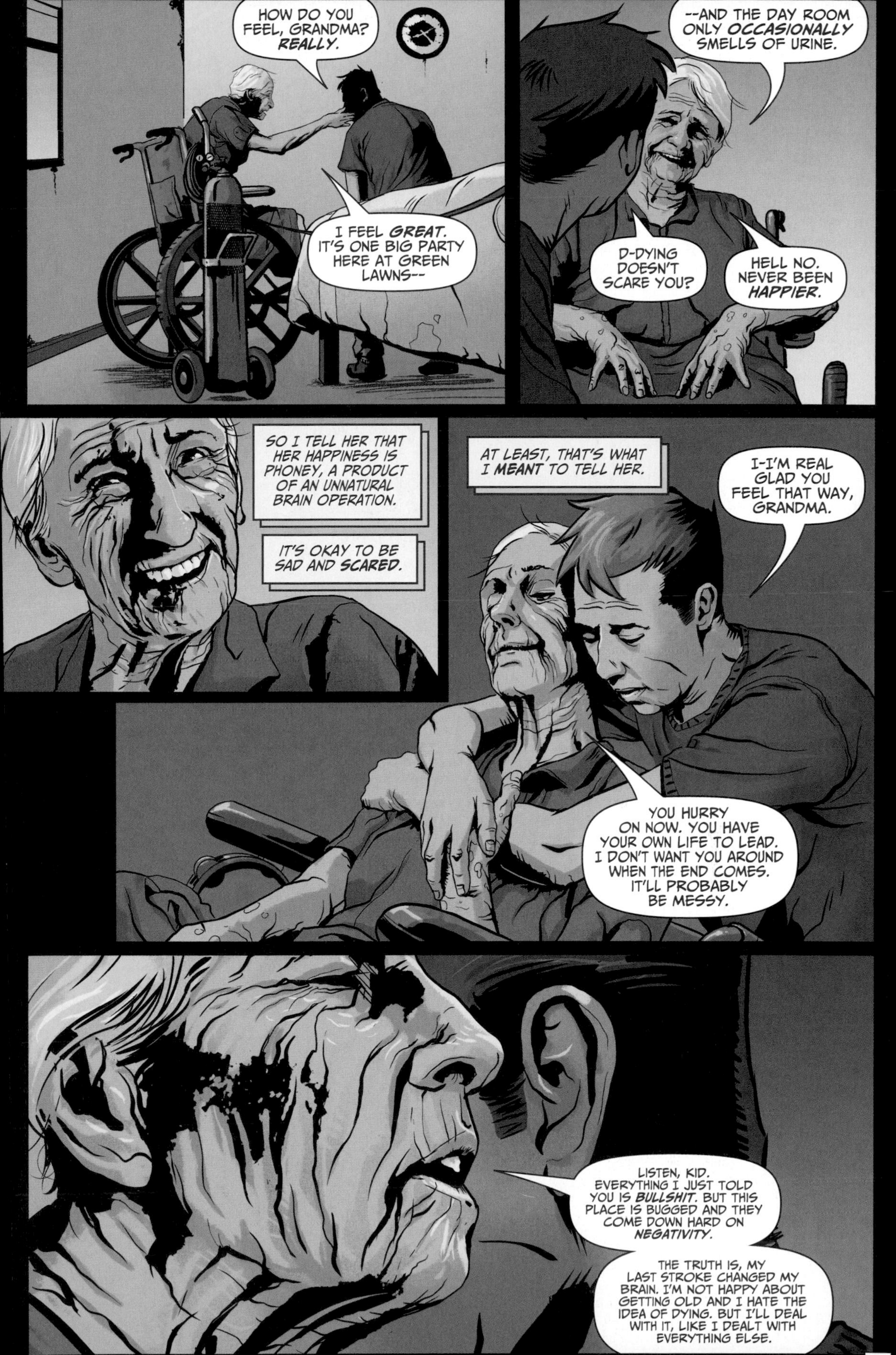
HOW DO YOU FEEL, GRANDMA? *REALLY*.
I FEEL *GREAT*. IT'S ONE BIG PARTY HERE AT GREEN LAWNS--
--AND THE DAY ROOM ONLY *OCCASIONALLY* SMELLS OF URINE.
D-DYING DOESN'T SCARE YOU?
HELL NO. NEVER BEEN *HAPPIER*.
SO I TELL HER THAT HER HAPPINESS IS PHONEY, A PRODUCT OF AN UNNATURAL BRAIN OPERATION.
IT'S OKAY TO BE SAD AND *SCARED*.
AT LEAST, THAT'S WHAT I *MEANT* TO TELL HER.
I-I'M REAL GLAD YOU FEEL THAT WAY, GRANDMA.
YOU HURRY ON NOW. YOU HAVE YOUR OWN LIFE TO LEAD. I DON'T WANT YOU AROUND WHEN THE END COMES. IT'LL PROBABLY BE MESSY.
LISTEN, KID. EVERYTHING I JUST TOLD YOU IS *BULLSHIT*. BUT THIS PLACE IS BUGGED AND THEY COME DOWN HARD ON *NEGATIVITY*.
THE TRUTH IS, MY LAST STROKE CHANGED MY BRAIN. I'M NOT HAPPY ABOUT GETTING OLD AND I HATE THE IDEA OF DYING. BUT I'LL DEAL WITH IT, LIKE I DEALT WITH EVERYTHING ELSE.

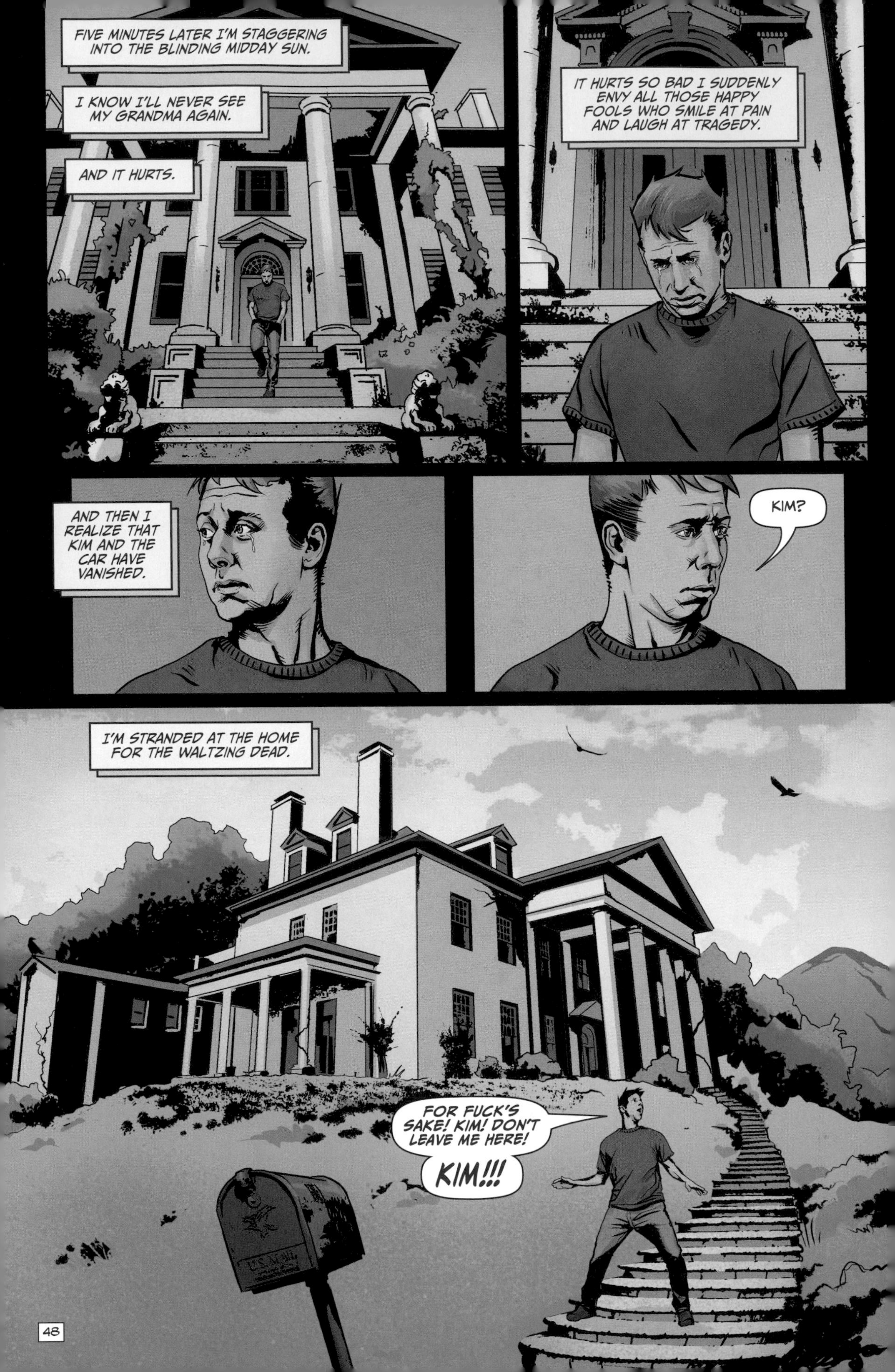

FIVE MINUTES LATER I'M STAGGERING INTO THE BLINDING MIDDAY SUN.
I KNOW I'LL NEVER SEE MY GRANDMA AGAIN.
AND IT HURTS.
IT HURTS SO BAD I SUDDENLY ENVY ALL THOSE HAPPY FOOLS WHO SMILE AT PAIN AND LAUGH AT TRAGEDY.
AND THEN I REALIZE THAT KIM AND THE CAR HAVE VANISHED.
KIM?
I'M STRANDED AT THE HOME FOR THE WALTZING DEAD.
FOR FUCK'S SAKE! KIM! DON'T LEAVE ME HERE!
KIM!!!

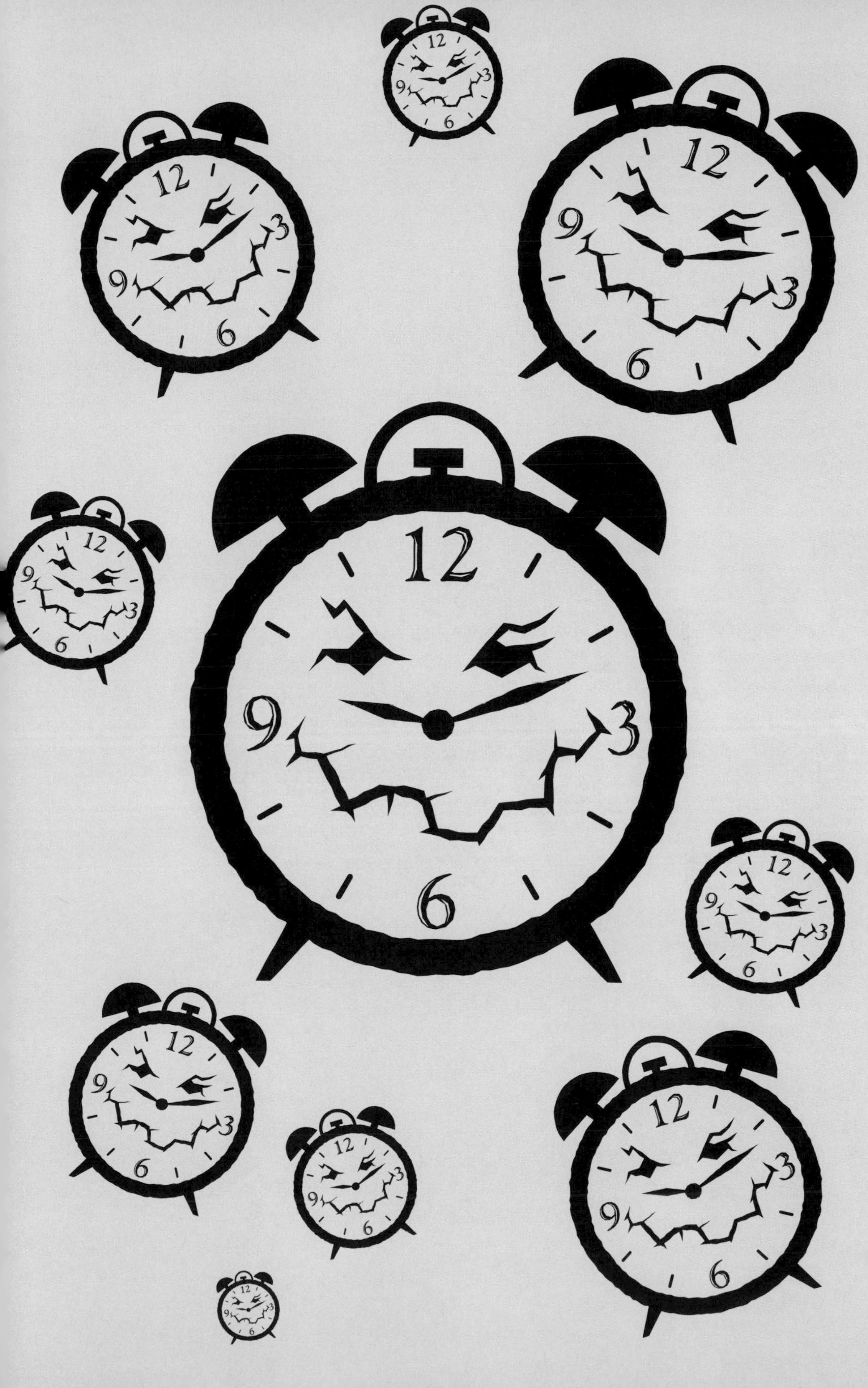

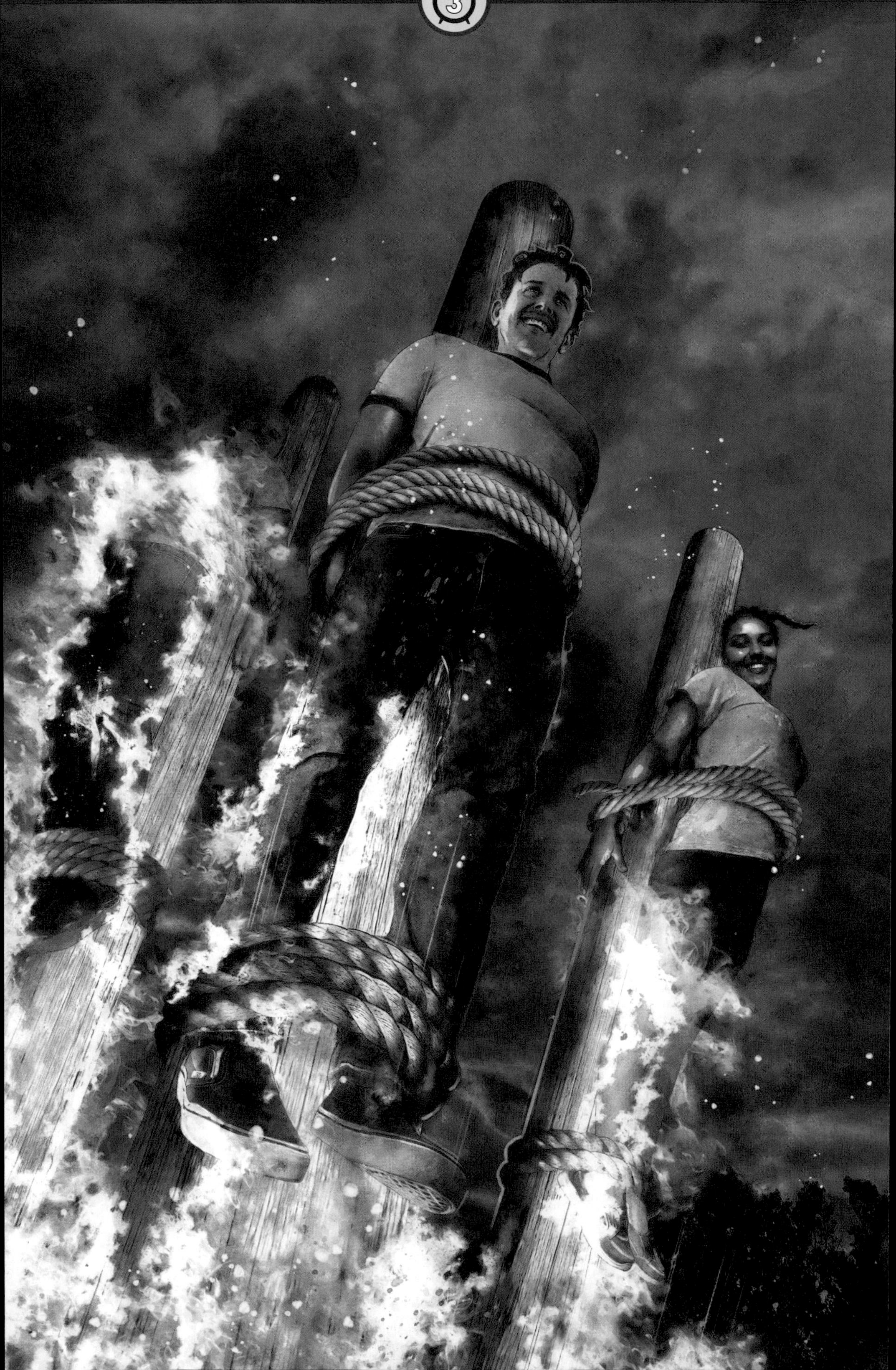

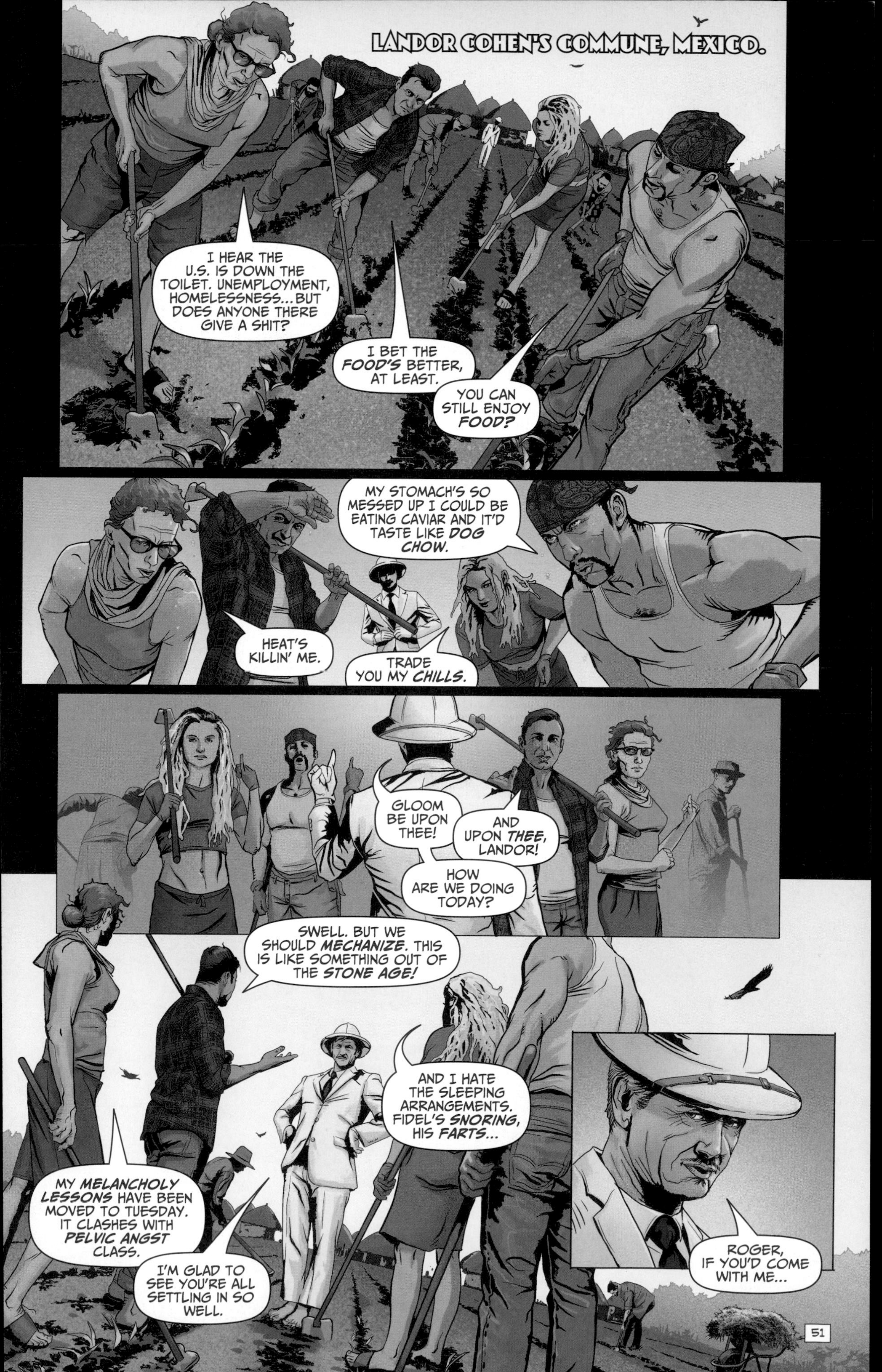

LANDOR COHEN'S COMMUNE, MEXICO.
I HEAR THE U.S. IS DOWN THE TOILET. UNEMPLOYMENT, HOMELESSNESS...BUT DOES ANYONE THERE GIVE A SHIT?
I BET THE FOOD'S BETTER, AT LEAST.
YOU CAN STILL ENJOY FOOD?
MY STOMACH'S SO MESSED UP I COULD BE EATING CAVIAR AND IT'D TASTE LIKE DOG CHOW.
HEAT'S KILLIN' ME.
TRADE YOU MY CHILLS.
GLOOM BE UPON THEE!
AND UPON THEE, LANDOR!
HOW ARE WE DOING TODAY?
SWELL. BUT WE SHOULD MECHANIZE. THIS IS LIKE SOMETHING OUT OF THE STONE AGE!
AND I HATE THE SLEEPING ARRANGEMENTS. FIDEL'S SNORING, HIS FARTS...
MY MELANCHOLY LESSONS HAVE BEEN MOVED TO TUESDAY. IT CLASHES WITH PELVIC ANGST CLASS.
I'M GLAD TO SEE YOU'RE ALL SETTLING IN SO WELL.
ROGER, IF YOU'D COME WITH ME...

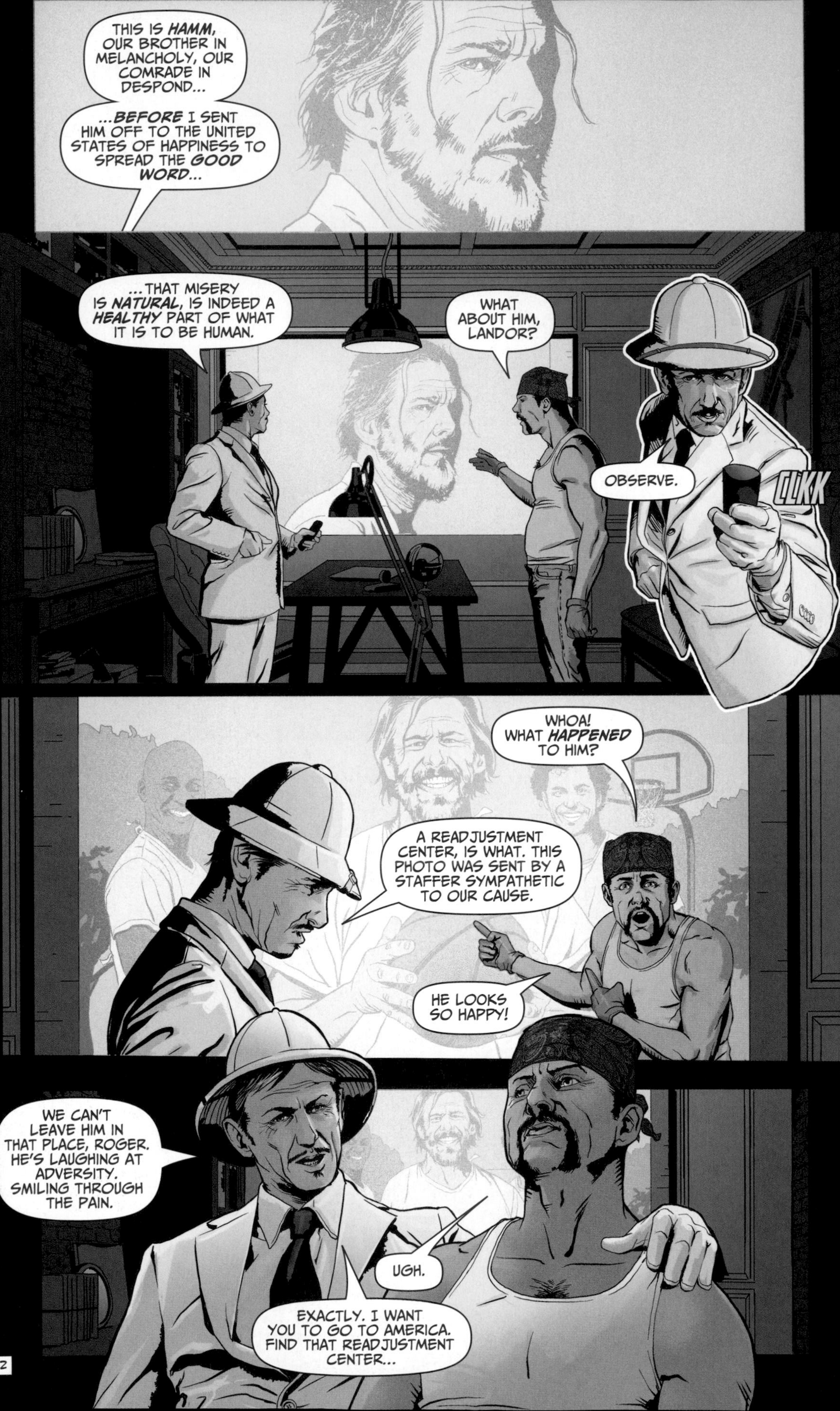
THIS IS HAMM, OUR BROTHER IN MELANCHOLY, OUR COMRADE IN DESPOND...
...BEFORE I SENT HIM OFF TO THE UNITED STATES OF HAPPINESS TO SPREAD THE GOOD WORD...
...THAT MISERY IS NATURAL, IS INDEED A HEALTHY PART OF WHAT IT IS TO BE HUMAN.
WHAT ABOUT HIM, LANDOR?
OBSERVE.
CLIKK
WHOA! WHAT HAPPENED TO HIM?
A READJUSTMENT CENTER, IS WHAT. THIS PHOTO WAS SENT BY A STAFFER SYMPATHETIC TO OUR CAUSE.
HE LOOKS SO HAPPY!
WE CAN'T LEAVE HIM IN THAT PLACE, ROGER. HE'S LAUGHING AT ADVERSITY. SMILING THROUGH THE PAIN.
UGH.
EXACTLY. I WANT YOU TO GO TO AMERICA. FIND THAT READJUSTMENT CENTER...

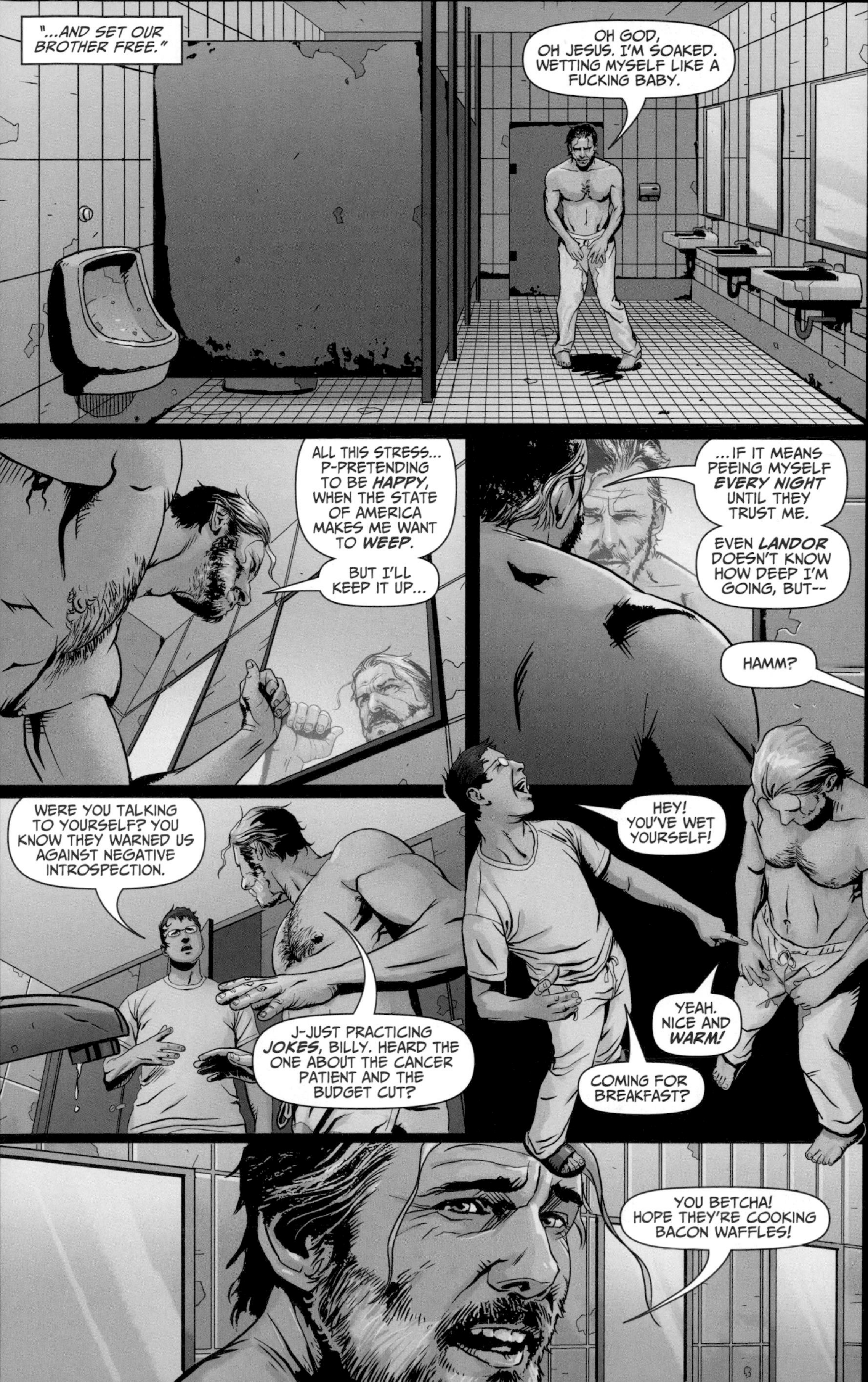
"...AND SET OUR BROTHER FREE."
OH GOD, OH JESUS. I'M SOAKED. WETTING MYSELF LIKE A FUCKING BABY.
ALL THIS STRESS... P-PRETENDING TO BE HAPPY, WHEN THE STATE OF AMERICA MAKES ME WANT TO WEEP.
BUT I'LL KEEP IT UP...
...IF IT MEANS PEEING MYSELF EVERY NIGHT UNTIL THEY TRUST ME.
EVEN LANDOR DOESN'T KNOW HOW DEEP I'M GOING, BUT--
HAMM?
WERE YOU TALKING TO YOURSELF? YOU KNOW THEY WARNED US AGAINST NEGATIVE INTROSPECTION.
J-JUST PRACTICING JOKES, BILLY. HEARD THE ONE ABOUT THE CANCER PATIENT AND THE BUDGET CUT?
HEY! YOU'VE WET YOURSELF!
YEAH. NICE AND WARM!
COMING FOR BREAKFAST?
YOU BETCHA! HOPE THEY'RE COOKING BACON WAFFLES!

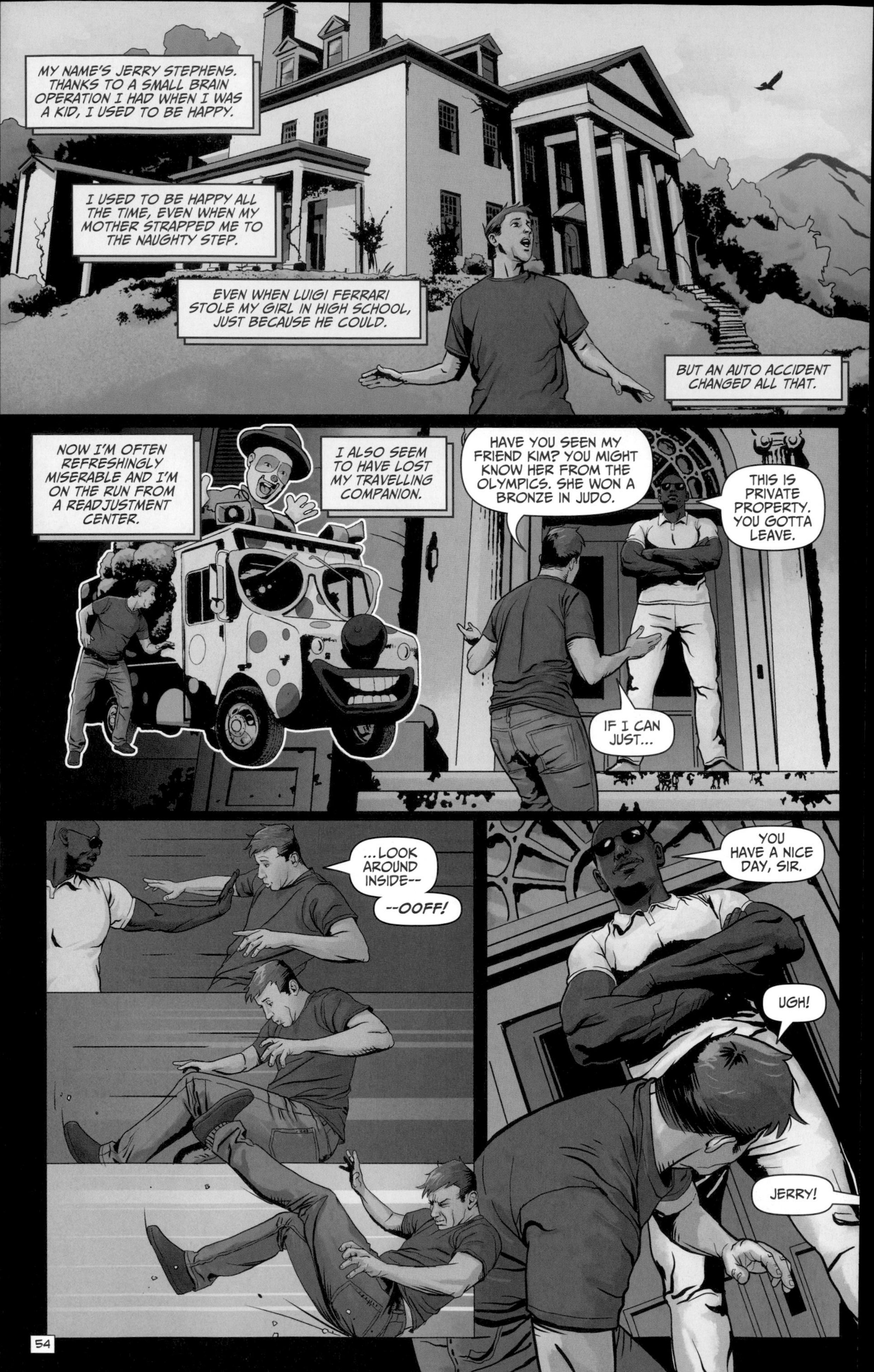

MY NAME'S JERRY STEPHENS. THANKS TO A SMALL BRAIN OPERATION I HAD WHEN I WAS A KID, I USED TO BE HAPPY.
I USED TO BE HAPPY ALL THE TIME, EVEN WHEN MY MOTHER STRAPPED ME TO THE NAUGHTY STEP.
EVEN WHEN LUIGI FERRARI STOLE MY GIRL IN HIGH SCHOOL, JUST BECAUSE HE COULD.
BUT AN AUTO ACCIDENT CHANGED ALL THAT.
NOW I'M OFTEN REFRESHINGLY MISERABLE AND I'M ON THE RUN FROM A READJUSTMENT CENTER.
I ALSO SEEM TO HAVE LOST MY TRAVELLING COMPANION.
HAVE YOU SEEN MY FRIEND KIM? YOU MIGHT KNOW HER FROM THE OLYMPICS. SHE WON A BRONZE IN JUDO.
THIS IS PRIVATE PROPERTY. YOU GOTTA LEAVE.
IF I CAN JUST...
...LOOK AROUND INSIDE--
--OOFF!
YOU HAVE A NICE DAY, SIR.
UGH!
JERRY!

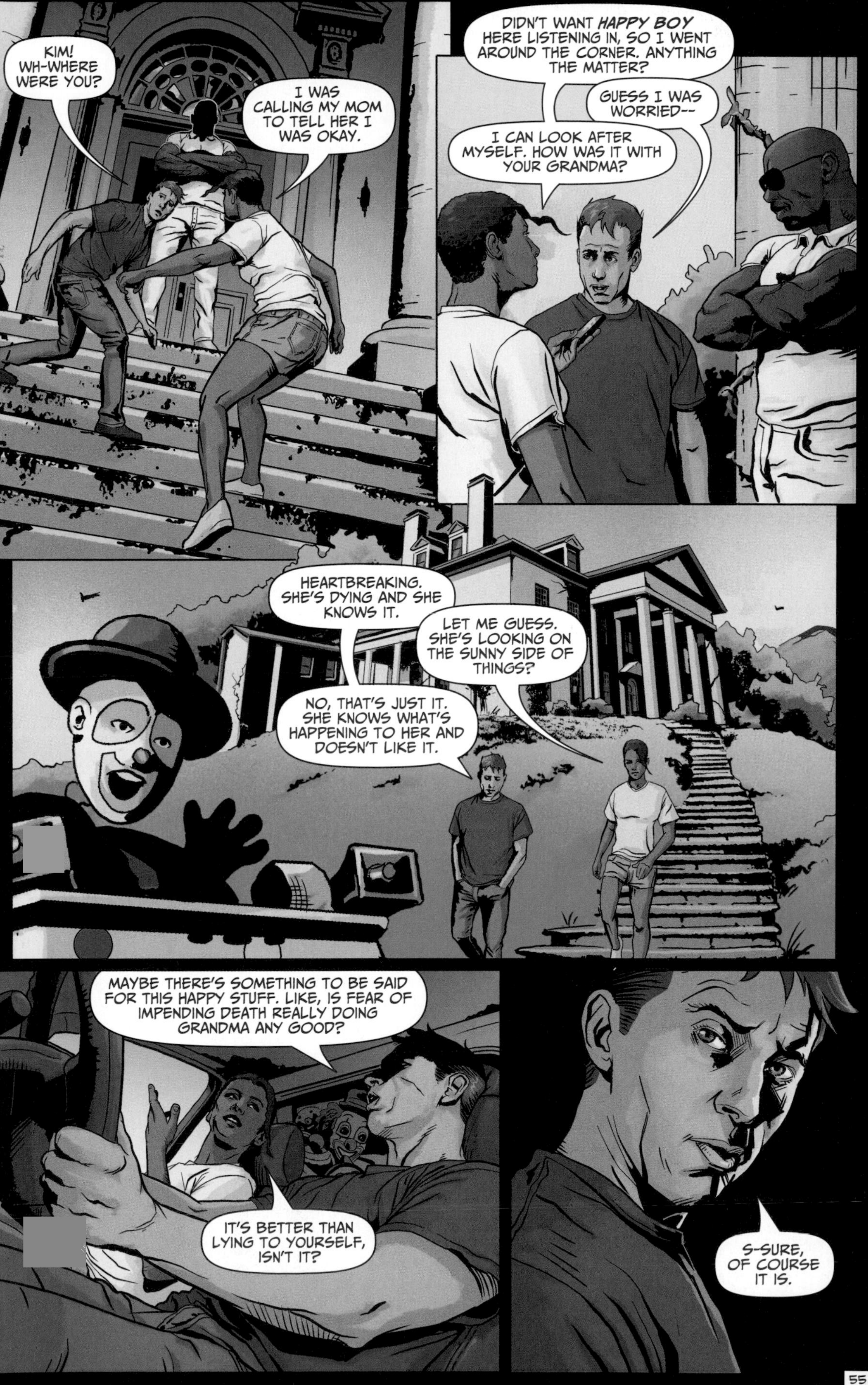
KIM! WH-WHERE WERE YOU?
I WAS CALLING MY MOM TO TELL HER I WAS OKAY.
DIDN'T WANT HAPPY BOY HERE LISTENING IN, SO I WENT AROUND THE CORNER. ANYTHING THE MATTER?
GUESS I WAS WORRIED--
I CAN LOOK AFTER MYSELF. HOW WAS IT WITH YOUR GRANDMA?
HEARTBREAKING. SHE'S DYING AND SHE KNOWS IT.
LET ME GUESS. SHE'S LOOKING ON THE SUNNY SIDE OF THINGS?
NO, THAT'S JUST IT. SHE KNOWS WHAT'S HAPPENING TO HER AND DOESN'T LIKE IT.
MAYBE THERE'S SOMETHING TO BE SAID FOR THIS HAPPY STUFF. LIKE, IS FEAR OF IMPENDING DEATH REALLY DOING GRANDMA ANY GOOD?
IT'S BETTER THAN LYING TO YOURSELF, ISN'T IT?
S-SURE, OF COURSE IT IS.

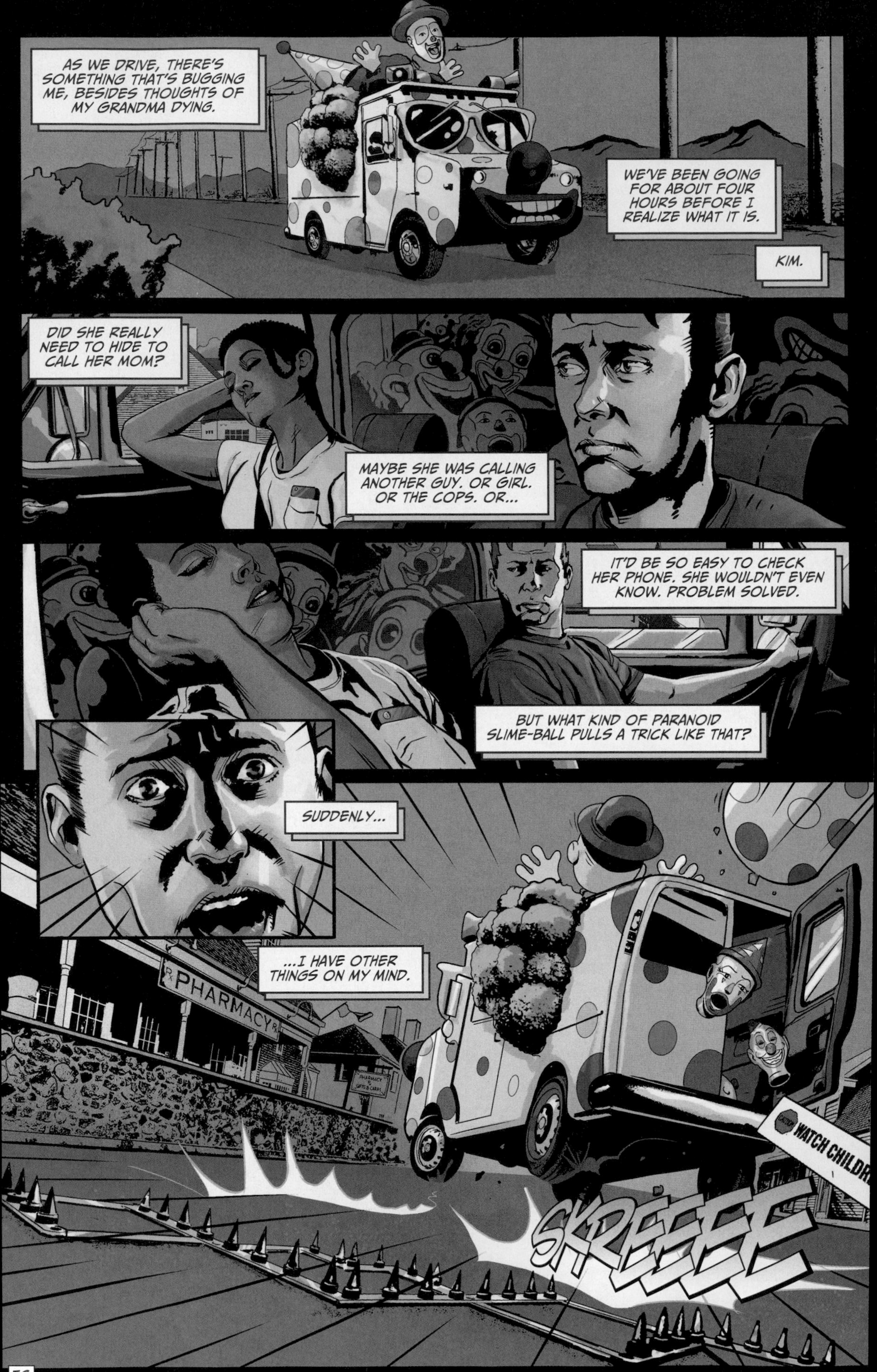
AS WE DRIVE, THERE'S SOMETHING THAT'S BUGGING ME, BESIDES THOUGHTS OF MY GRANDMA DYING.
WE'VE BEEN GOING FOR ABOUT FOUR HOURS BEFORE I REALIZE WHAT IT IS.
KIM.
DID SHE REALLY NEED TO HIDE TO CALL HER MOM?
MAYBE SHE WAS CALLING ANOTHER GUY. OR GIRL. OR THE COPS. OR...
IT'D BE SO EASY TO CHECK HER PHONE. SHE WOULDN'T EVEN KNOW. PROBLEM SOLVED.
BUT WHAT KIND OF PARANOID SLIME-BALL PULLS A TRICK LIKE THAT?
SUDDENLY...
...I HAVE OTHER THINGS ON MY MIND.
PHARMACY
WATCH CHILDR
SKREEEEE

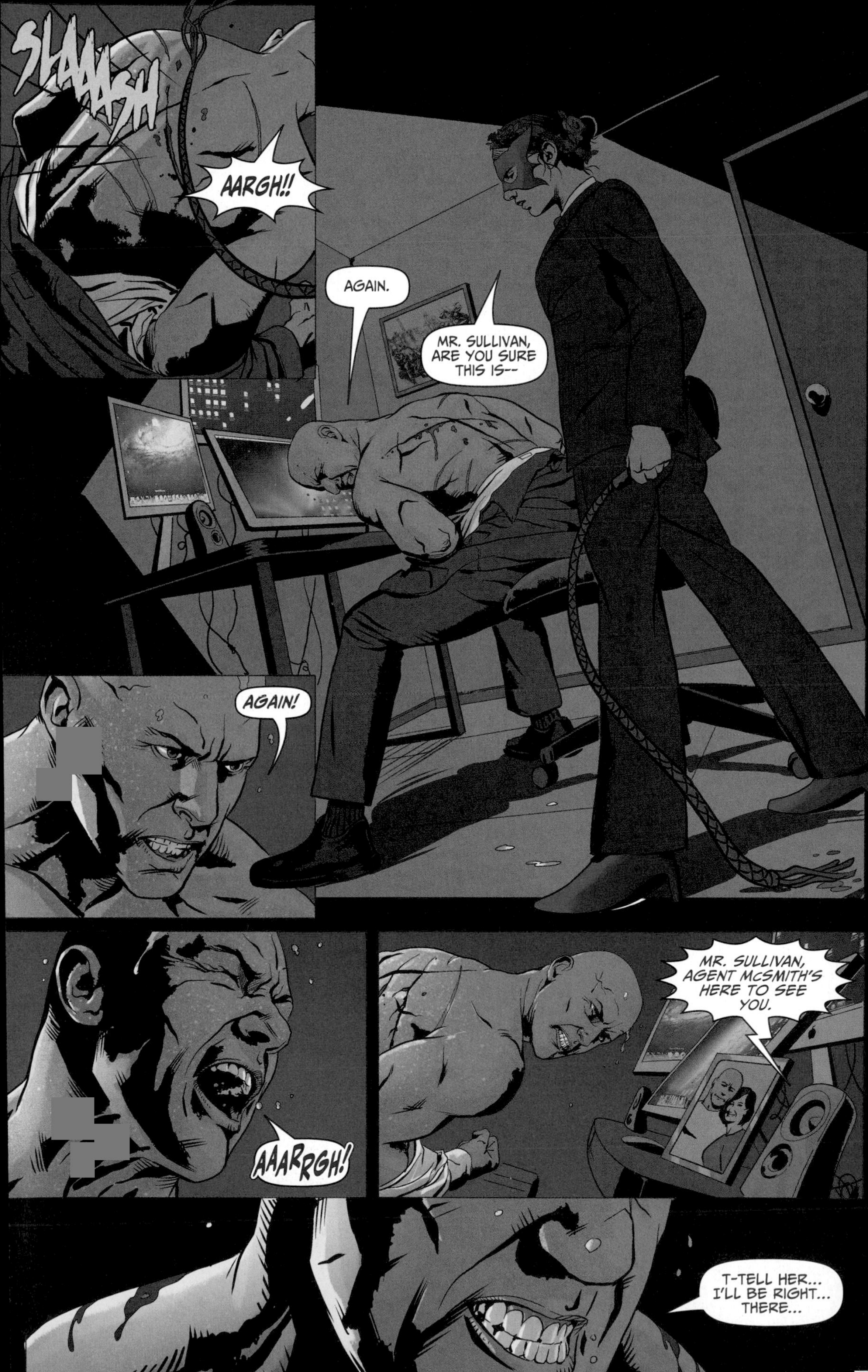
SLAAASH
AARGH!!
AGAIN.
MR. SULLIVAN, ARE YOU SURE THIS IS--
AGAIN!
AAARRGH!
MR. SULLIVAN, AGENT McSMITH'S HERE TO SEE YOU.
T-TELL HER... I'LL BE RIGHT... THERE...

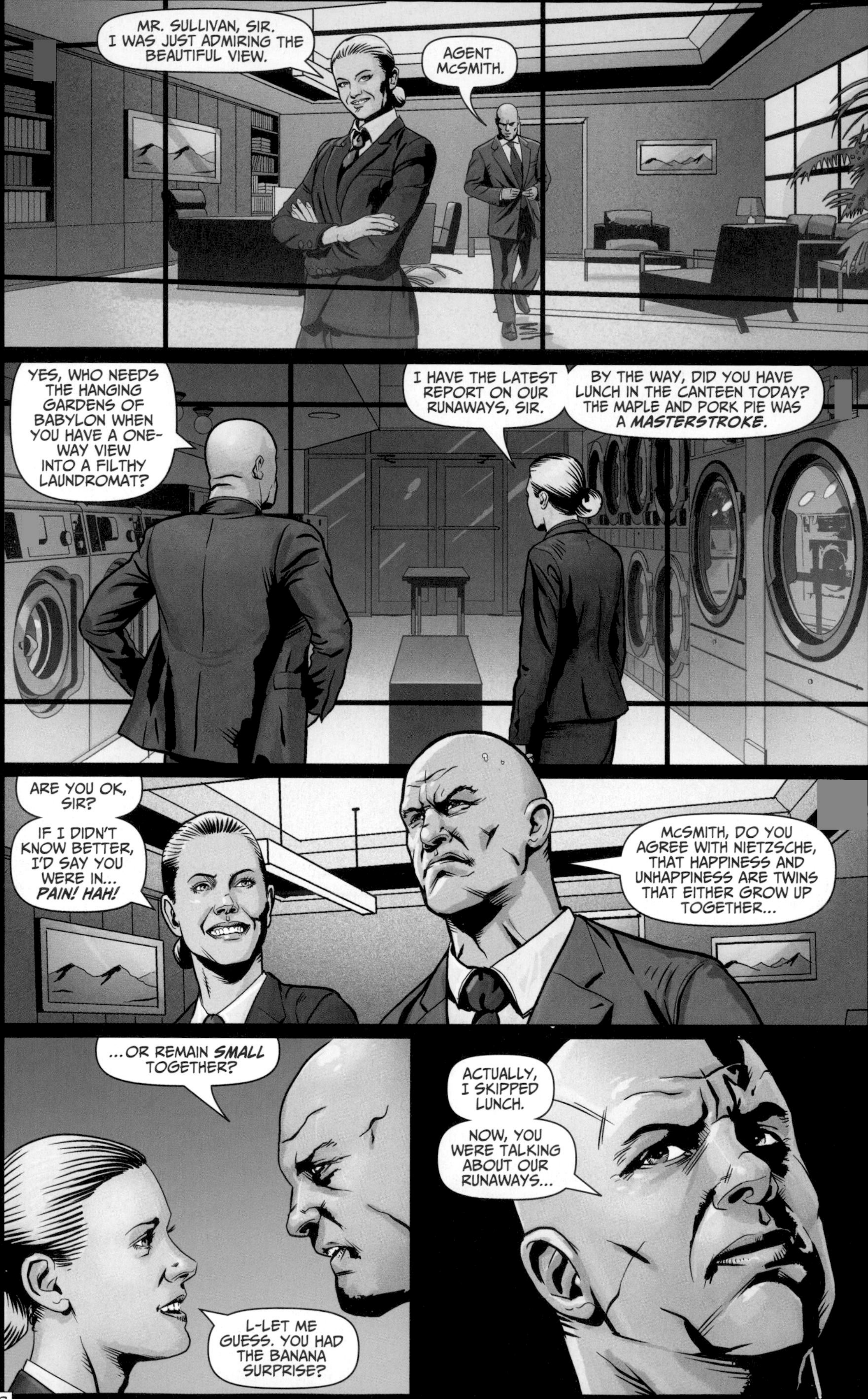
MR. SULLIVAN, SIR. I WAS JUST ADMIRING THE BEAUTIFUL VIEW.
AGENT McSMITH.
YES, WHO NEEDS THE HANGING GARDENS OF BABYLON WHEN YOU HAVE A ONE-WAY VIEW INTO A FILTHY LAUNDROMAT?
I HAVE THE LATEST REPORT ON OUR RUNAWAYS, SIR.
BY THE WAY, DID YOU HAVE LUNCH IN THE CANTEEN TODAY? THE MAPLE AND PORK PIE WAS A MASTERSTROKE.
ARE YOU OK, SIR?
IF I DIDN'T KNOW BETTER, I'D SAY YOU WERE IN... PAIN! HAH!
McSMITH, DO YOU AGREE WITH NIETZSCHE, THAT HAPPINESS AND UNHAPPINESS ARE TWINS THAT EITHER GROW UP TOGETHER...
...OR REMAIN SMALL TOGETHER?
L-LET ME GUESS. YOU HAD THE BANANA SURPRISE?
ACTUALLY, I SKIPPED LUNCH.
NOW, YOU WERE TALKING ABOUT OUR RUNAWAYS...

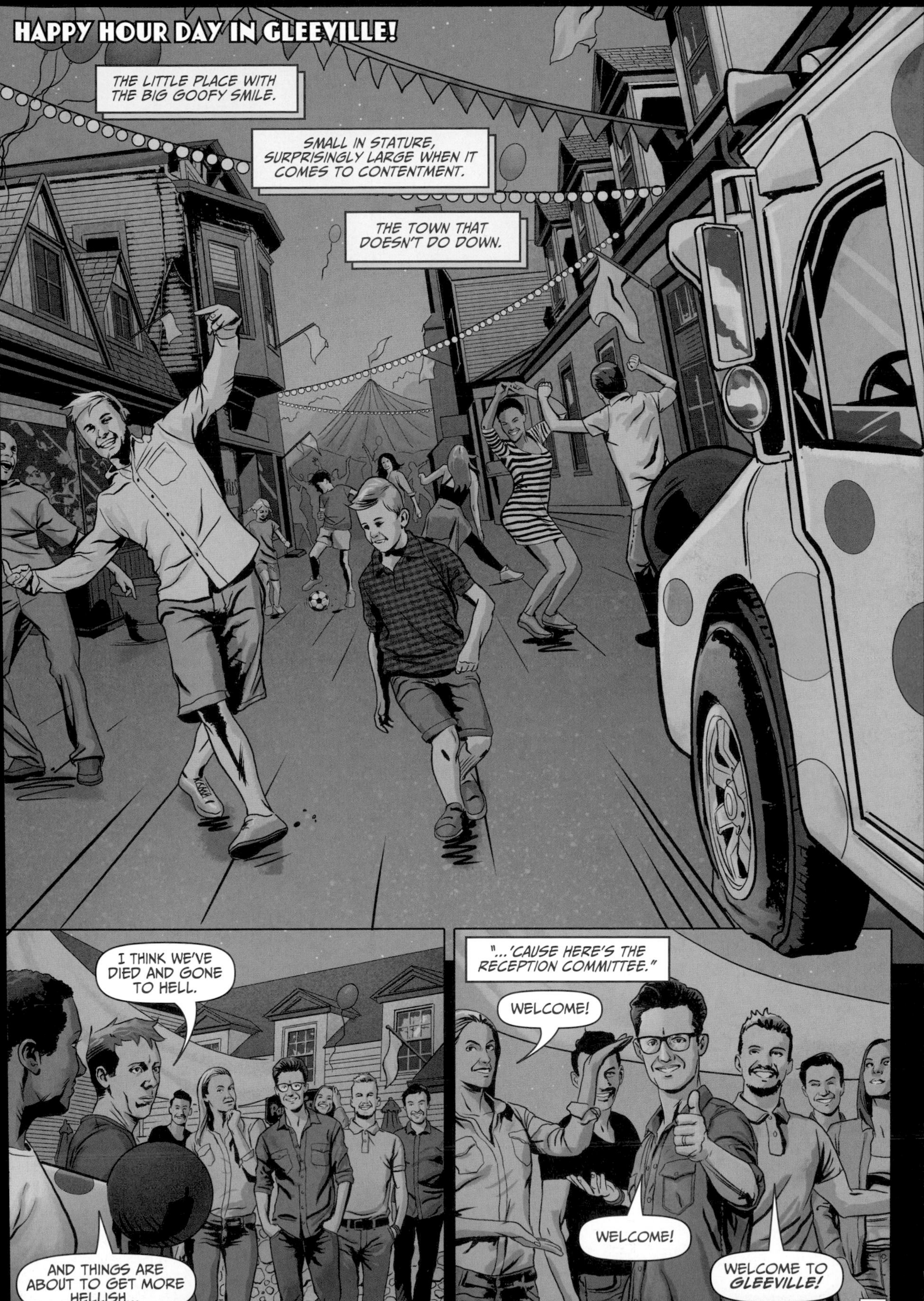
HAPPY HOUR DAY IN GLEEVILLE!
THE LITTLE PLACE WITH THE BIG GOOFY SMILE.
SMALL IN STATURE, SURPRISINGLY LARGE WHEN IT COMES TO CONTENTMENT.
THE TOWN THAT DOESN'T DO DOWN.
I THINK WE'VE DIED AND GONE TO HELL.
AND THINGS ARE ABOUT TO GET MORE HELLISH...
"...'CAUSE HERE'S THE RECEPTION COMMITTEE."
WELCOME!
WELCOME!
WELCOME TO *GLEEVILLE!*

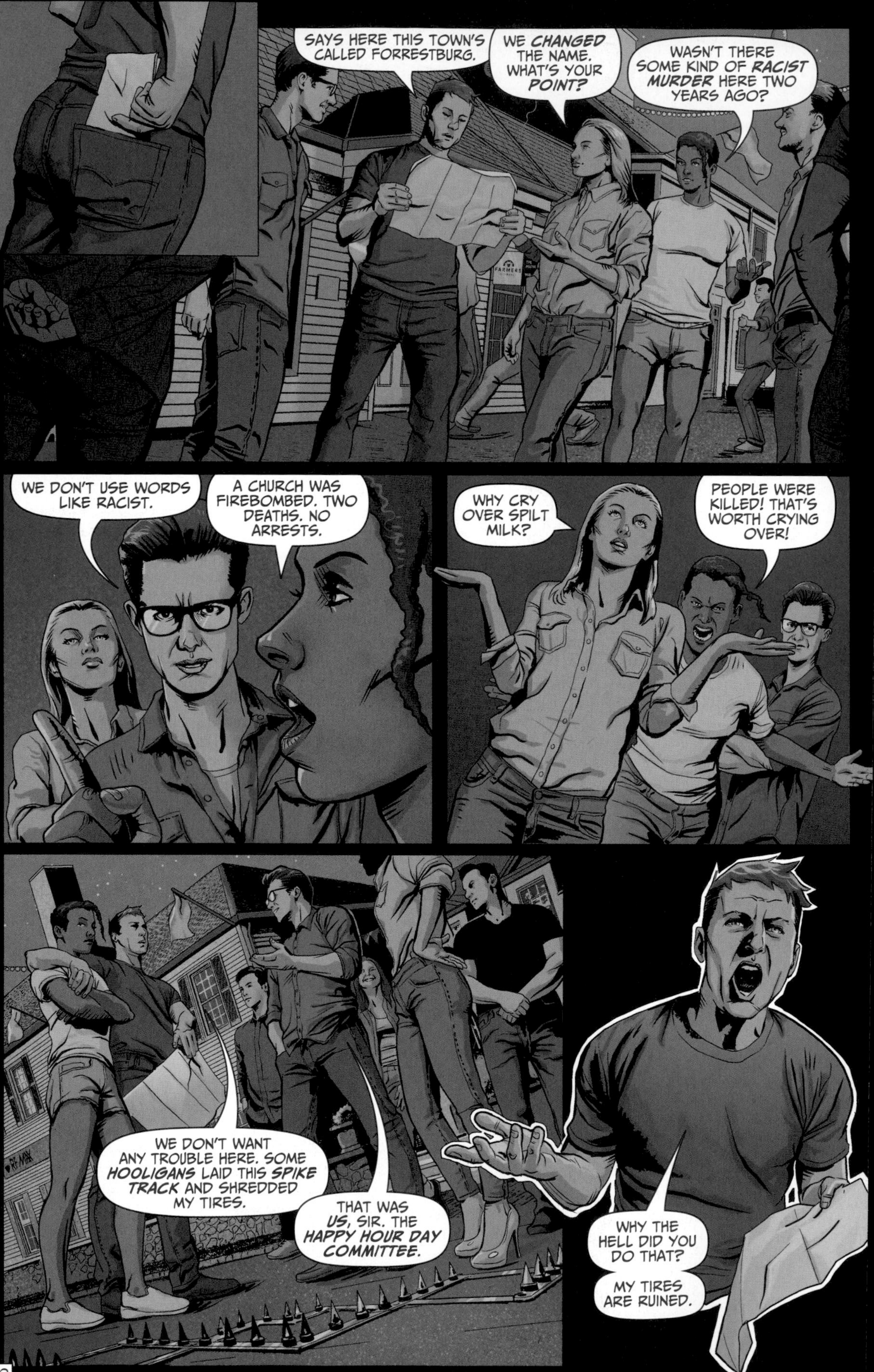
SAYS HERE THIS TOWN'S CALLED FORRESTBURG.
WE CHANGED THE NAME. WHAT'S YOUR POINT?
WASN'T THERE SOME KIND OF RACIST MURDER HERE TWO YEARS AGO?
WE DON'T USE WORDS LIKE RACIST.
A CHURCH WAS FIREBOMBED. TWO DEATHS. NO ARRESTS.
WHY CRY OVER SPILT MILK?
PEOPLE WERE KILLED! THAT'S WORTH CRYING OVER!
WE DON'T WANT ANY TROUBLE HERE. SOME HOOLIGANS LAID THIS SPIKE TRACK AND SHREDDED MY TIRES.
THAT WAS US, SIR. THE HAPPY HOUR DAY COMMITTEE.
WHY THE HELL DID YOU DO THAT?
MY TIRES ARE RUINED.

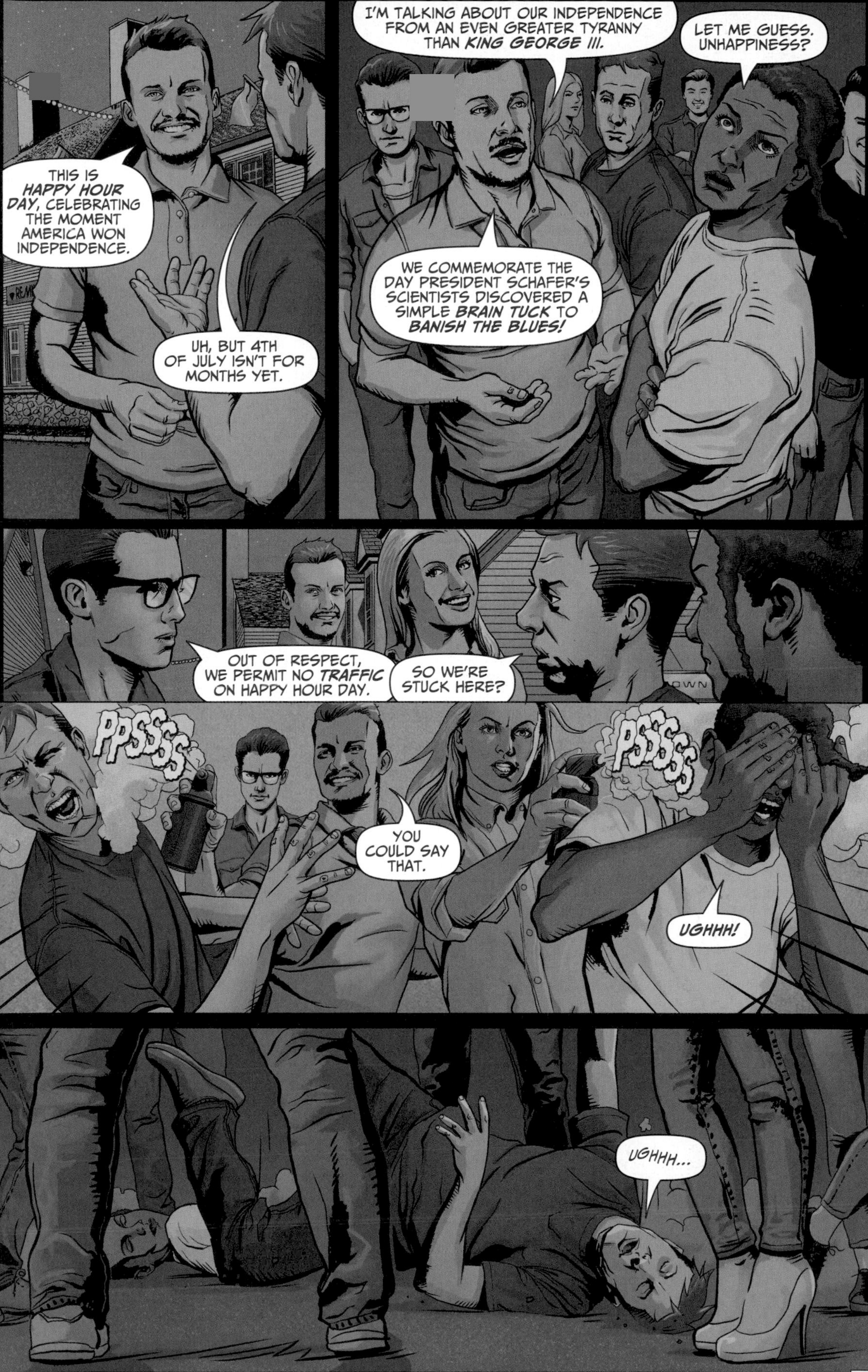
THIS IS *HAPPY HOUR DAY*, CELEBRATING THE MOMENT AMERICA WON INDEPENDENCE.
UH, BUT 4TH OF JULY ISN'T FOR MONTHS YET.
I'M TALKING ABOUT OUR INDEPENDENCE FROM AN EVEN GREATER TYRANNY THAN *KING GEORGE III.*
LET ME GUESS. UNHAPPINESS?
WE COMMEMORATE THE DAY PRESIDENT SCHAFER'S SCIENTISTS DISCOVERED A SIMPLE *BRAIN TUCK* TO *BANISH THE BLUES!*
OUT OF RESPECT, WE PERMIT NO *TRAFFIC* ON HAPPY HOUR DAY.
SO WE'RE STUCK HERE?
PPSSSS
YOU COULD SAY THAT.
PSSSSS
UGHHH!
UGHHH...

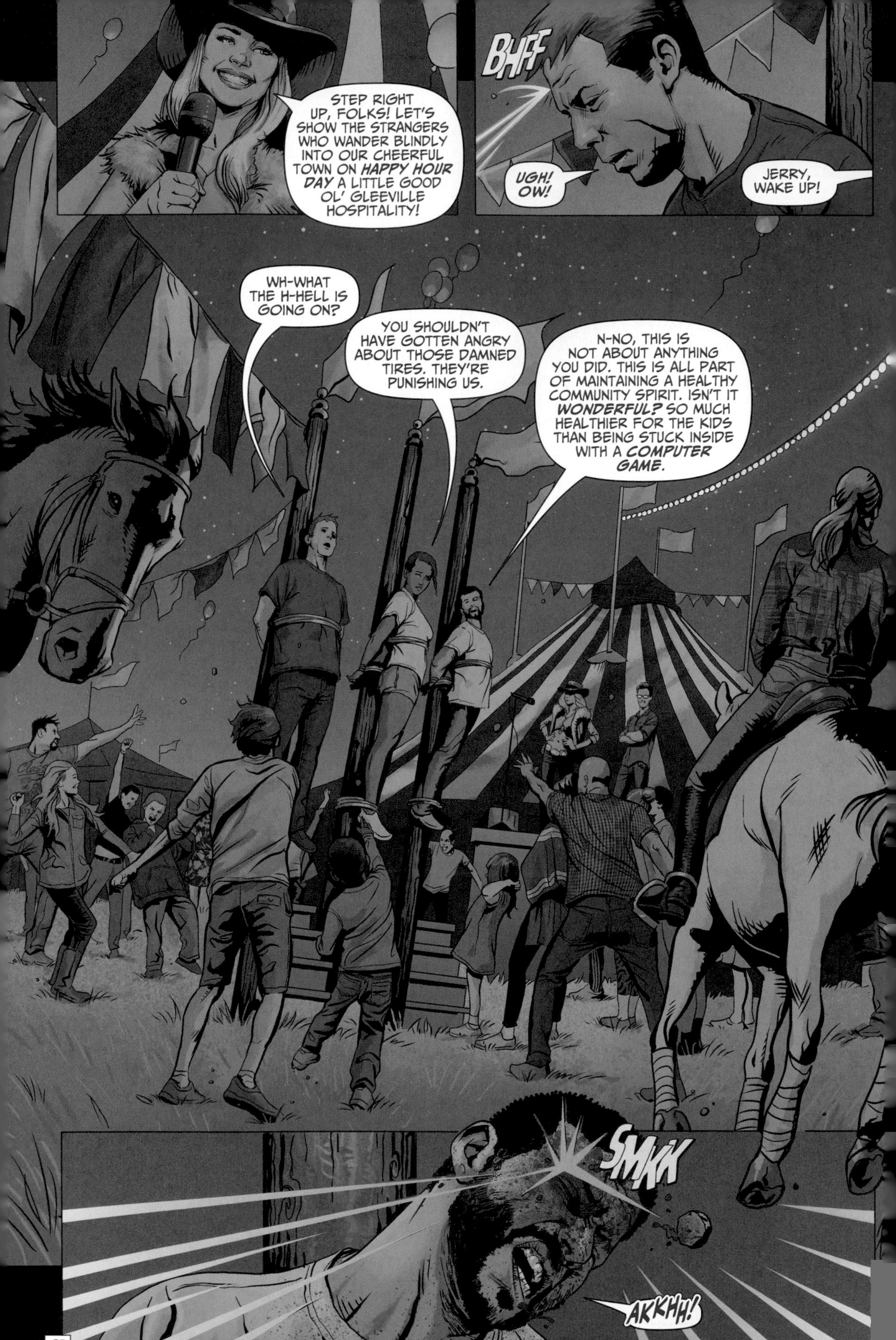
STEP RIGHT UP, FOLKS! LET'S SHOW THE STRANGERS WHO WANDER BLINDLY INTO OUR CHEERFUL TOWN ON *HAPPY HOUR DAY* A LITTLE GOOD OL' GLEEVILLE HOSPITALITY!
BHFF
UGH! OW!
JERRY, WAKE UP!
WH-WHAT THE H-HELL IS GOING ON?
YOU SHOULDN'T HAVE GOTTEN ANGRY ABOUT THOSE DAMNED TIRES. THEY'RE PUNISHING US.
N-NO, THIS IS NOT ABOUT ANYTHING YOU DID. THIS IS ALL PART OF MAINTAINING A HEALTHY COMMUNITY SPIRIT. ISN'T IT *WONDERFUL?* SO MUCH HEALTHIER FOR THE KIDS THAN BEING STUCK INSIDE WITH A *COMPUTER GAME*.
SMKK
AKKHH!

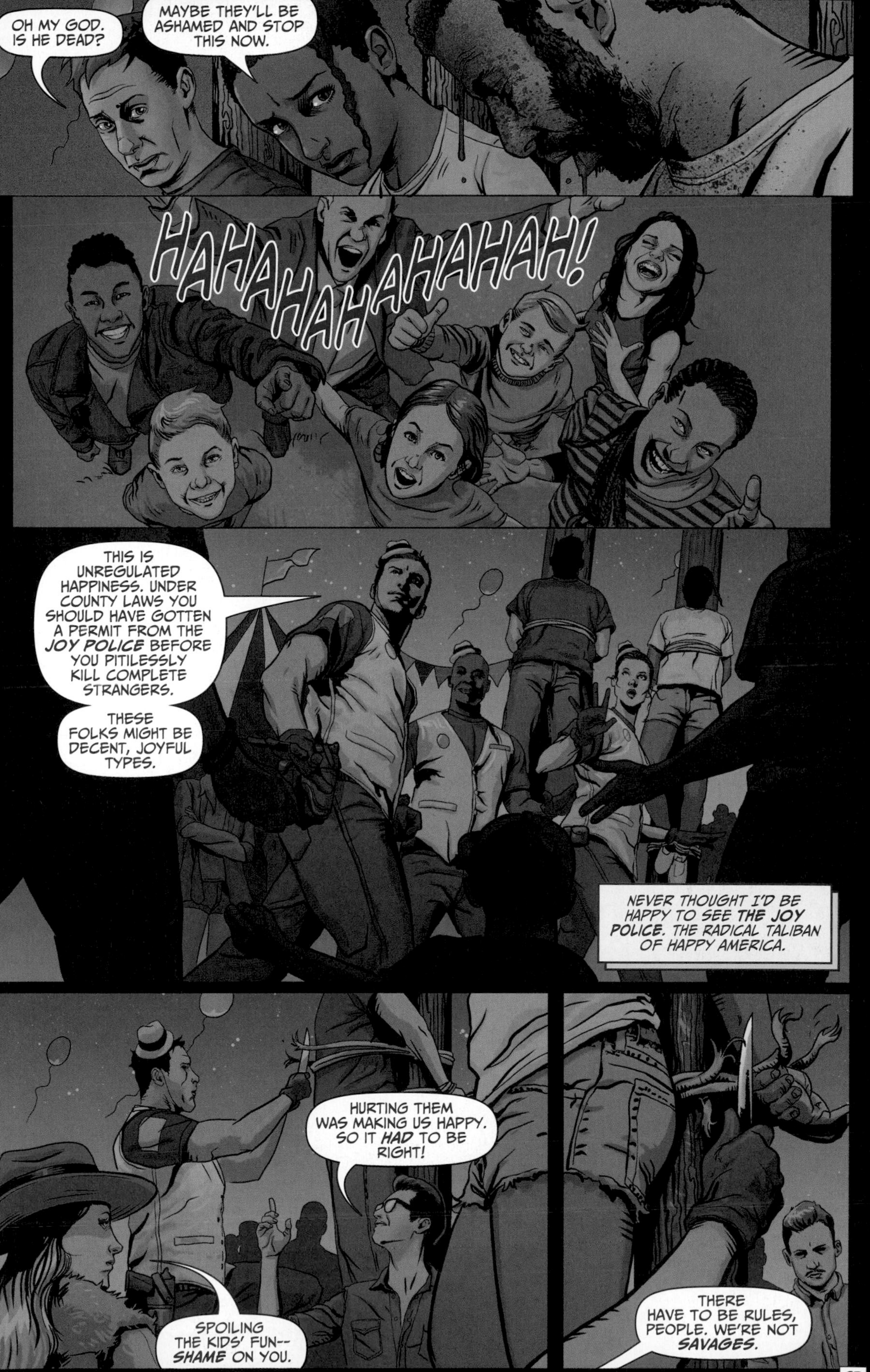
OH MY GOD. IS HE DEAD?
MAYBE THEY'LL BE ASHAMED AND STOP THIS NOW.
HAHAHAHAHAHAH!
THIS IS UNREGULATED HAPPINESS. UNDER COUNTY LAWS YOU SHOULD HAVE GOTTEN A PERMIT FROM THE JOY POLICE BEFORE YOU PITILESSLY KILL COMPLETE STRANGERS.
THESE FOLKS MIGHT BE DECENT, JOYFUL TYPES.
NEVER THOUGHT I'D BE HAPPY TO SEE THE JOY POLICE. THE RADICAL TALIBAN OF HAPPY AMERICA.
HURTING THEM WAS MAKING US HAPPY. SO IT HAD TO BE RIGHT!
SPOILING THE KIDS' FUN-- SHAME ON YOU.
THERE HAVE TO BE RULES, PEOPLE. WE'RE NOT SAVAGES.

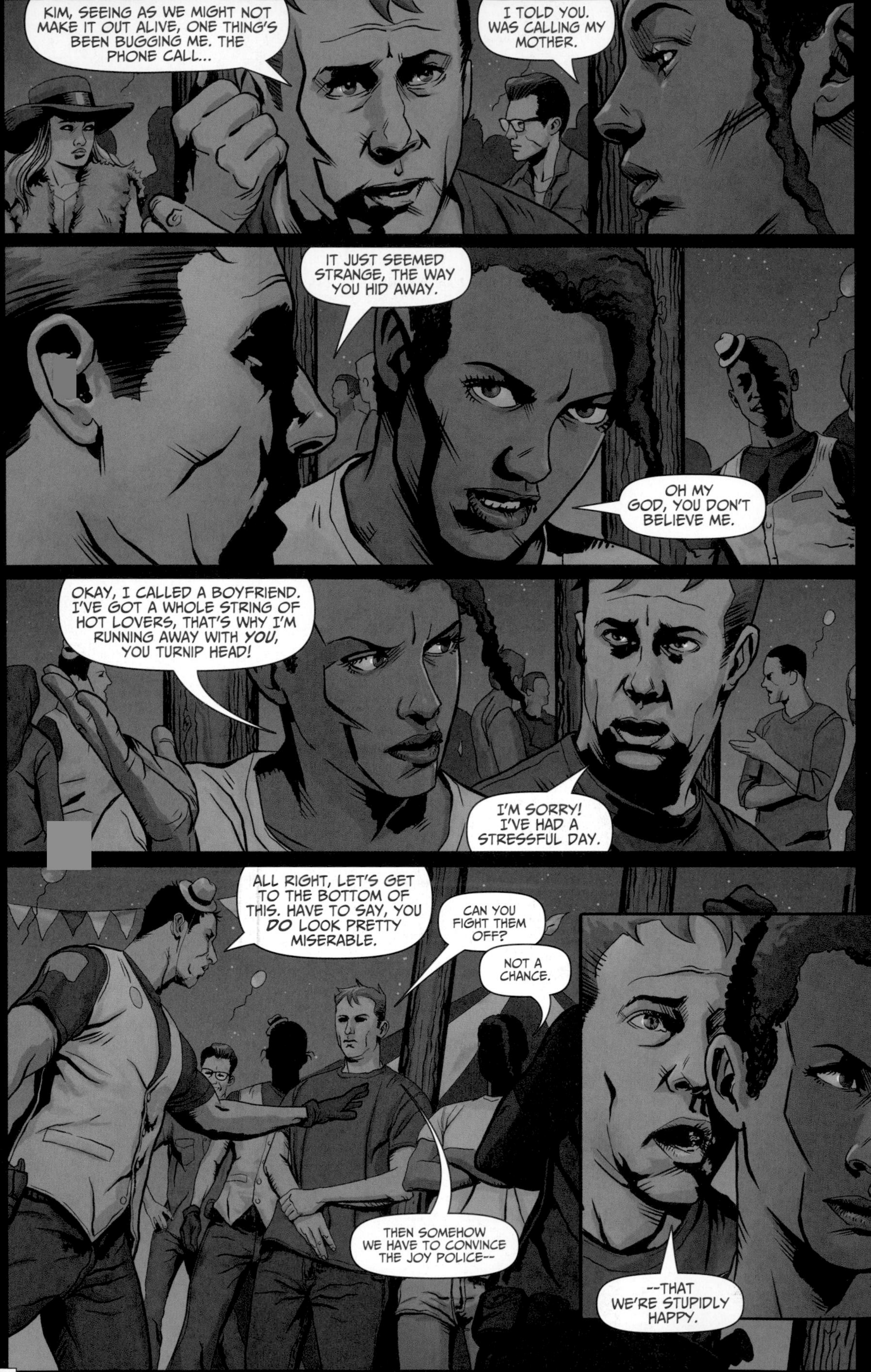
KIM, SEEING AS WE MIGHT NOT MAKE IT OUT ALIVE, ONE THING'S BEEN BUGGING ME. THE PHONE CALL...
I TOLD YOU. WAS CALLING MY MOTHER.
IT JUST SEEMED STRANGE, THE WAY YOU HID AWAY.
OH MY GOD, YOU DON'T BELIEVE ME.
OKAY, I CALLED A BOYFRIEND. I'VE GOT A WHOLE STRING OF HOT LOVERS, THAT'S WHY I'M RUNNING AWAY WITH *YOU*, YOU TURNIP HEAD!
I'M SORRY! I'VE HAD A STRESSFUL DAY.
ALL RIGHT, LET'S GET TO THE BOTTOM OF THIS. HAVE TO SAY, YOU *DO* LOOK PRETTY MISERABLE.
CAN YOU FIGHT THEM OFF?
NOT A CHANCE.
THEN SOMEHOW WE HAVE TO CONVINCE THE JOY POLICE--
--THAT WE'RE STUPIDLY HAPPY.

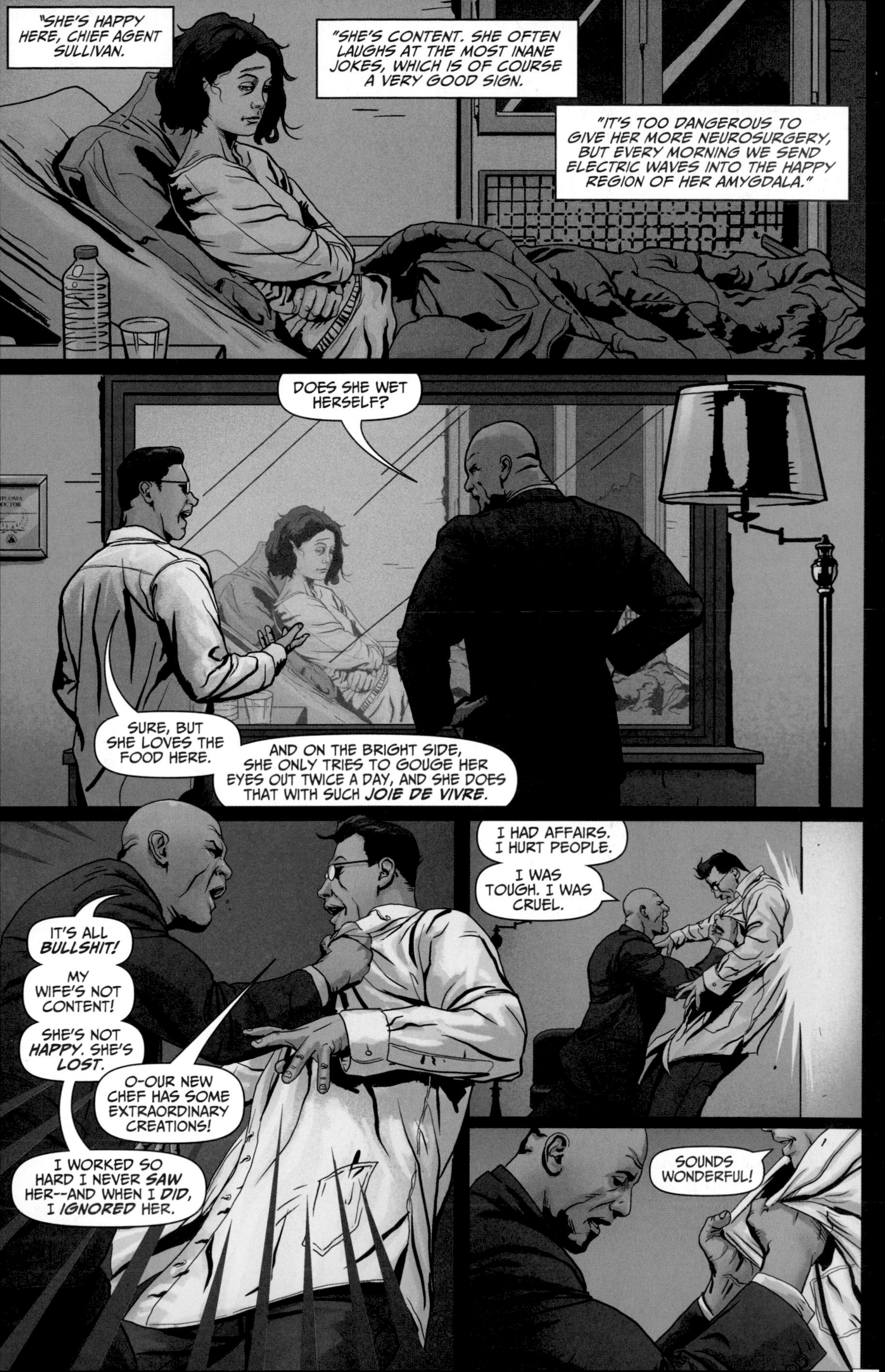
"SHE'S HAPPY HERE, CHIEF AGENT SULLIVAN.
"SHE'S CONTENT. SHE OFTEN LAUGHS AT THE MOST INANE JOKES, WHICH IS OF COURSE A VERY GOOD SIGN.
"IT'S TOO DANGEROUS TO GIVE HER MORE NEUROSURGERY, BUT EVERY MORNING WE SEND ELECTRIC WAVES INTO THE HAPPY REGION OF HER AMYGDALA."
DOES SHE WET HERSELF?
SURE, BUT SHE LOVES THE FOOD HERE.
AND ON THE BRIGHT SIDE, SHE ONLY TRIES TO GOUGE HER EYES OUT TWICE A DAY, AND SHE DOES THAT WITH SUCH JOIE DE VIVRE.
IT'S ALL BULLSHIT!
MY WIFE'S NOT CONTENT!
SHE'S NOT HAPPY. SHE'S LOST.
O-OUR NEW CHEF HAS SOME EXTRAORDINARY CREATIONS!
I WORKED SO HARD I NEVER SAW HER--AND WHEN I DID, I IGNORED HER.
I HAD AFFAIRS. I HURT PEOPLE.
I WAS TOUGH. I WAS CRUEL.
SOUNDS WONDERFUL!

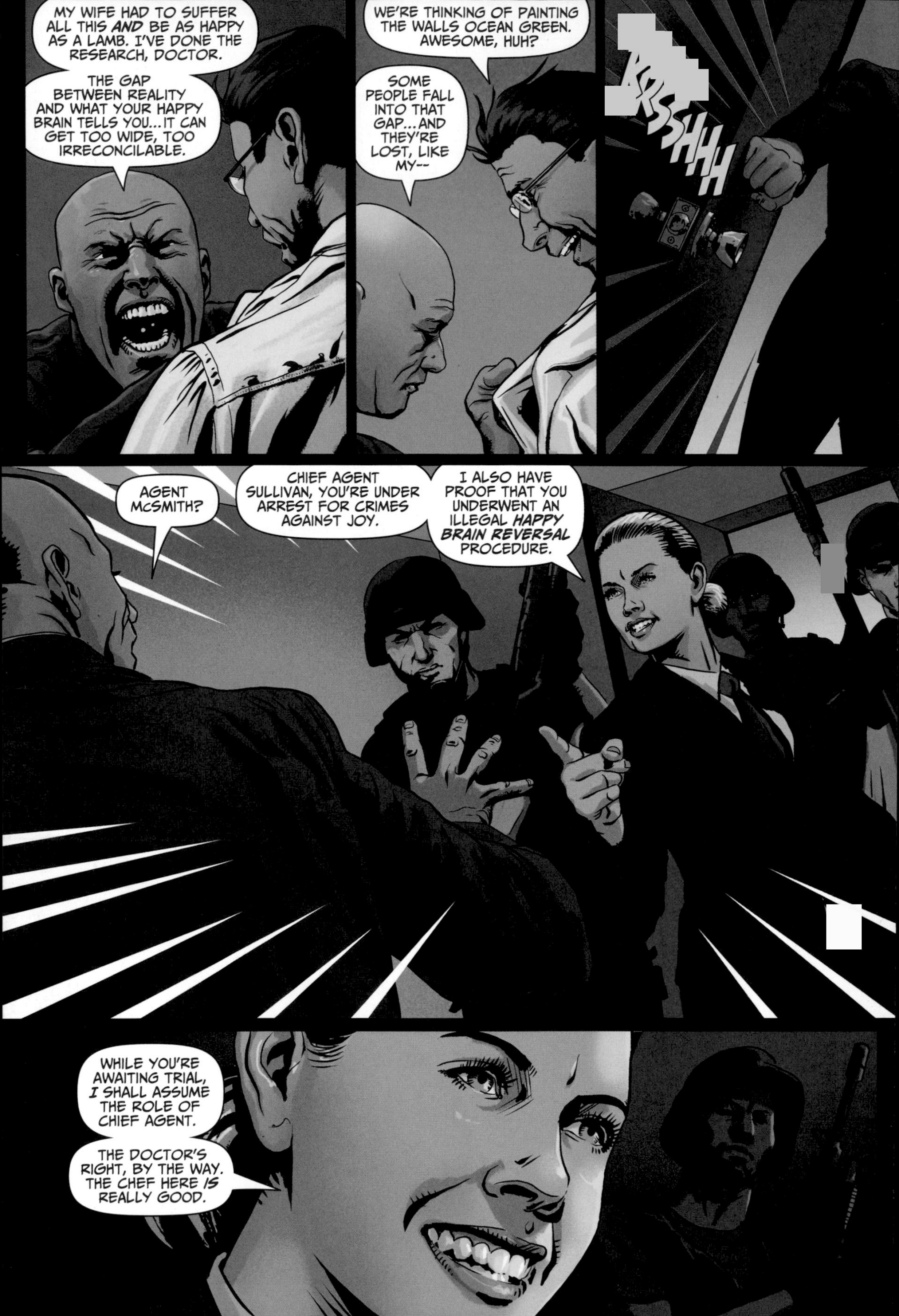

MY WIFE HAD TO SUFFER ALL THIS *AND* BE AS HAPPY AS A LAMB. I'VE DONE THE RESEARCH, DOCTOR.
THE GAP BETWEEN REALITY AND WHAT YOUR HAPPY BRAIN TELLS YOU... IT CAN GET TOO WIDE, TOO IRRECONCILABLE.
WE'RE THINKING OF PAINTING THE WALLS OCEAN GREEN. AWESOME, HUH?
SOME PEOPLE FALL INTO THAT GAP... AND THEY'RE LOST, LIKE MY--
AGENT McSMITH?
CHIEF AGENT SULLIVAN, YOU'RE UNDER ARREST FOR CRIMES AGAINST JOY.
I ALSO HAVE PROOF THAT YOU UNDERWENT AN ILLEGAL *HAPPY BRAIN REVERSAL* PROCEDURE.
WHILE YOU'RE AWAITING TRIAL, *I* SHALL ASSUME THE ROLE OF CHIEF AGENT.
THE DOCTOR'S RIGHT, BY THE WAY. THE CHEF HERE *IS* REALLY GOOD.

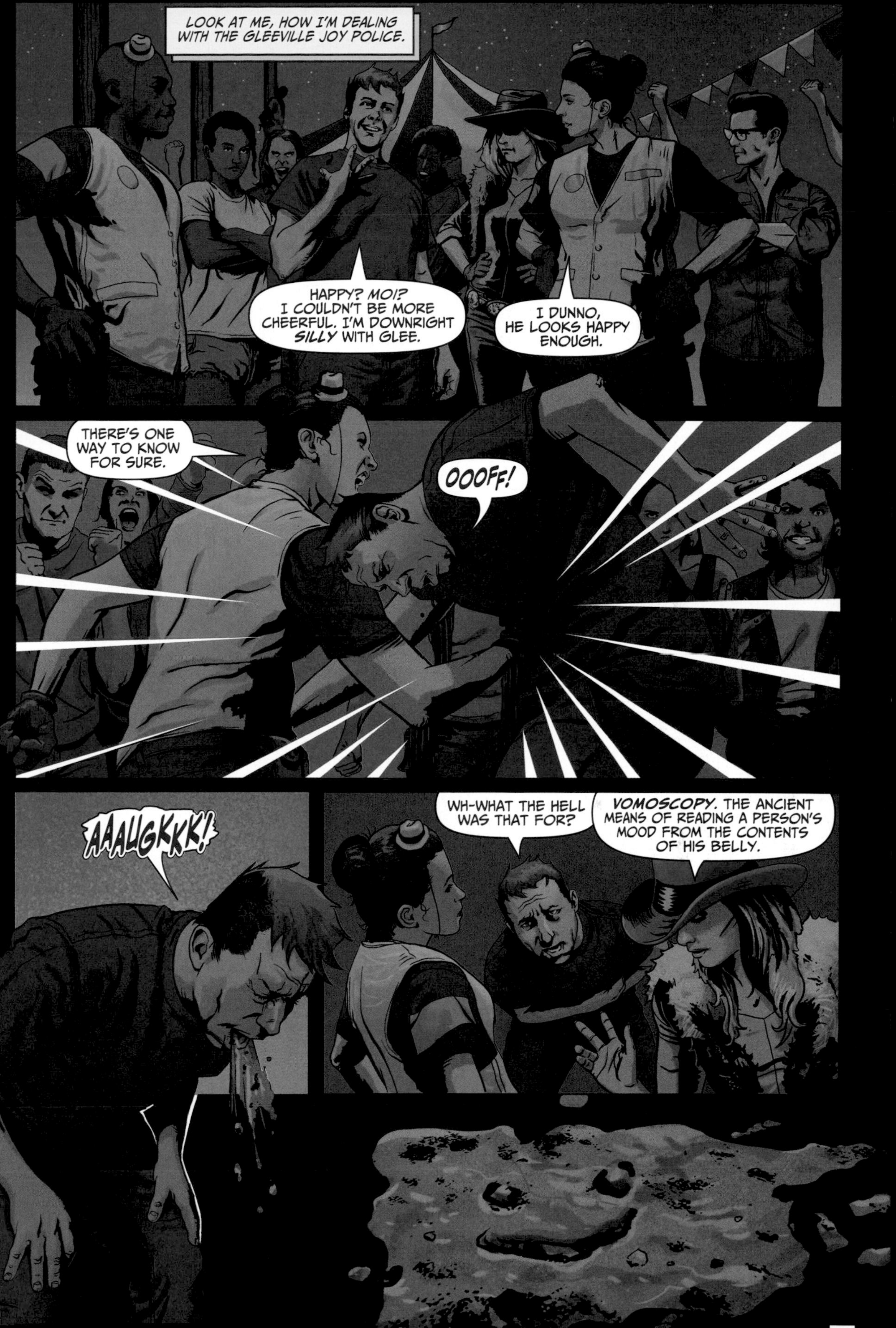
LOOK AT ME, HOW I'M DEALING WITH THE GLEEVILLE JOY POLICE.
HAPPY? MOI!? I COULDN'T BE MORE CHEERFUL. I'M DOWNRIGHT SILLY WITH GLEE.
I DUNNO, HE LOOKS HAPPY ENOUGH.
THERE'S ONE WAY TO KNOW FOR SURE.
OOOFF!
AAAUGKKK!
WH-WHAT THE HELL WAS THAT FOR?
VOMOSCOPY. THE ANCIENT MEANS OF READING A PERSON'S MOOD FROM THE CONTENTS OF HIS BELLY.

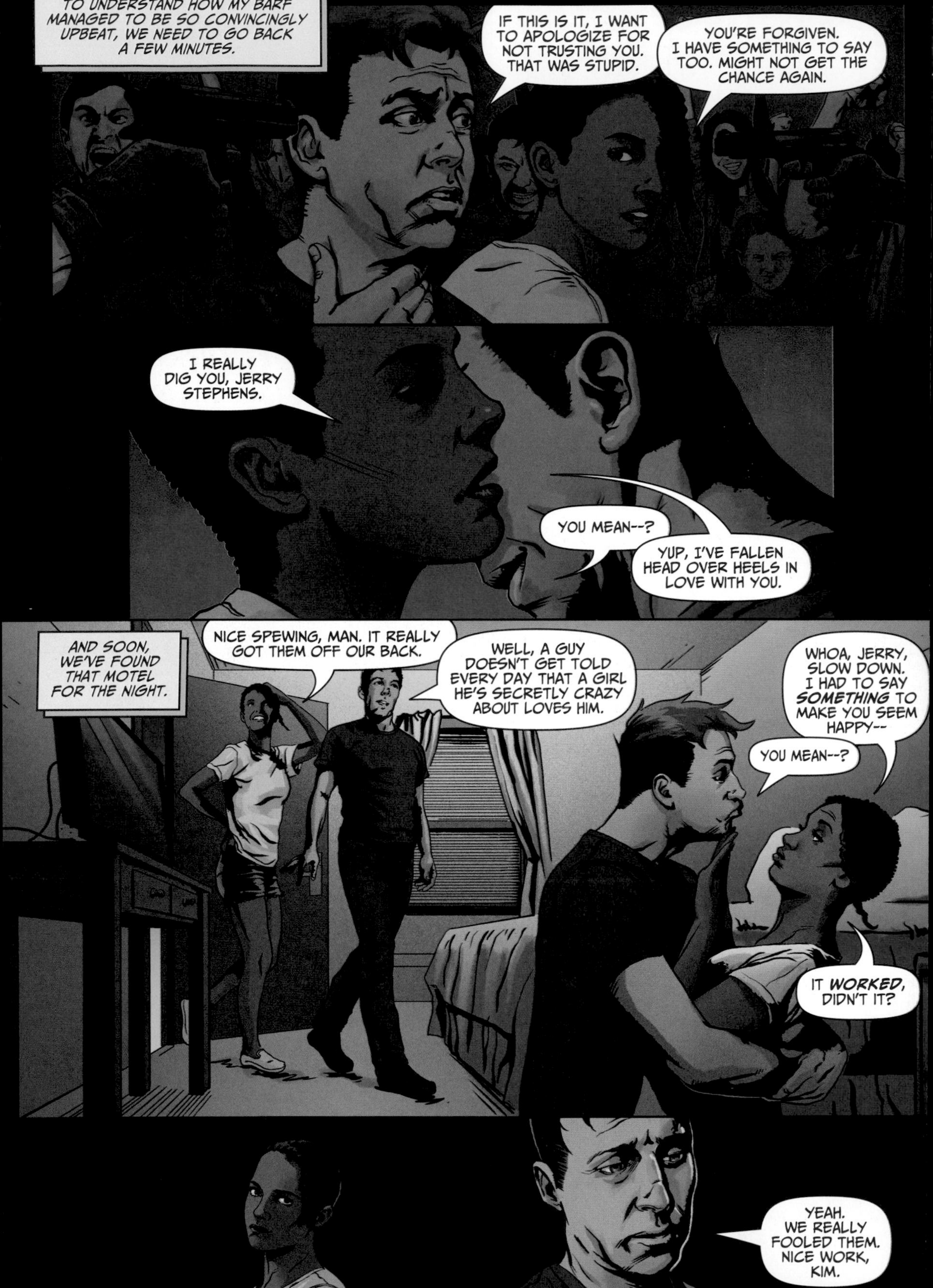
TO UNDERSTAND HOW MY BARF MANAGED TO BE SO CONVINCINGLY UPBEAT, WE NEED TO GO BACK A FEW MINUTES.
IF THIS IS IT, I WANT TO APOLOGIZE FOR NOT TRUSTING YOU. THAT WAS STUPID.
YOU'RE FORGIVEN. I HAVE SOMETHING TO SAY TOO. MIGHT NOT GET THE CHANCE AGAIN.
I REALLY DIG YOU, JERRY STEPHENS.
YOU MEAN--?
YUP, I'VE FALLEN HEAD OVER HEELS IN LOVE WITH YOU.
AND SOON, WE'VE FOUND THAT MOTEL FOR THE NIGHT.
NICE SPEWING, MAN. IT REALLY GOT THEM OFF OUR BACK.
WELL, A GUY DOESN'T GET TOLD EVERY DAY THAT A GIRL HE'S SECRETLY CRAZY ABOUT LOVES HIM.
WHOA, JERRY, SLOW DOWN. I HAD TO SAY *SOMETHING* TO MAKE YOU SEEM HAPPY--
YOU MEAN--?
IT *WORKED*, DIDN'T IT?
YEAH. WE REALLY FOOLED THEM. NICE WORK, KIM.

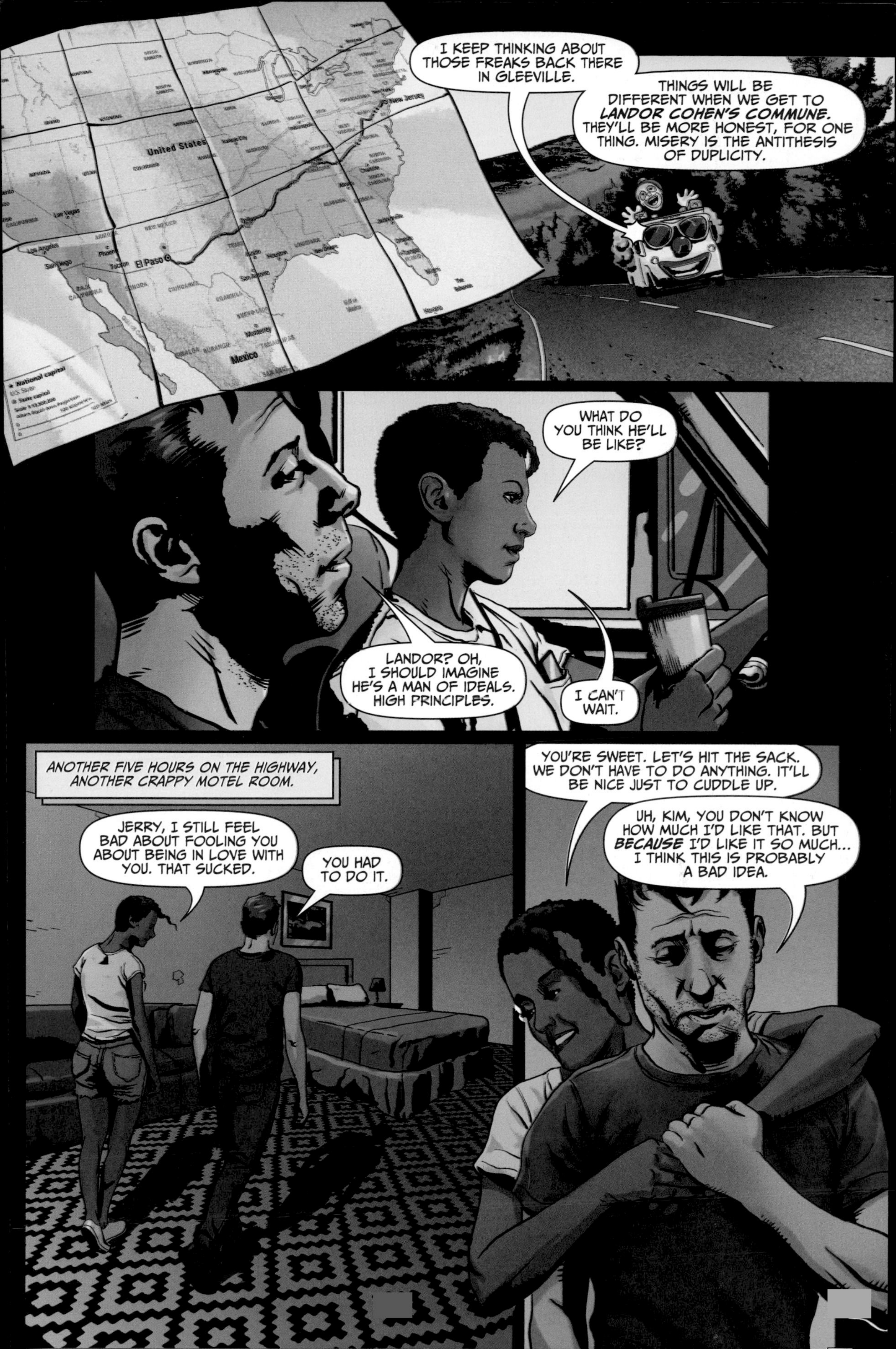

United States
El Paso
Mexico
I KEEP THINKING ABOUT THOSE FREAKS BACK THERE IN GLEEVILLE.
THINGS WILL BE DIFFERENT WHEN WE GET TO *LANDOR COHEN'S COMMUNE.* THEY'LL BE MORE HONEST, FOR ONE THING. MISERY IS THE ANTITHESIS OF DUPLICITY.
WHAT DO YOU THINK HE'LL BE LIKE?
LANDOR? OH, I SHOULD IMAGINE HE'S A MAN OF IDEALS. HIGH PRINCIPLES.
I CAN'T WAIT.
ANOTHER FIVE HOURS ON THE HIGHWAY, ANOTHER CRAPPY MOTEL ROOM.
JERRY, I STILL FEEL BAD ABOUT FOOLING YOU ABOUT BEING IN LOVE WITH YOU. THAT SUCKED.
YOU HAD TO DO IT.
YOU'RE SWEET. LET'S HIT THE SACK. WE DON'T HAVE TO DO ANYTHING. IT'LL BE NICE JUST TO CUDDLE UP.
UH, KIM, YOU DON'T KNOW HOW MUCH I'D LIKE THAT. BUT *BECAUSE* I'D LIKE IT SO MUCH... I THINK THIS IS PROBABLY A BAD IDEA.

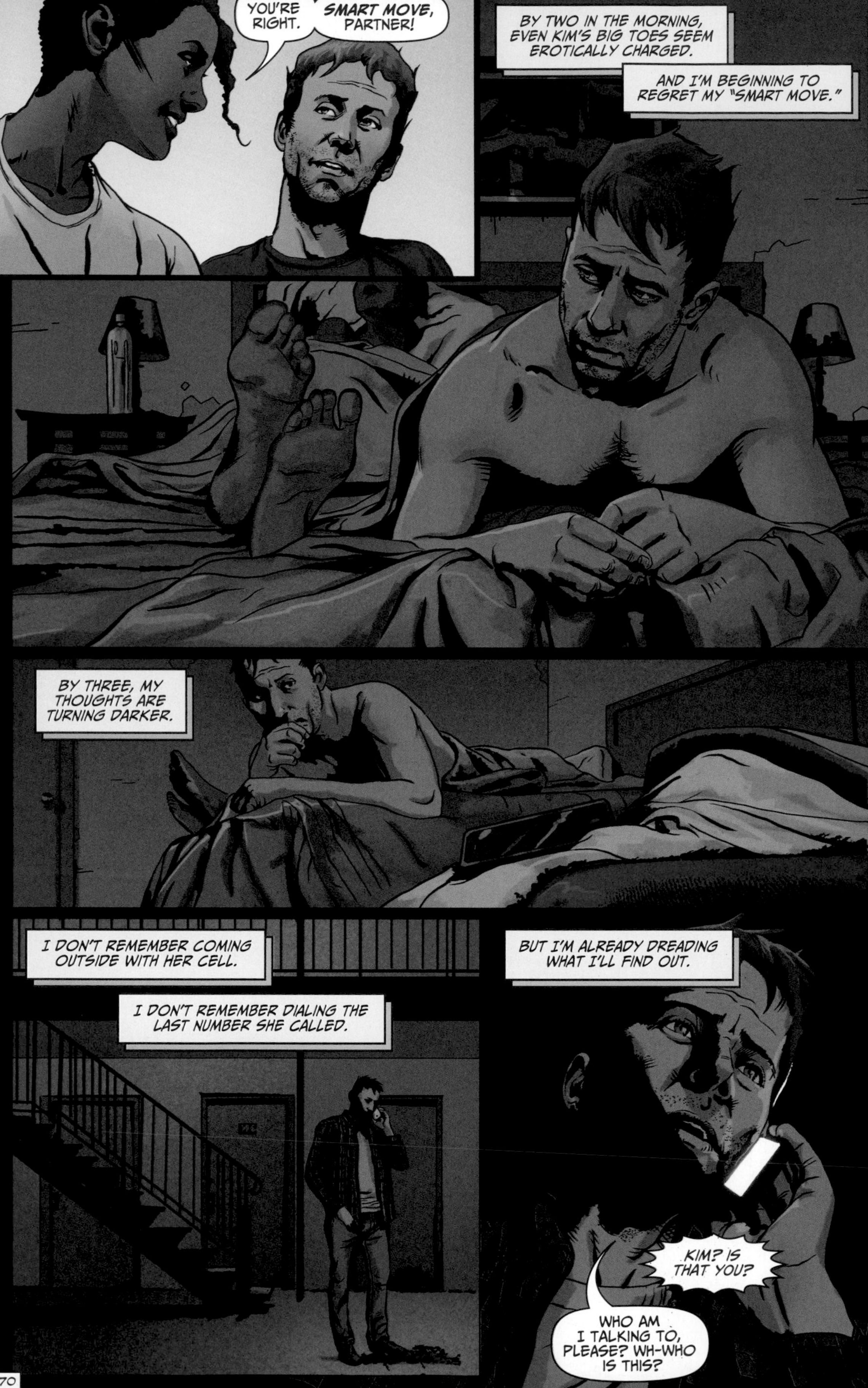

YOU'RE RIGHT.
SMART MOVE, PARTNER!
BY TWO IN THE MORNING, EVEN KIM'S BIG TOES SEEM EROTICALLY CHARGED.
AND I'M BEGINNING TO REGRET MY "SMART MOVE."
BY THREE, MY THOUGHTS ARE TURNING DARKER.
I DON'T REMEMBER COMING OUTSIDE WITH HER CELL.
I DON'T REMEMBER DIALING THE LAST NUMBER SHE CALLED.
BUT I'M ALREADY DREADING WHAT I'LL FIND OUT.
KIM? IS THAT YOU?
WHO AM I TALKING TO, PLEASE? WH-WHO IS THIS?

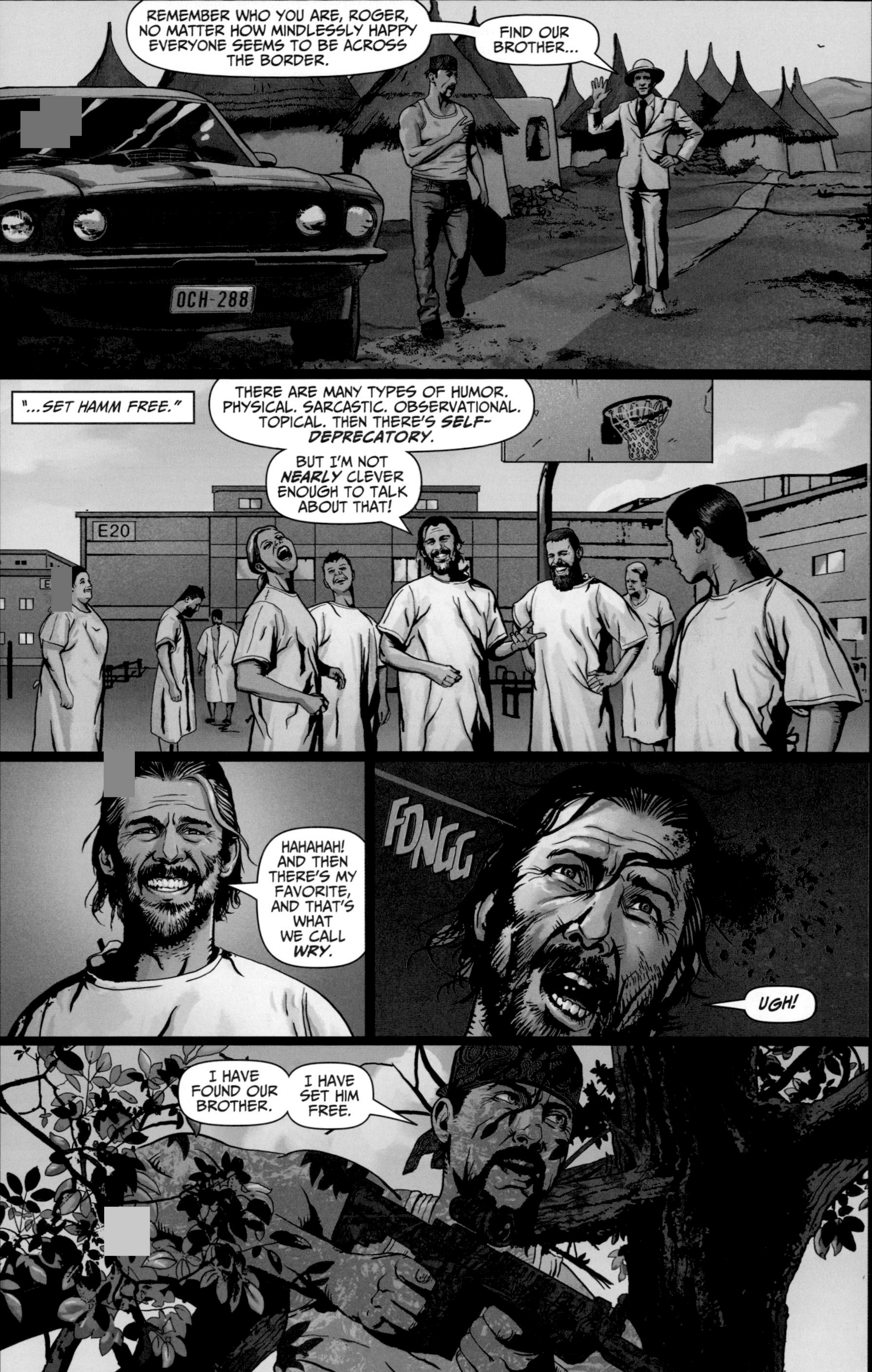
REMEMBER WHO YOU ARE, ROGER, NO MATTER HOW MINDLESSLY HAPPY EVERYONE SEEMS TO BE ACROSS THE BORDER.
FIND OUR BROTHER...
OCH-288
"...SET HAMM FREE."
THERE ARE MANY TYPES OF HUMOR. PHYSICAL. SARCASTIC. OBSERVATIONAL. TOPICAL. THEN THERE'S SELF-DEPRECATORY.
BUT I'M NOT NEARLY CLEVER ENOUGH TO TALK ABOUT THAT!
E20
HAHAHAH! AND THEN THERE'S MY FAVORITE, AND THAT'S WHAT WE CALL WRY.
FDNGG
UGH!
I HAVE FOUND OUR BROTHER.
I HAVE SET HIM FREE.

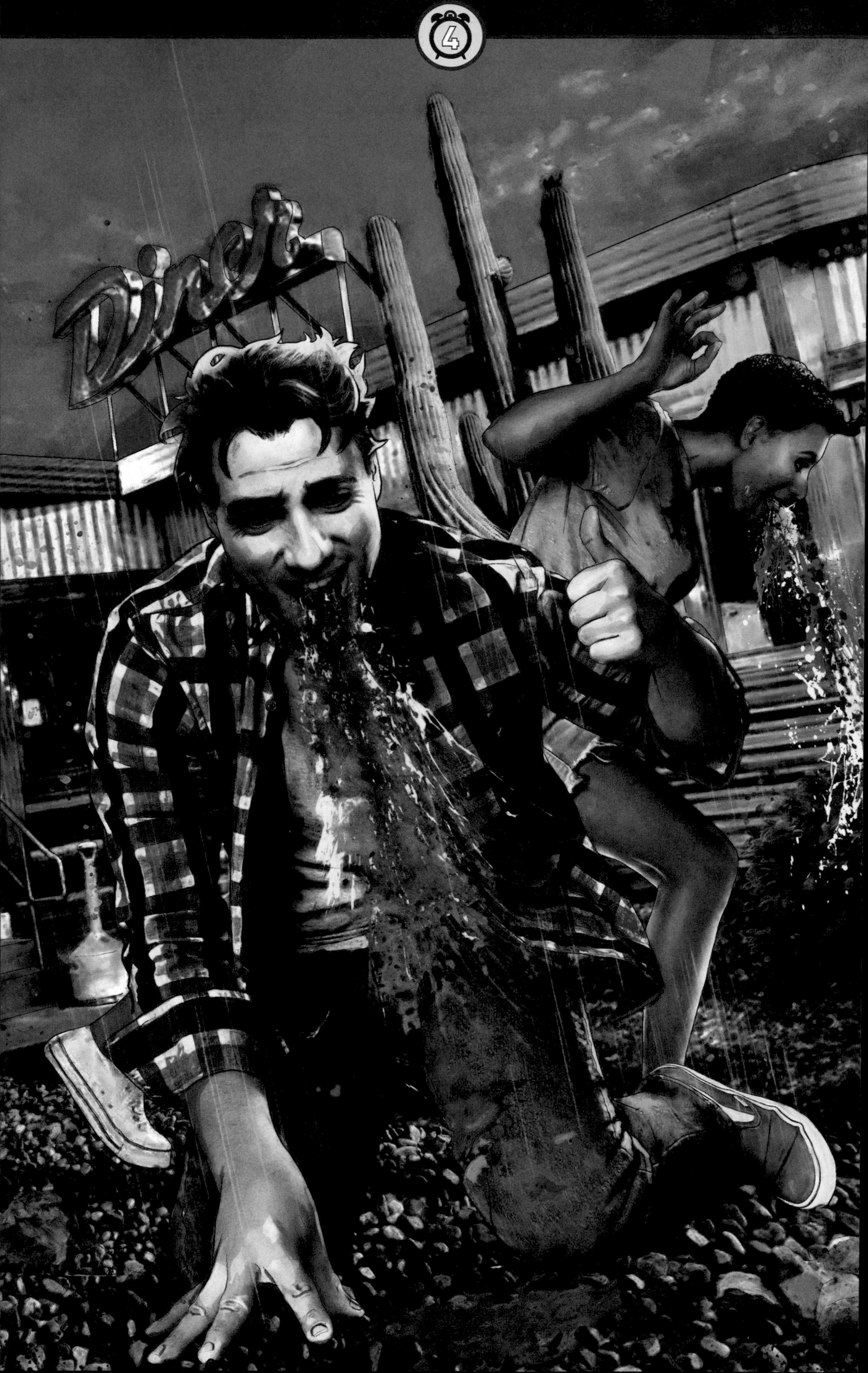
4
Diner

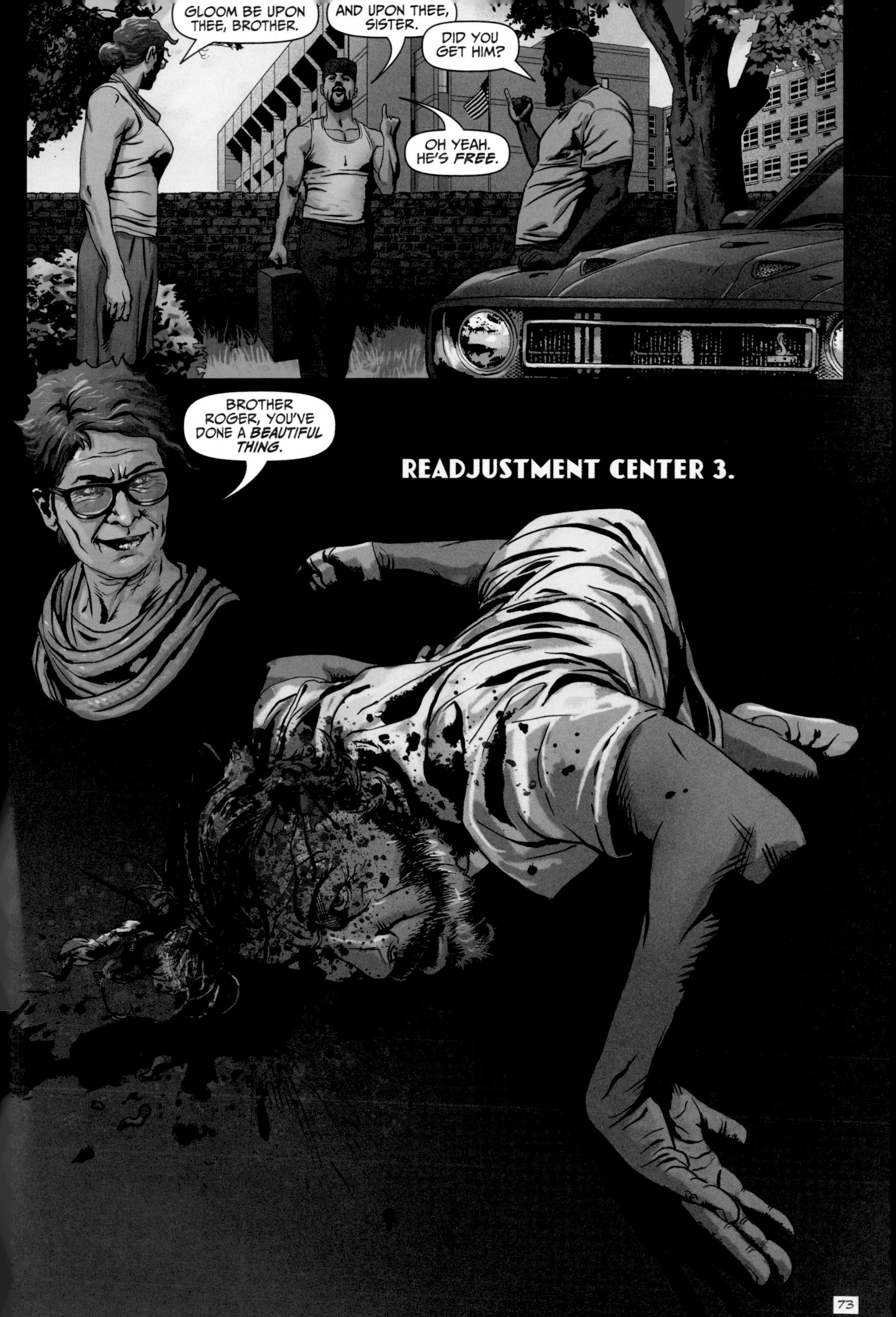
GLOOM BE UPON THEE, BROTHER.
AND UPON THEE, SISTER.
DID YOU GET HIM?
OH YEAH. HE'S *FREE*.
BROTHER ROGER, YOU'VE DONE A *BEAUTIFUL* THING.
READJUSTMENT CENTER 3.

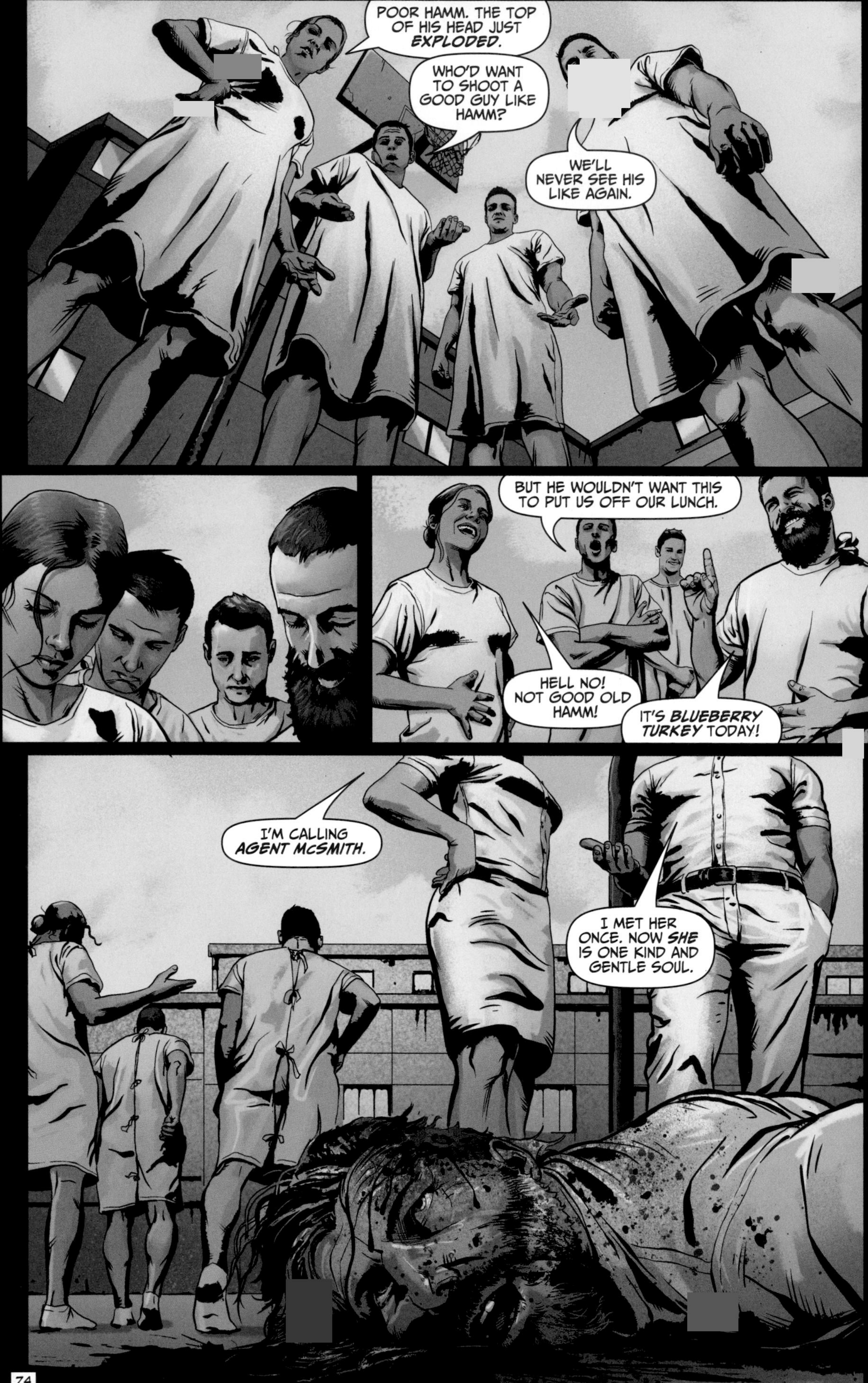
POOR HAMM. THE TOP OF HIS HEAD JUST EXPLODED.
WHO'D WANT TO SHOOT A GOOD GUY LIKE HAMM?
WE'LL NEVER SEE HIS LIKE AGAIN.
BUT HE WOULDN'T WANT THIS TO PUT US OFF OUR LUNCH.
HELL NO! NOT GOOD OLD HAMM!
IT'S BLUEBERRY TURKEY TODAY!
I'M CALLING AGENT McSMITH.
I MET HER ONCE. NOW SHE IS ONE KIND AND GENTLE SOUL.

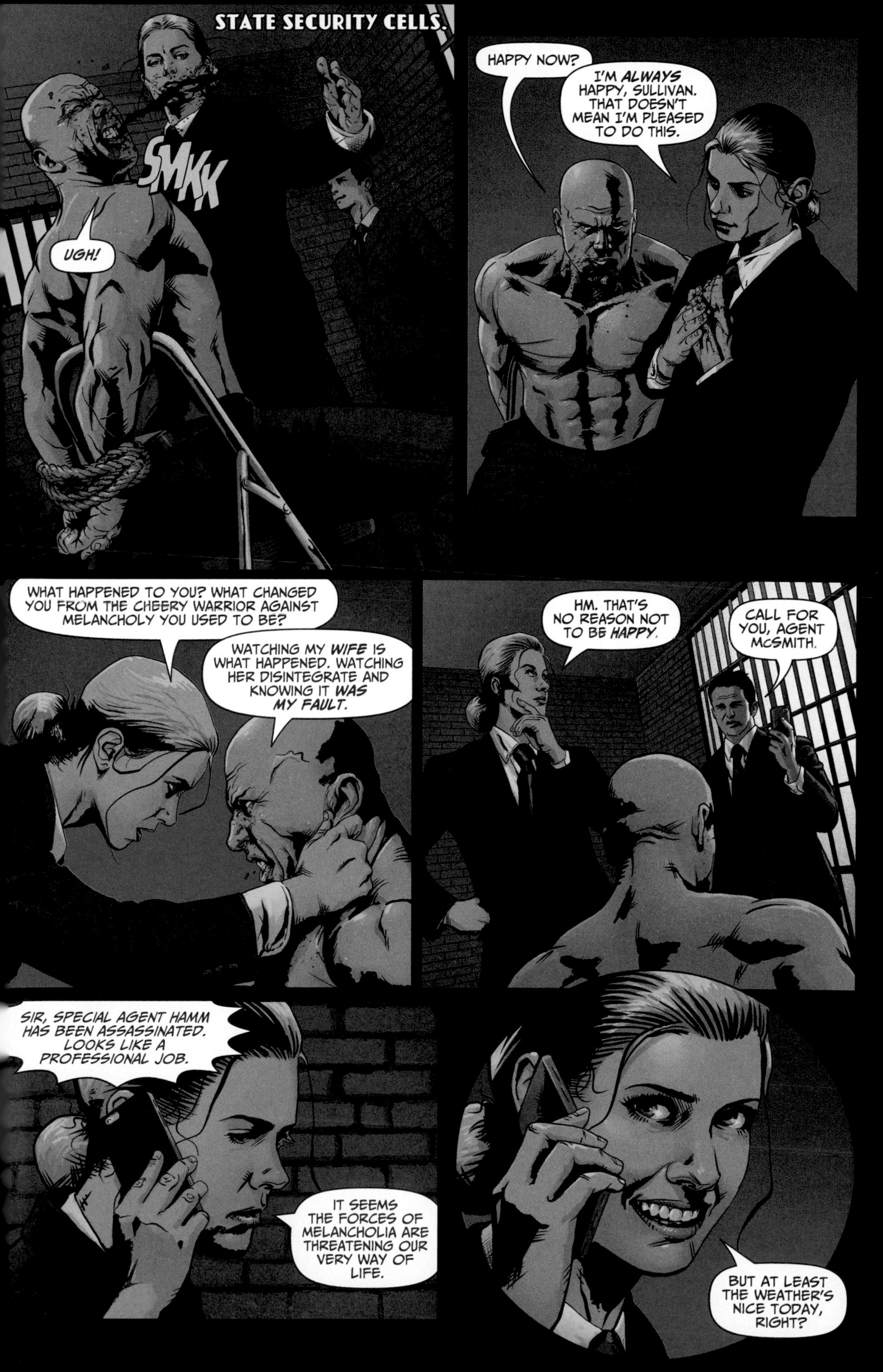
STATE SECURITY CELLS.
SMKK
UGH!
HAPPY NOW?
I'M ALWAYS HAPPY, SULLIVAN. THAT DOESN'T MEAN I'M PLEASED TO DO THIS.
WHAT HAPPENED TO YOU? WHAT CHANGED YOU FROM THE CHEERY WARRIOR AGAINST MELANCHOLY YOU USED TO BE?
WATCHING MY WIFE IS WHAT HAPPENED. WATCHING HER DISINTEGRATE AND KNOWING IT WAS MY FAULT.
HM. THAT'S NO REASON NOT TO BE HAPPY.
CALL FOR YOU, AGENT McSMITH.
SIR, SPECIAL AGENT HAMM HAS BEEN ASSASSINATED. LOOKS LIKE A PROFESSIONAL JOB.
IT SEEMS THE FORCES OF MELANCHOLIA ARE THREATENING OUR VERY WAY OF LIFE.
BUT AT LEAST THE WEATHER'S NICE TODAY, RIGHT?

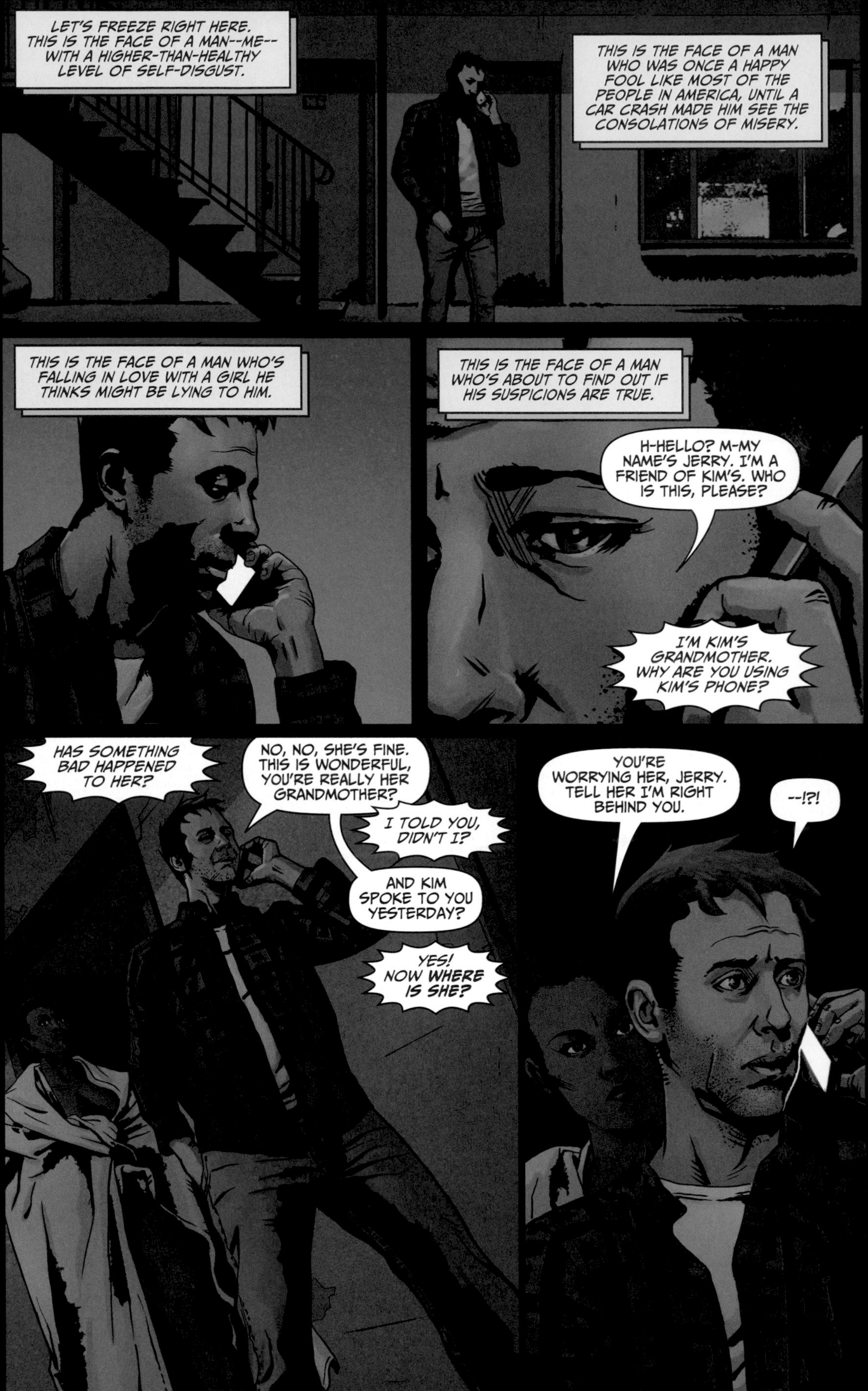
LET'S FREEZE RIGHT HERE. THIS IS THE FACE OF A MAN--ME--WITH A HIGHER-THAN-HEALTHY LEVEL OF SELF-DISGUST.
THIS IS THE FACE OF A MAN WHO WAS ONCE A HAPPY FOOL LIKE MOST OF THE PEOPLE IN AMERICA, UNTIL A CAR CRASH MADE HIM SEE THE CONSOLATIONS OF MISERY.
THIS IS THE FACE OF A MAN WHO'S FALLING IN LOVE WITH A GIRL HE THINKS MIGHT BE LYING TO HIM.
THIS IS THE FACE OF A MAN WHO'S ABOUT TO FIND OUT IF HIS SUSPICIONS ARE TRUE.
H-HELLO? M-MY NAME'S JERRY. I'M A FRIEND OF KIM'S. WHO IS THIS, PLEASE?
I'M KIM'S GRANDMOTHER. WHY ARE YOU USING KIM'S PHONE?
HAS SOMETHING BAD HAPPENED TO HER?
NO, NO, SHE'S FINE. THIS IS WONDERFUL, YOU'RE REALLY HER GRANDMOTHER?
I TOLD YOU, DIDN'T I?
AND KIM SPOKE TO YOU YESTERDAY?
YES! NOW WHERE IS SHE?
YOU'RE WORRYING HER, JERRY. TELL HER I'M RIGHT BEHIND YOU.
--!?!

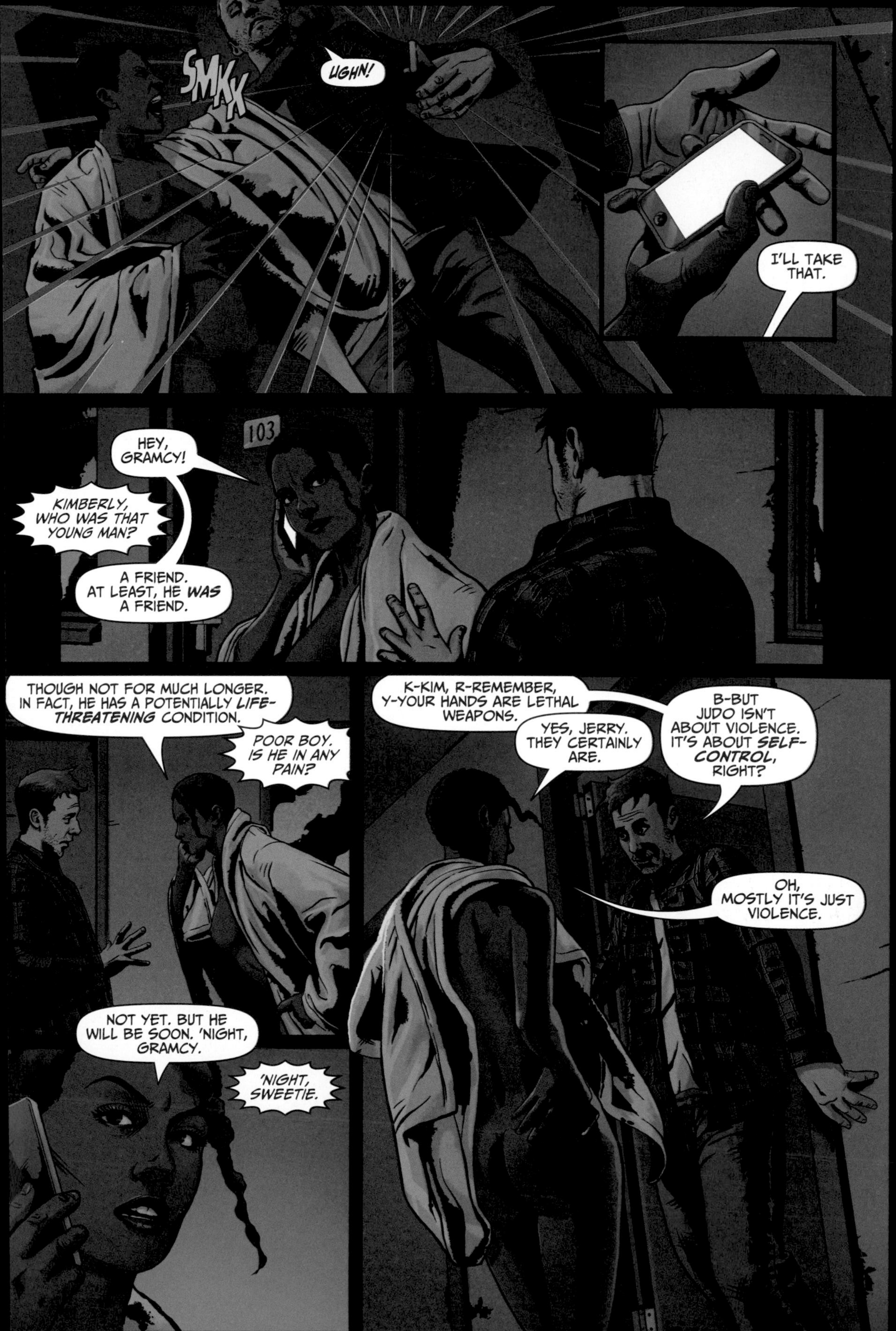
SMKK
UGHN!
I'LL TAKE THAT.
HEY, GRAMCY!
KIMBERLY, WHO WAS THAT YOUNG MAN?
A FRIEND. AT LEAST, HE WAS A FRIEND.
THOUGH NOT FOR MUCH LONGER. IN FACT, HE HAS A POTENTIALLY LIFE-THREATENING CONDITION.
POOR BOY. IS HE IN ANY PAIN?
NOT YET. BUT HE WILL BE SOON. 'NIGHT, GRAMCY.
'NIGHT, SWEETIE.
K-KIM, R-REMEMBER, Y-YOUR HANDS ARE LETHAL WEAPONS.
YES, JERRY. THEY CERTAINLY ARE.
B-BUT JUDO ISN'T ABOUT VIOLENCE. IT'S ABOUT SELF-CONTROL, RIGHT?
OH, MOSTLY IT'S JUST VIOLENCE.

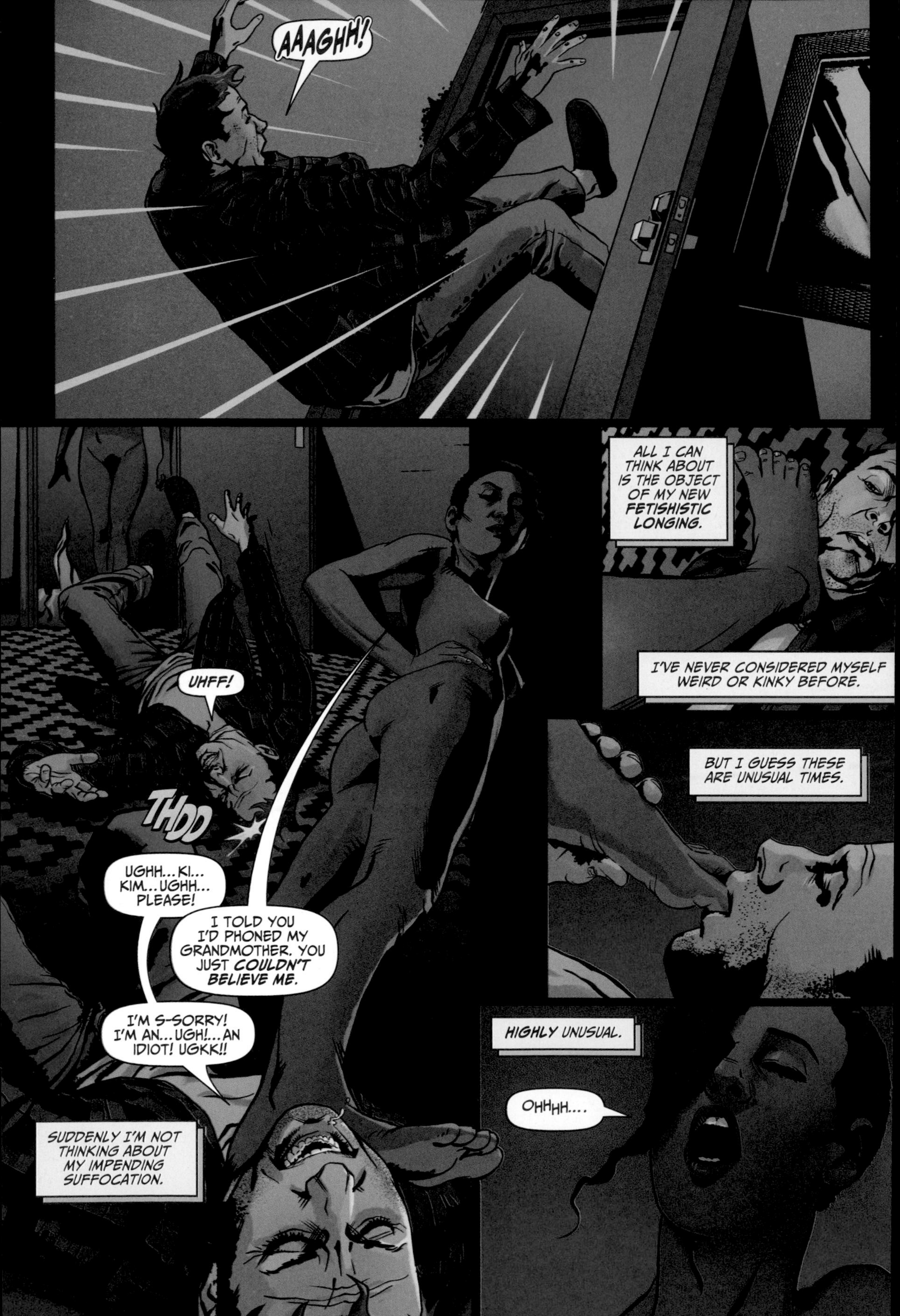

AAAGHH!
UHFF!
THDD
UGHH... KI... KIM... UGHH... PLEASE!
I TOLD YOU I'D PHONED MY GRANDMOTHER. YOU JUST COULDN'T BELIEVE ME.
I'M S-SORRY! I'M AN... UGH!... AN IDIOT! UGKK!!
SUDDENLY I'M NOT THINKING ABOUT MY IMPENDING SUFFOCATION.
ALL I CAN THINK ABOUT IS THE OBJECT OF MY NEW FETISHISTIC LONGING.
I'VE NEVER CONSIDERED MYSELF WEIRD OR KINKY BEFORE.
BUT I GUESS THESE ARE UNUSUAL TIMES.
HIGHLY UNUSUAL.
OHHHH....

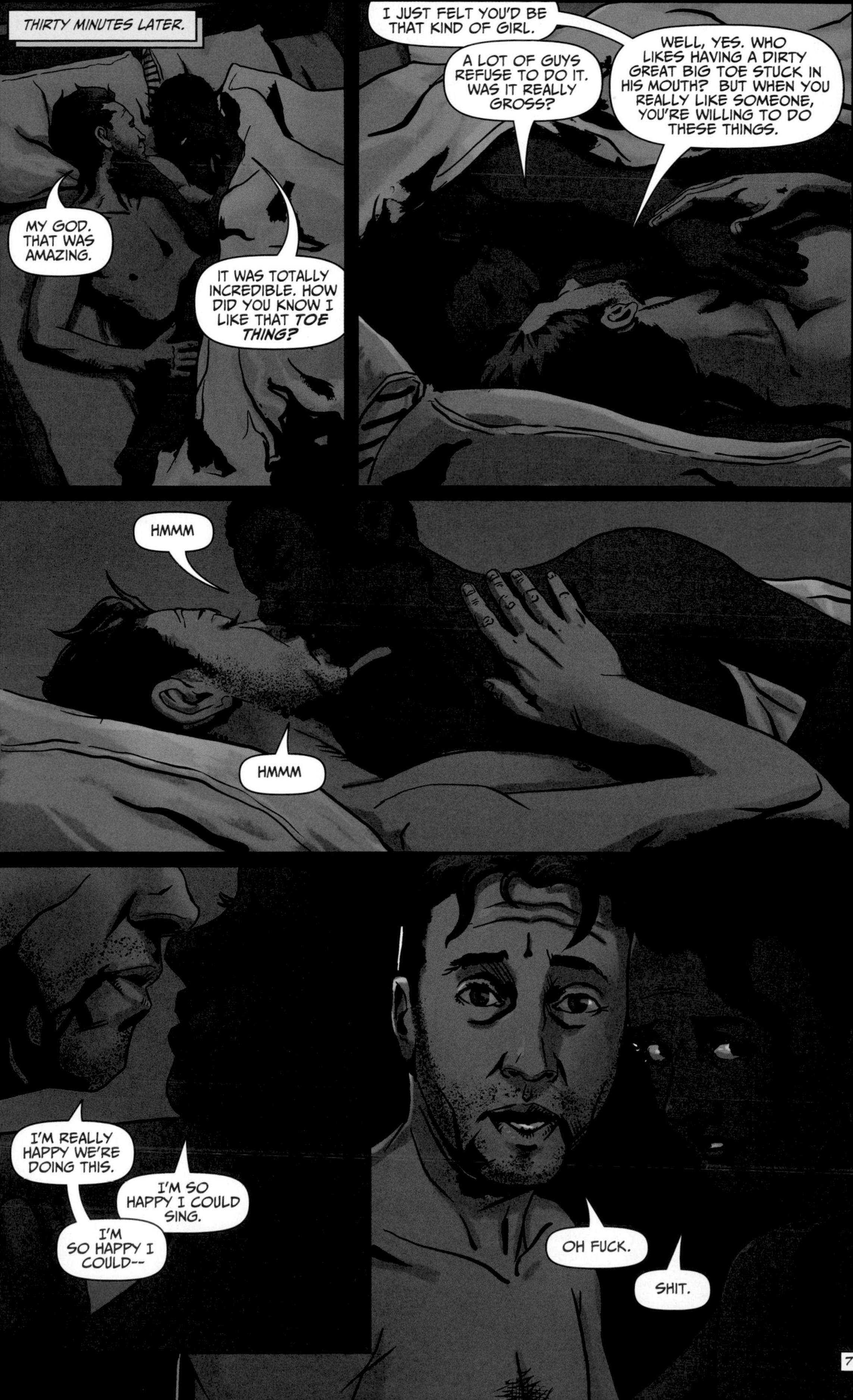
THIRTY MINUTES LATER.
MY GOD. THAT WAS AMAZING.
IT WAS TOTALLY INCREDIBLE. HOW DID YOU KNOW I LIKE THAT *TOE THING?*
I JUST FELT YOU'D BE THAT KIND OF GIRL.
A LOT OF GUYS REFUSE TO DO IT. WAS IT REALLY GROSS?
WELL, YES. WHO LIKES HAVING A DIRTY GREAT BIG TOE STUCK IN HIS MOUTH? BUT WHEN YOU REALLY LIKE SOMEONE, YOU'RE WILLING TO DO THESE THINGS.
HMMM
HMMM
I'M REALLY HAPPY WE'RE DOING THIS.
I'M SO HAPPY I COULD SING.
I'M SO HAPPY I COULD--
OH FUCK.
SHIT.

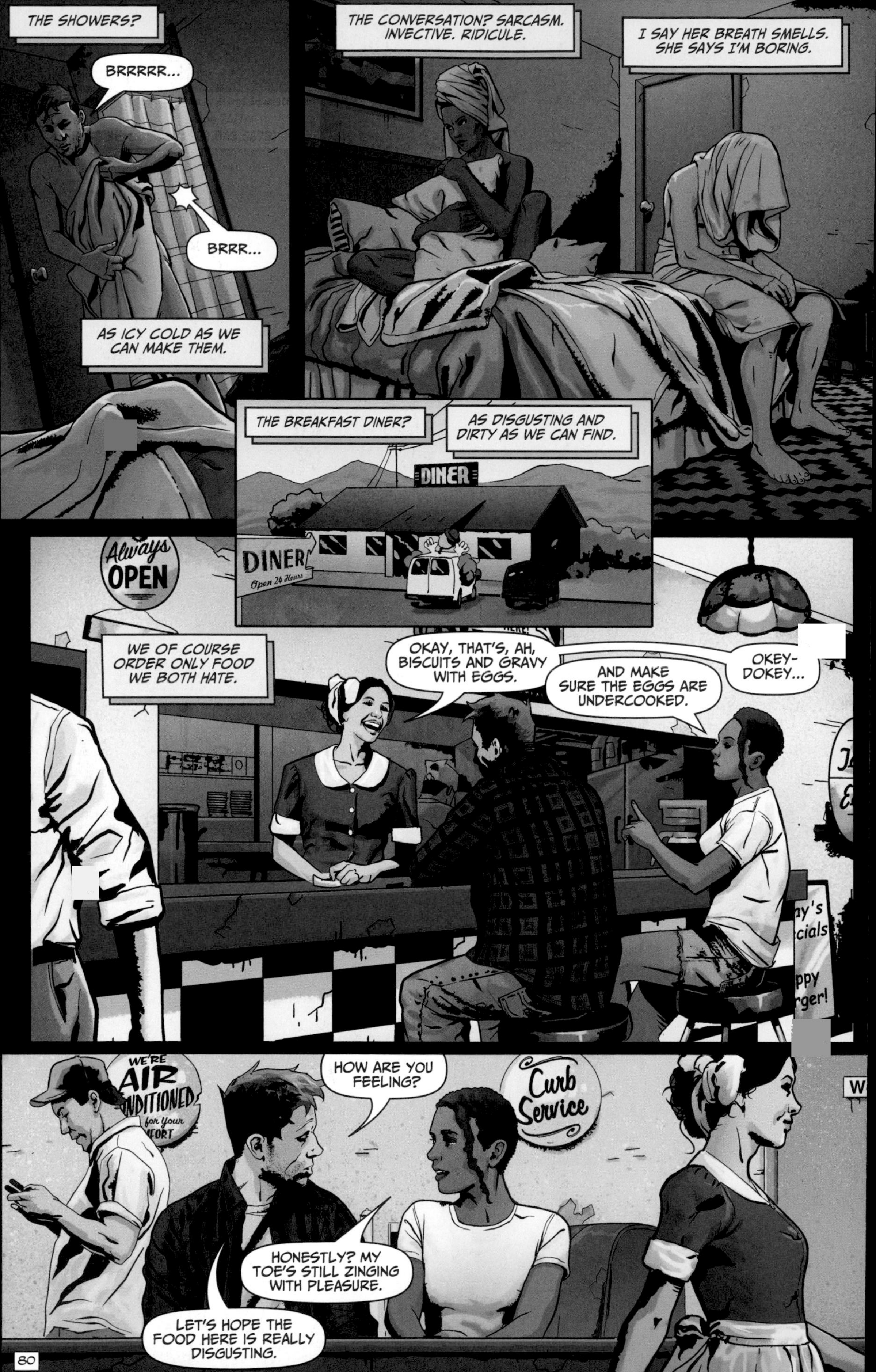
THE SHOWERS?
BRRRRR...
BRRR...
AS ICY COLD AS WE CAN MAKE THEM.
THE CONVERSATION? SARCASM. INVECTIVE. RIDICULE.
I SAY HER BREATH SMELLS. SHE SAYS I'M BORING.
THE BREAKFAST DINER?
AS DISGUSTING AND DIRTY AS WE CAN FIND.
DINER
DINER
Open 24 Hours
Always OPEN
WE OF COURSE ORDER ONLY FOOD WE BOTH HATE.
OKAY, THAT'S, AH, BISCUITS AND GRAVY WITH EGGS.
AND MAKE SURE THE EGGS ARE UNDERCOOKED.
OKEY-DOKEY...
HOW ARE YOU FEELING?
Curb Service
HONESTLY? MY TOE'S STILL ZINGING WITH PLEASURE.
LET'S HOPE THE FOOD HERE IS REALLY DISGUSTING.

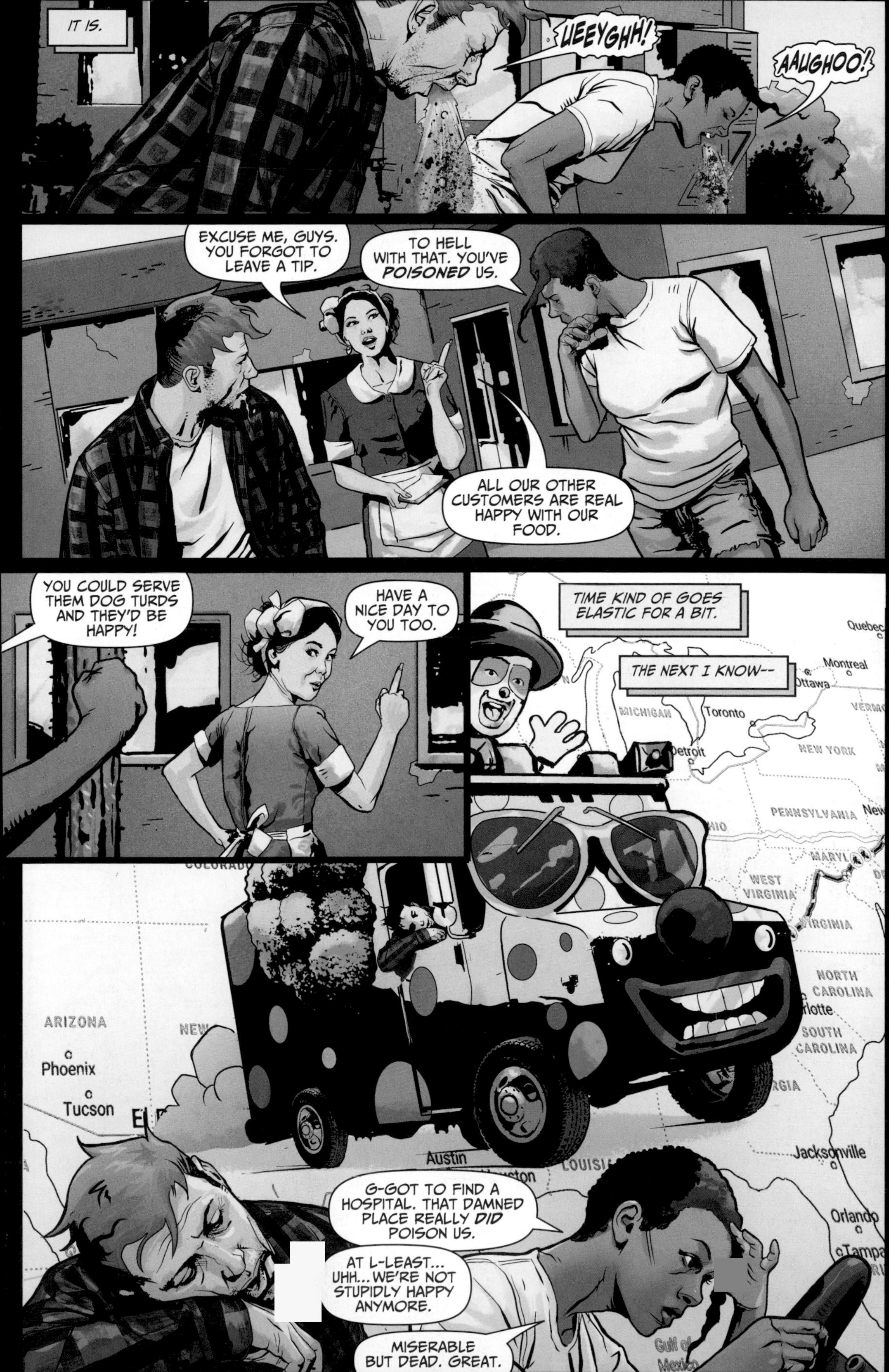
IT IS.
UEEYGHH!
AAUGHOO!
EXCUSE ME, GUYS. YOU FORGOT TO LEAVE A TIP.
TO HELL WITH THAT. YOU'VE POISONED US.
ALL OUR OTHER CUSTOMERS ARE REAL HAPPY WITH OUR FOOD.
YOU COULD SERVE THEM DOG TURDS AND THEY'D BE HAPPY!
HAVE A NICE DAY TO YOU TOO.
TIME KIND OF GOES ELASTIC FOR A BIT.
THE NEXT I KNOW--
Quebec
Montreal
Ottawa
MICHIGAN
Toronto
Detroit
NEW YORK
PENNSYLVANIA
WEST VIRGINIA
VIRGINIA
NORTH CAROLINA
SOUTH CAROLINA
ARIZONA
Phoenix
Tucson
Austin
Jacksonville
Orlando
G-GOT TO FIND A HOSPITAL. THAT DAMNED PLACE REALLY DID POISON US.
AT L-LEAST... UHH... WE'RE NOT STUPIDLY HAPPY ANYMORE.
MISERABLE BUT DEAD. GREAT.
Gulf of Mexico

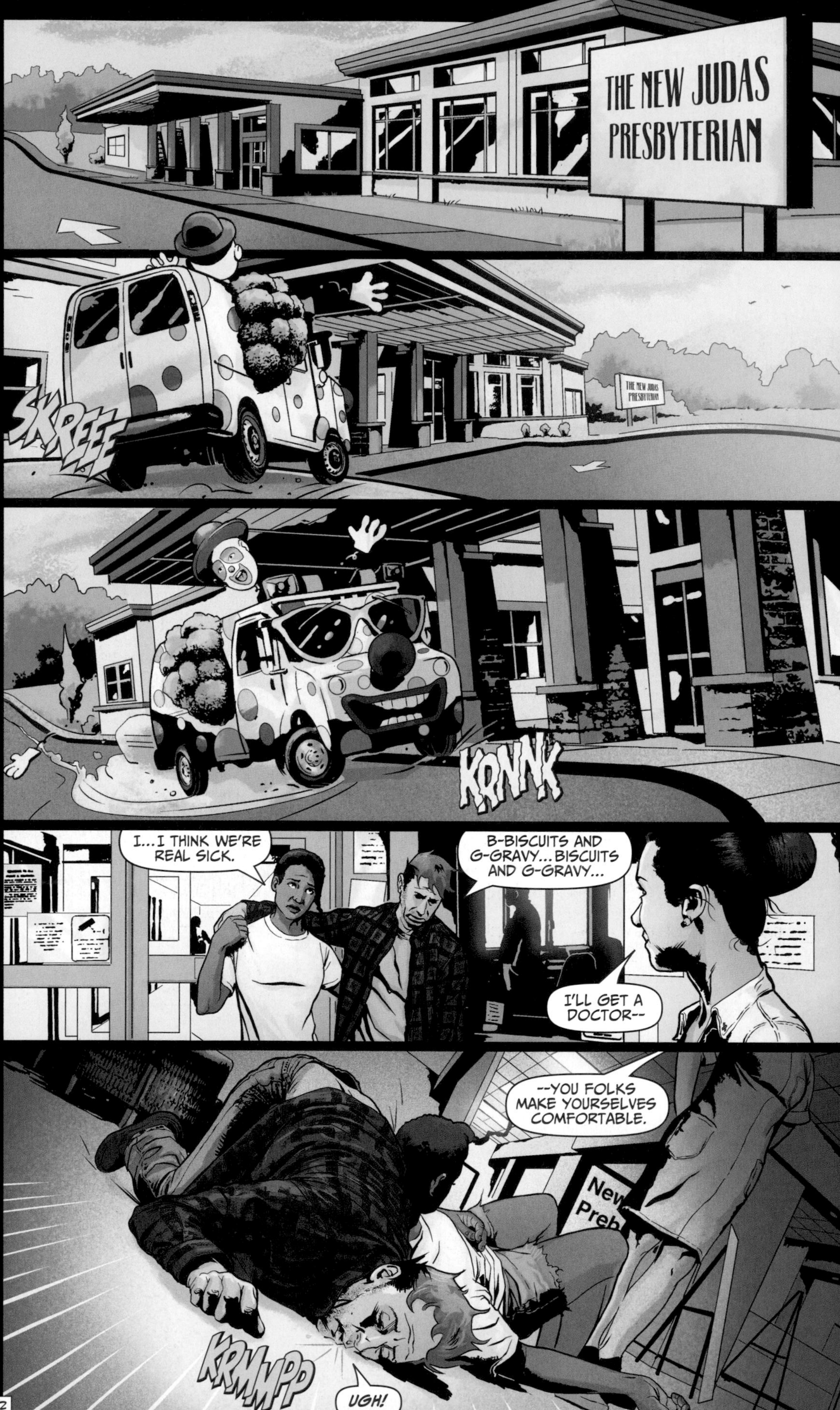

THE NEW JUDAS PRESBYTERIAN
SKREEE
THE NEW JUDAS PRESBYTERIAN
KONNK
I...I THINK WE'RE REAL SICK.
B-BISCUITS AND G-GRAVY...BISCUITS AND G-GRAVY...
I'LL GET A DOCTOR--
--YOU FOLKS MAKE YOURSELVES COMFORTABLE.
KRMMPP
UGH!

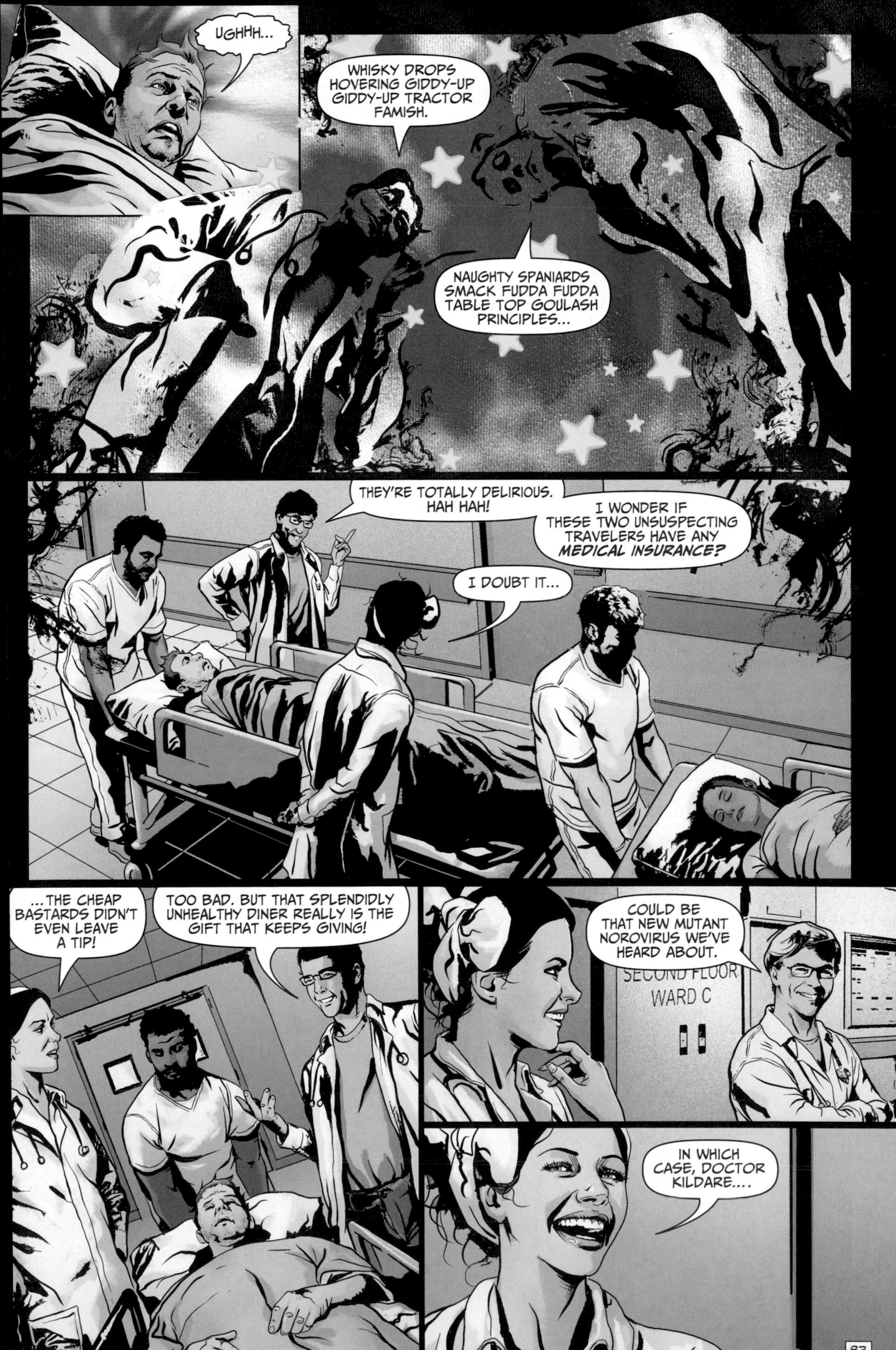
UGHHH...
WHISKY DROPS HOVERING GIDDY-UP GIDDY-UP TRACTOR FAMISH.
NAUGHTY SPANIARDS SMACK FUDDA FUDDA TABLE TOP GOULASH PRINCIPLES...
THEY'RE TOTALLY DELIRIOUS. HAH HAH!
I WONDER IF THESE TWO UNSUSPECTING TRAVELERS HAVE ANY MEDICAL INSURANCE?
I DOUBT IT...
...THE CHEAP BASTARDS DIDN'T EVEN LEAVE A TIP!
TOO BAD. BUT THAT SPLENDIDLY UNHEALTHY DINER REALLY IS THE GIFT THAT KEEPS GIVING!
COULD BE THAT NEW MUTANT NOROVIRUS WE'VE HEARD ABOUT.
SECOND FLOOR
WARD C
IN WHICH CASE, DOCTOR KILDARE....

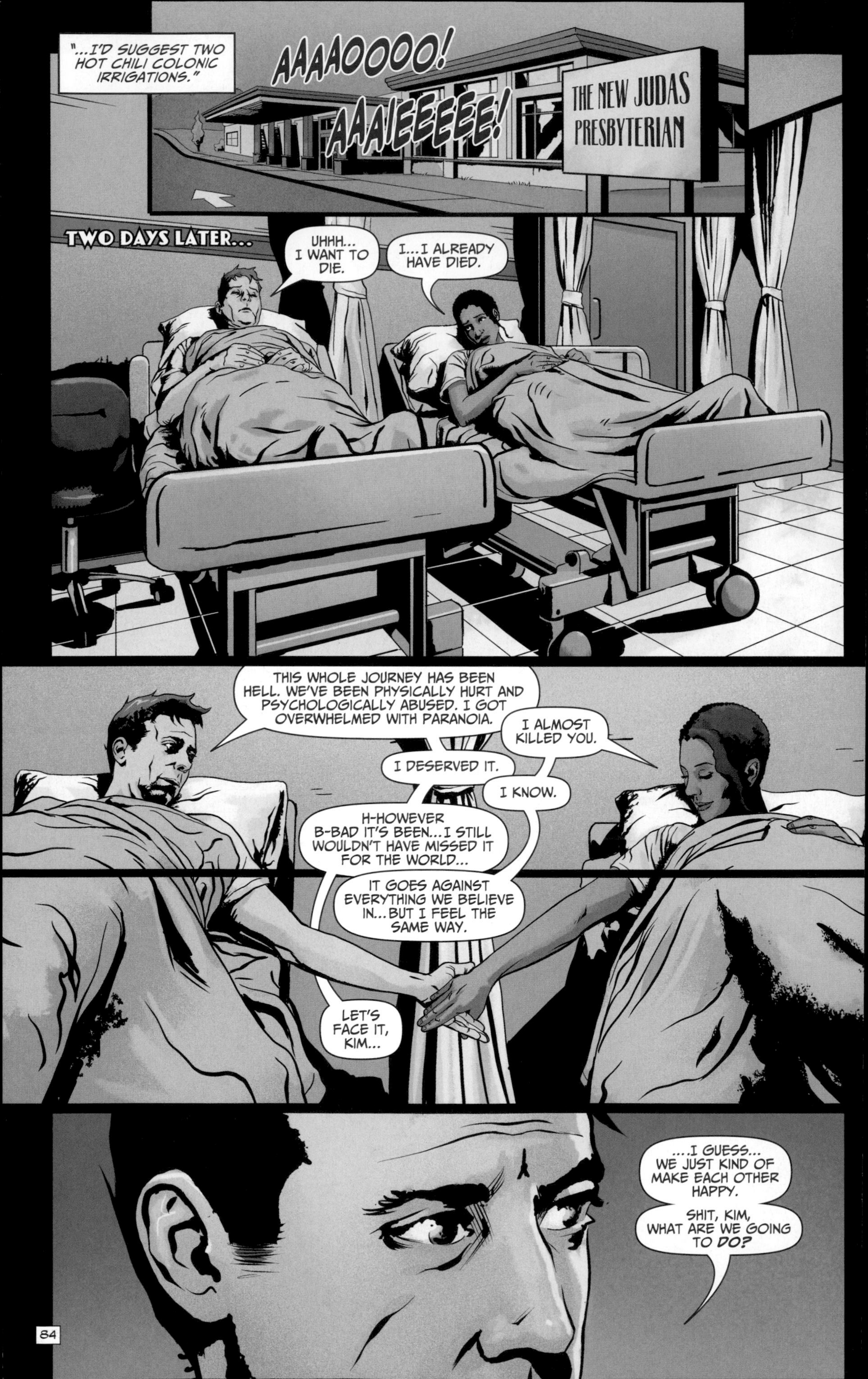
"...I'D SUGGEST TWO HOT CHILI COLONIC IRRIGATIONS."
AAAAOOOO!
AAAIEEEEE!
THE NEW JUDAS PRESBYTERIAN
TWO DAYS LATER...
UHHH... I WANT TO DIE.
I...I ALREADY HAVE DIED.
THIS WHOLE JOURNEY HAS BEEN HELL. WE'VE BEEN PHYSICALLY HURT AND PSYCHOLOGICALLY ABUSED. I GOT OVERWHELMED WITH PARANOIA.
I ALMOST KILLED YOU.
I DESERVED IT.
I KNOW.
H-HOWEVER B-BAD IT'S BEEN...I STILL WOULDN'T HAVE MISSED IT FOR THE WORLD...
IT GOES AGAINST EVERYTHING WE BELIEVE IN...BUT I FEEL THE SAME WAY.
LET'S FACE IT, KIM...
....I GUESS... WE JUST KIND OF MAKE EACH OTHER HAPPY.
SHIT, KIM, WHAT ARE WE GOING TO *DO?*

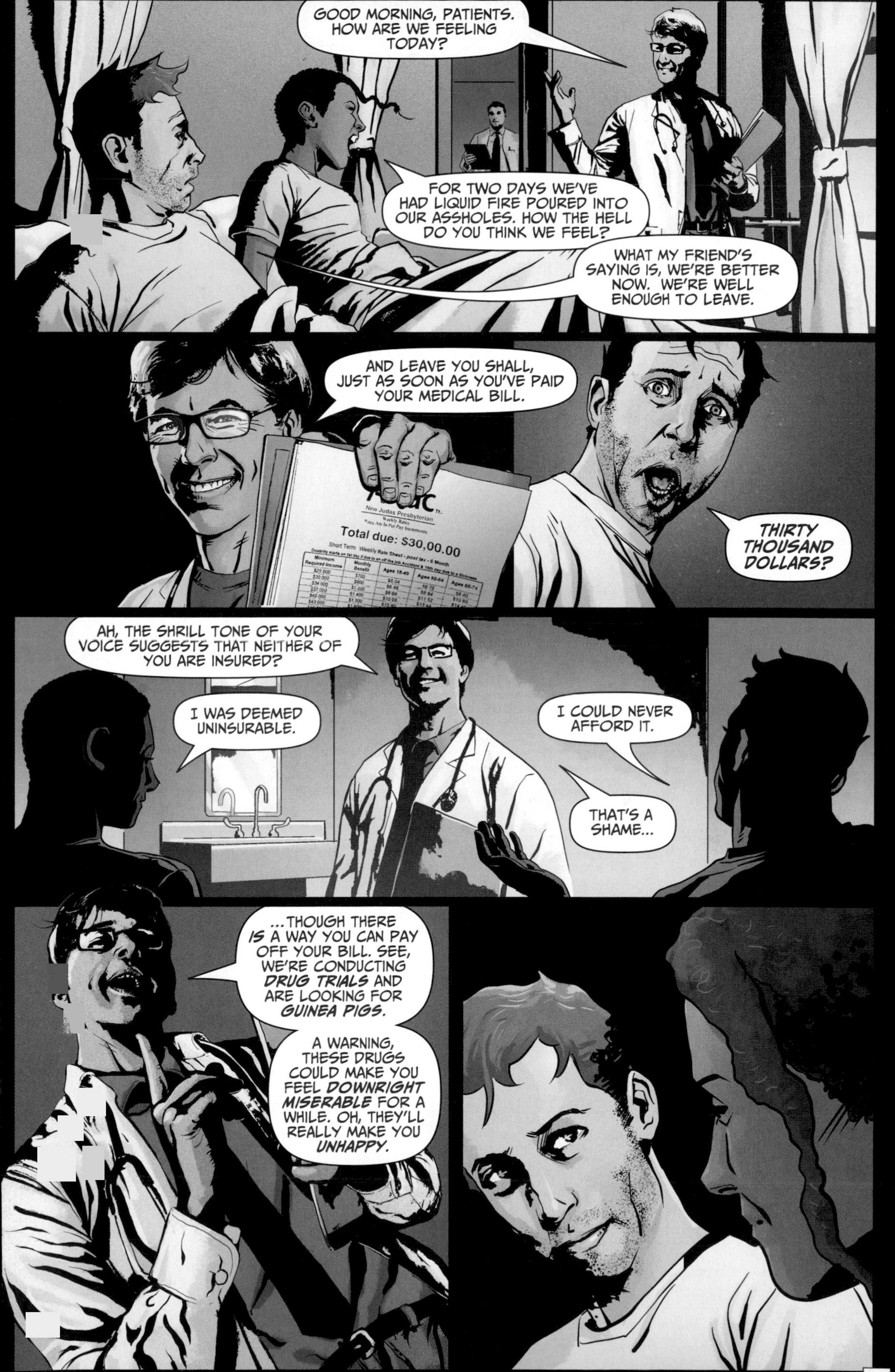
GOOD MORNING, PATIENTS. HOW ARE WE FEELING TODAY?
FOR TWO DAYS WE'VE HAD LIQUID FIRE POURED INTO OUR ASSHOLES. HOW THE HELL DO YOU THINK WE FEEL?
WHAT MY FRIEND'S SAYING IS, WE'RE BETTER NOW. WE'RE WELL ENOUGH TO LEAVE.
AND LEAVE YOU SHALL, JUST AS SOON AS YOU'VE PAID YOUR MEDICAL BILL.
New Judas Presbyterian
Weekly Rates
Total due: $30,00.00
Short Term Weekly Rate Sheet - post tax - 6 Month
THIRTY THOUSAND DOLLARS?
AH, THE SHRILL TONE OF YOUR VOICE SUGGESTS THAT NEITHER OF YOU ARE INSURED?
I WAS DEEMED UNINSURABLE.
I COULD NEVER AFFORD IT.
THAT'S A SHAME...
...THOUGH THERE *IS* A WAY YOU CAN PAY OFF YOUR BILL. SEE, WE'RE CONDUCTING ***DRUG TRIALS*** AND ARE LOOKING FOR ***GUINEA PIGS***.
A WARNING, THESE DRUGS COULD MAKE YOU FEEL ***DOWNRIGHT MISERABLE*** FOR A WHILE. OH, THEY'LL REALLY MAKE YOU ***UNHAPPY***.

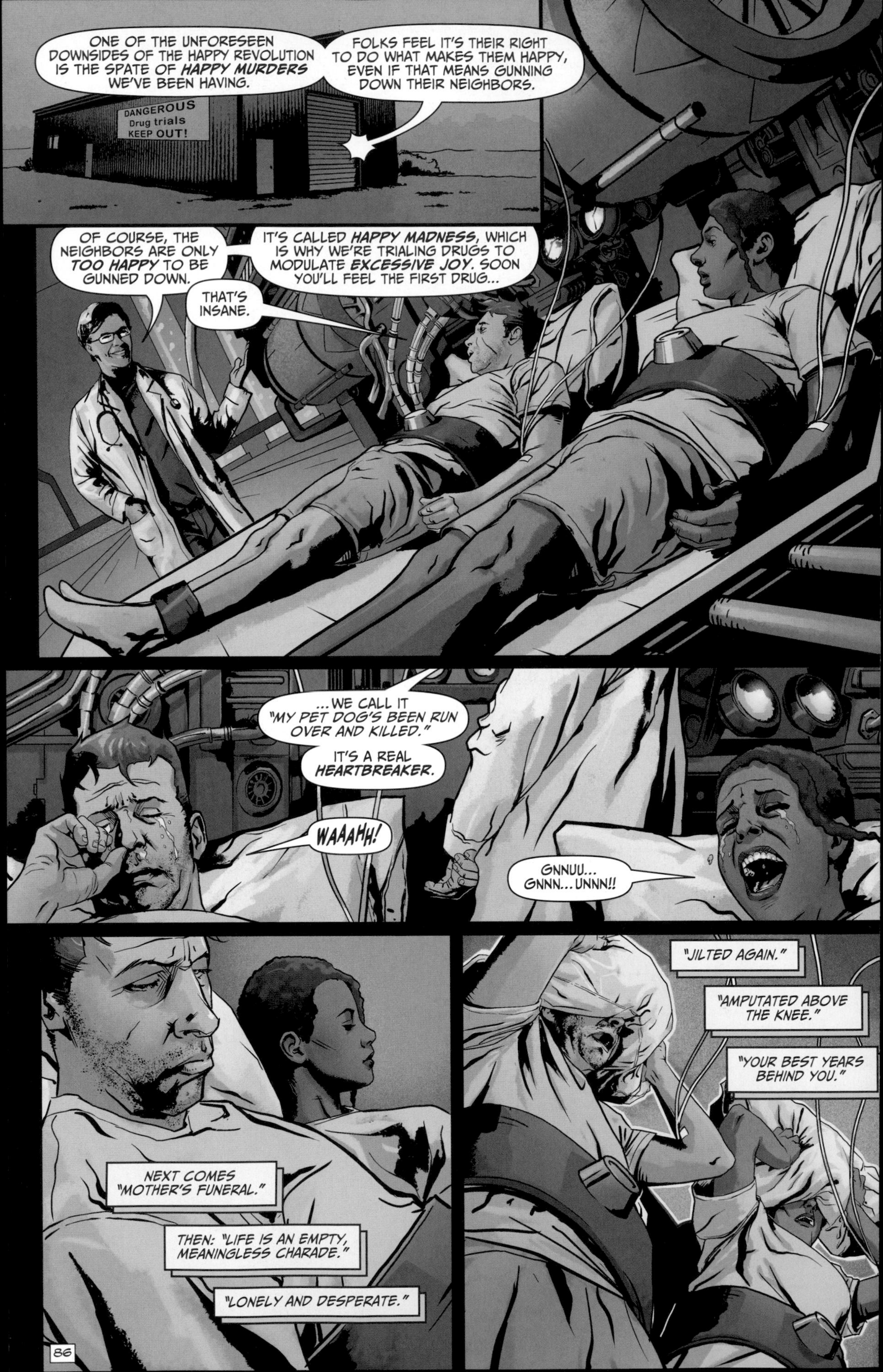

ONE OF THE UNFORESEEN DOWNSIDES OF THE HAPPY REVOLUTION IS THE SPATE OF *HAPPY MURDERS* WE'VE BEEN HAVING.
FOLKS FEEL IT'S THEIR RIGHT TO DO WHAT MAKES THEM HAPPY, EVEN IF THAT MEANS GUNNING DOWN THEIR NEIGHBORS.
DANGEROUS Drug trials KEEP OUT!
OF COURSE, THE NEIGHBORS ARE ONLY *TOO HAPPY* TO BE GUNNED DOWN.
IT'S CALLED *HAPPY MADNESS*, WHICH IS WHY WE'RE TRIALING DRUGS TO MODULATE *EXCESSIVE JOY*. SOON YOU'LL FEEL THE FIRST DRUG...
THAT'S INSANE.
...WE CALL IT *"MY PET DOG'S BEEN RUN OVER AND KILLED."*
IT'S A REAL *HEARTBREAKER*.
WAAAHH!
GNNUU... GNNN... UNNN!!
NEXT COMES "MOTHER'S FUNERAL."
THEN: "LIFE IS AN EMPTY, MEANINGLESS CHARADE."
"LONELY AND DESPERATE."
"JILTED AGAIN."
"AMPUTATED ABOVE THE KNEE."
"YOUR BEST YEARS BEHIND YOU."

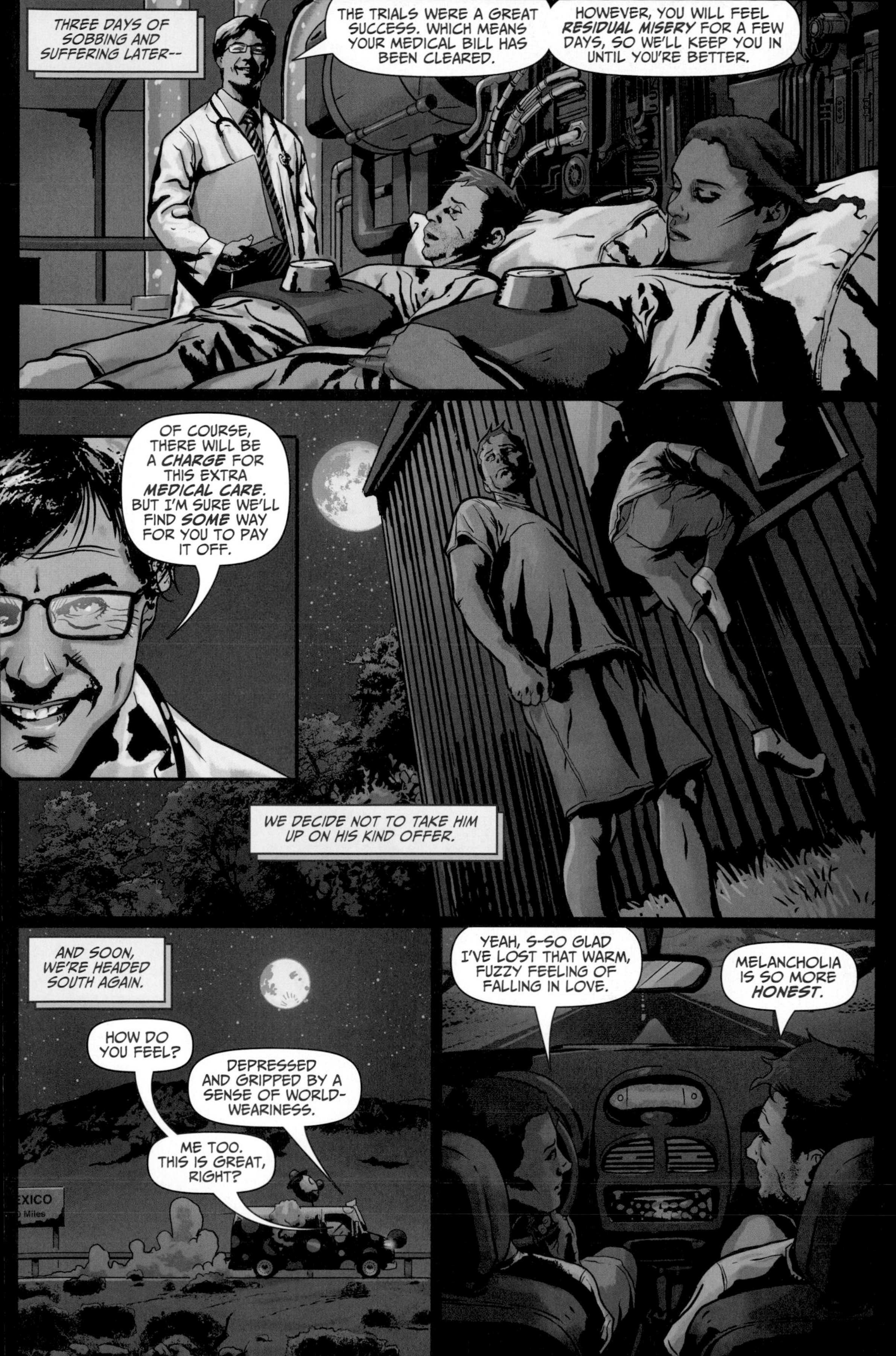
THREE DAYS OF SOBBING AND SUFFERING LATER--
THE TRIALS WERE A GREAT SUCCESS. WHICH MEANS YOUR MEDICAL BILL HAS BEEN CLEARED.
HOWEVER, YOU WILL FEEL RESIDUAL MISERY FOR A FEW DAYS, SO WE'LL KEEP YOU IN UNTIL YOU'RE BETTER.
OF COURSE, THERE WILL BE A CHARGE FOR THIS EXTRA MEDICAL CARE. BUT I'M SURE WE'LL FIND SOME WAY FOR YOU TO PAY IT OFF.
WE DECIDE NOT TO TAKE HIM UP ON HIS KIND OFFER.
AND SOON, WE'RE HEADED SOUTH AGAIN.
HOW DO YOU FEEL?
DEPRESSED AND GRIPPED BY A SENSE OF WORLD-WEARINESS.
ME TOO. THIS IS GREAT, RIGHT?
YEAH, S-SO GLAD I'VE LOST THAT WARM, FUZZY FEELING OF FALLING IN LOVE.
MELANCHOLIA IS SO MORE HONEST.

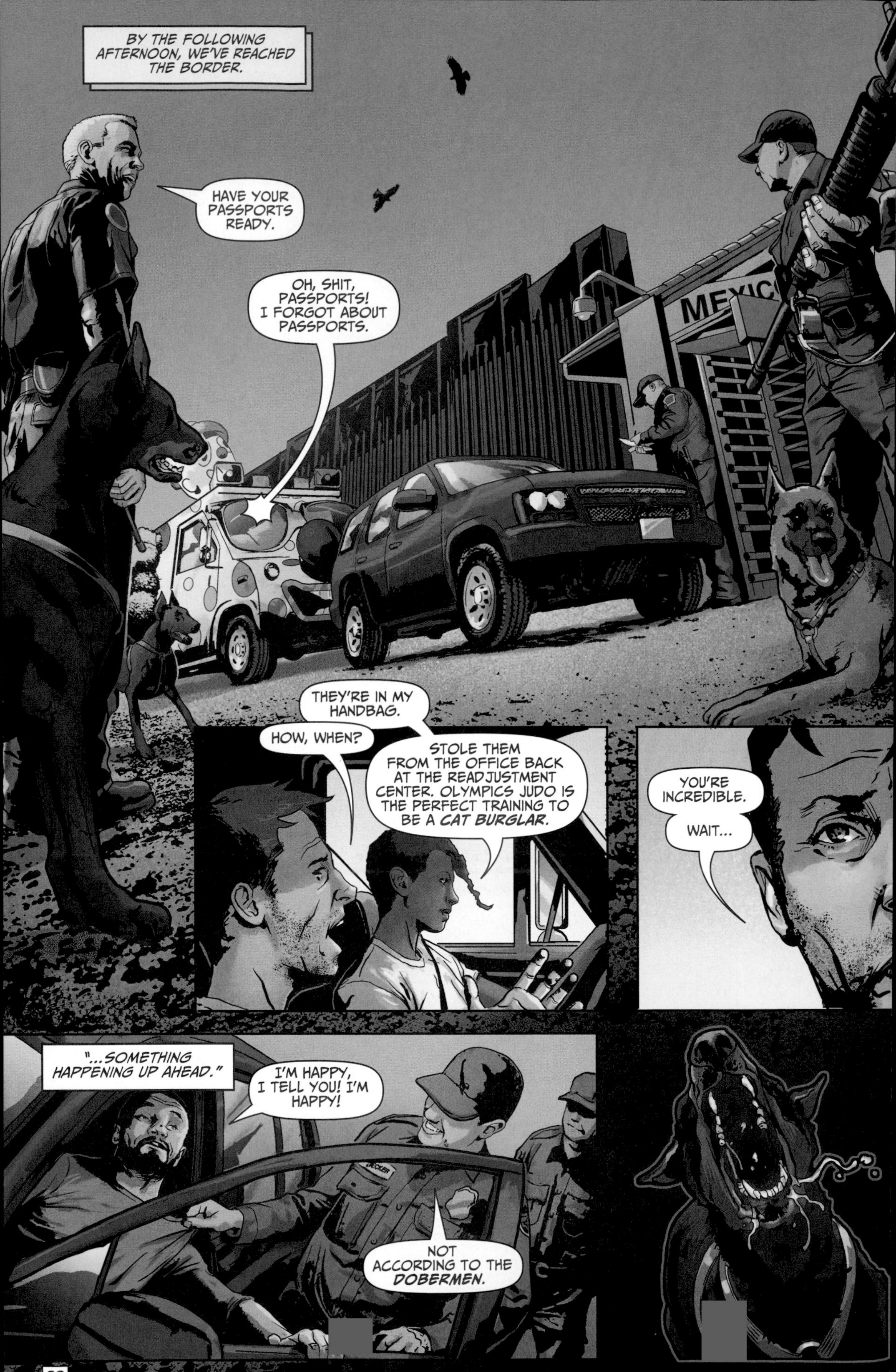
BY THE FOLLOWING AFTERNOON, WE'VE REACHED THE BORDER.
HAVE YOUR PASSPORTS READY.
OH, SHIT, PASSPORTS! I FORGOT ABOUT PASSPORTS.
MEXICO
THEY'RE IN MY HANDBAG.
HOW, WHEN?
STOLE THEM FROM THE OFFICE BACK AT THE READJUSTMENT CENTER. OLYMPICS JUDO IS THE PERFECT TRAINING TO BE A CAT BURGLAR.
YOU'RE INCREDIBLE.
WAIT...
"...SOMETHING HAPPENING UP AHEAD."
I'M HAPPY, I TELL YOU! I'M HAPPY!
NOT ACCORDING TO THE DOBERMEN.

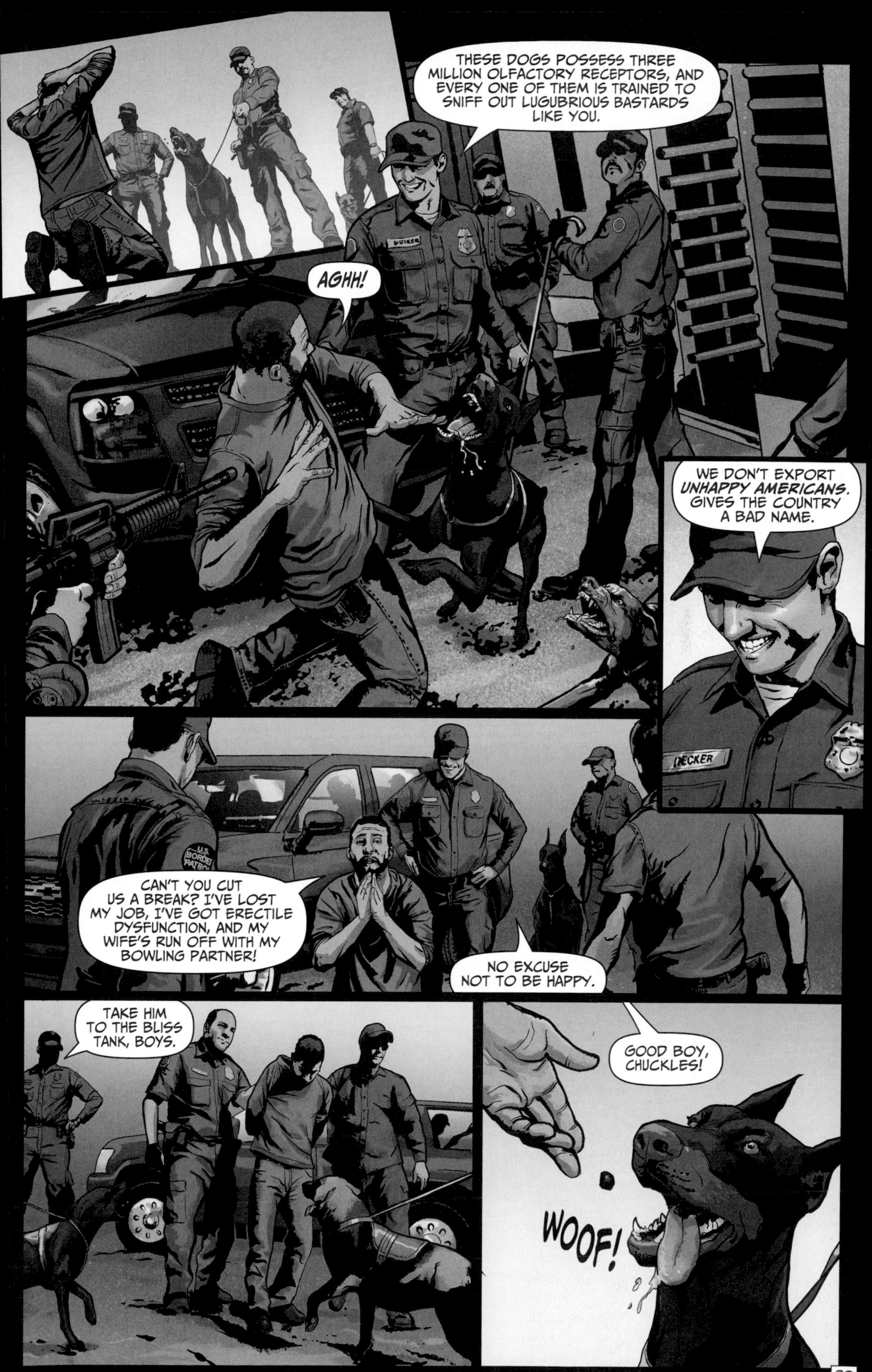

THESE DOGS POSSESS THREE MILLION OLFACTORY RECEPTORS, AND EVERY ONE OF THEM IS TRAINED TO SNIFF OUT LUGUBRIOUS BASTARDS LIKE YOU.
AGHH!
WE DON'T EXPORT *UNHAPPY AMERICANS*. GIVES THE COUNTRY A BAD NAME.
CAN'T YOU CUT US A BREAK? I'VE LOST MY JOB, I'VE GOT ERECTILE DYSFUNCTION, AND MY WIFE'S RUN OFF WITH MY BOWLING PARTNER!
NO EXCUSE NOT TO BE HAPPY.
TAKE HIM TO THE BLISS TANK, BOYS.
GOOD BOY, CHUCKLES!
WOOF!

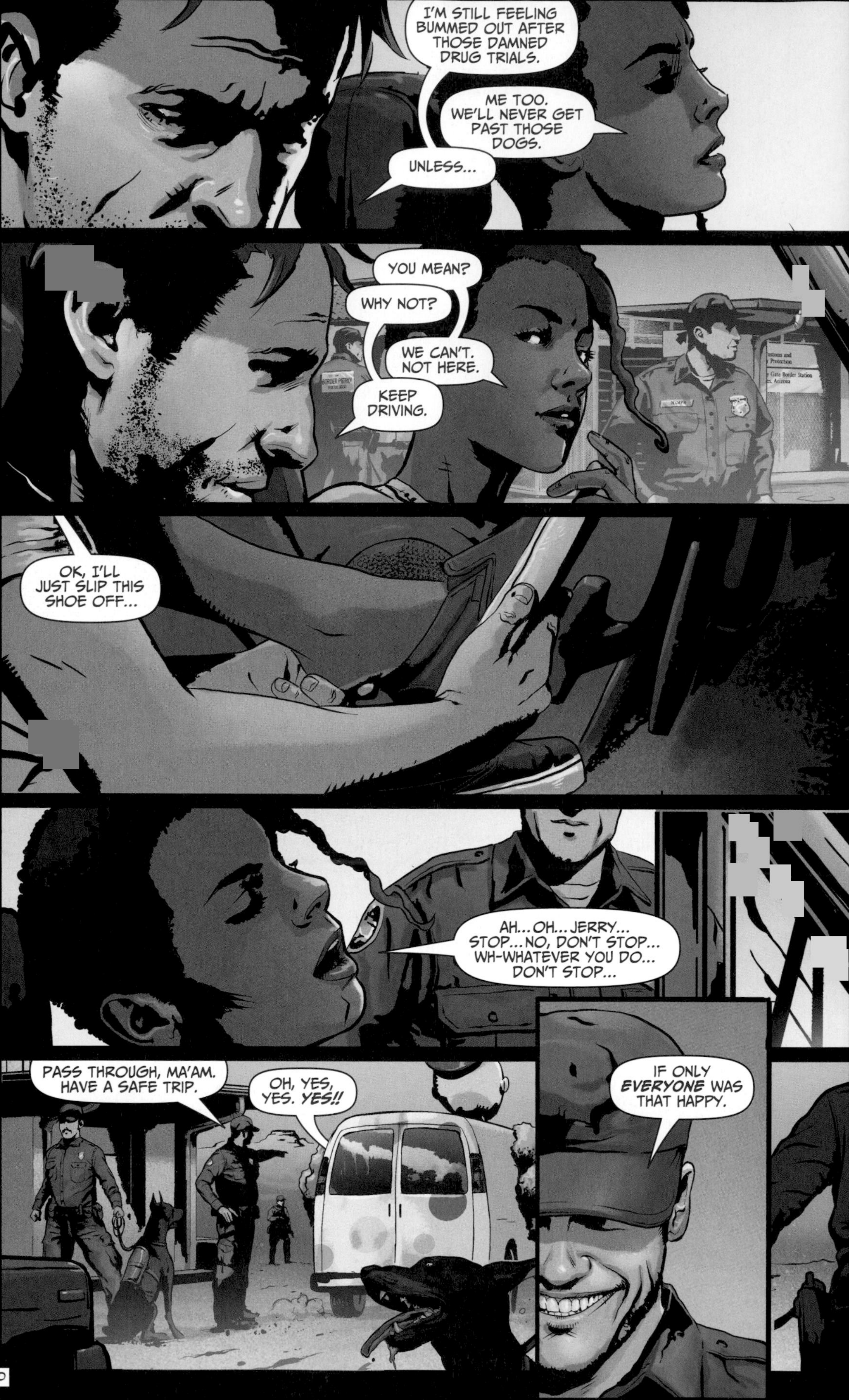
I'M STILL FEELING BUMMED OUT AFTER THOSE DAMNED DRUG TRIALS.
ME TOO. WE'LL NEVER GET PAST THOSE DOGS.
UNLESS...
YOU MEAN?
WHY NOT?
WE CAN'T. NOT HERE.
KEEP DRIVING.
OK, I'LL JUST SLIP THIS SHOE OFF...
AH...OH...JERRY... STOP...NO, DON'T STOP... WH-WHATEVER YOU DO... DON'T STOP...
PASS THROUGH, MA'AM. HAVE A SAFE TRIP.
OH, YES, YES. YES!!
IF ONLY EVERYONE WAS THAT HAPPY.

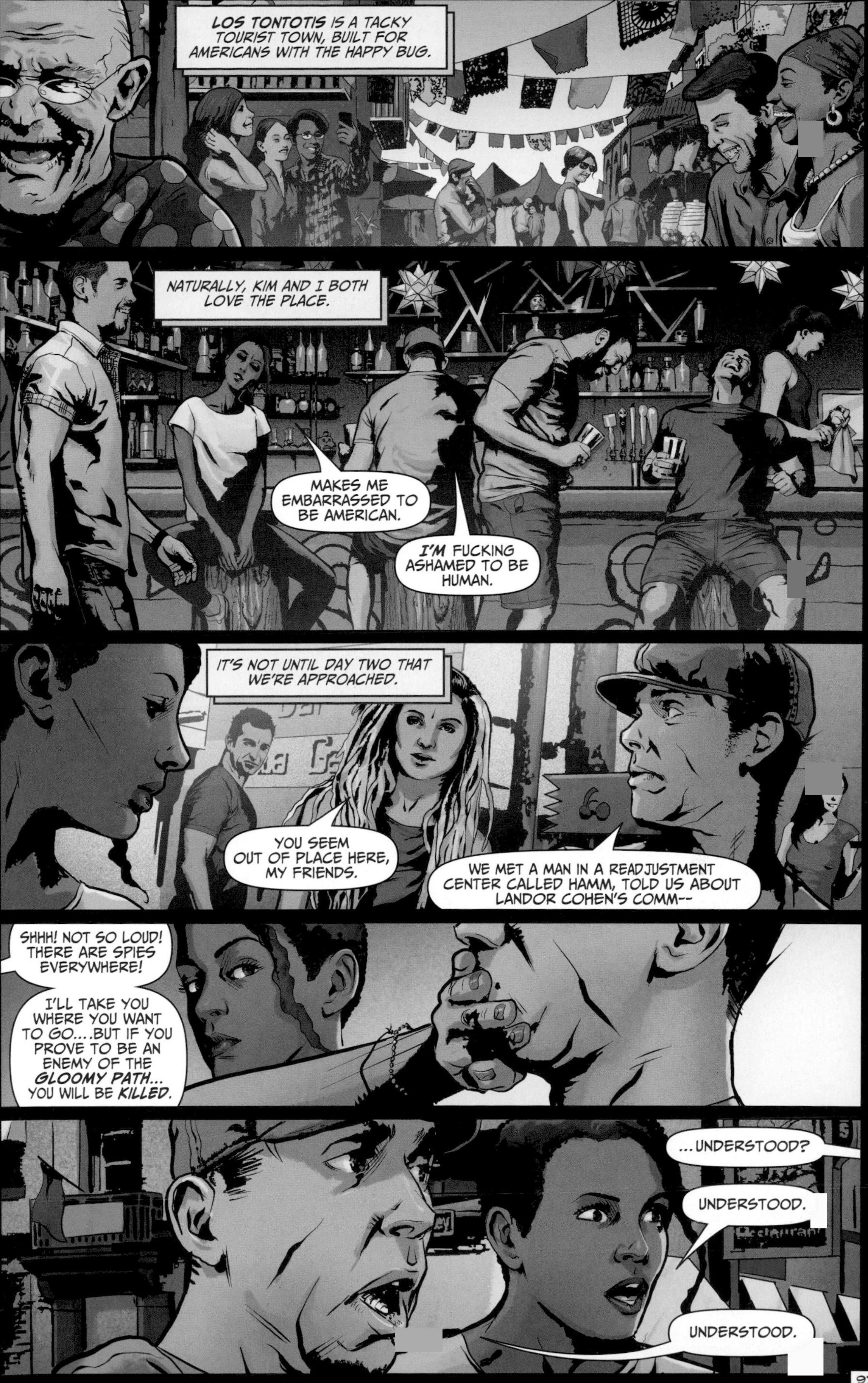

LOS TONTOTIS IS A TACKY TOURIST TOWN, BUILT FOR AMERICANS WITH THE HAPPY BUG.
NATURALLY, KIM AND I BOTH LOVE THE PLACE.
MAKES ME EMBARRASSED TO BE AMERICAN.
I'M FUCKING ASHAMED TO BE HUMAN.
IT'S NOT UNTIL DAY TWO THAT WE'RE APPROACHED.
YOU SEEM OUT OF PLACE HERE, MY FRIENDS.
WE MET A MAN IN A READJUSTMENT CENTER CALLED HAMM, TOLD US ABOUT LANDOR COHEN'S COMM--
SHHH! NOT SO LOUD! THERE ARE SPIES EVERYWHERE!
I'LL TAKE YOU WHERE YOU WANT TO GO....BUT IF YOU PROVE TO BE AN ENEMY OF THE GLOOMY PATH... YOU WILL BE KILLED.
...UNDERSTOOD?
UNDERSTOOD.
UNDERSTOOD.

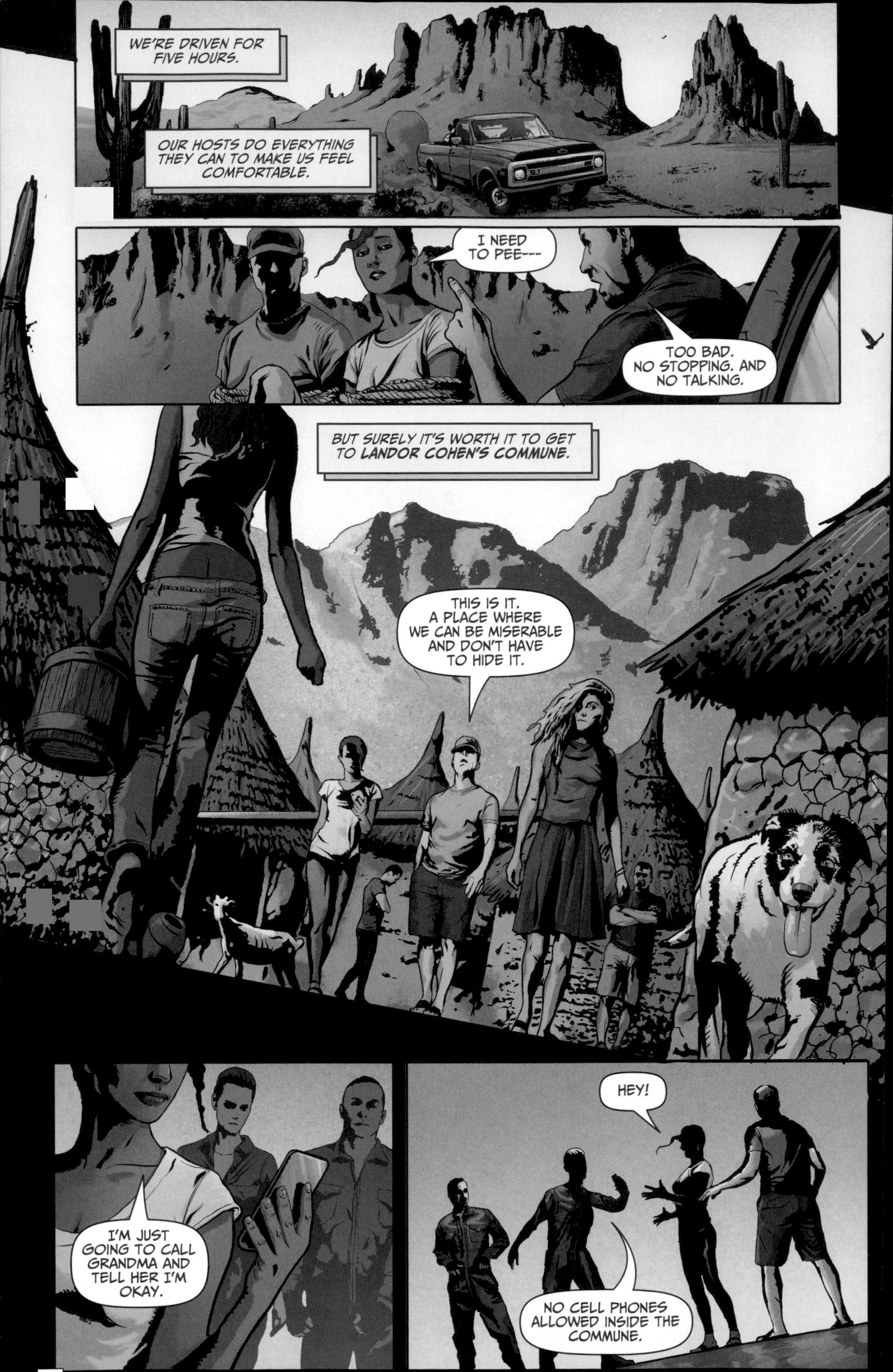
WE'RE DRIVEN FOR FIVE HOURS.
OUR HOSTS DO EVERYTHING THEY CAN TO MAKE US FEEL COMFORTABLE.
I NEED TO PEE---
TOO BAD. NO STOPPING. AND NO TALKING.
BUT SURELY IT'S WORTH IT TO GET TO LANDOR COHEN'S COMMUNE.
THIS IS IT. A PLACE WHERE WE CAN BE MISERABLE AND DON'T HAVE TO HIDE IT.
I'M JUST GOING TO CALL GRANDMA AND TELL HER I'M OKAY.
HEY!
NO CELL PHONES ALLOWED INSIDE THE COMMUNE.

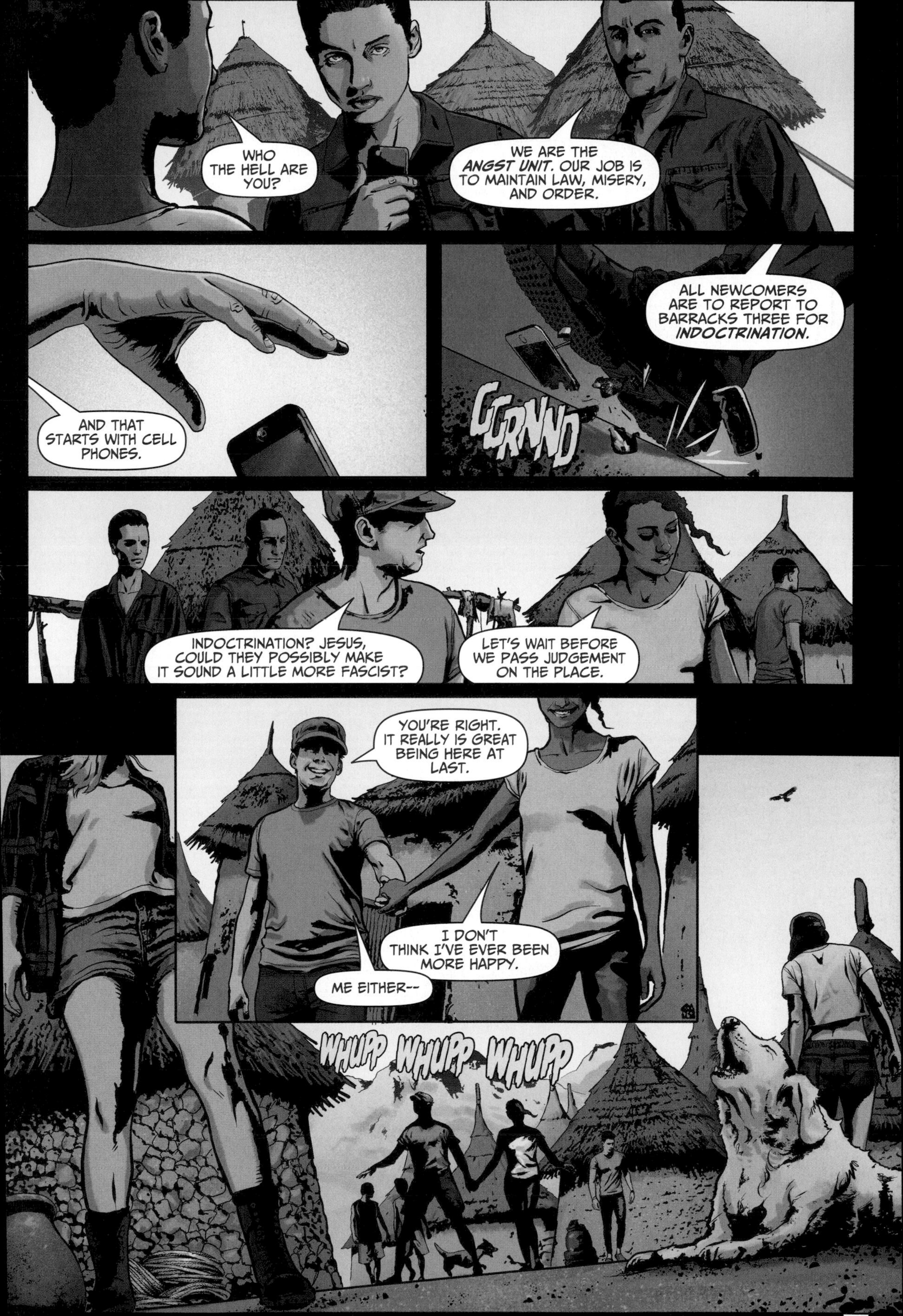
WHO THE HELL ARE YOU?
WE ARE THE *ANGST UNIT*. OUR JOB IS TO MAINTAIN LAW, MISERY, AND ORDER.
AND THAT STARTS WITH CELL PHONES.
ALL NEWCOMERS ARE TO REPORT TO BARRACKS THREE FOR *INDOCTRINATION.*
GGRNND
INDOCTRINATION? JESUS, COULD THEY POSSIBLY MAKE IT SOUND A LITTLE MORE FASCIST?
LET'S WAIT BEFORE WE PASS JUDGEMENT ON THE PLACE.
YOU'RE RIGHT. IT REALLY IS GREAT BEING HERE AT LAST.
I DON'T THINK I'VE EVER BEEN MORE HAPPY.
ME EITHER--
WHUPP WHUPP WHUPP

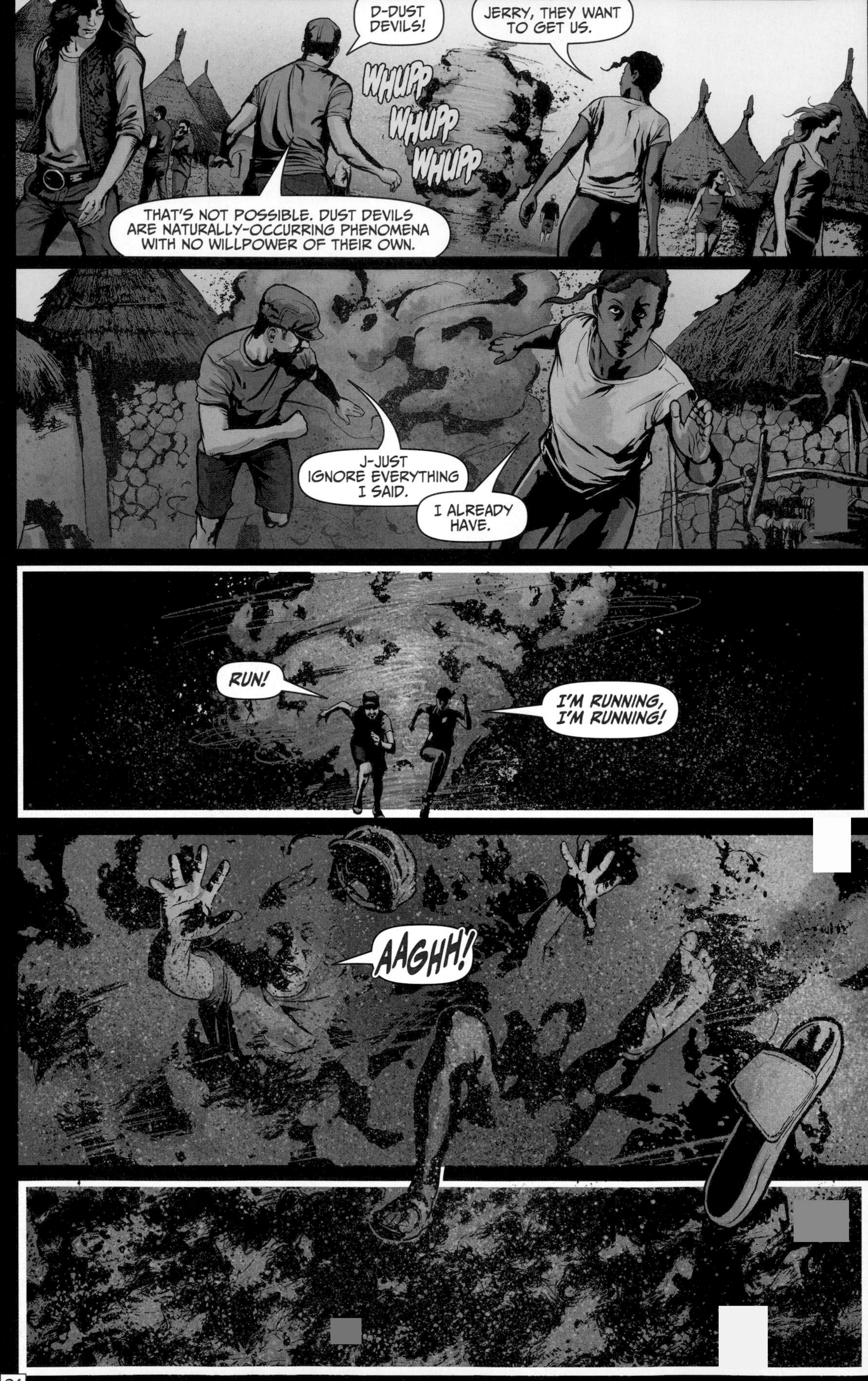
D-DUST DEVILS!
JERRY, THEY WANT TO GET US.
WHUPP WHUPP WHUPP
THAT'S NOT POSSIBLE. DUST DEVILS ARE NATURALLY-OCCURRING PHENOMENA WITH NO WILLPOWER OF THEIR OWN.
J-JUST IGNORE EVERYTHING I SAID.
I ALREADY HAVE.
RUN!
I'M RUNNING, I'M RUNNING!
AAGHH!

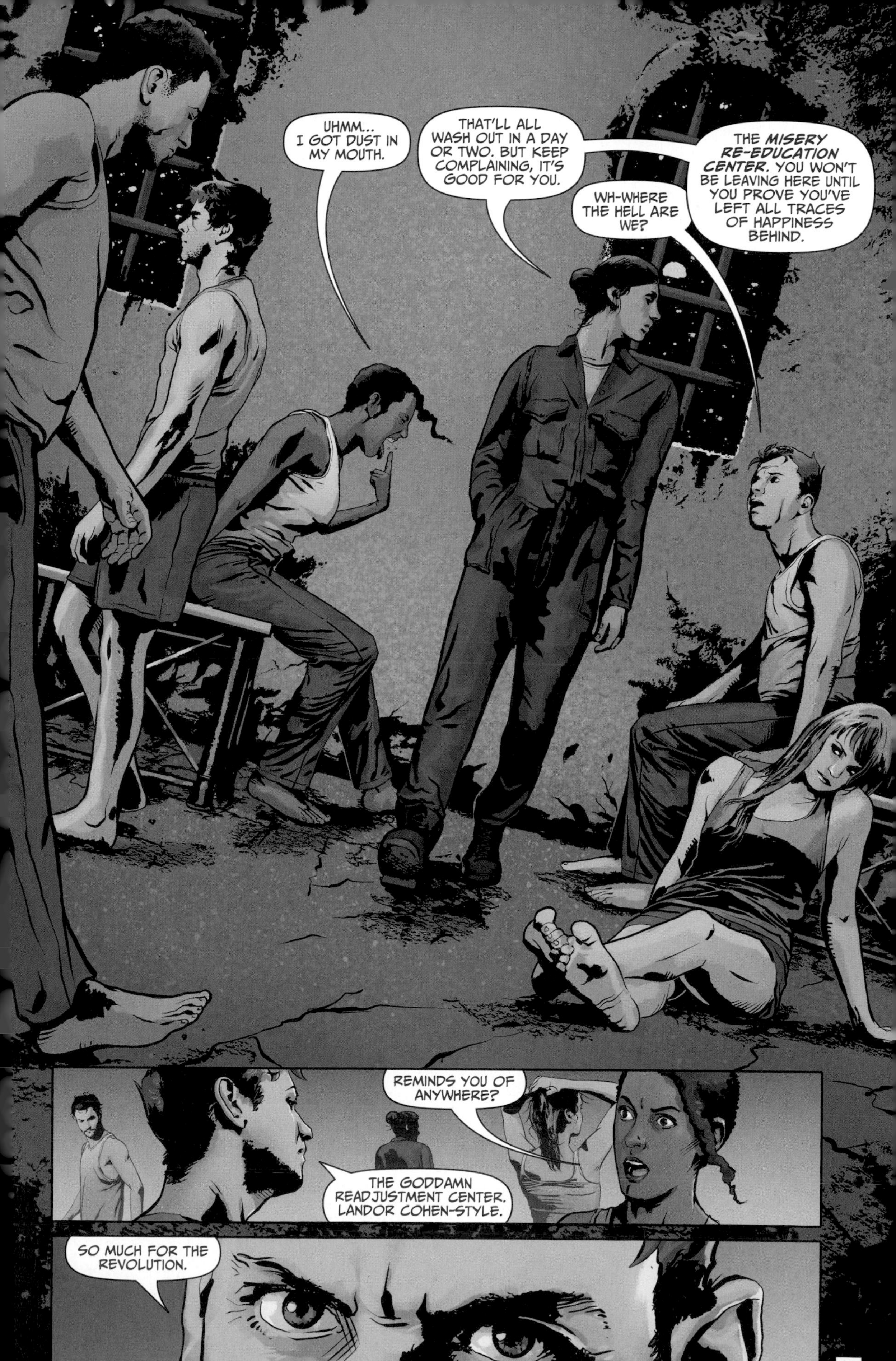
UHMM.. I GOT DUST IN MY MOUTH.
THAT'LL ALL WASH OUT IN A DAY OR TWO. BUT KEEP COMPLAINING, IT'S GOOD FOR YOU.
WH-WHERE THE HELL ARE WE?
THE MISERY RE-EDUCATION CENTER. YOU WON'T BE LEAVING HERE UNTIL YOU PROVE YOU'VE LEFT ALL TRACES OF HAPPINESS BEHIND.
REMINDS YOU OF ANYWHERE?
THE GODDAMN READJUSTMENT CENTER. LANDOR COHEN-STYLE.
SO MUCH FOR THE REVOLUTION.

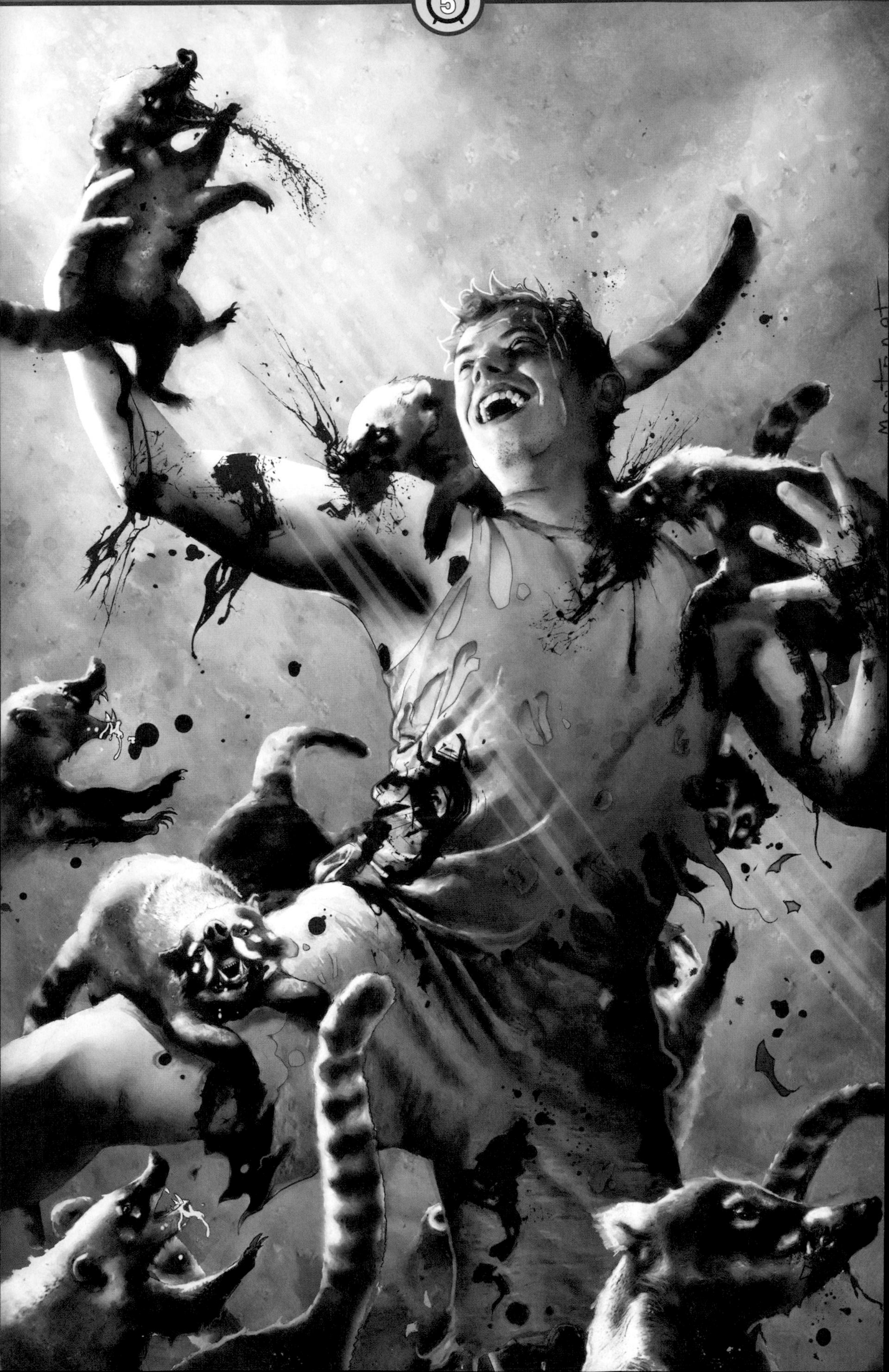

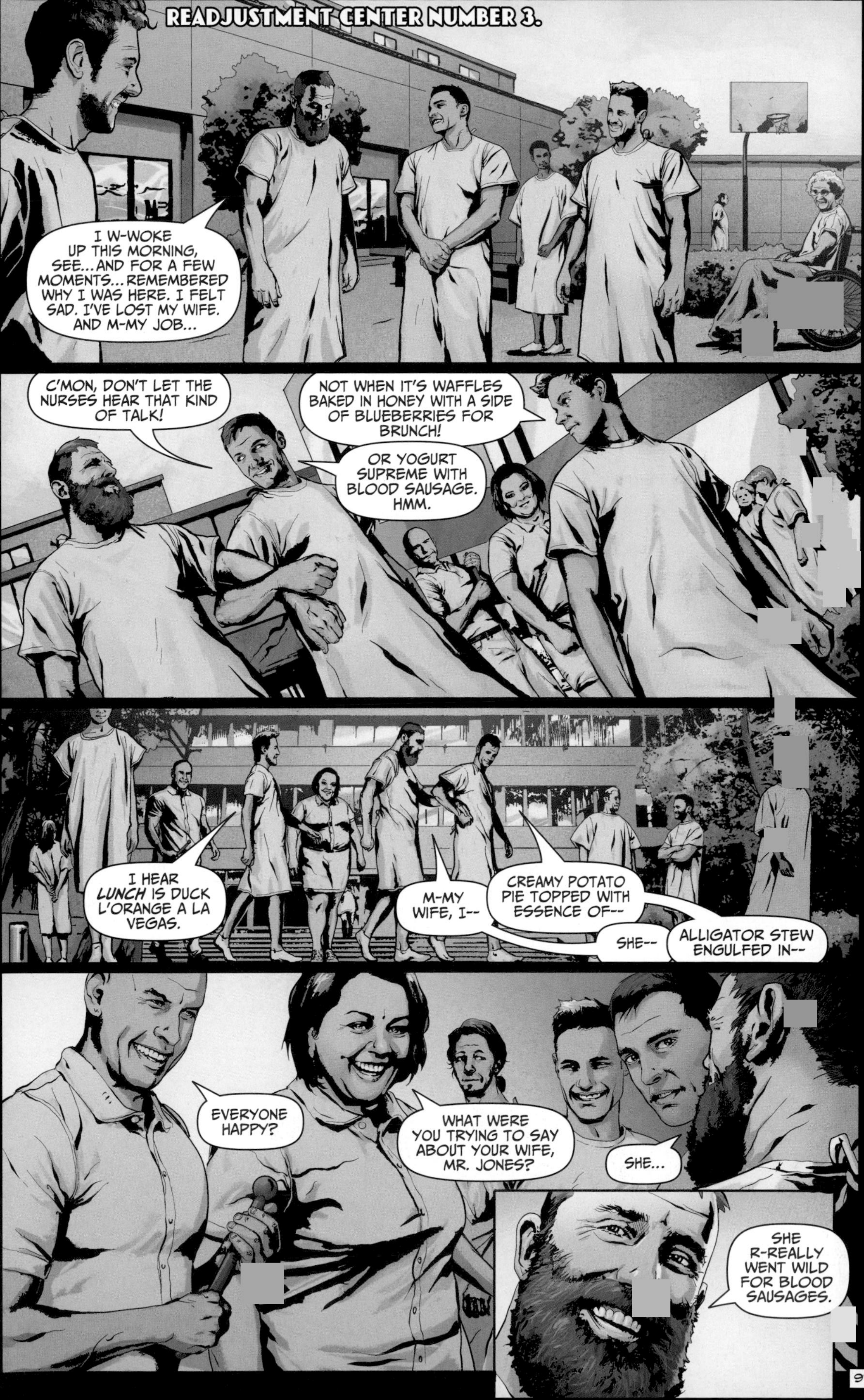
READJUSTMENT CENTER NUMBER 3.
I W-WOKE UP THIS MORNING, SEE...AND FOR A FEW MOMENTS...REMEMBERED WHY I WAS HERE. I FELT SAD. I'VE LOST MY WIFE. AND M-MY JOB...
C'MON, DON'T LET THE NURSES HEAR THAT KIND OF TALK!
NOT WHEN IT'S WAFFLES BAKED IN HONEY WITH A SIDE OF BLUEBERRIES FOR BRUNCH!
OR YOGURT SUPREME WITH BLOOD SAUSAGE. HMM.
I HEAR LUNCH IS DUCK L'ORANGE A LA VEGAS.
M-MY WIFE, I--
CREAMY POTATO PIE TOPPED WITH ESSENCE OF--
SHE--
ALLIGATOR STEW ENGULFED IN--
EVERYONE HAPPY?
WHAT WERE YOU TRYING TO SAY ABOUT YOUR WIFE, MR. JONES?
SHE...
SHE R-REALLY WENT WILD FOR BLOOD SAUSAGES.

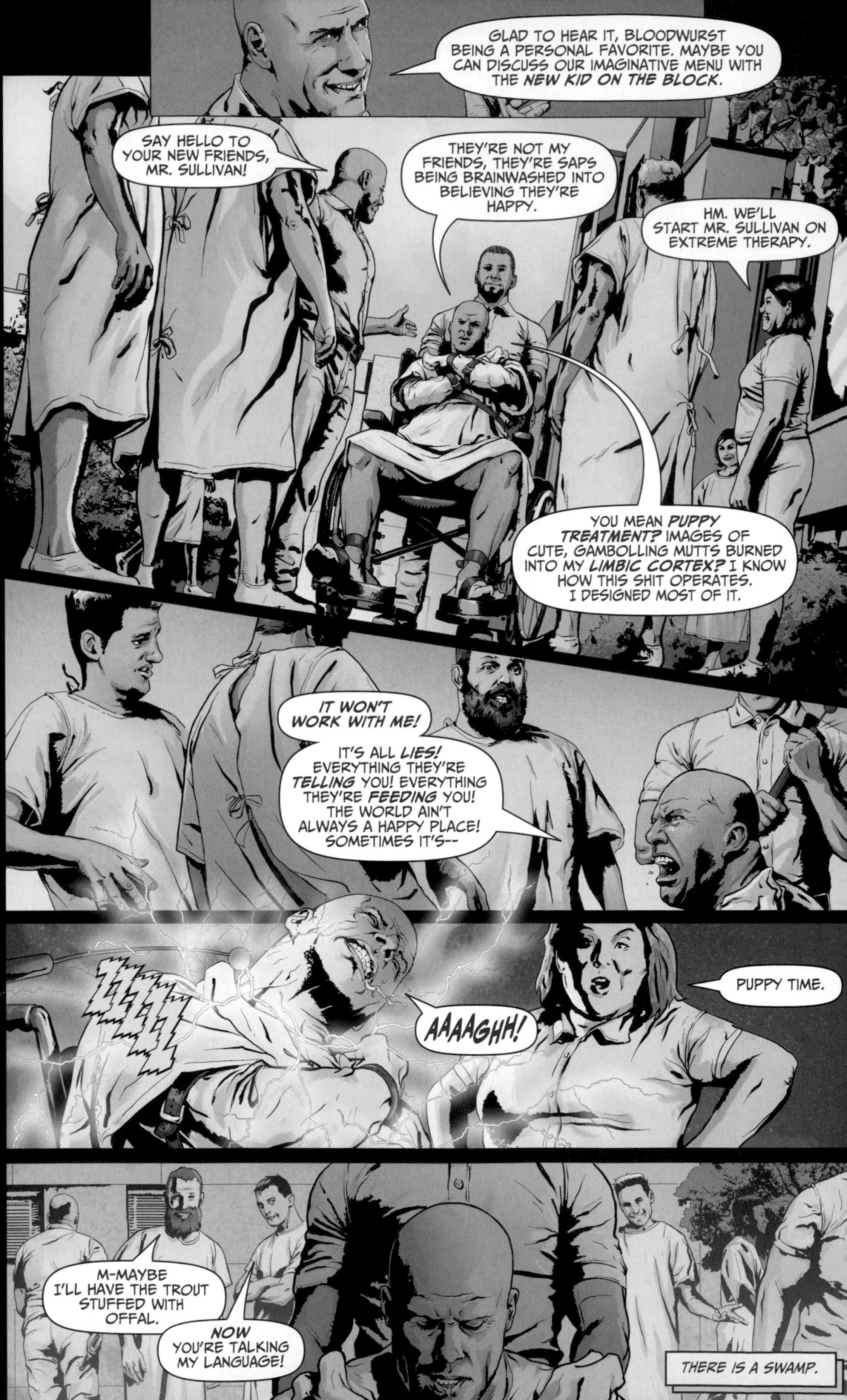

GLAD TO HEAR IT, BLOODWURST BEING A PERSONAL FAVORITE. MAYBE YOU CAN DISCUSS OUR IMAGINATIVE MENU WITH THE *NEW KID ON THE BLOCK*.
SAY HELLO TO YOUR NEW FRIENDS, MR. SULLIVAN!
THEY'RE NOT MY FRIENDS, THEY'RE SAPS BEING BRAINWASHED INTO BELIEVING THEY'RE HAPPY.
HM. WE'LL START MR. SULLIVAN ON EXTREME THERAPY.
YOU MEAN *PUPPY TREATMENT?* IMAGES OF CUTE, GAMBOLLING MUTTS BURNED INTO MY *LIMBIC CORTEX?* I KNOW HOW THIS SHIT OPERATES. I DESIGNED MOST OF IT.
IT WON'T WORK WITH ME!
IT'S ALL *LIES!* EVERYTHING THEY'RE *TELLING* YOU! EVERYTHING THEY'RE *FEEDING* YOU! THE WORLD AIN'T ALWAYS A HAPPY PLACE! SOMETIMES IT'S--
ZZZT
AAAAGHH!
PUPPY TIME.
M-MAYBE I'LL HAVE THE TROUT STUFFED WITH OFFAL.
NOW YOU'RE TALKING MY LANGUAGE!
THERE IS A SWAMP.

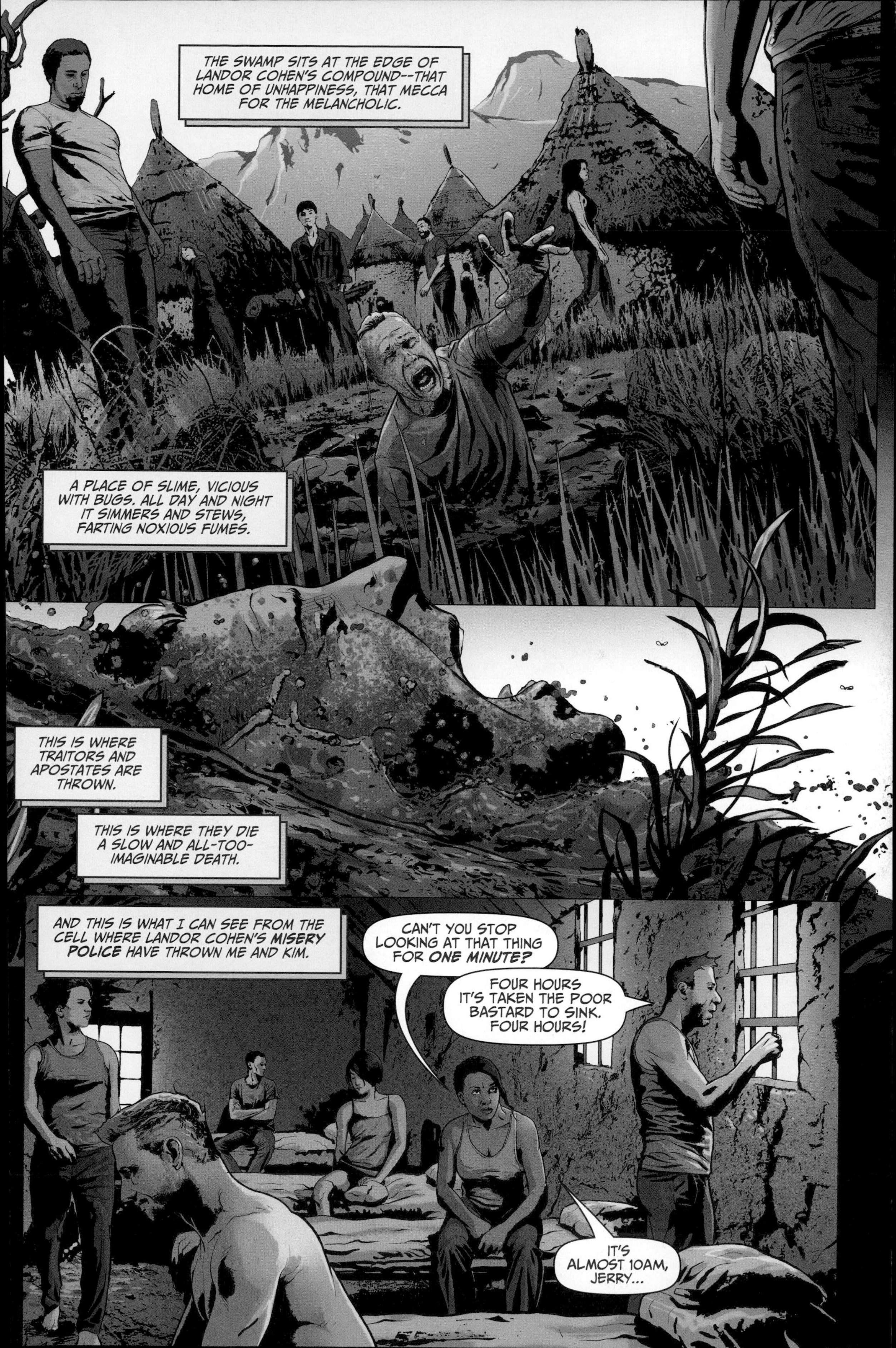
THE SWAMP SITS AT THE EDGE OF LANDOR COHEN'S COMPOUND--THAT HOME OF UNHAPPINESS, THAT MECCA FOR THE MELANCHOLIC.
A PLACE OF SLIME, VICIOUS WITH BUGS. ALL DAY AND NIGHT IT SIMMERS AND STEWS, FARTING NOXIOUS FUMES.
THIS IS WHERE TRAITORS AND APOSTATES ARE THROWN.
THIS IS WHERE THEY DIE A SLOW AND ALL-TOO-IMAGINABLE DEATH.
AND THIS IS WHAT I CAN SEE FROM THE CELL WHERE LANDOR COHEN'S MISERY POLICE HAVE THROWN ME AND KIM.
CAN'T YOU STOP LOOKING AT THAT THING FOR ONE MINUTE?
FOUR HOURS IT'S TAKEN THE POOR BASTARD TO SINK. FOUR HOURS!
IT'S ALMOST 10AM, JERRY...

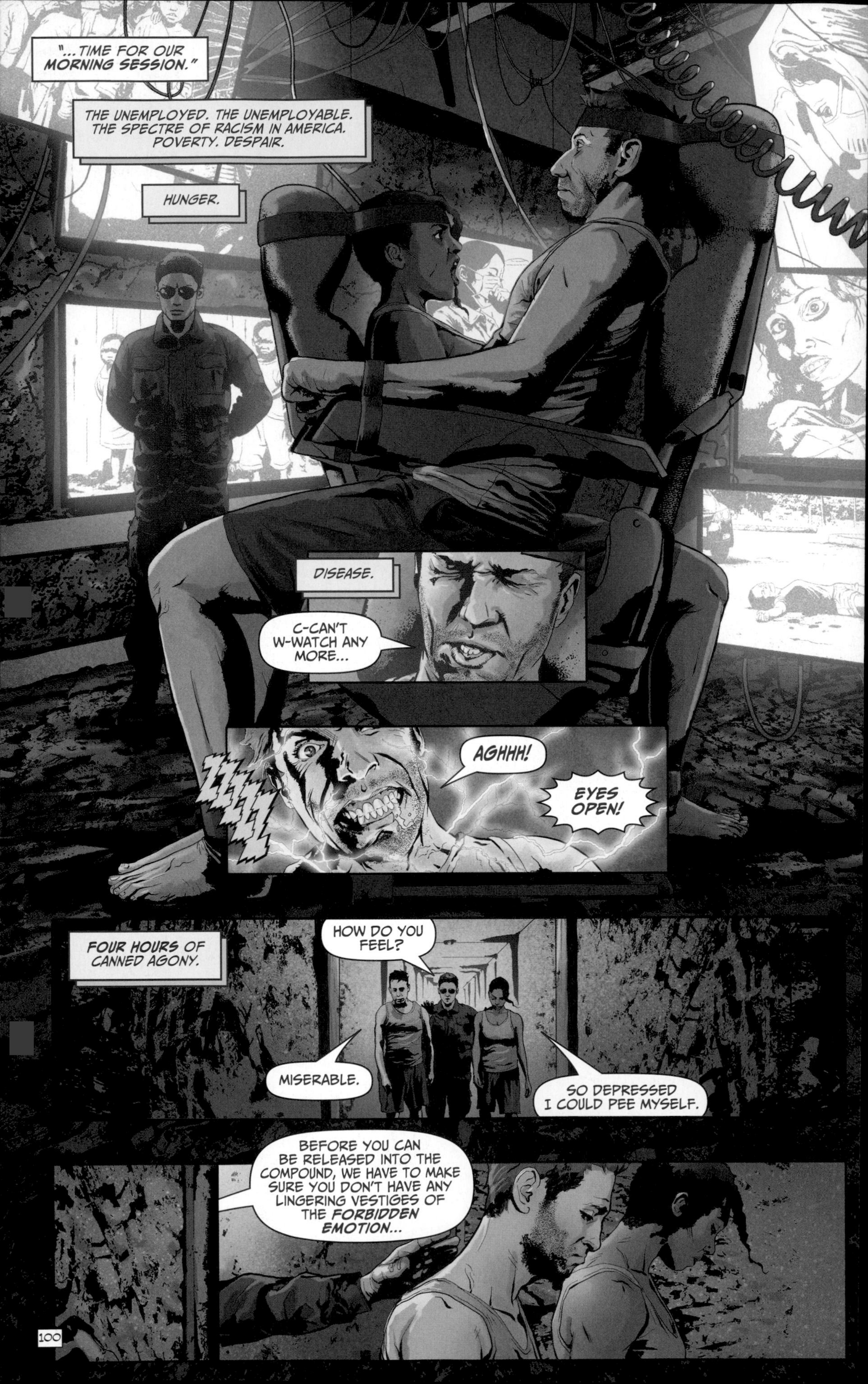
"...TIME FOR OUR MORNING SESSION."
THE UNEMPLOYED. THE UNEMPLOYABLE. THE SPECTRE OF RACISM IN AMERICA. POVERTY. DESPAIR.
HUNGER.
DISEASE.
C-CAN'T W-WATCH ANY MORE...
AGHHH!
EYES OPEN!
FOUR HOURS OF CANNED AGONY.
HOW DO YOU FEEL?
MISERABLE.
SO DEPRESSED I COULD PEE MYSELF.
BEFORE YOU CAN BE RELEASED INTO THE COMPOUND, WE HAVE TO MAKE SURE YOU DON'T HAVE ANY LINGERING VESTIGES OF THE FORBIDDEN EMOTION...

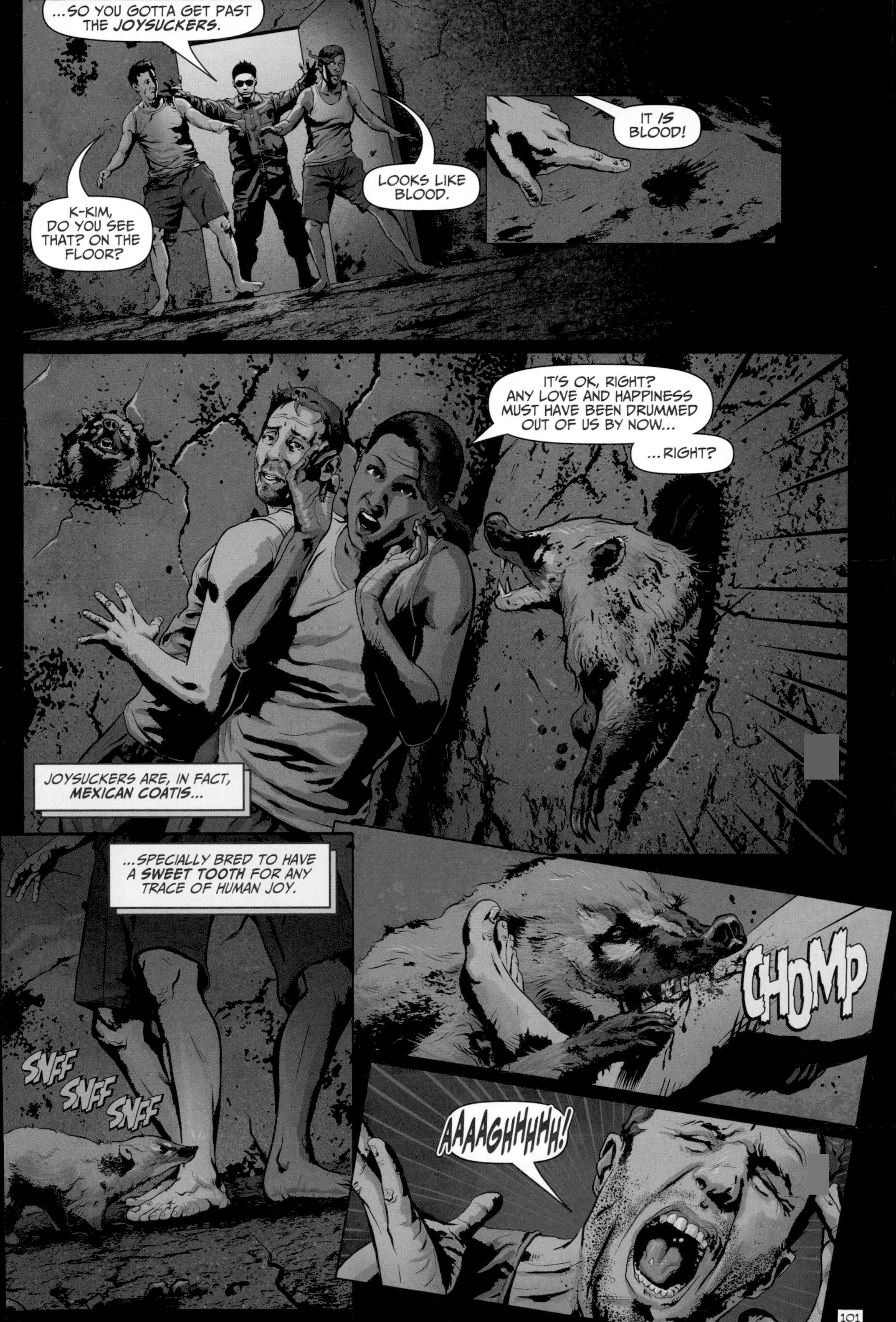
...SO YOU GOTTA GET PAST THE *JOYSUCKERS.*
K-KIM, DO YOU SEE THAT? ON THE FLOOR?
LOOKS LIKE BLOOD.
IT *IS* BLOOD!
IT'S OK, RIGHT? ANY LOVE AND HAPPINESS MUST HAVE BEEN DRUMMED OUT OF US BY NOW...
...RIGHT?
JOYSUCKERS ARE, IN FACT, **MEXICAN COATIS...**
...SPECIALLY BRED TO HAVE A **SWEET TOOTH** FOR ANY TRACE OF HUMAN JOY.
SNFF SNFF SNFF
CHOMP
AAAAGHHHHH!

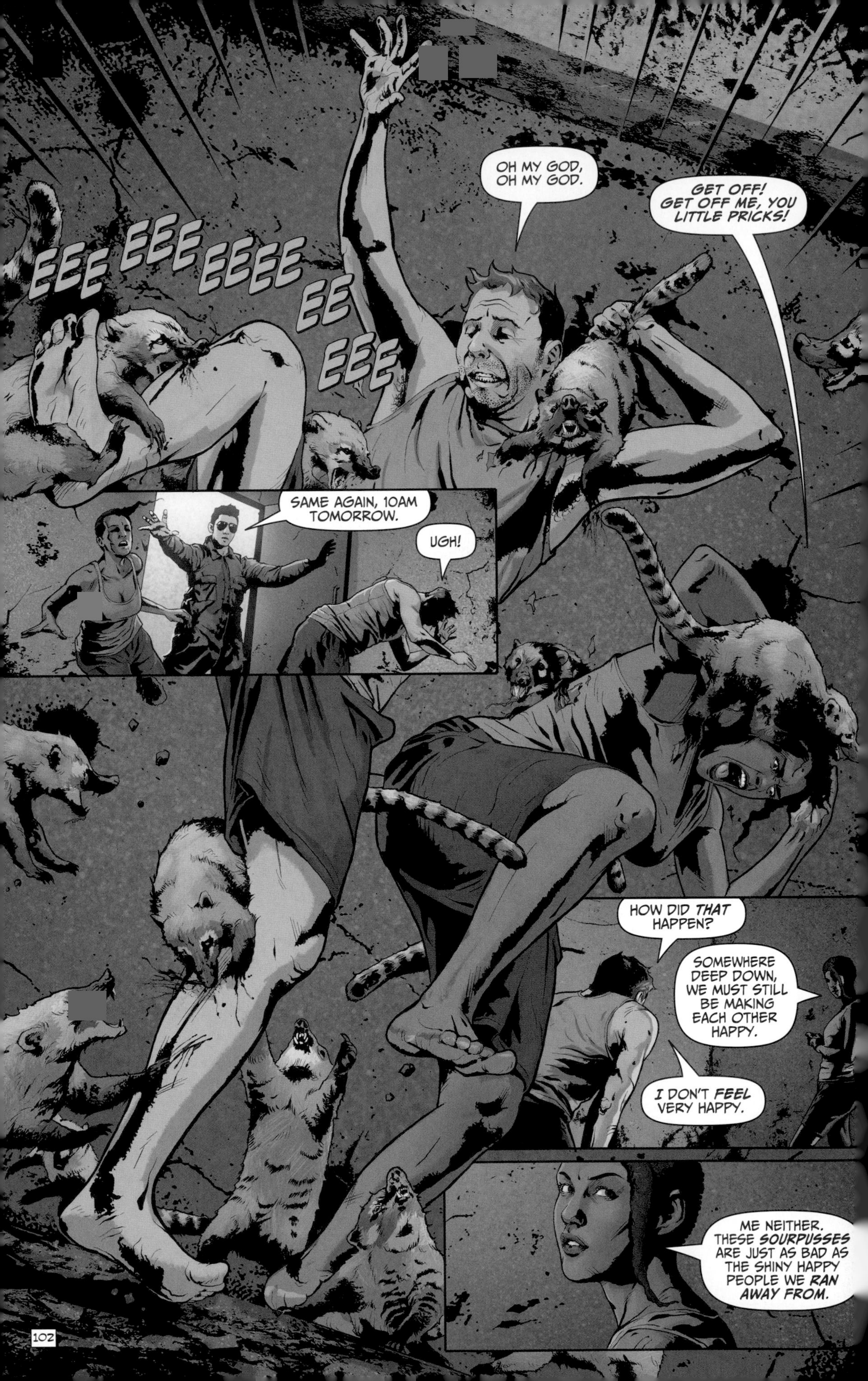
EEE EEE EEEE EE EEE
OH MY GOD, OH MY GOD.
GET OFF! GET OFF ME, YOU LITTLE PRICKS!
SAME AGAIN, 10AM TOMORROW.
UGH!
HOW DID *THAT* HAPPEN?
SOMEWHERE DEEP DOWN, WE MUST STILL BE MAKING EACH OTHER HAPPY.
I DON'T *FEEL* VERY HAPPY.
ME NEITHER. THESE ***SOURPUSSES*** ARE JUST AS BAD AS THE SHINY HAPPY PEOPLE WE ***RAN AWAY FROM.***

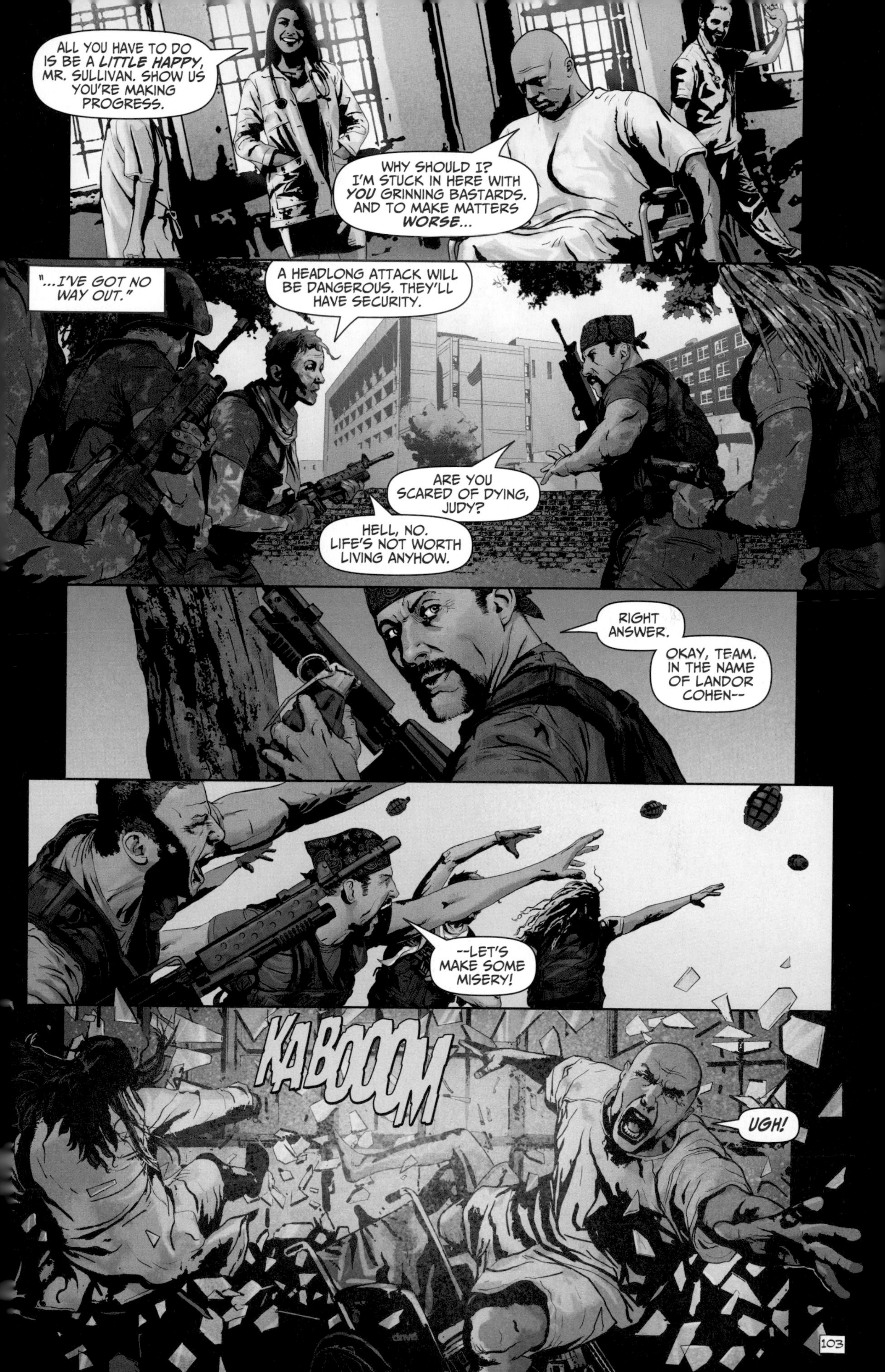
ALL YOU HAVE TO DO IS BE A *LITTLE HAPPY*, MR. SULLIVAN. SHOW US YOU'RE MAKING PROGRESS.
WHY SHOULD I? I'M STUCK IN HERE WITH *YOU* GRINNING BASTARDS. AND TO MAKE MATTERS *WORSE*...
"...I'VE GOT NO WAY OUT."
A HEADLONG ATTACK WILL BE DANGEROUS. THEY'LL HAVE SECURITY.
ARE YOU SCARED OF DYING, JUDY?
HELL, NO. LIFE'S NOT WORTH LIVING ANYHOW.
RIGHT ANSWER.
OKAY, TEAM. IN THE NAME OF LANDOR COHEN--
--LET'S MAKE SOME MISERY!
KABOOOM
UGH!

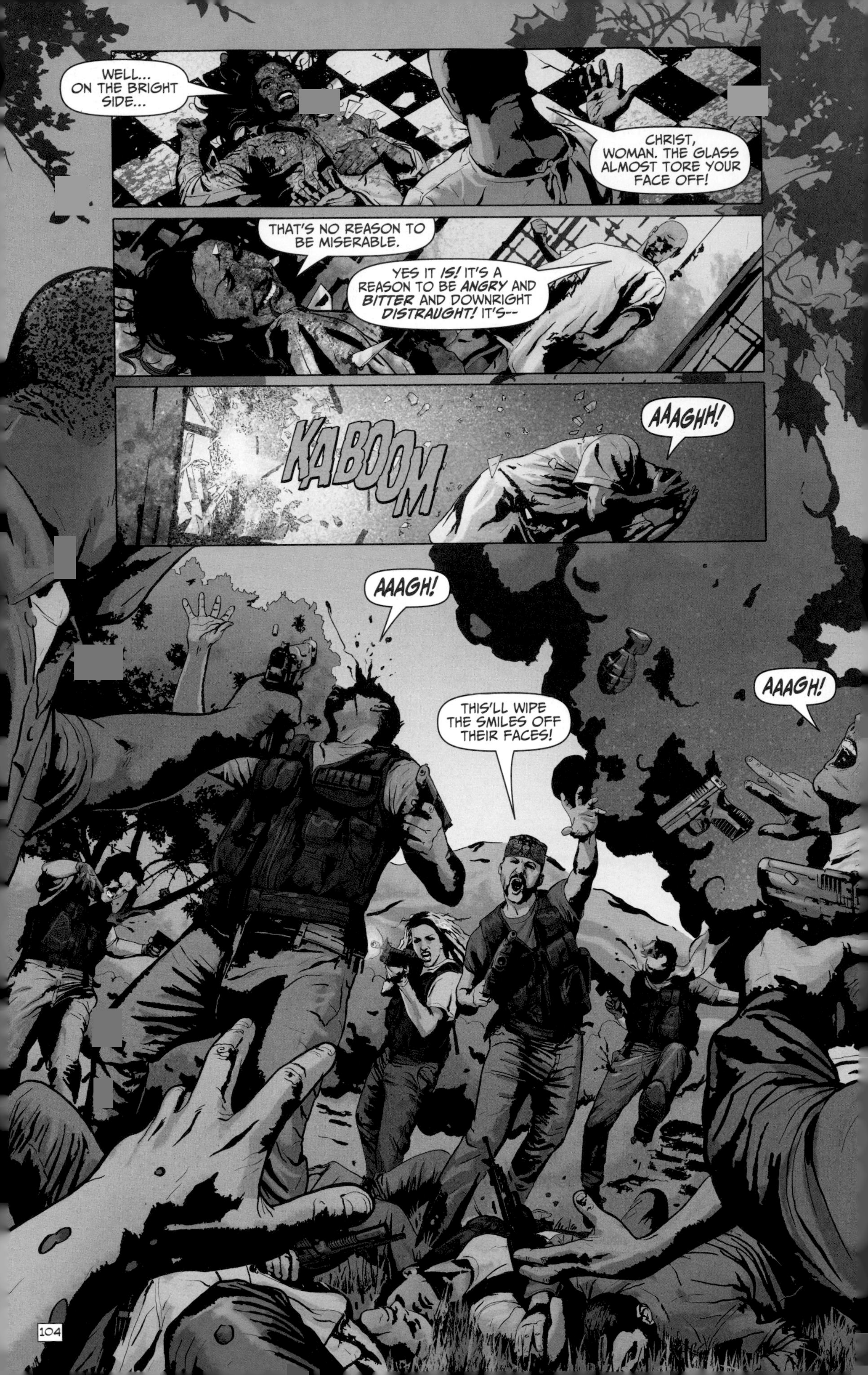
WELL... ON THE BRIGHT SIDE...
CHRIST, WOMAN. THE GLASS ALMOST TORE YOUR FACE OFF!
THAT'S NO REASON TO BE MISERABLE.
YES IT *IS!* IT'S A REASON TO BE *ANGRY* AND *BITTER* AND DOWNRIGHT *DISTRAUGHT!* IT'S--
KABOOM
AAAGHH!
AAAGH!
THIS'LL WIPE THE SMILES OFF THEIR FACES!
AAAGH!

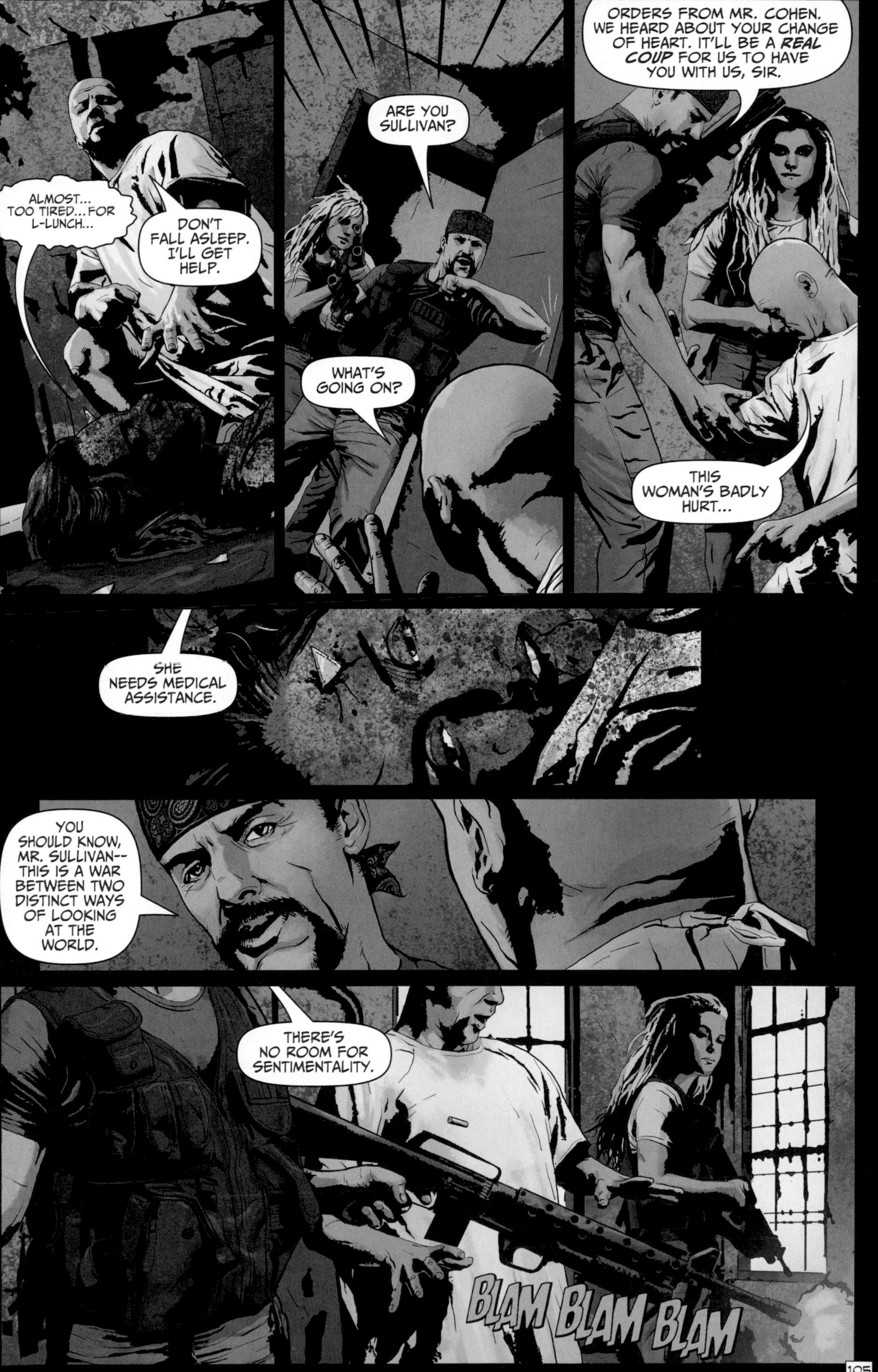
ALMOST... TOO TIRED... FOR L-LUNCH...
DON'T FALL ASLEEP. I'LL GET HELP.
ARE YOU SULLIVAN?
WHAT'S GOING ON?
ORDERS FROM MR. COHEN. WE HEARD ABOUT YOUR CHANGE OF HEART. IT'LL BE A *REAL COUP* FOR US TO HAVE YOU WITH US, SIR.
THIS WOMAN'S BADLY HURT...
SHE NEEDS MEDICAL ASSISTANCE.
YOU SHOULD KNOW, MR. SULLIVAN-- THIS IS A WAR BETWEEN TWO DISTINCT WAYS OF LOOKING AT THE WORLD.
THERE'S NO ROOM FOR SENTIMENTALITY.
BLAM BLAM BLAM

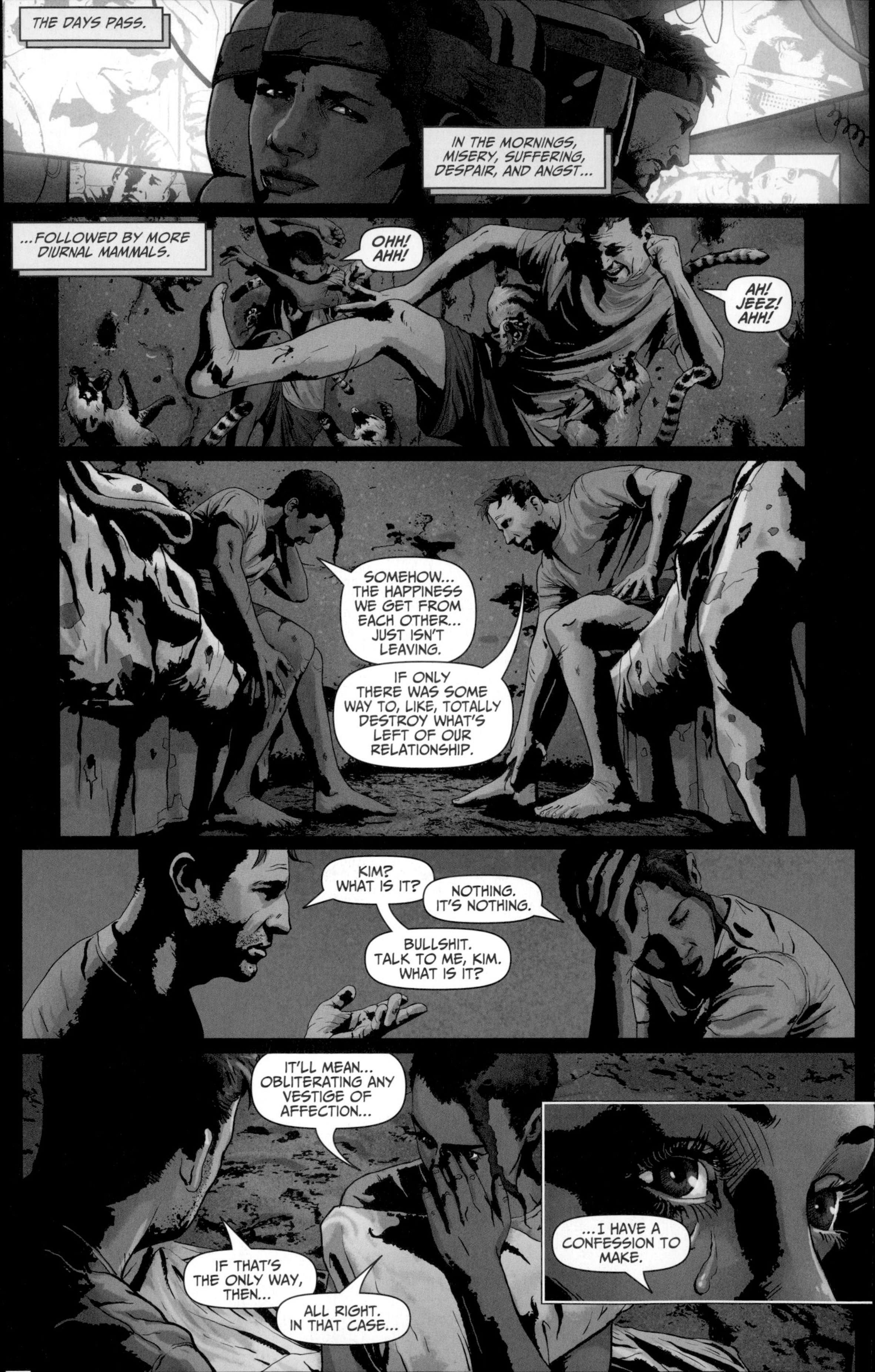
THE DAYS PASS.
IN THE MORNINGS, MISERY, SUFFERING, DESPAIR, AND ANGST...
...FOLLOWED BY MORE DIURNAL MAMMALS.
OHH! AHH!
AH! JEEZ! AHH!
SOMEHOW... THE HAPPINESS WE GET FROM EACH OTHER... JUST ISN'T LEAVING.
IF ONLY THERE WAS SOME WAY TO, LIKE, TOTALLY DESTROY WHAT'S LEFT OF OUR RELATIONSHIP.
KIM? WHAT IS IT?
NOTHING. IT'S NOTHING.
BULLSHIT. TALK TO ME, KIM. WHAT IS IT?
IT'LL MEAN... OBLITERATING ANY VESTIGE OF AFFECTION...
IF THAT'S THE ONLY WAY, THEN...
ALL RIGHT. IN THAT CASE...
...I HAVE A CONFESSION TO MAKE.

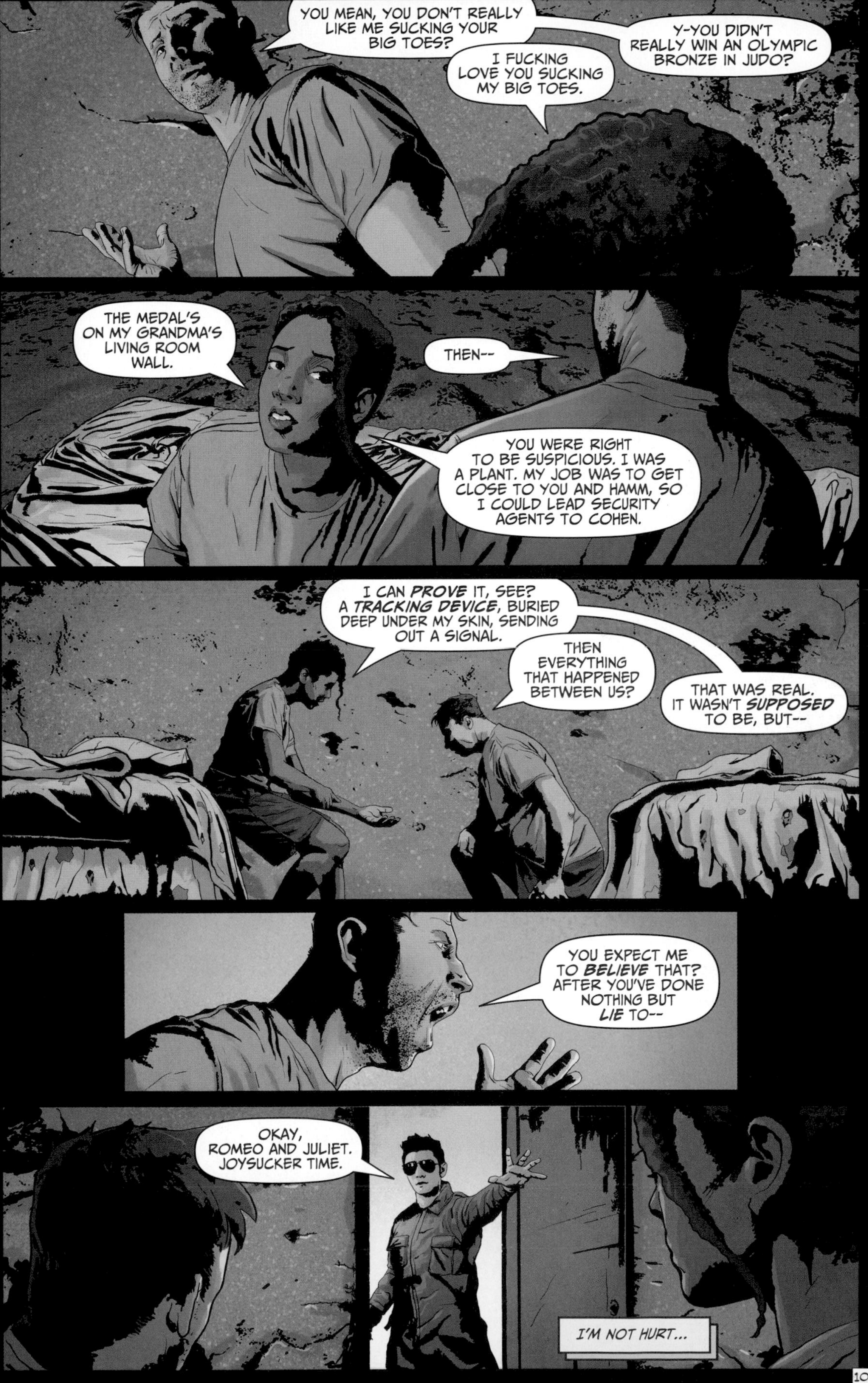
YOU MEAN, YOU DON'T REALLY LIKE ME SUCKING YOUR BIG TOES?
I FUCKING LOVE YOU SUCKING MY BIG TOES.
Y-YOU DIDN'T REALLY WIN AN OLYMPIC BRONZE IN JUDO?
THE MEDAL'S ON MY GRANDMA'S LIVING ROOM WALL.
THEN--
YOU WERE RIGHT TO BE SUSPICIOUS. I WAS A PLANT. MY JOB WAS TO GET CLOSE TO YOU AND HAMM, SO I COULD LEAD SECURITY AGENTS TO COHEN.
I CAN PROVE IT, SEE? A TRACKING DEVICE, BURIED DEEP UNDER MY SKIN, SENDING OUT A SIGNAL.
THEN EVERYTHING THAT HAPPENED BETWEEN US?
THAT WAS REAL. IT WASN'T SUPPOSED TO BE, BUT--
YOU EXPECT ME TO BELIEVE THAT? AFTER YOU'VE DONE NOTHING BUT LIE TO--
OKAY, ROMEO AND JULIET. JOYSUCKER TIME.
I'M NOT HURT...

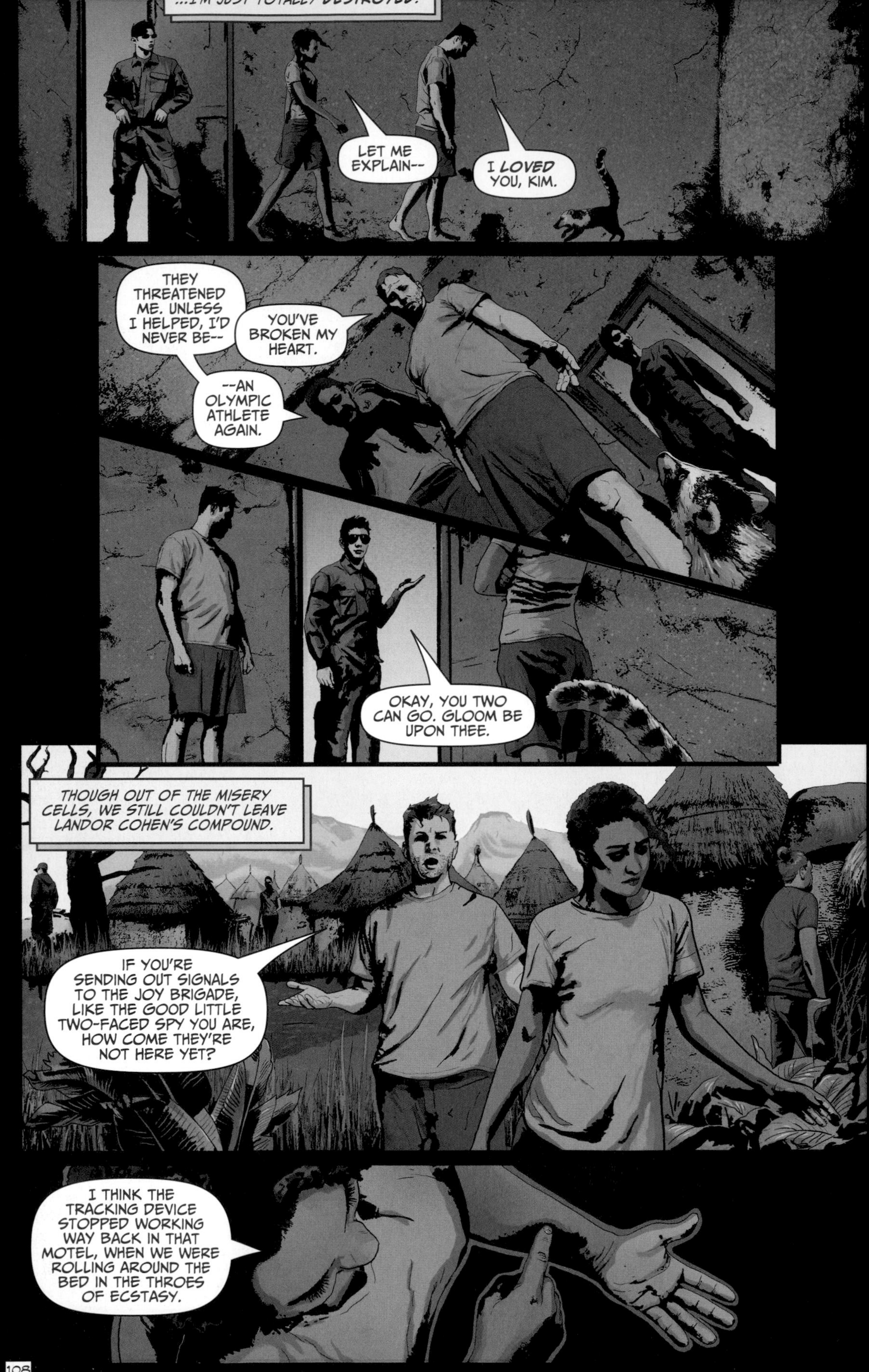

...I'M JUST TOTALLY DESTROYED.
LET ME EXPLAIN--
I LOVED YOU, KIM.
THEY THREATENED ME. UNLESS I HELPED, I'D NEVER BE--
YOU'VE BROKEN MY HEART.
--AN OLYMPIC ATHLETE AGAIN.
OKAY, YOU TWO CAN GO. GLOOM BE UPON THEE.
THOUGH OUT OF THE MISERY CELLS, WE STILL COULDN'T LEAVE LANDOR COHEN'S COMPOUND.
IF YOU'RE SENDING OUT SIGNALS TO THE JOY BRIGADE, LIKE THE GOOD LITTLE TWO-FACED SPY YOU ARE, HOW COME THEY'RE NOT HERE YET?
I THINK THE TRACKING DEVICE STOPPED WORKING WAY BACK IN THAT MOTEL, WHEN WE WERE ROLLING AROUND THE BED IN THE THROES OF ECSTASY.

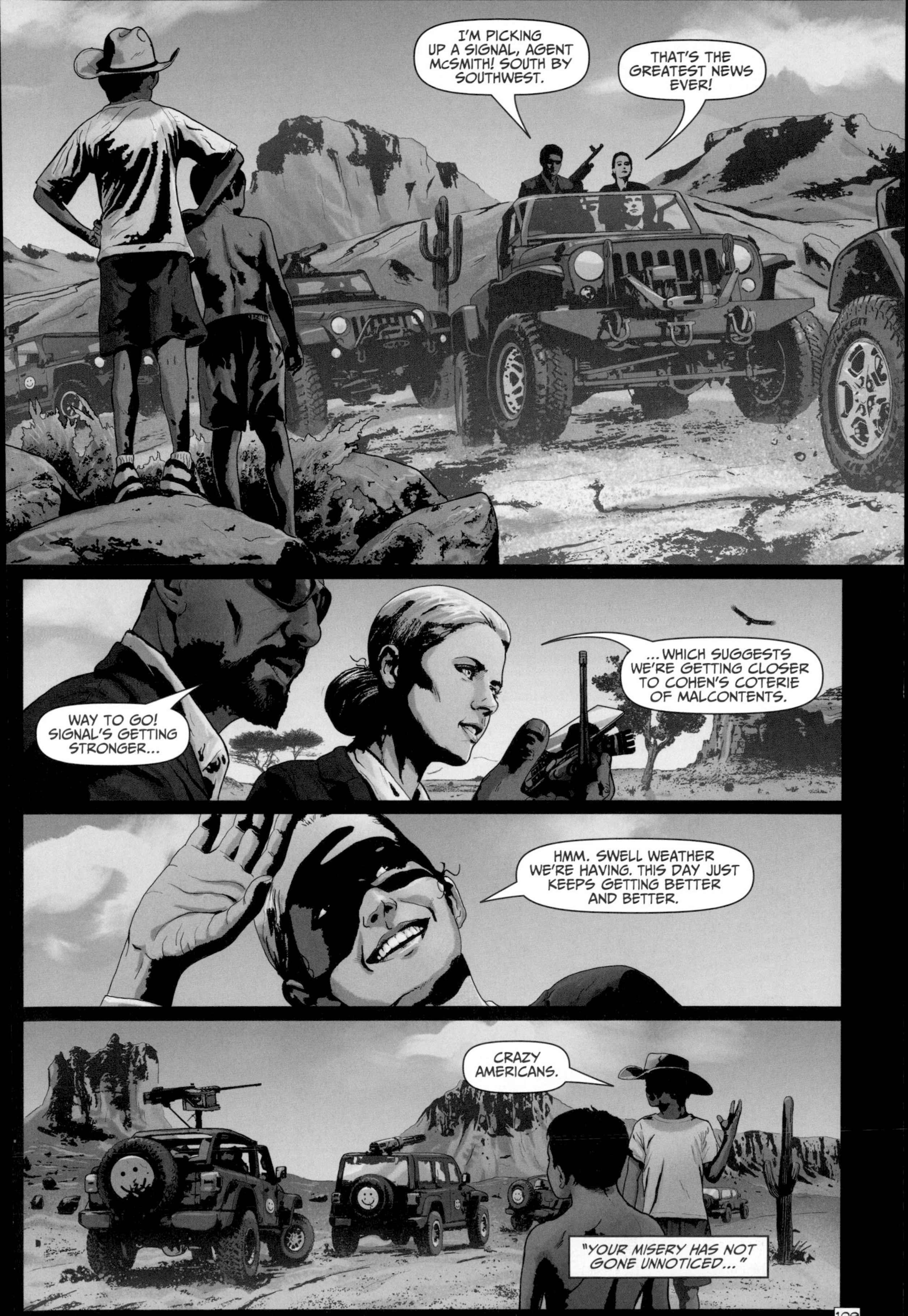
I'M PICKING UP A SIGNAL, AGENT McSMITH! SOUTH BY SOUTHWEST.
THAT'S THE GREATEST NEWS EVER!
WAY TO GO! SIGNAL'S GETTING STRONGER...
...WHICH SUGGESTS WE'RE GETTING CLOSER TO COHEN'S COTERIE OF MALCONTENTS.
HMM. SWELL WEATHER WE'RE HAVING. THIS DAY JUST KEEPS GETTING BETTER AND BETTER.
CRAZY AMERICANS.
"YOUR MISERY HAS NOT GONE UNNOTICED..."

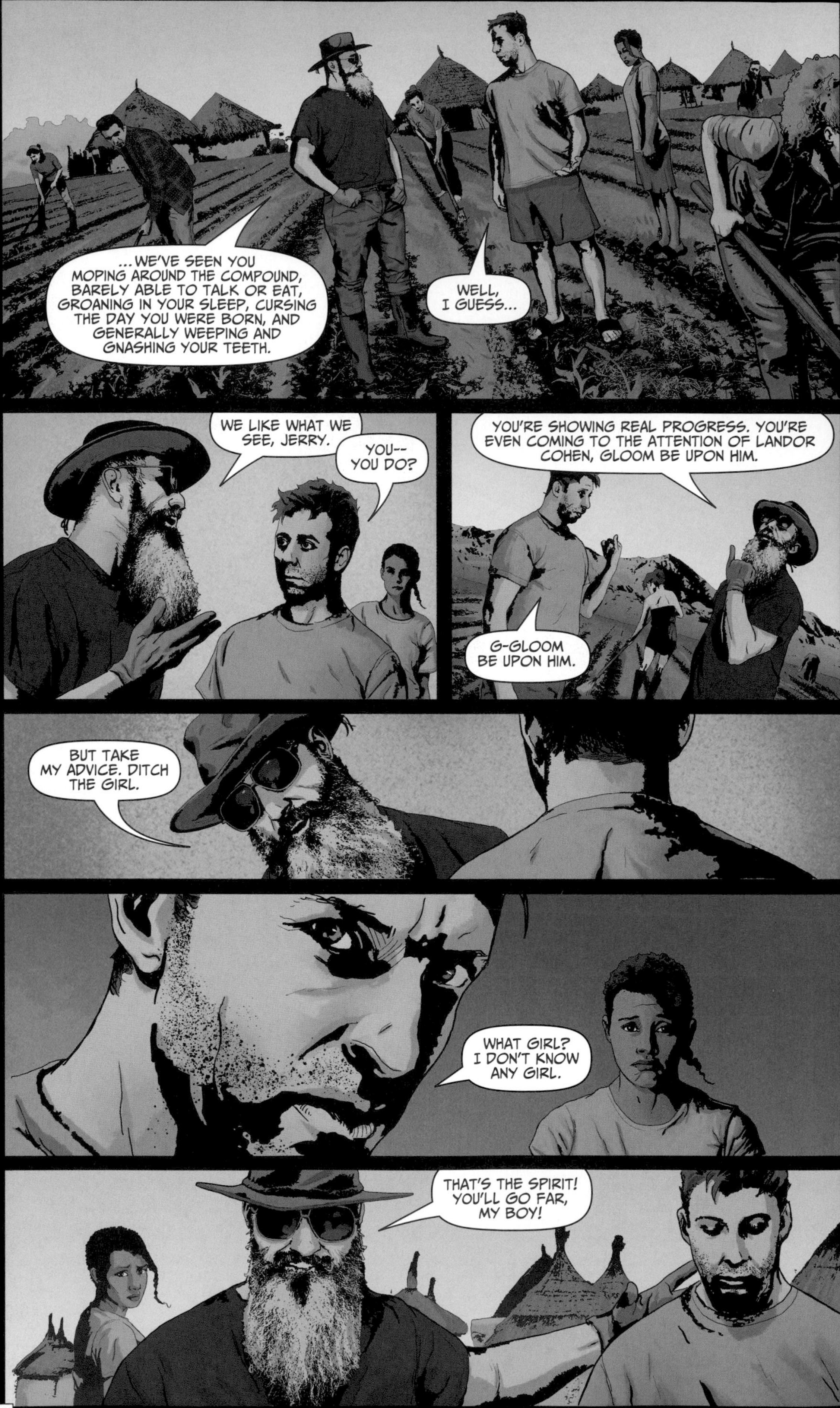
...WE'VE SEEN YOU MOPING AROUND THE COMPOUND, BARELY ABLE TO TALK OR EAT, GROANING IN YOUR SLEEP, CURSING THE DAY YOU WERE BORN, AND GENERALLY WEEPING AND GNASHING YOUR TEETH.
WELL, I GUESS...
WE LIKE WHAT WE SEE, JERRY.
YOU-- YOU DO?
YOU'RE SHOWING REAL PROGRESS. YOU'RE EVEN COMING TO THE ATTENTION OF LANDOR COHEN, GLOOM BE UPON HIM.
G-GLOOM BE UPON HIM.
BUT TAKE MY ADVICE. DITCH THE GIRL.
WHAT GIRL? I DON'T KNOW ANY GIRL.
THAT'S THE SPIRIT! YOU'LL GO FAR, MY BOY!

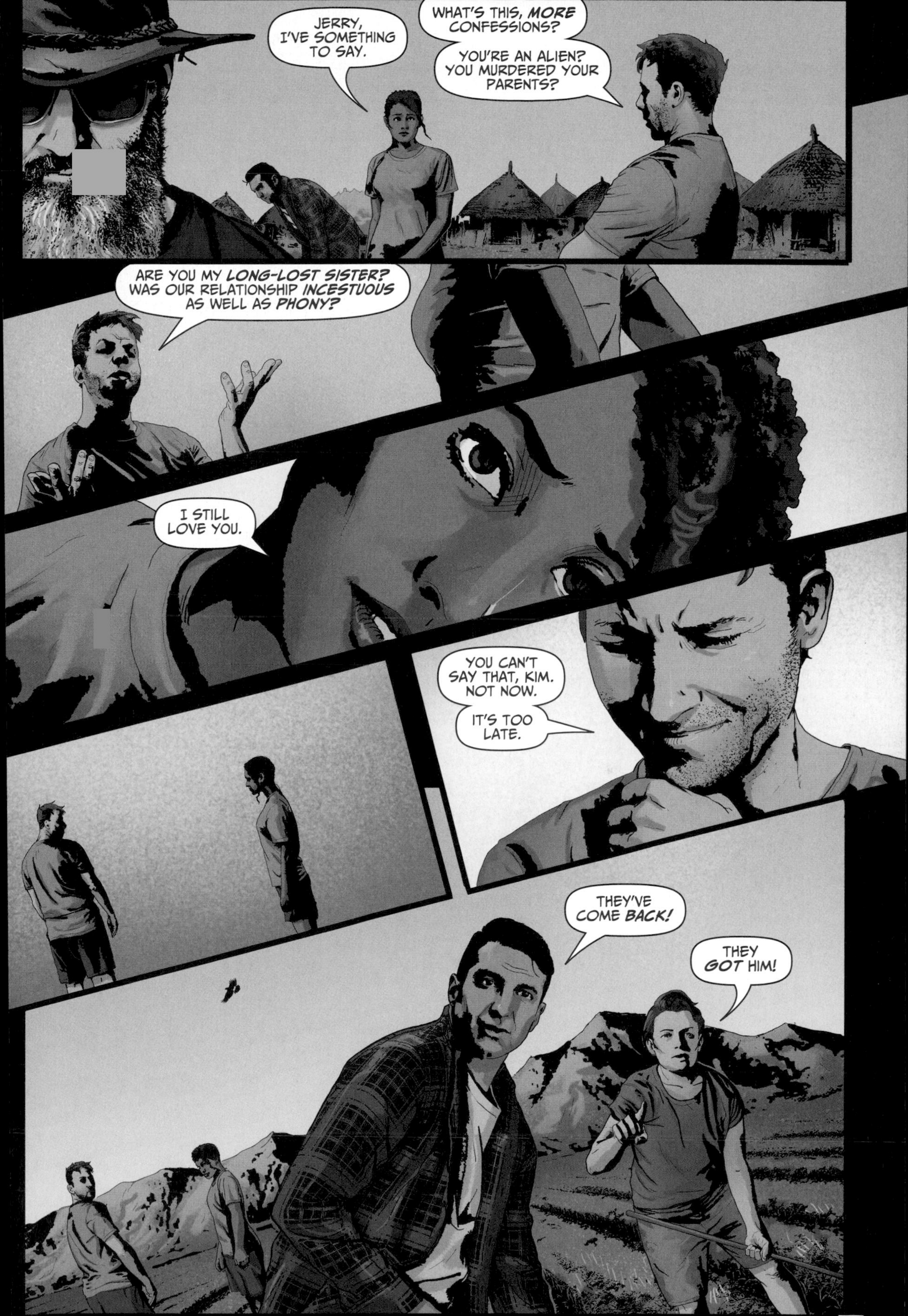
JERRY, I'VE SOMETHING TO SAY.
WHAT'S THIS, MORE CONFESSIONS?
YOU'RE AN ALIEN? YOU MURDERED YOUR PARENTS?
ARE YOU MY LONG-LOST SISTER? WAS OUR RELATIONSHIP INCESTUOUS AS WELL AS PHONY?
I STILL LOVE YOU.
YOU CAN'T SAY THAT, KIM. NOT NOW.
IT'S TOO LATE.
THEY'VE COME BACK!
THEY GOT HIM!

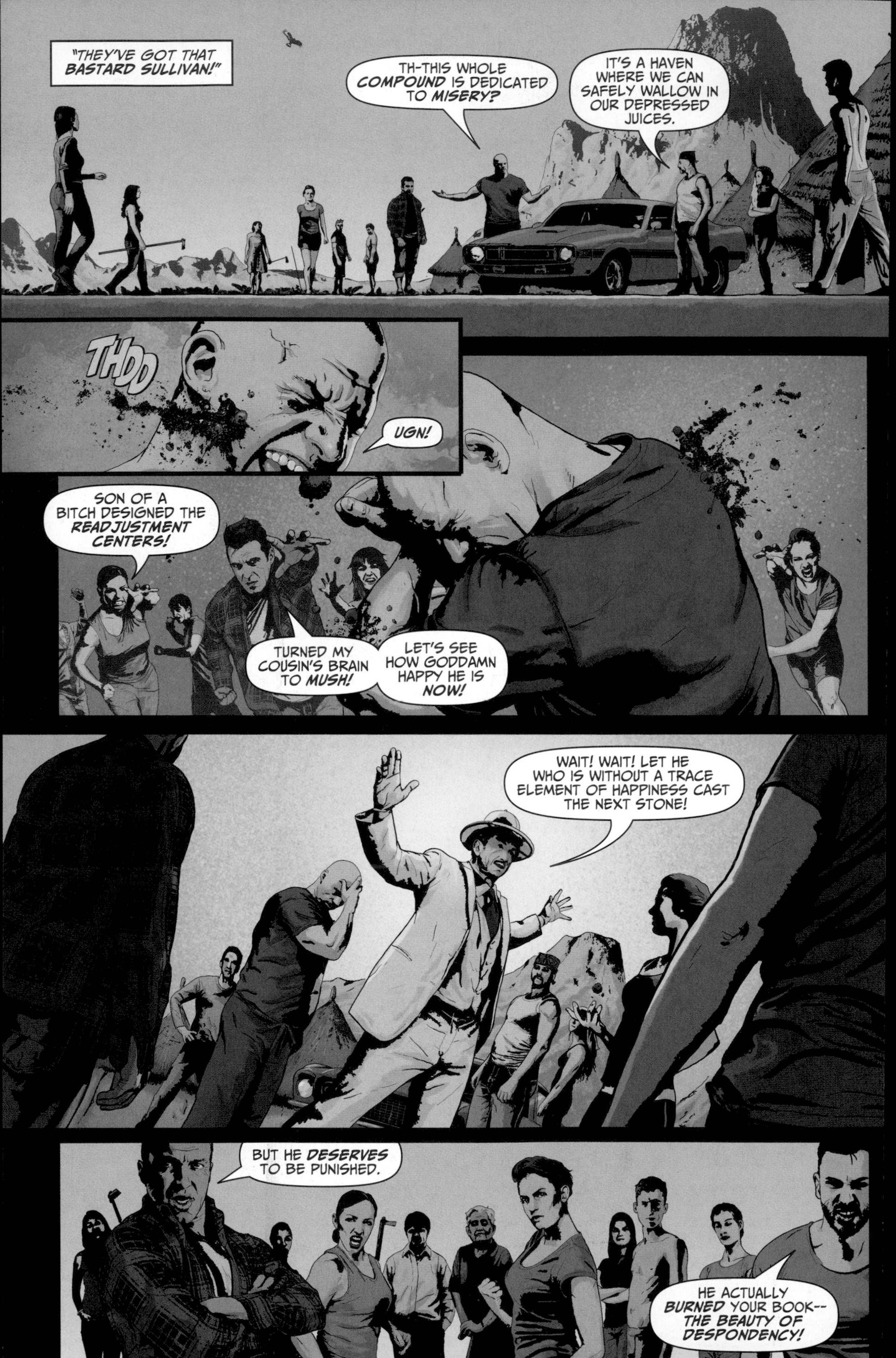
"THEY'VE GOT THAT BASTARD SULLIVAN!"
TH-THIS WHOLE COMPOUND IS DEDICATED TO MISERY?
IT'S A HAVEN WHERE WE CAN SAFELY WALLOW IN OUR DEPRESSED JUICES.
THDD
UGN!
SON OF A BITCH DESIGNED THE READJUSTMENT CENTERS!
TURNED MY COUSIN'S BRAIN TO MUSH!
LET'S SEE HOW GODDAMN HAPPY HE IS NOW!
WAIT! WAIT! LET HE WHO IS WITHOUT A TRACE ELEMENT OF HAPPINESS CAST THE NEXT STONE!
BUT HE DESERVES TO BE PUNISHED.
HE ACTUALLY BURNED YOUR BOOK-- THE BEAUTY OF DESPONDENCY!

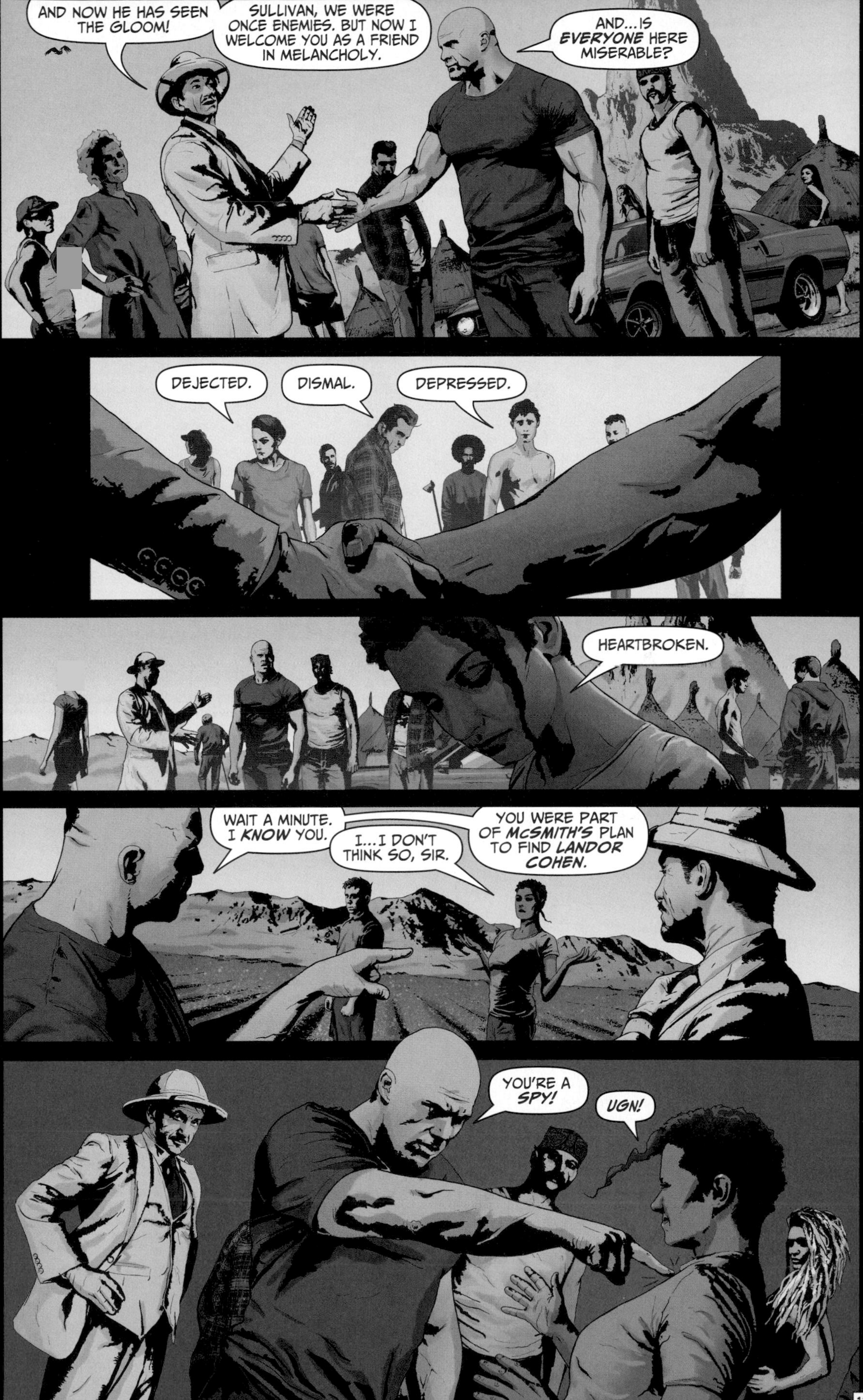
AND NOW HE HAS SEEN THE GLOOM!
SULLIVAN, WE WERE ONCE ENEMIES. BUT NOW I WELCOME YOU AS A FRIEND IN MELANCHOLY.
AND...IS *EVERYONE* HERE MISERABLE?
DEJECTED.
DISMAL.
DEPRESSED.
HEARTBROKEN.
WAIT A MINUTE. I *KNOW* YOU.
I...I DON'T THINK SO, SIR.
YOU WERE PART OF *McSMITH'S* PLAN TO FIND *LANDOR COHEN.*
YOU'RE A *SPY!*
UGN!

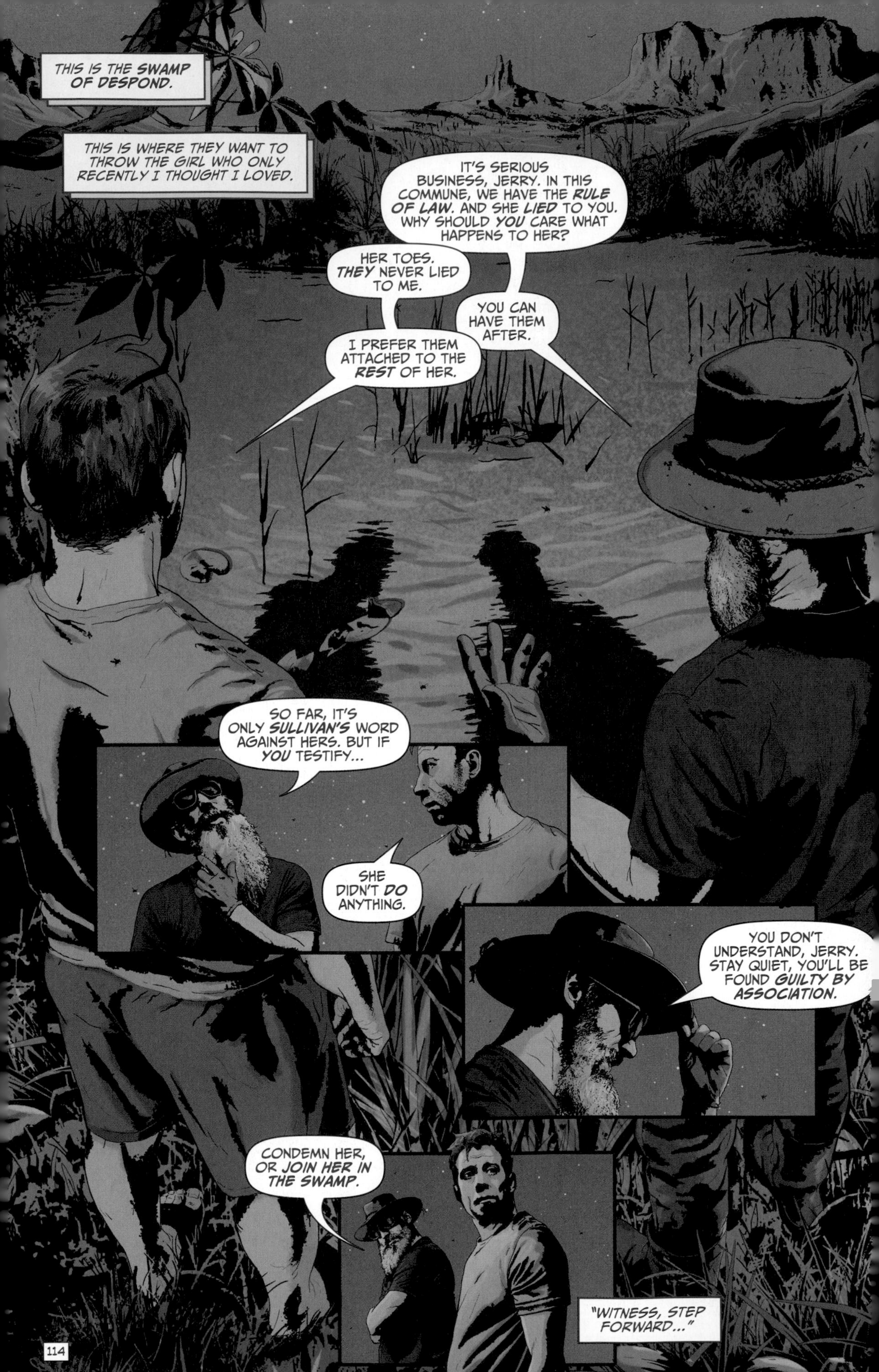
THIS IS THE SWAMP OF DESPOND.
THIS IS WHERE THEY WANT TO THROW THE GIRL WHO ONLY RECENTLY I THOUGHT I LOVED.
IT'S SERIOUS BUSINESS, JERRY. IN THIS COMMUNE, WE HAVE THE RULE OF LAW. AND SHE LIED TO YOU. WHY SHOULD YOU CARE WHAT HAPPENS TO HER?
HER TOES. THEY NEVER LIED TO ME.
YOU CAN HAVE THEM AFTER.
I PREFER THEM ATTACHED TO THE REST OF HER.
SO FAR, IT'S ONLY SULLIVAN'S WORD AGAINST HERS. BUT IF YOU TESTIFY...
SHE DIDN'T DO ANYTHING.
YOU DON'T UNDERSTAND, JERRY. STAY QUIET, YOU'LL BE FOUND GUILTY BY ASSOCIATION.
CONDEMN HER, OR JOIN HER IN THE SWAMP.
"WITNESS, STEP FORWARD..."

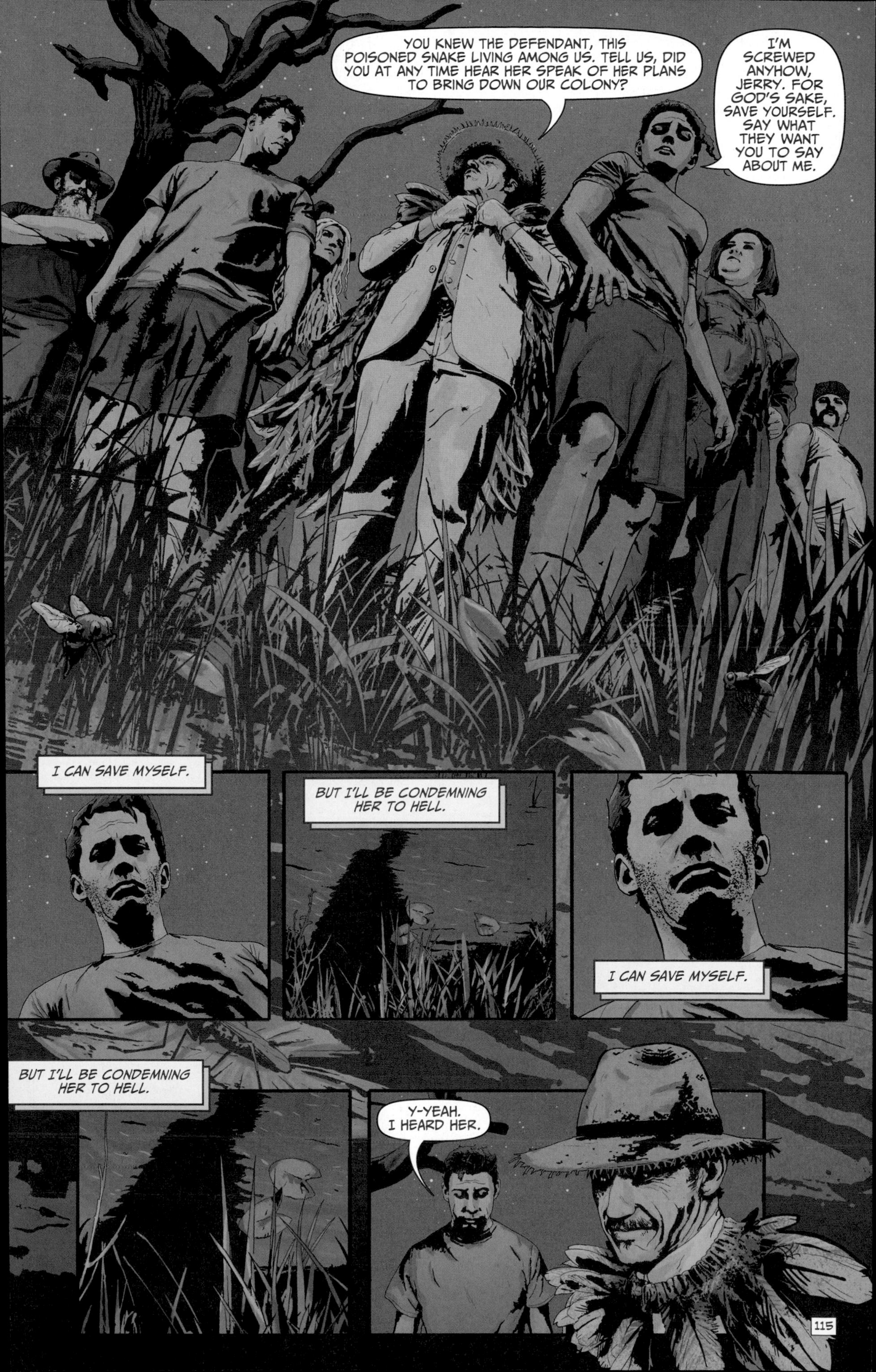
YOU KNEW THE DEFENDANT, THIS POISONED SNAKE LIVING AMONG US. TELL US, DID YOU AT ANY TIME HEAR HER SPEAK OF HER PLANS TO BRING DOWN OUR COLONY?
I'M SCREWED ANYHOW, JERRY. FOR GOD'S SAKE, SAVE YOURSELF. SAY WHAT THEY WANT YOU TO SAY ABOUT ME.
I CAN SAVE MYSELF.
BUT I'LL BE CONDEMNING HER TO HELL.
I CAN SAVE MYSELF.
BUT I'LL BE CONDEMNING HER TO HELL.
Y-YEAH. I HEARD HER.

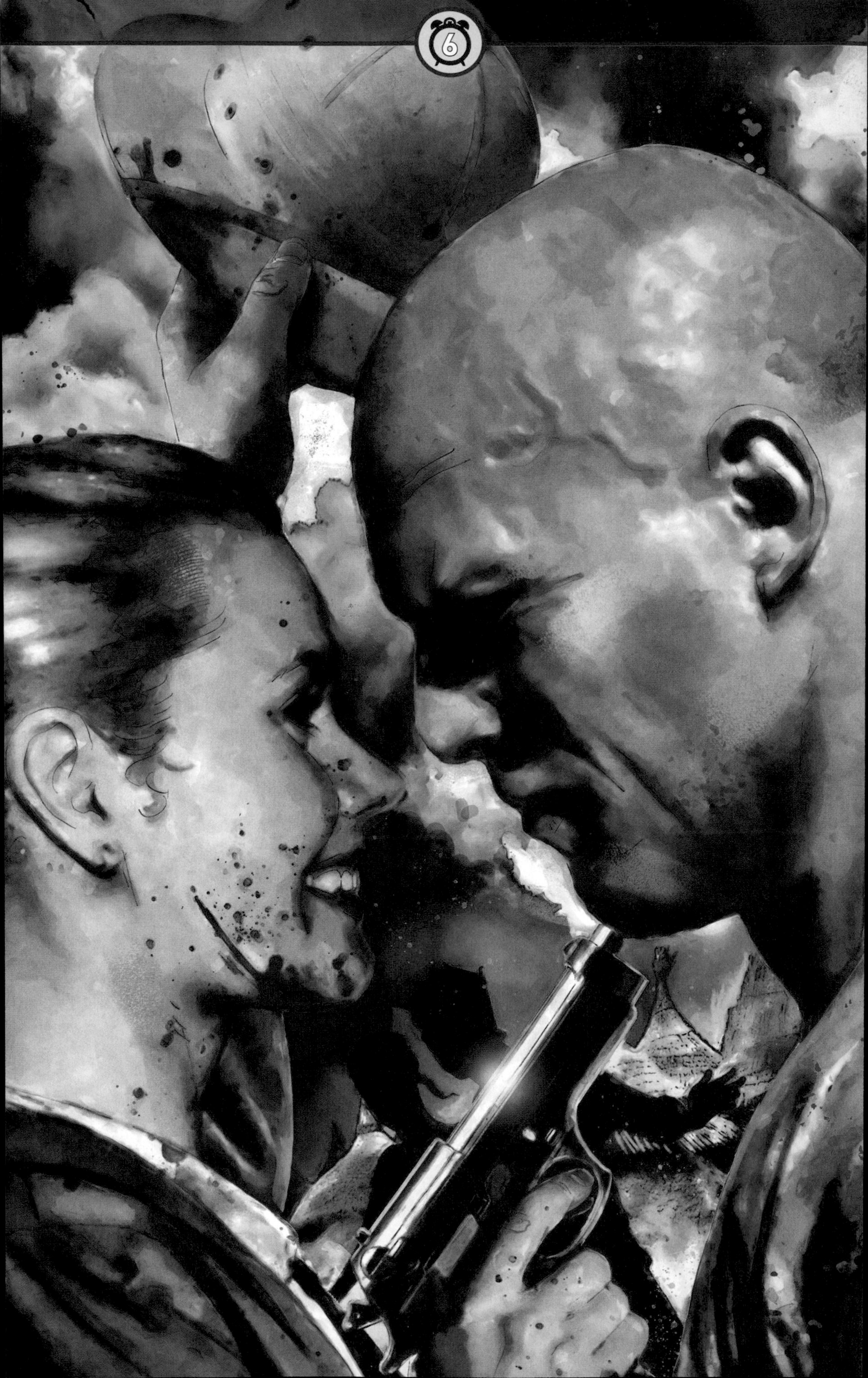

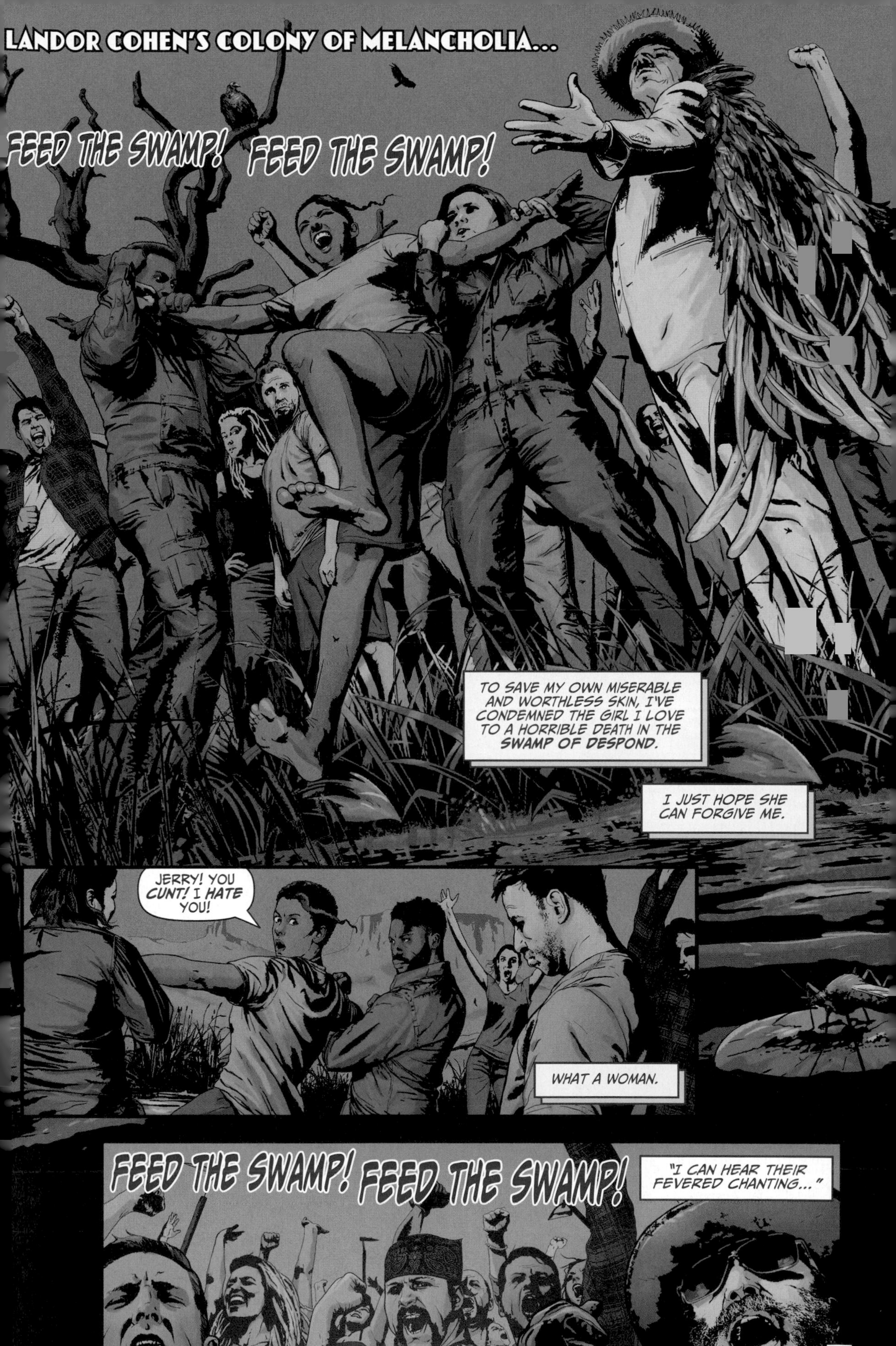
LANDOR COHEN'S COLONY OF MELANCHOLIA...
FEED THE SWAMP! FEED THE SWAMP!
TO SAVE MY OWN MISERABLE AND WORTHLESS SKIN, I'VE CONDEMNED THE GIRL I LOVE TO A HORRIBLE DEATH IN THE SWAMP OF DESPOND.
I JUST HOPE SHE CAN FORGIVE ME.
JERRY! YOU CUNT! I HATE YOU!
WHAT A WOMAN.
FEED THE SWAMP! FEED THE SWAMP!
"I CAN HEAR THEIR FEVERED CHANTING..."

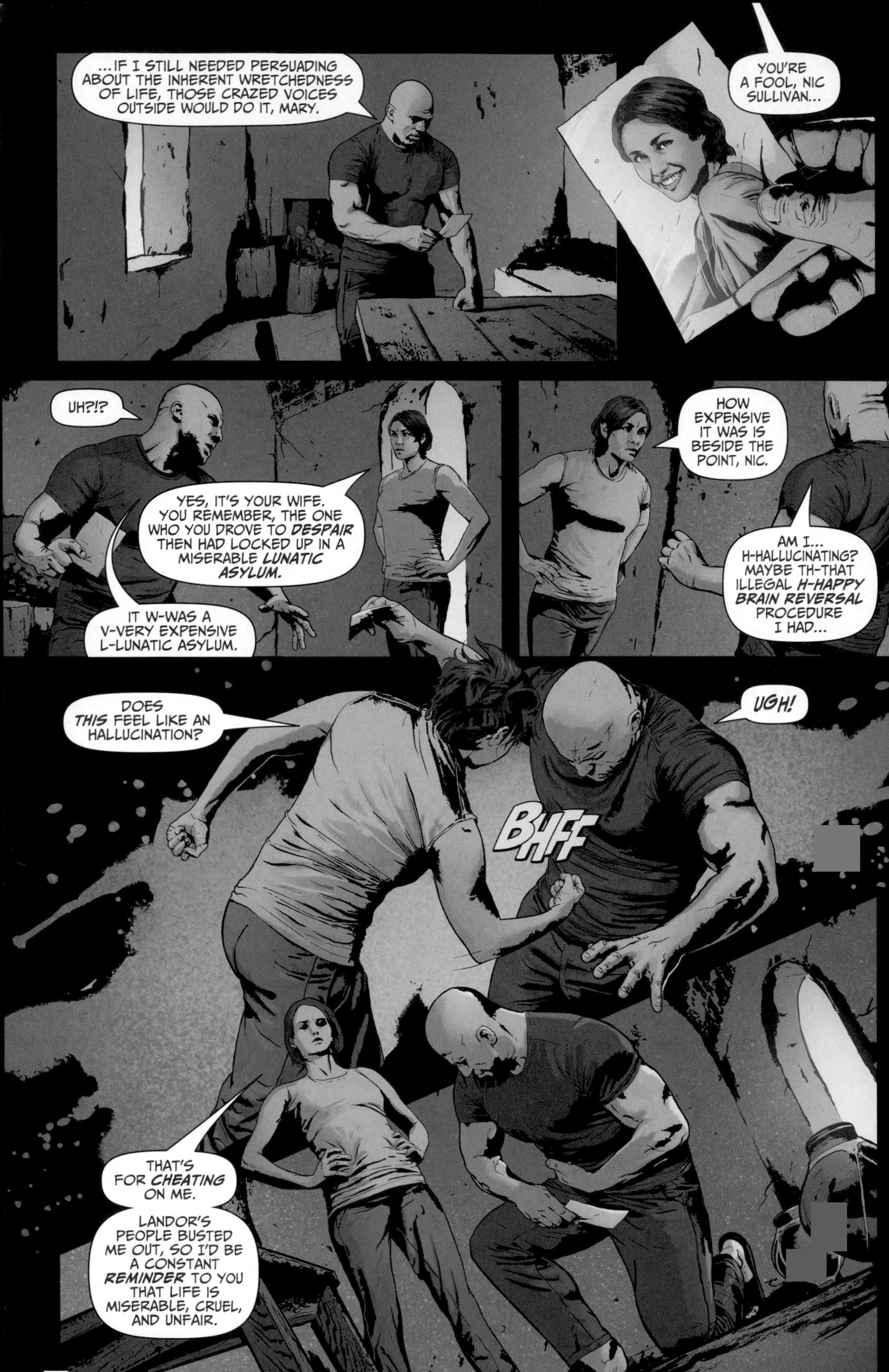

...IF I STILL NEEDED PERSUADING ABOUT THE INHERENT WRETCHEDNESS OF LIFE, THOSE CRAZED VOICES OUTSIDE WOULD DO IT, MARY.
YOU'RE A FOOL, NIC SULLIVAN...
UH?!?
YES, IT'S YOUR WIFE. YOU REMEMBER, THE ONE WHO YOU DROVE TO DESPAIR THEN HAD LOCKED UP IN A MISERABLE LUNATIC ASYLUM.
IT W-WAS A V-VERY EXPENSIVE L-LUNATIC ASYLUM.
HOW EXPENSIVE IT WAS IS BESIDE THE POINT, NIC.
AM I... H-HALLUCINATING? MAYBE TH-THAT ILLEGAL H-HAPPY BRAIN REVERSAL PROCEDURE I HAD...
DOES THIS FEEL LIKE AN HALLUCINATION?
UGH!
BHFF
THAT'S FOR CHEATING ON ME.
LANDOR'S PEOPLE BUSTED ME OUT, SO I'D BE A CONSTANT REMINDER TO YOU THAT LIFE IS MISERABLE, CRUEL, AND UNFAIR.

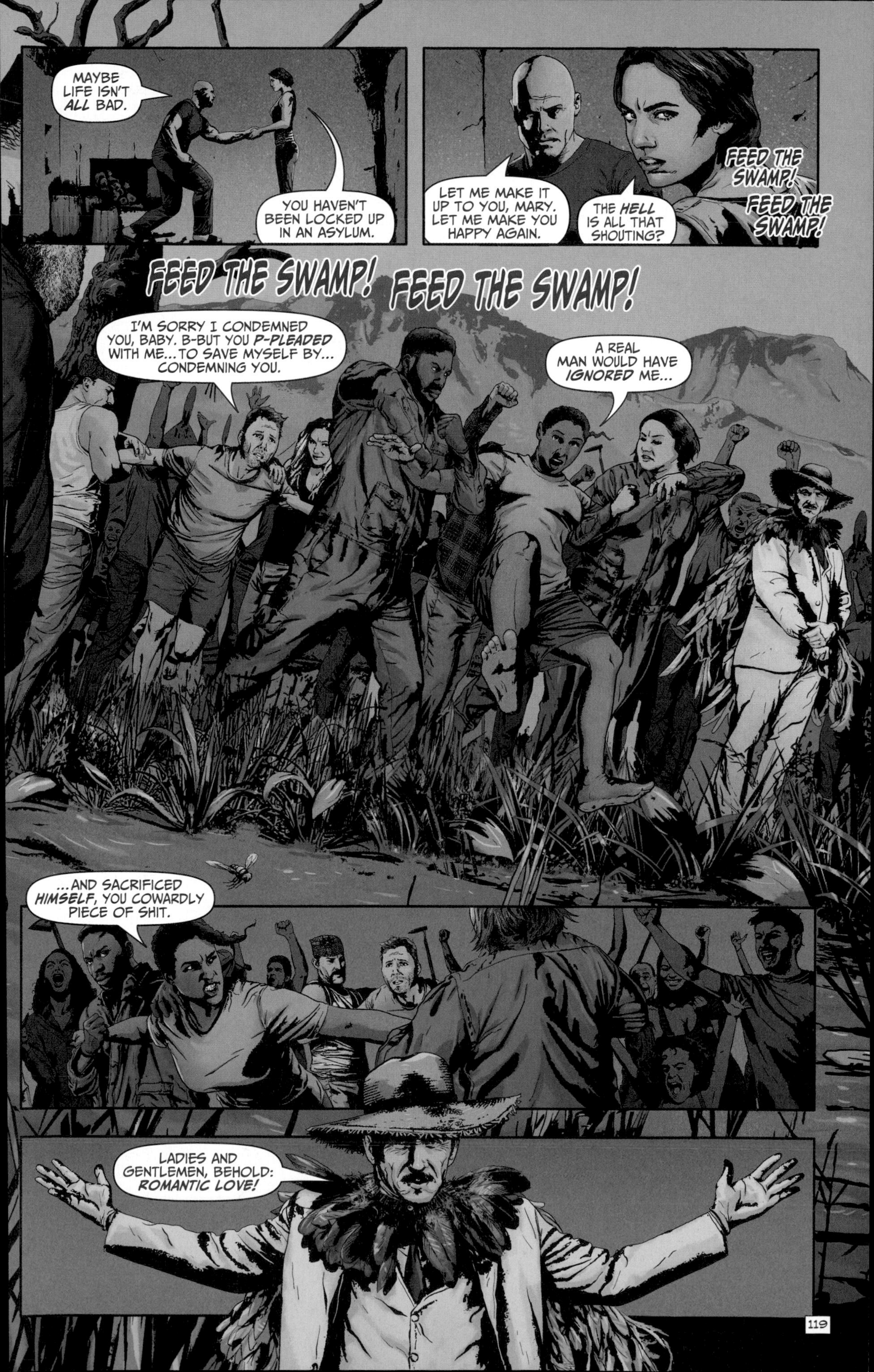
MAYBE LIFE ISN'T ALL BAD.
YOU HAVEN'T BEEN LOCKED UP IN AN ASYLUM.
LET ME MAKE IT UP TO YOU, MARY. LET ME MAKE YOU HAPPY AGAIN.
THE HELL IS ALL THAT SHOUTING?
FEED THE SWAMP!
FEED THE SWAMP!
FEED THE SWAMP!
FEED THE SWAMP!
I'M SORRY I CONDEMNED YOU, BABY. B-BUT YOU P-PLEADED WITH ME... TO SAVE MYSELF BY... CONDEMNING YOU.
A REAL MAN WOULD HAVE IGNORED ME...
...AND SACRIFICED HIMSELF, YOU COWARDLY PIECE OF SHIT.
LADIES AND GENTLEMEN, BEHOLD: ROMANTIC LOVE!

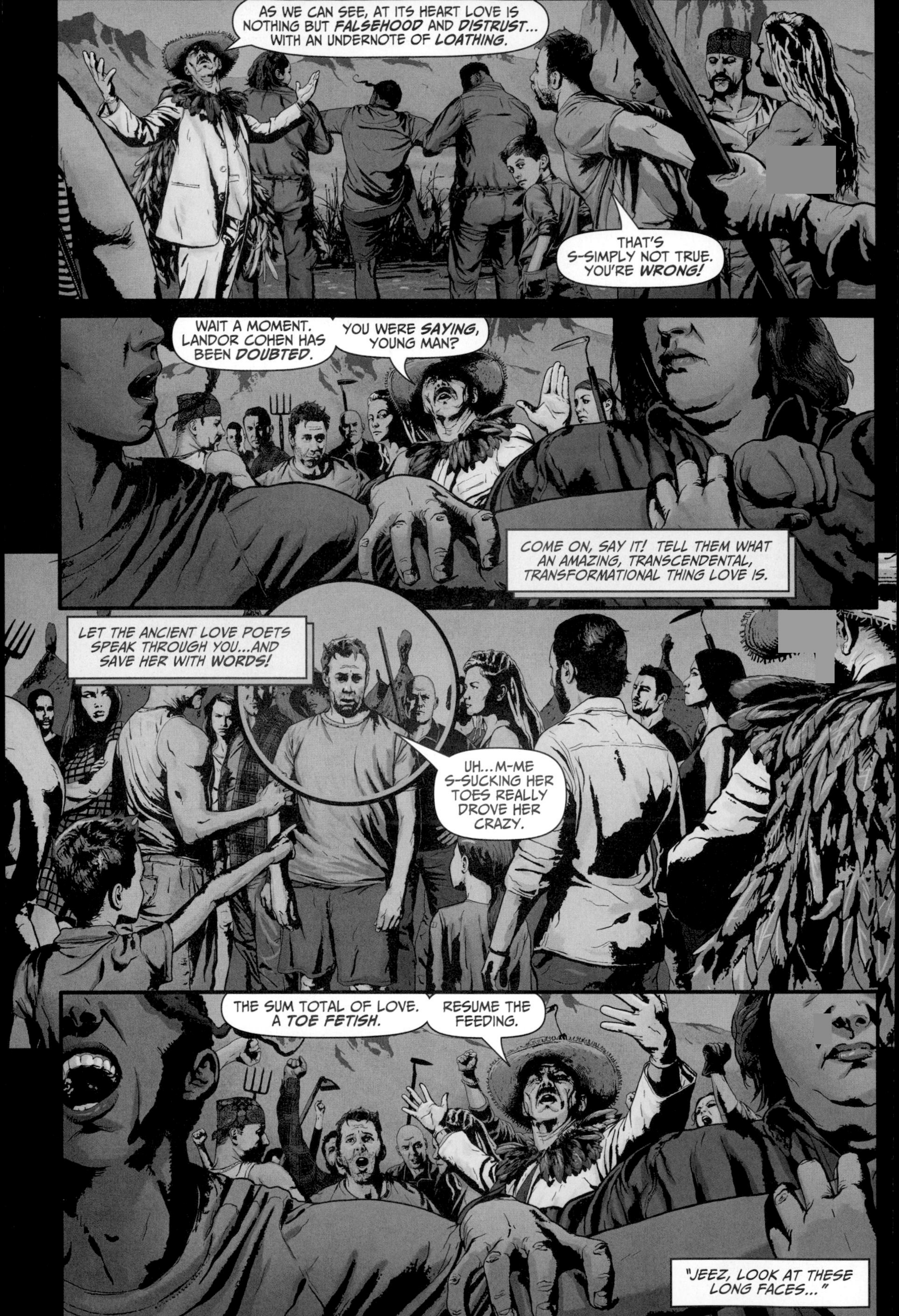

AS WE CAN SEE, AT ITS HEART LOVE IS NOTHING BUT FALSEHOOD AND DISTRUST... WITH AN UNDERNOTE OF LOATHING.
THAT'S S-SIMPLY NOT TRUE. YOU'RE WRONG!
WAIT A MOMENT. LANDOR COHEN HAS BEEN DOUBTED.
YOU WERE SAYING, YOUNG MAN?
COME ON, SAY IT! TELL THEM WHAT AN AMAZING, TRANSCENDENTAL, TRANSFORMATIONAL THING LOVE IS.
LET THE ANCIENT LOVE POETS SPEAK THROUGH YOU...AND SAVE HER WITH WORDS!
UH...M-ME S-SUCKING HER TOES REALLY DROVE HER CRAZY.
THE SUM TOTAL OF LOVE. A TOE FETISH.
RESUME THE FEEDING.
"JEEZ, LOOK AT THESE LONG FACES..."

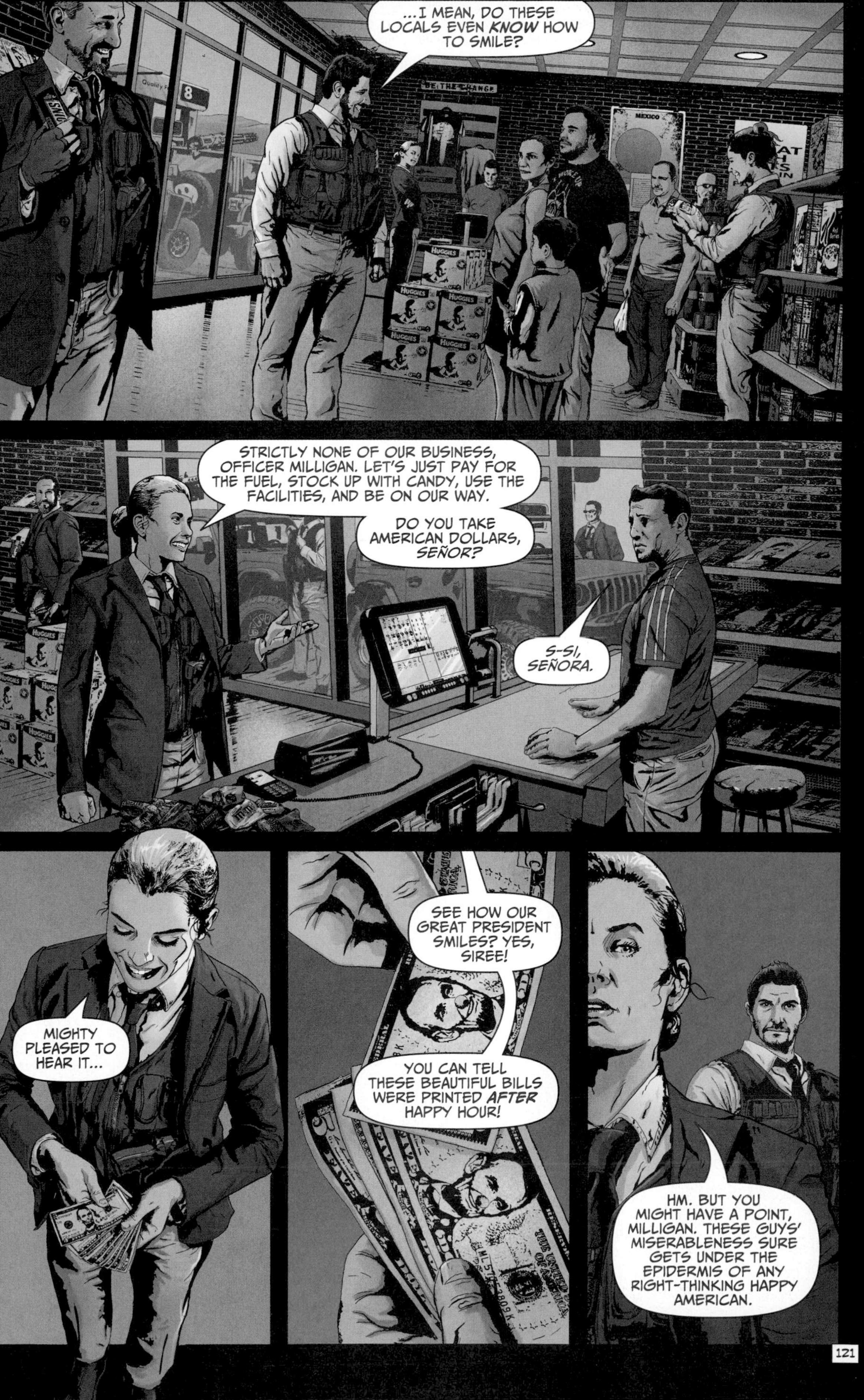
...I MEAN, DO THESE LOCALS EVEN *KNOW* HOW TO SMILE?
STRICTLY NONE OF OUR BUSINESS, OFFICER MILLIGAN. LET'S JUST PAY FOR THE FUEL, STOCK UP WITH CANDY, USE THE FACILITIES, AND BE ON OUR WAY.
DO YOU TAKE AMERICAN DOLLARS, *SEÑOR?*
S-SI, SEÑORA.
MIGHTY PLEASED TO HEAR IT...
SEE HOW OUR GREAT PRESIDENT SMILES? YES, SIREE!
YOU CAN TELL THESE BEAUTIFUL BILLS WERE PRINTED *AFTER* HAPPY HOUR!
HM. BUT YOU MIGHT HAVE A POINT, MILLIGAN. THESE GUYS' MISERABLENESS SURE GETS UNDER THE EPIDERMIS OF ANY RIGHT-THINKING HAPPY AMERICAN.

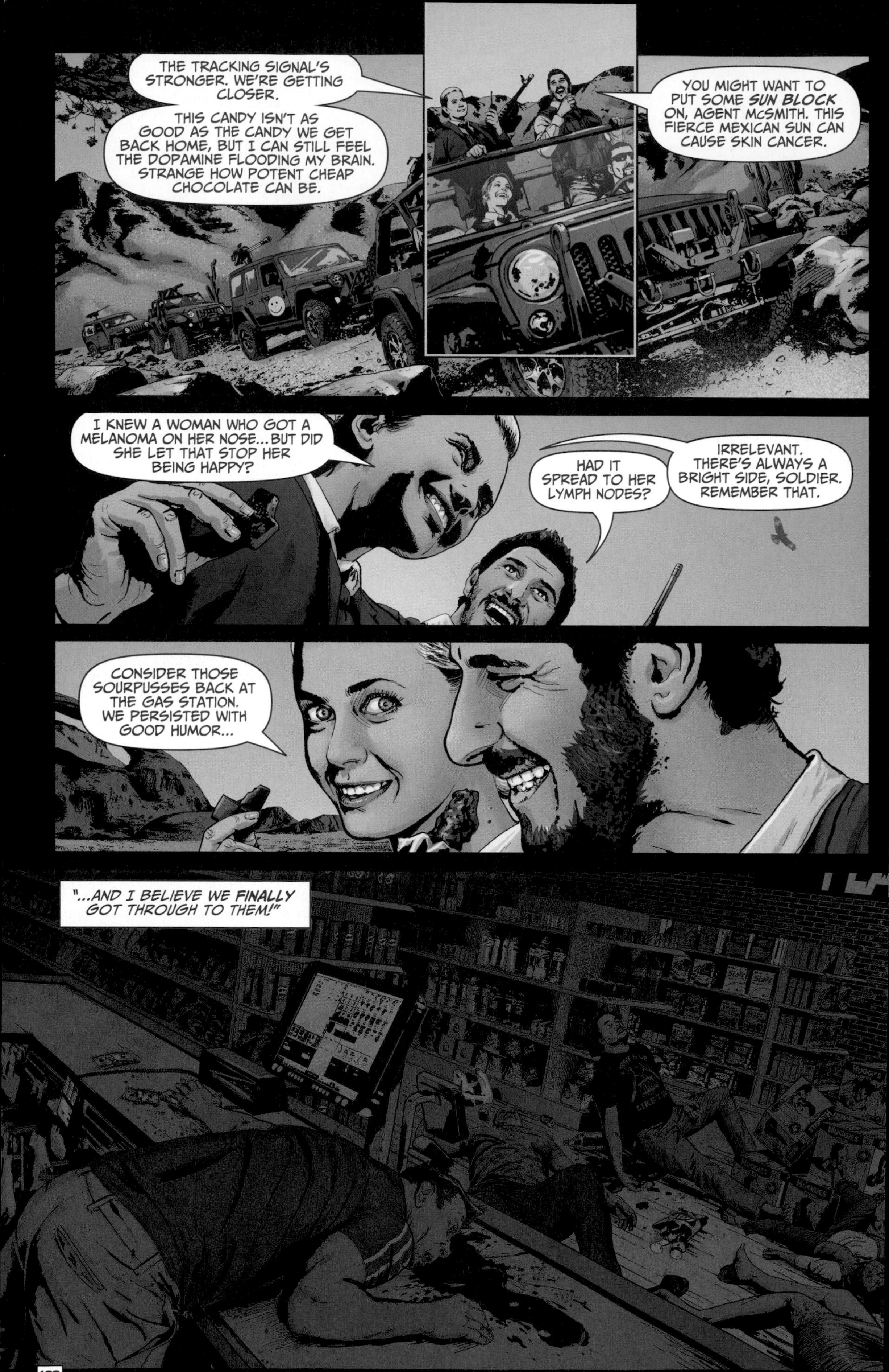
THE TRACKING SIGNAL'S STRONGER. WE'RE GETTING CLOSER.
THIS CANDY ISN'T AS GOOD AS THE CANDY WE GET BACK HOME, BUT I CAN STILL FEEL THE DOPAMINE FLOODING MY BRAIN. STRANGE HOW POTENT CHEAP CHOCOLATE CAN BE.
YOU MIGHT WANT TO PUT SOME SUN BLOCK ON, AGENT McSMITH. THIS FIERCE MEXICAN SUN CAN CAUSE SKIN CANCER.
I KNEW A WOMAN WHO GOT A MELANOMA ON HER NOSE...BUT DID SHE LET THAT STOP HER BEING HAPPY?
HAD IT SPREAD TO HER LYMPH NODES?
IRRELEVANT. THERE'S ALWAYS A BRIGHT SIDE, SOLDIER. REMEMBER THAT.
CONSIDER THOSE SOURPUSSES BACK AT THE GAS STATION. WE PERSISTED WITH GOOD HUMOR...
"...AND I BELIEVE WE FINALLY GOT THROUGH TO THEM!"

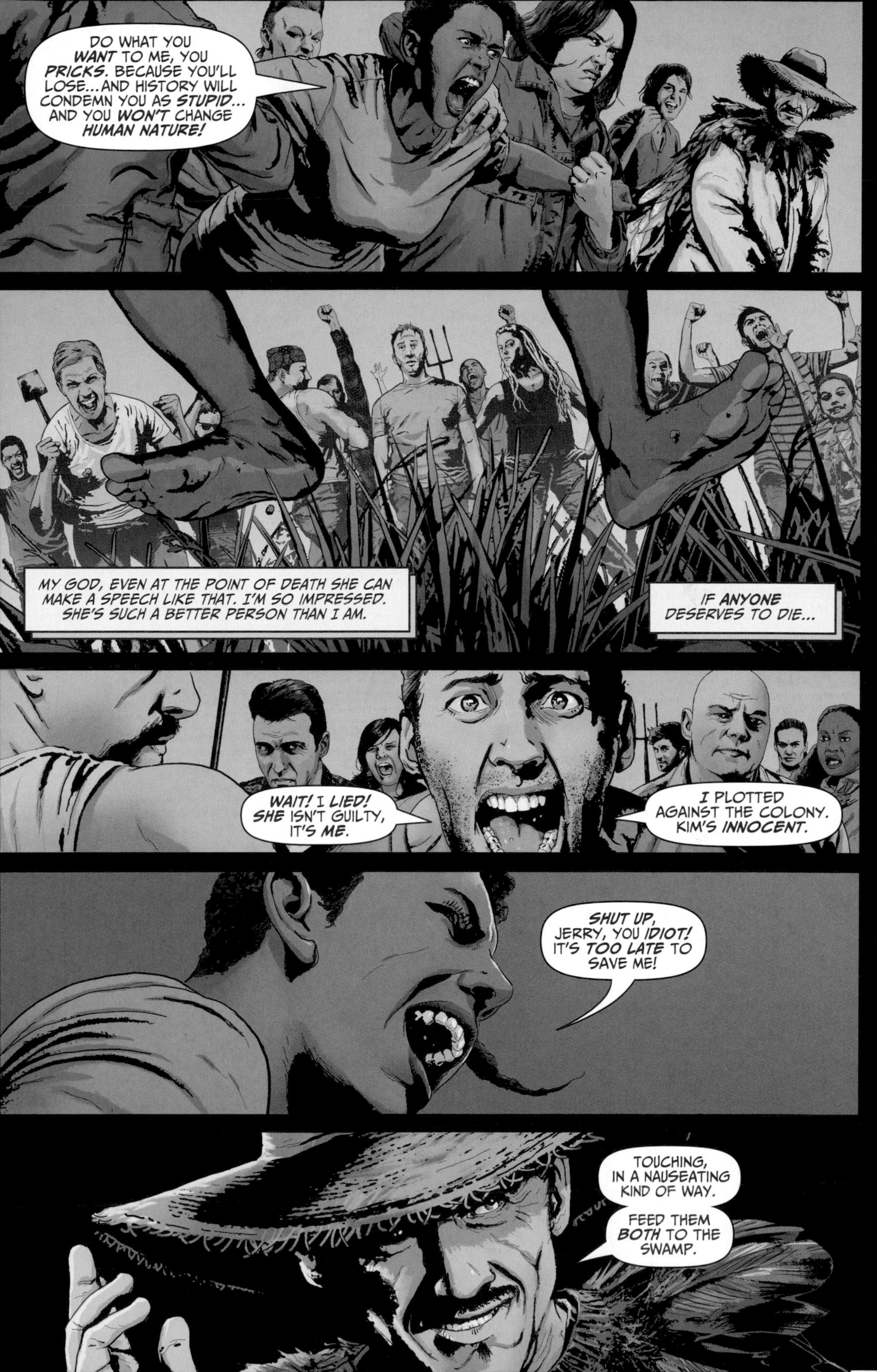
DO WHAT YOU WANT TO ME, YOU PRICKS. BECAUSE YOU'LL LOSE...AND HISTORY WILL CONDEMN YOU AS STUPID... AND YOU WON'T CHANGE HUMAN NATURE!
MY GOD, EVEN AT THE POINT OF DEATH SHE CAN MAKE A SPEECH LIKE THAT. I'M SO IMPRESSED. SHE'S SUCH A BETTER PERSON THAN I AM.
IF ANYONE DESERVES TO DIE...
WAIT! I LIED! SHE ISN'T GUILTY, IT'S ME.
I PLOTTED AGAINST THE COLONY. KIM'S INNOCENT.
SHUT UP, JERRY, YOU IDIOT! IT'S TOO LATE TO SAVE ME!
TOUCHING, IN A NAUSEATING KIND OF WAY.
FEED THEM BOTH TO THE SWAMP.

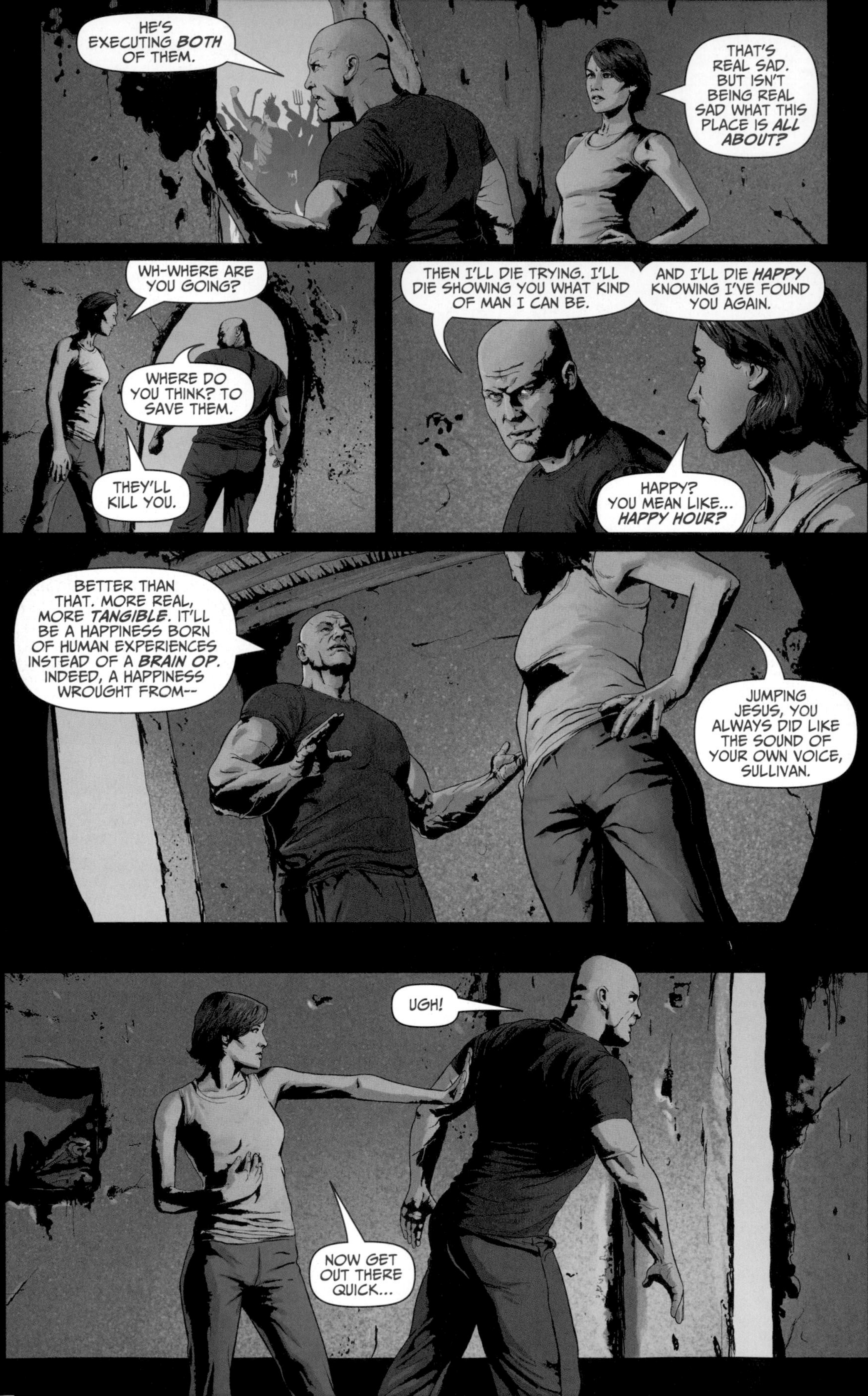
HE'S EXECUTING BOTH OF THEM.
THAT'S REAL SAD. BUT ISN'T BEING REAL SAD WHAT THIS PLACE IS ALL ABOUT?
WH-WHERE ARE YOU GOING?
WHERE DO YOU THINK? TO SAVE THEM.
THEY'LL KILL YOU.
THEN I'LL DIE TRYING. I'LL DIE SHOWING YOU WHAT KIND OF MAN I CAN BE.
AND I'LL DIE HAPPY KNOWING I'VE FOUND YOU AGAIN.
HAPPY? YOU MEAN LIKE... HAPPY HOUR?
BETTER THAN THAT. MORE REAL, MORE TANGIBLE. IT'LL BE A HAPPINESS BORN OF HUMAN EXPERIENCES INSTEAD OF A BRAIN OP. INDEED, A HAPPINESS WROUGHT FROM--
JUMPING JESUS, YOU ALWAYS DID LIKE THE SOUND OF YOUR OWN VOICE, SULLIVAN.
UGH!
NOW GET OUT THERE QUICK...

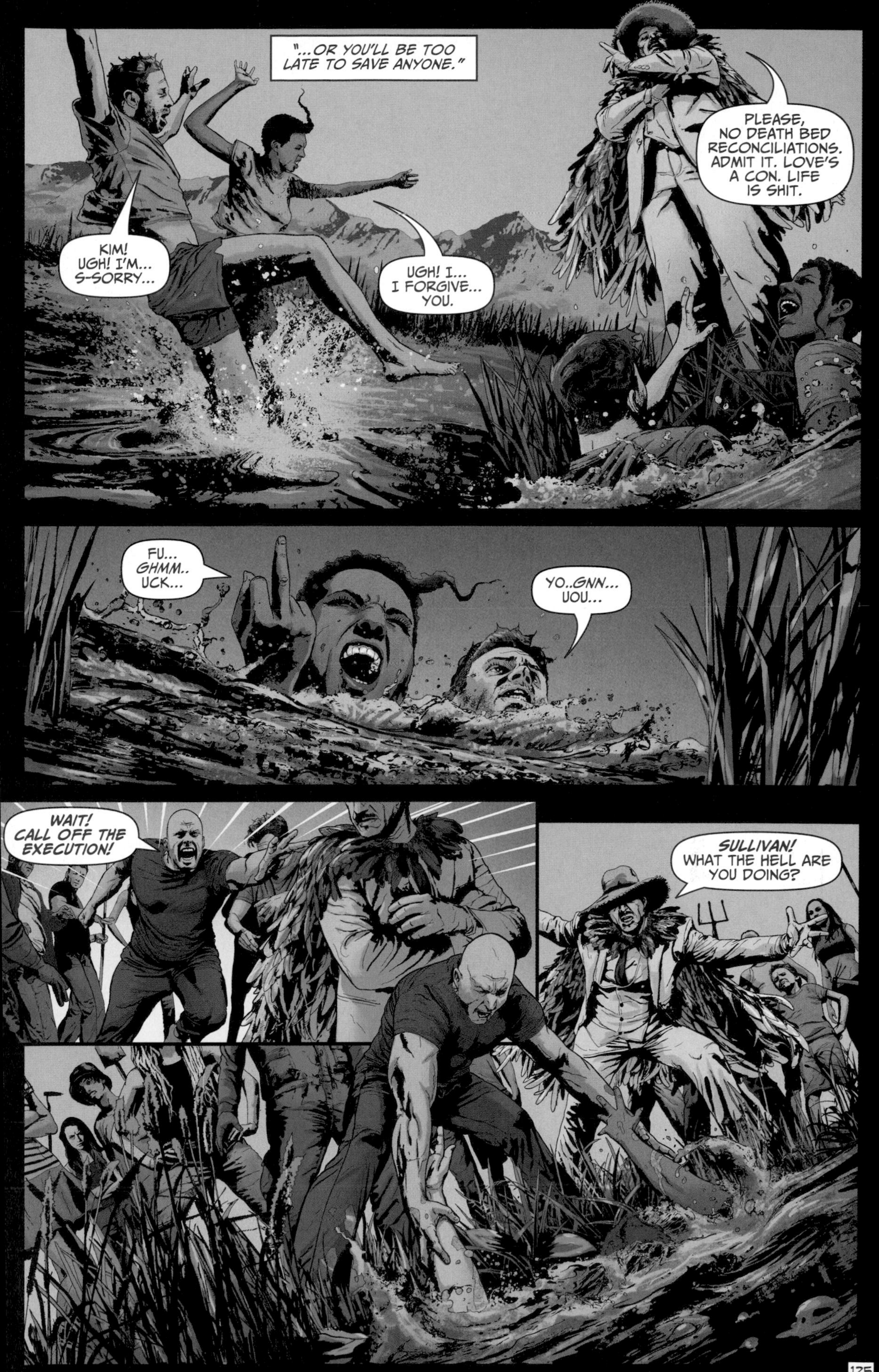
"...OR YOU'LL BE TOO LATE TO SAVE ANYONE."
KIM! UGH! I'M... S-SORRY...
UGH! I... I FORGIVE... YOU.
PLEASE, NO DEATH BED RECONCILIATIONS. ADMIT IT. LOVE'S A CON. LIFE IS SHIT.
FU... GHMM.. UCK...
YO..GNN... UOU...
WAIT! CALL OFF THE EXECUTION!
SULLIVAN! WHAT THE HELL ARE YOU DOING?

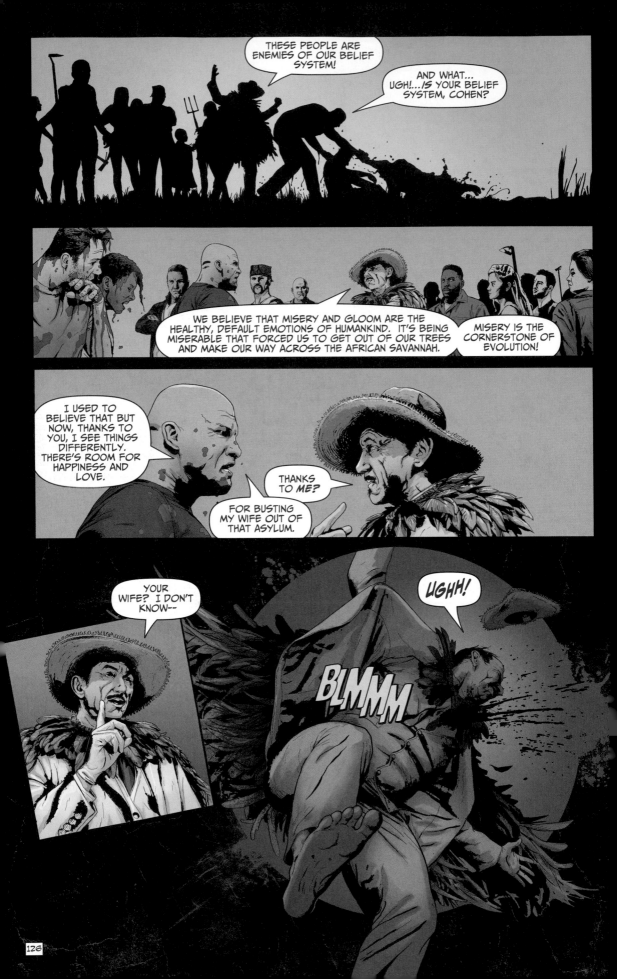

THESE PEOPLE ARE ENEMIES OF OUR BELIEF SYSTEM!

AND WHAT... UGH!...*IS* YOUR BELIEF SYSTEM, COHEN?

WE BELIEVE THAT MISERY AND GLOOM ARE THE HEALTHY, DEFAULT EMOTIONS OF HUMANKIND. IT'S BEING MISERABLE THAT FORCED US TO GET OUT OF OUR TREES AND MAKE OUR WAY ACROSS THE AFRICAN SAVANNAH.

MISERY IS THE CORNERSTONE OF EVOLUTION!

I USED TO BELIEVE THAT BUT NOW, THANKS TO YOU, I SEE THINGS DIFFERENTLY. THERE'S ROOM FOR HAPPINESS AND LOVE.

THANKS TO *ME?*

FOR BUSTING MY WIFE OUT OF THAT ASYLUM.

YOUR WIFE? I DON'T KNOW--

UGHH!

BLMMM

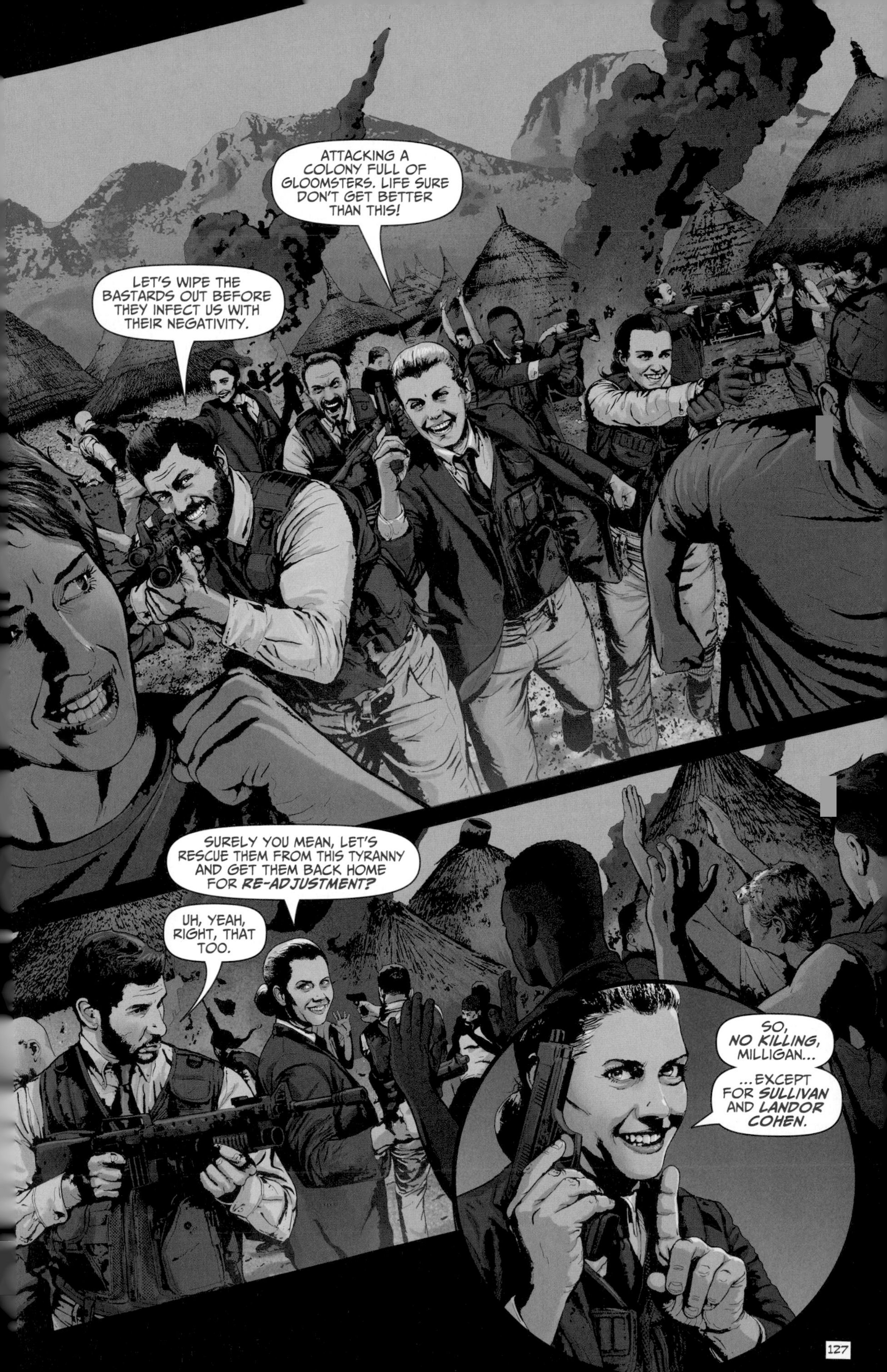
LET'S WIPE THE BASTARDS OUT BEFORE THEY INFECT US WITH THEIR NEGATIVITY.
ATTACKING A COLONY FULL OF GLOOMSTERS. LIFE SURE DON'T GET BETTER THAN THIS!
SURELY YOU MEAN, LET'S RESCUE THEM FROM THIS TYRANNY AND GET THEM BACK HOME FOR *RE-ADJUSTMENT?*
UH, YEAH, RIGHT, THAT TOO.
SO, *NO KILLING,* MILLIGAN...
...EXCEPT FOR *SULLIVAN* AND *LANDOR COHEN.*

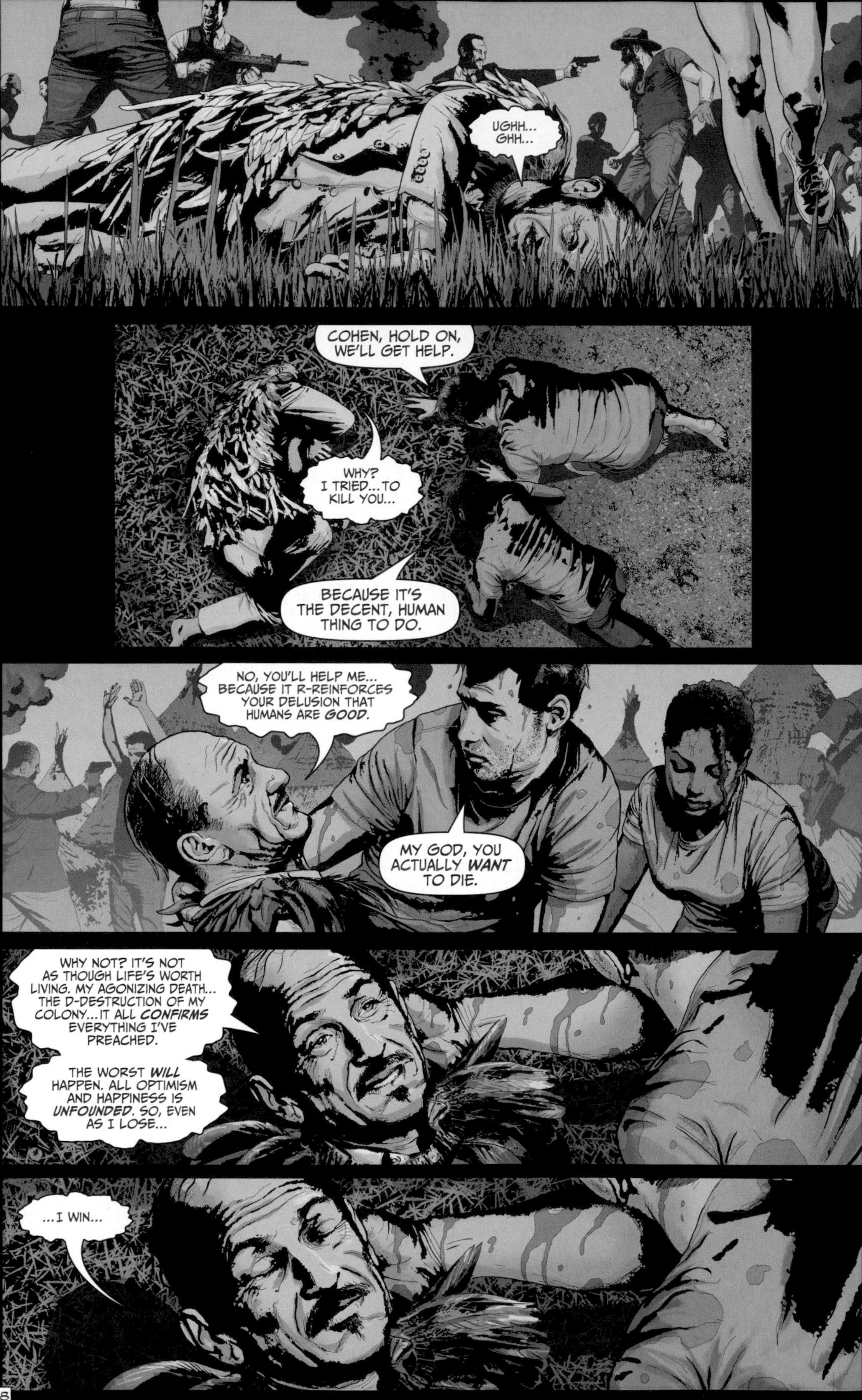
UGHH... GHH...
COHEN, HOLD ON, WE'LL GET HELP.
WHY? I TRIED...TO KILL YOU...
BECAUSE IT'S THE DECENT, HUMAN THING TO DO.
NO, YOU'LL HELP ME... BECAUSE IT R-REINFORCES YOUR DELUSION THAT HUMANS ARE GOOD.
MY GOD, YOU ACTUALLY WANT TO DIE.
WHY NOT? IT'S NOT AS THOUGH LIFE'S WORTH LIVING. MY AGONIZING DEATH... THE D-DESTRUCTION OF MY COLONY...IT ALL CONFIRMS EVERYTHING I'VE PREACHED.
THE WORST WILL HAPPEN. ALL OPTIMISM AND HAPPINESS IS UNFOUNDED. SO, EVEN AS I LOSE...
...I WIN...

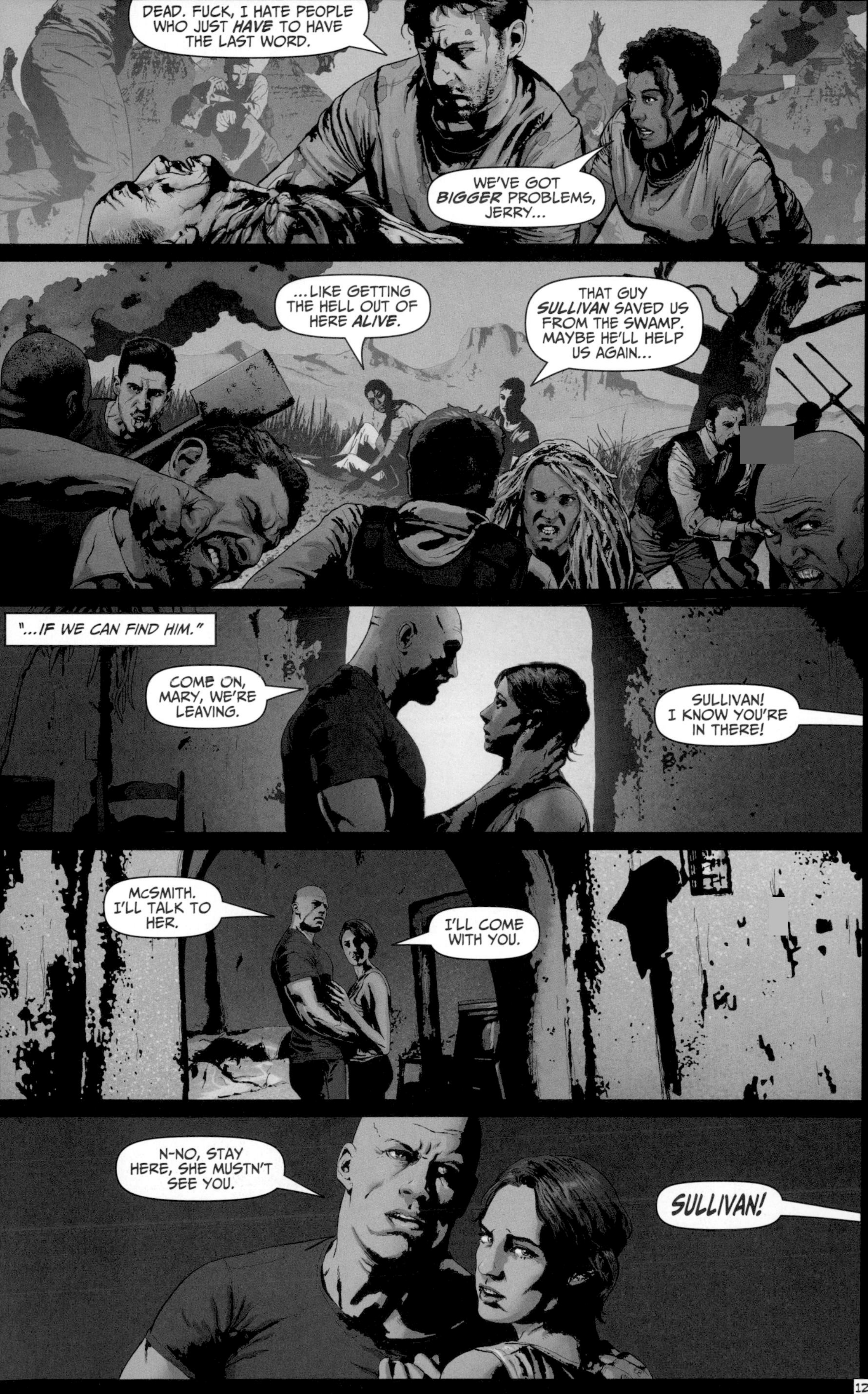
DEAD. FUCK, I HATE PEOPLE WHO JUST HAVE TO HAVE THE LAST WORD.
WE'VE GOT BIGGER PROBLEMS, JERRY...
...LIKE GETTING THE HELL OUT OF HERE ALIVE.
THAT GUY SULLIVAN SAVED US FROM THE SWAMP. MAYBE HE'LL HELP US AGAIN...
"...IF WE CAN FIND HIM."
COME ON, MARY, WE'RE LEAVING.
SULLIVAN! I KNOW YOU'RE IN THERE!
McSMITH. I'LL TALK TO HER.
I'LL COME WITH YOU.
N-NO, STAY HERE, SHE MUSTN'T SEE YOU.
SULLIVAN!

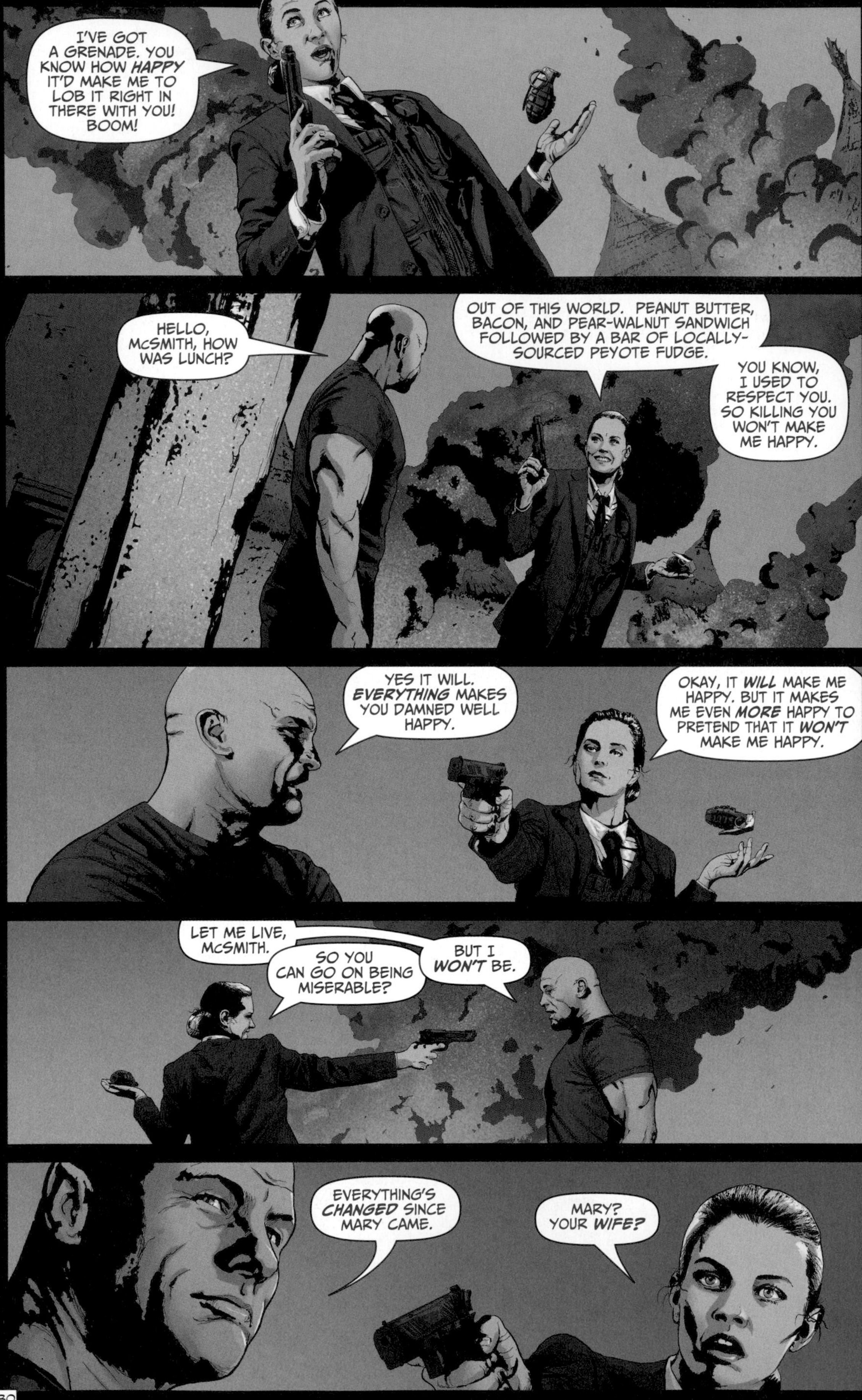
I'VE GOT A GRENADE. YOU KNOW HOW HAPPY IT'D MAKE ME TO LOB IT RIGHT IN THERE WITH YOU! BOOM!
HELLO, McSMITH, HOW WAS LUNCH?
OUT OF THIS WORLD. PEANUT BUTTER, BACON, AND PEAR-WALNUT SANDWICH FOLLOWED BY A BAR OF LOCALLY-SOURCED PEYOTE FUDGE.
YOU KNOW, I USED TO RESPECT YOU. SO KILLING YOU WON'T MAKE ME HAPPY.
YES IT WILL. EVERYTHING MAKES YOU DAMNED WELL HAPPY.
OKAY, IT WILL MAKE ME HAPPY. BUT IT MAKES ME EVEN MORE HAPPY TO PRETEND THAT IT WON'T MAKE ME HAPPY.
LET ME LIVE, McSMITH.
SO YOU CAN GO ON BEING MISERABLE?
BUT I WON'T BE.
EVERYTHING'S CHANGED SINCE MARY CAME.
MARY? YOUR WIFE?

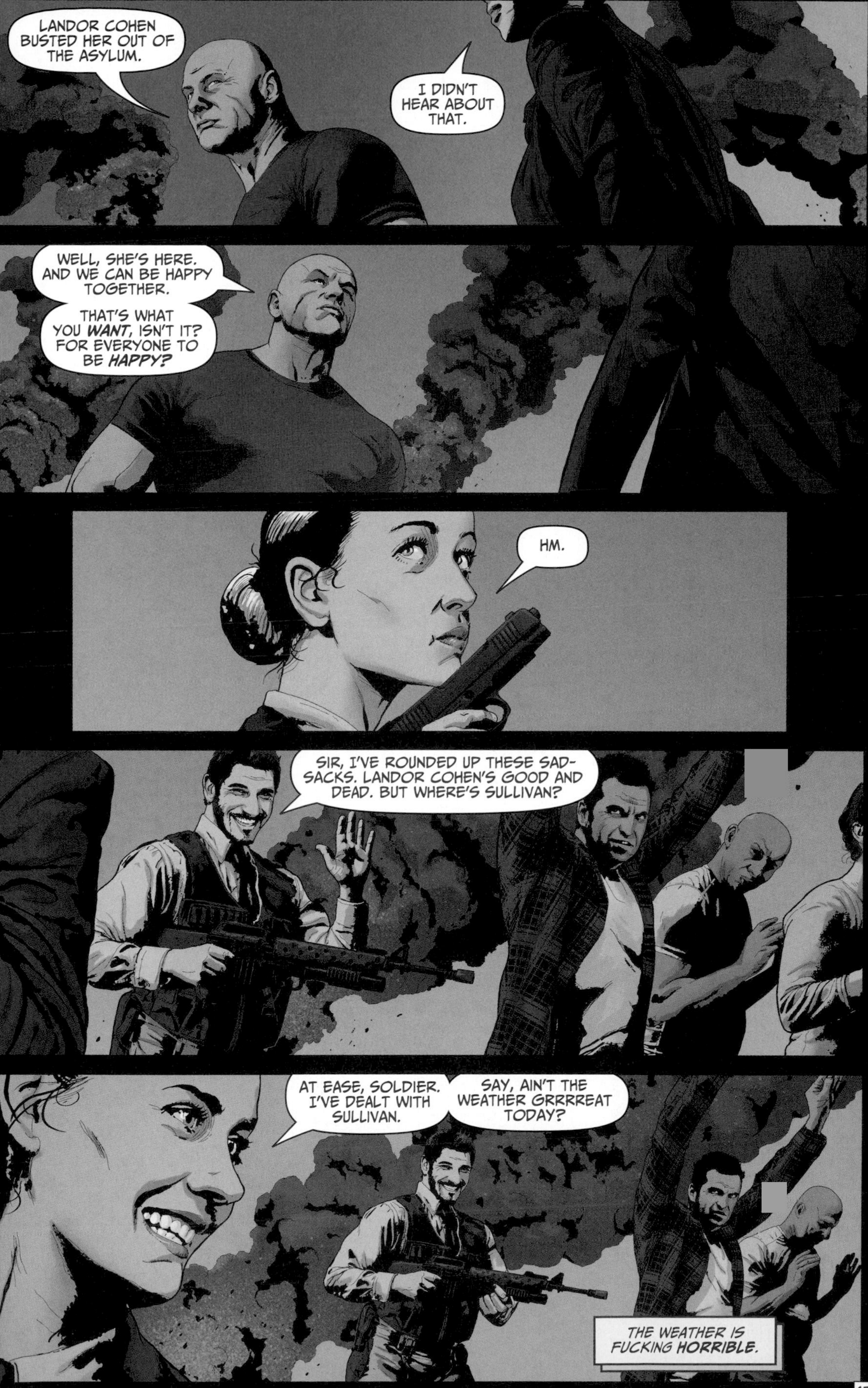
LANDOR COHEN BUSTED HER OUT OF THE ASYLUM.
I DIDN'T HEAR ABOUT THAT.
WELL, SHE'S HERE. AND WE CAN BE HAPPY TOGETHER.
THAT'S WHAT YOU *WANT*, ISN'T IT? FOR EVERYONE TO BE *HAPPY?*
HM.
SIR, I'VE ROUNDED UP THESE SAD-SACKS. LANDOR COHEN'S GOOD AND DEAD. BUT WHERE'S SULLIVAN?
AT EASE, SOLDIER. I'VE DEALT WITH SULLIVAN.
SAY, AIN'T THE WEATHER GRRRREAT TODAY?
THE WEATHER IS FUCKING ***HORRIBLE.***

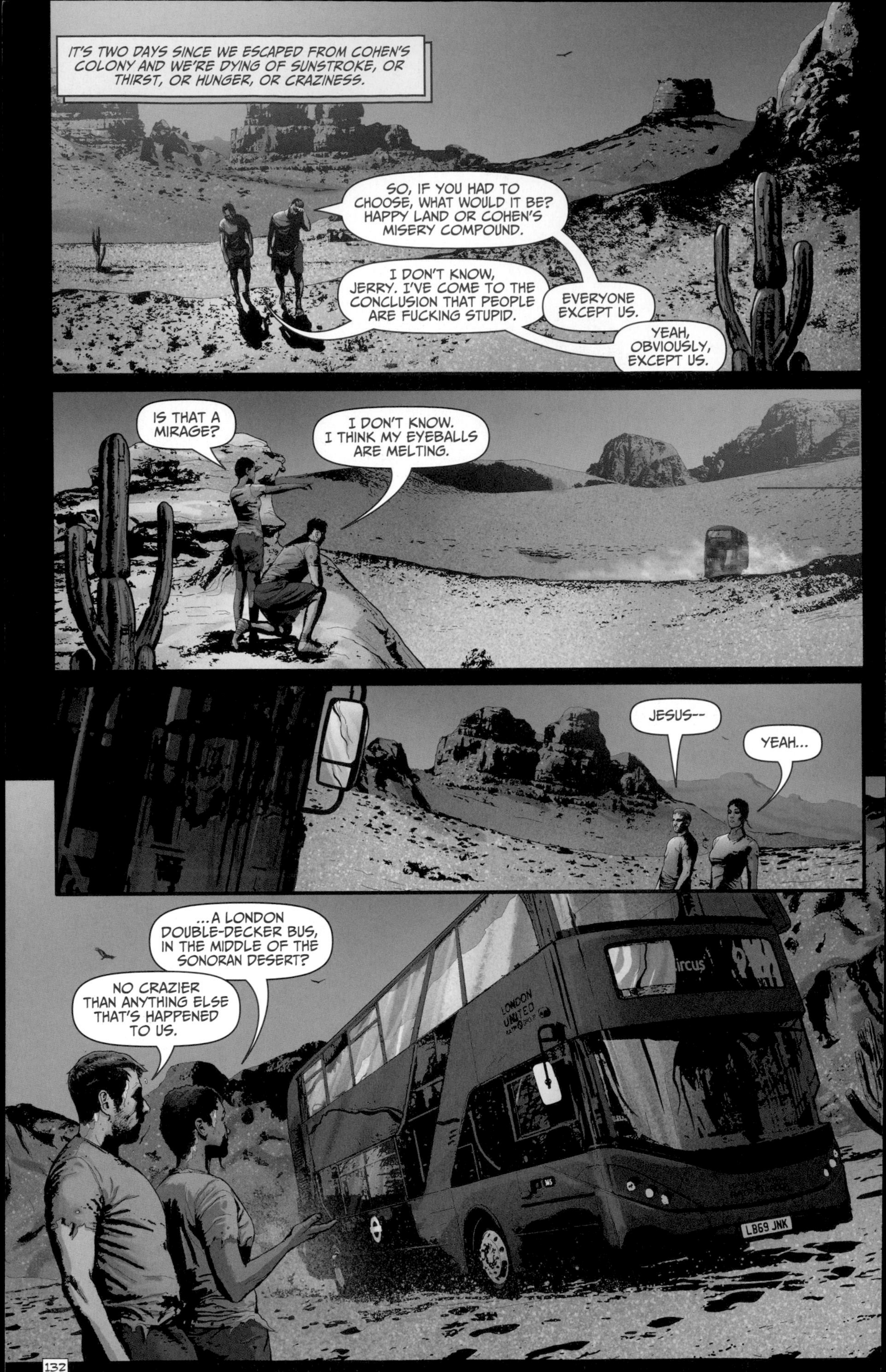
IT'S TWO DAYS SINCE WE ESCAPED FROM COHEN'S COLONY AND WE'RE DYING OF SUNSTROKE, OR THIRST, OR HUNGER, OR CRAZINESS.
SO, IF YOU HAD TO CHOOSE, WHAT WOULD IT BE? HAPPY LAND OR COHEN'S MISERY COMPOUND.
I DON'T KNOW, JERRY. I'VE COME TO THE CONCLUSION THAT PEOPLE ARE FUCKING STUPID.
EVERYONE EXCEPT US.
YEAH, OBVIOUSLY, EXCEPT US.
IS THAT A MIRAGE?
I DON'T KNOW. I THINK MY EYEBALLS ARE MELTING.
JESUS--
YEAH...
...A LONDON DOUBLE-DECKER BUS, IN THE MIDDLE OF THE SONORAN DESERT?
NO CRAZIER THAN ANYTHING ELSE THAT'S HAPPENED TO US.
LONDON UNITED
LB69 JNK

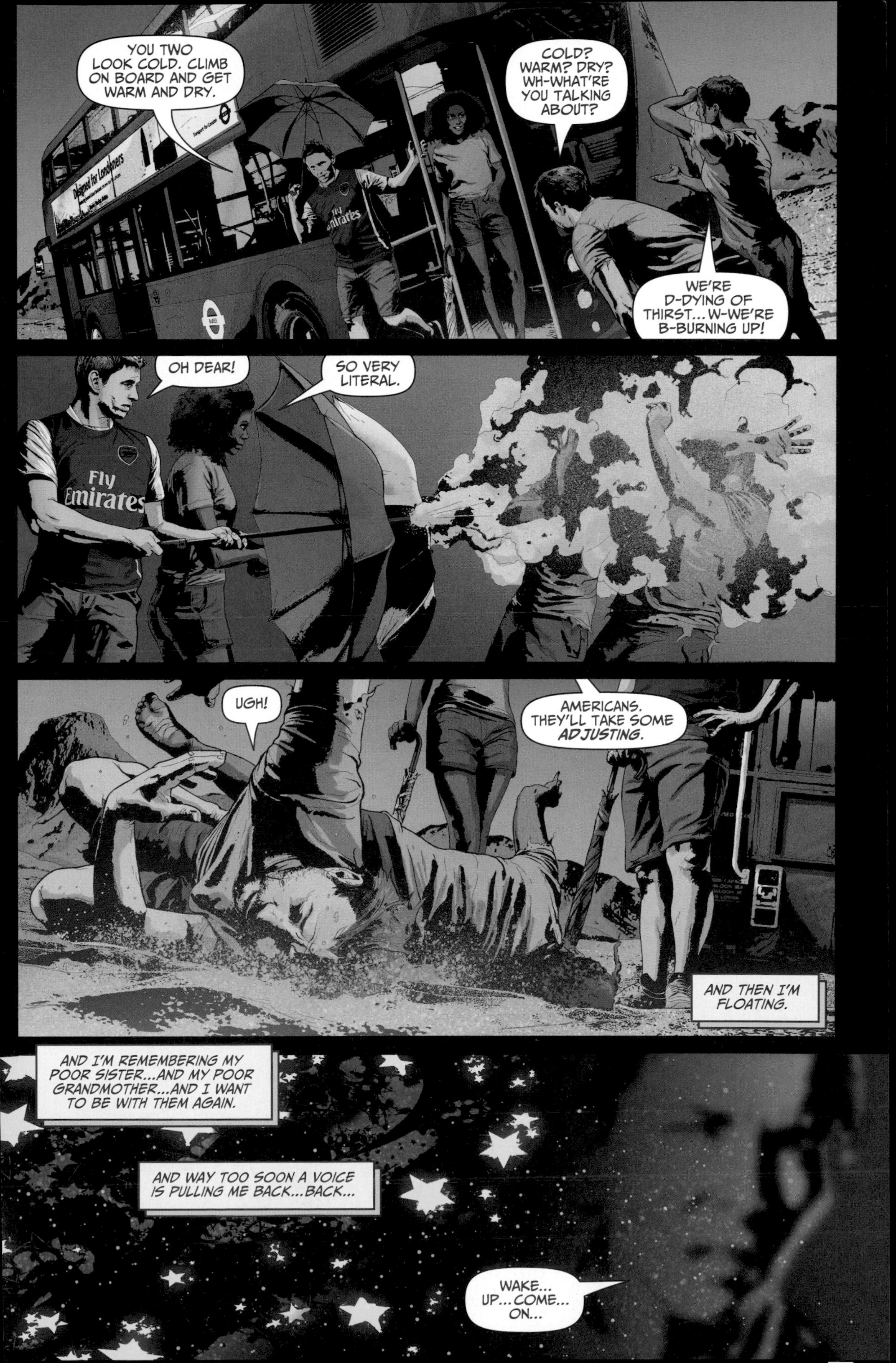

YOU TWO LOOK COLD. CLIMB ON BOARD AND GET WARM AND DRY.
COLD? WARM? DRY? WH-WHAT'RE YOU TALKING ABOUT?
WE'RE D-DYING OF THIRST... W-WE'RE B-BURNING UP!
Designed for Londoners
Fly Emirates
OH DEAR!
SO VERY LITERAL.
Fly Emirates
UGH!
AMERICANS. THEY'LL TAKE SOME *ADJUSTING*.
AND THEN I'M FLOATING.
AND I'M REMEMBERING MY POOR SISTER...AND MY POOR GRANDMOTHER...AND I WANT TO BE WITH THEM AGAIN.
AND WAY TOO SOON A VOICE IS PULLING ME BACK...BACK...
WAKE... UP...COME... ON...

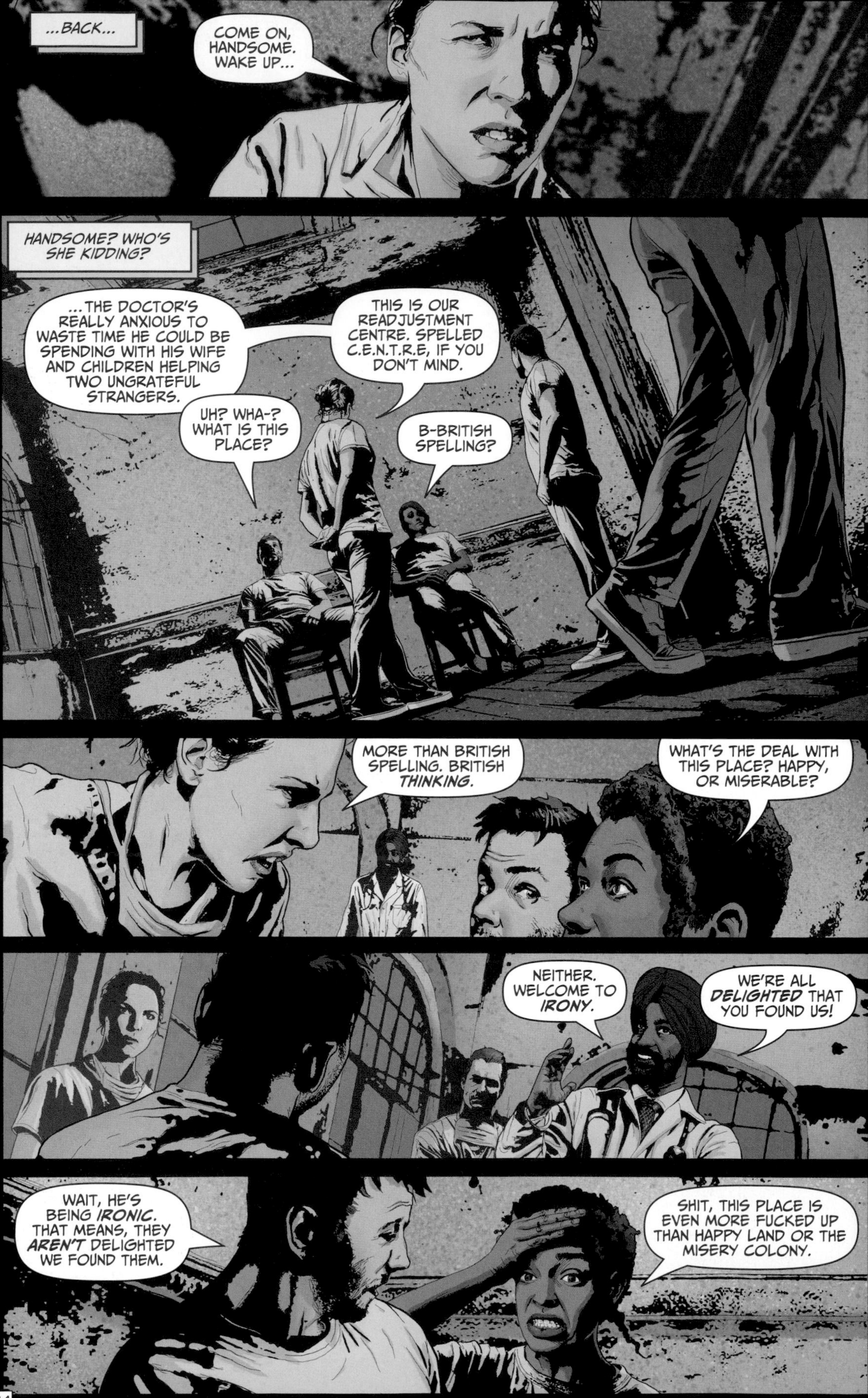
...BACK...
COME ON, HANDSOME. WAKE UP...
HANDSOME? WHO'S SHE KIDDING?
...THE DOCTOR'S REALLY ANXIOUS TO WASTE TIME HE COULD BE SPENDING WITH HIS WIFE AND CHILDREN HELPING TWO UNGRATEFUL STRANGERS.
UH? WHA-? WHAT IS THIS PLACE?
THIS IS OUR READJUSTMENT CENTRE. SPELLED C.E.N.T.R.E, IF YOU DON'T MIND.
B-BRITISH SPELLING?
MORE THAN BRITISH SPELLING. BRITISH THINKING.
WHAT'S THE DEAL WITH THIS PLACE? HAPPY, OR MISERABLE?
NEITHER. WELCOME TO IRONY.
WE'RE ALL DELIGHTED THAT YOU FOUND US!
WAIT, HE'S BEING IRONIC. THAT MEANS, THEY AREN'T DELIGHTED WE FOUND THEM.
SHIT, THIS PLACE IS EVEN MORE FUCKED UP THAN HAPPY LAND OR THE MISERY COLONY.

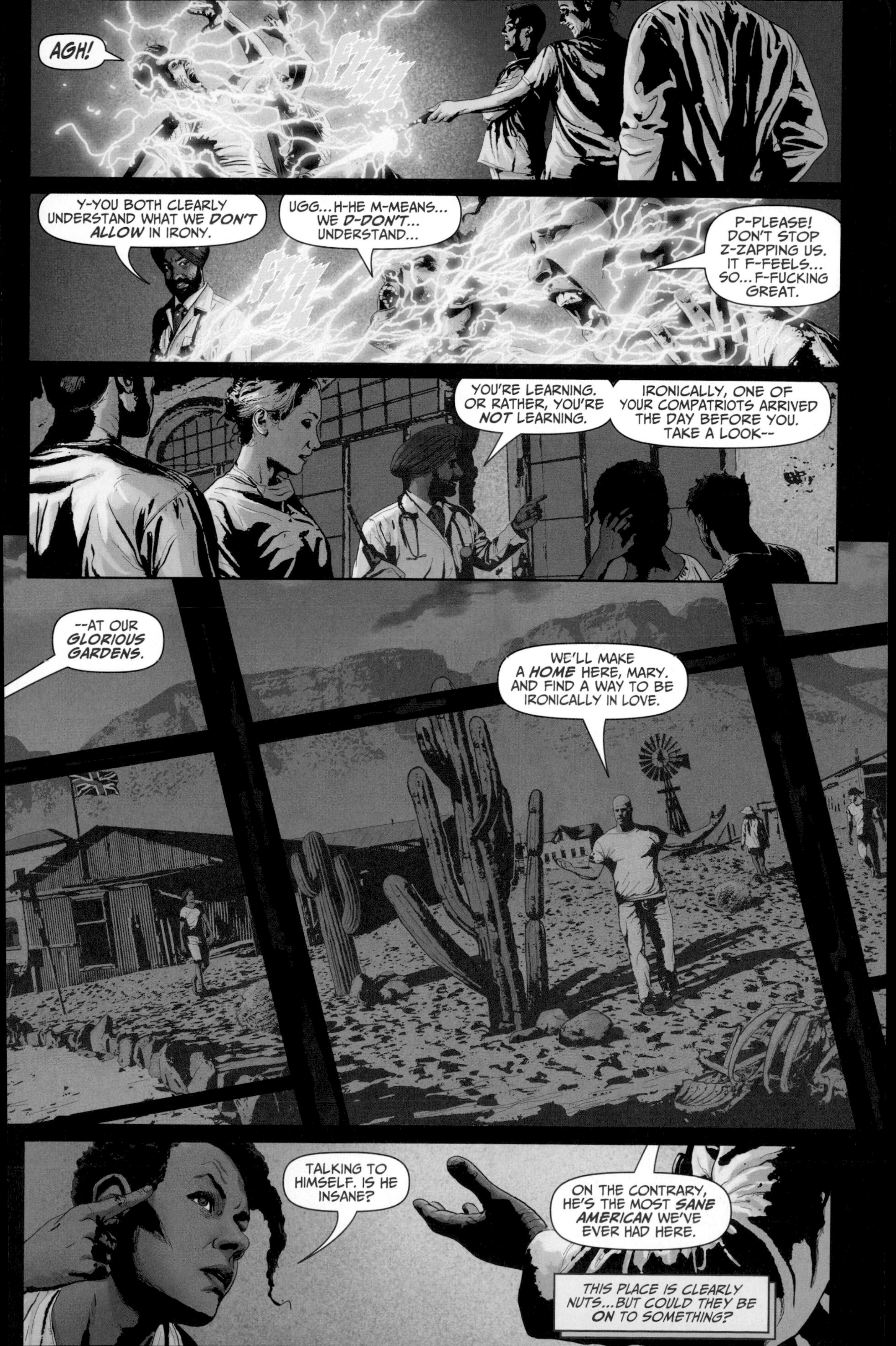
AGH!
FZZZZ
Y-YOU BOTH CLEARLY UNDERSTAND WHAT WE DON'T ALLOW IN IRONY.
UGG...H-HE M-MEANS... WE D-DON'T... UNDERSTAND...
FZZZ
P-PLEASE! DON'T STOP Z-ZAPPING US. IT F-FEELS... SO...F-FUCKING GREAT.
YOU'RE LEARNING. OR RATHER, YOU'RE NOT LEARNING.
IRONICALLY, ONE OF YOUR COMPATRIOTS ARRIVED THE DAY BEFORE YOU. TAKE A LOOK--
--AT OUR GLORIOUS GARDENS.
WE'LL MAKE A HOME HERE, MARY. AND FIND A WAY TO BE IRONICALLY IN LOVE.
TALKING TO HIMSELF. IS HE INSANE?
ON THE CONTRARY, HE'S THE MOST SANE AMERICAN WE'VE EVER HAD HERE.
THIS PLACE IS CLEARLY NUTS...BUT COULD THEY BE ON TO SOMETHING?

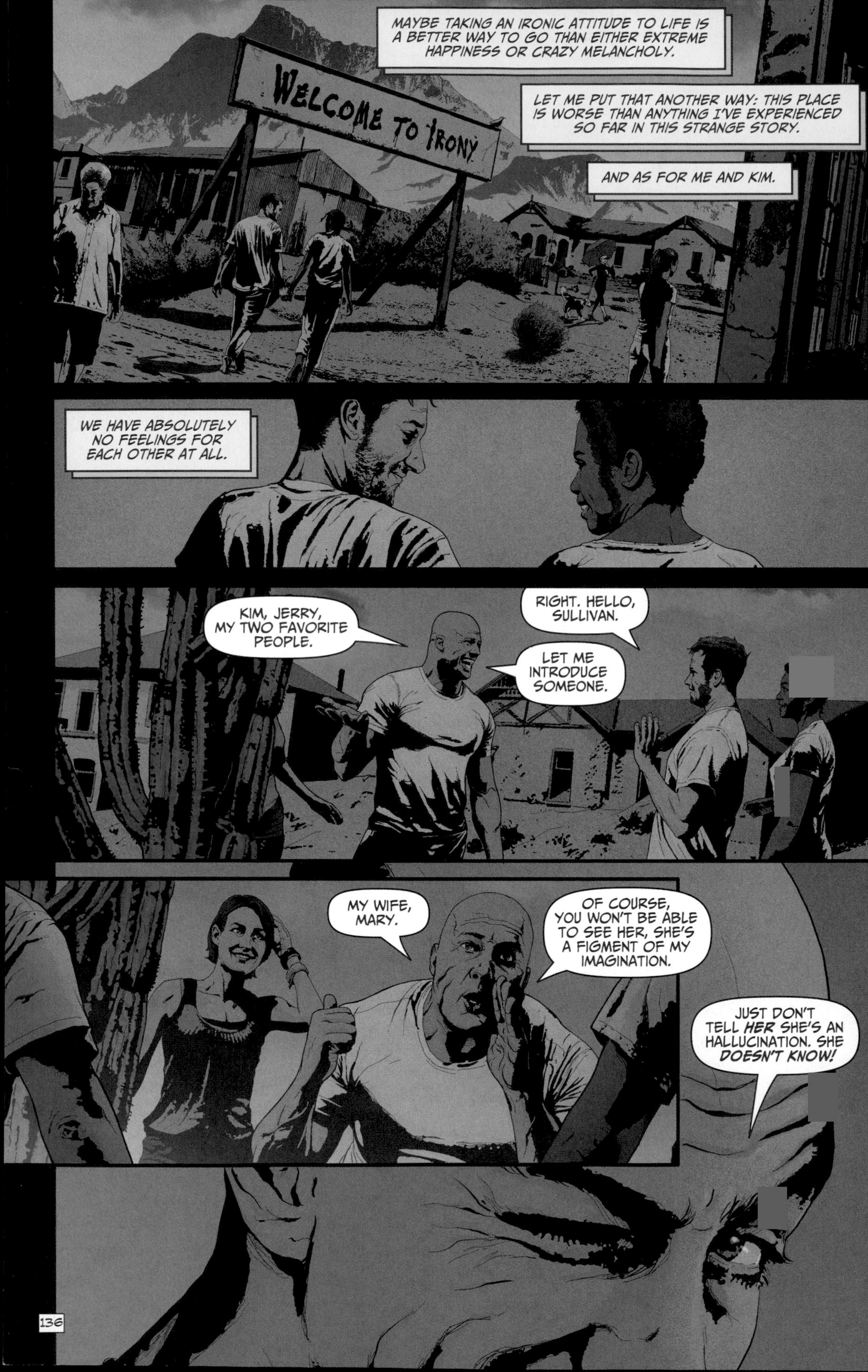
MAYBE TAKING AN IRONIC ATTITUDE TO LIFE IS A BETTER WAY TO GO THAN EITHER EXTREME HAPPINESS OR CRAZY MELANCHOLY.
WELCOME TO IRONY
LET ME PUT THAT ANOTHER WAY: THIS PLACE IS WORSE THAN ANYTHING I'VE EXPERIENCED SO FAR IN THIS STRANGE STORY.
AND AS FOR ME AND KIM.
WE HAVE ABSOLUTELY NO FEELINGS FOR EACH OTHER AT ALL.
KIM, JERRY, MY TWO FAVORITE PEOPLE.
RIGHT. HELLO, SULLIVAN.
LET ME INTRODUCE SOMEONE.
MY WIFE, MARY.
OF COURSE, YOU WON'T BE ABLE TO SEE HER, SHE'S A FIGMENT OF MY IMAGINATION.
JUST DON'T TELL *HER* SHE'S AN HALLUCINATION. SHE *DOESN'T KNOW!*

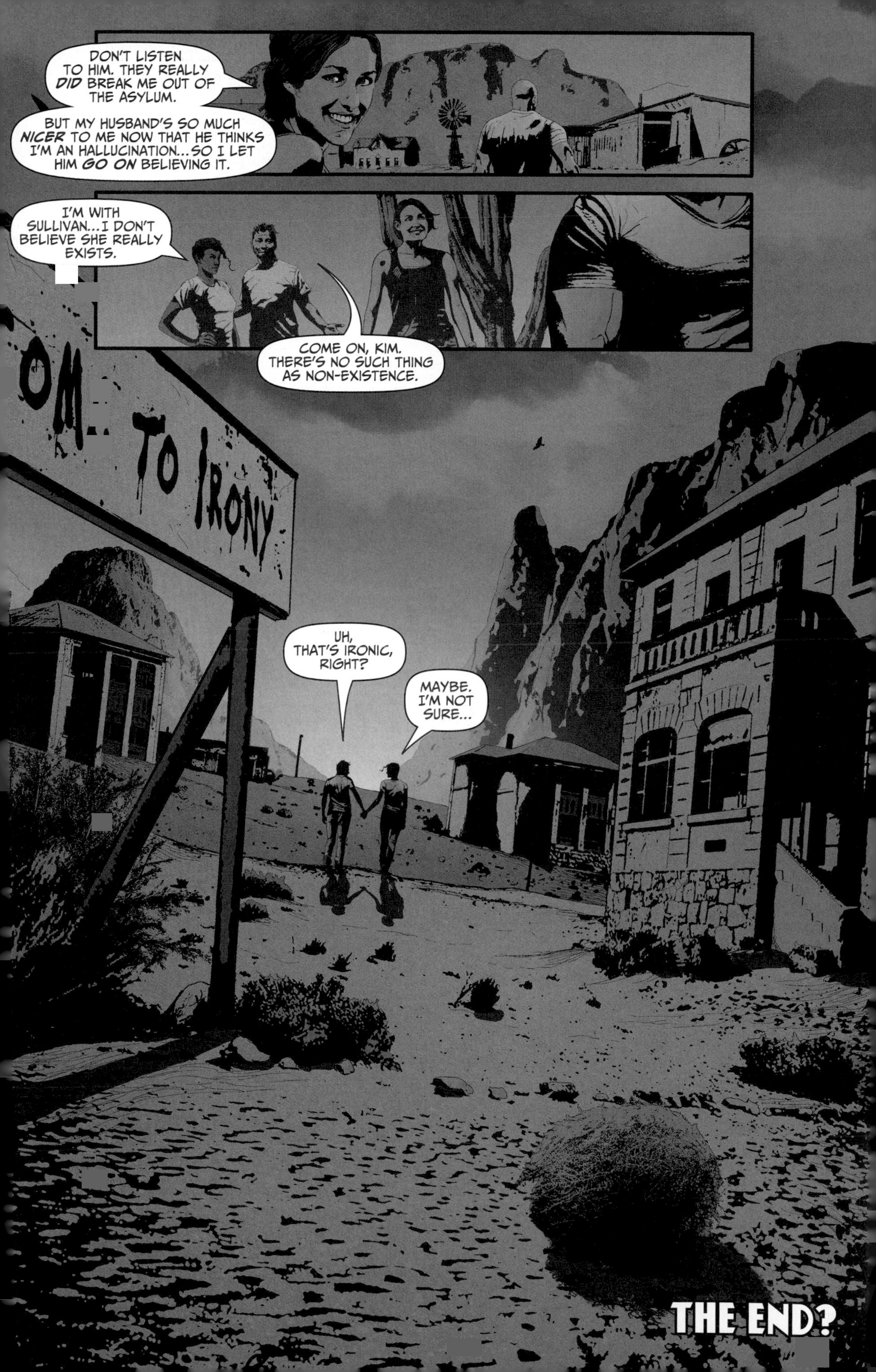
DON'T LISTEN TO HIM. THEY REALLY DID BREAK ME OUT OF THE ASYLUM.
BUT MY HUSBAND'S SO MUCH NICER TO ME NOW THAT HE THINKS I'M AN HALLUCINATION...SO I LET HIM GO ON BELIEVING IT.
I'M WITH SULLIVAN...I DON'T BELIEVE SHE REALLY EXISTS.
COME ON, KIM. THERE'S NO SUCH THING AS NON-EXISTENCE.
OM TO IRONY
UH, THAT'S IRONIC, RIGHT?
MAYBE. I'M NOT SURE...
THE END?

Jerry Stephens

I wanted Jerry to look like a weenie. Skinny, a bit of a belly, poor posture most of the time, etc. Then in some defining moments, we see that although not physically strong, he can be strong-willed. I tried to show that most in his eyes that would go from his usual lost puppy dog look to eyes of determination.

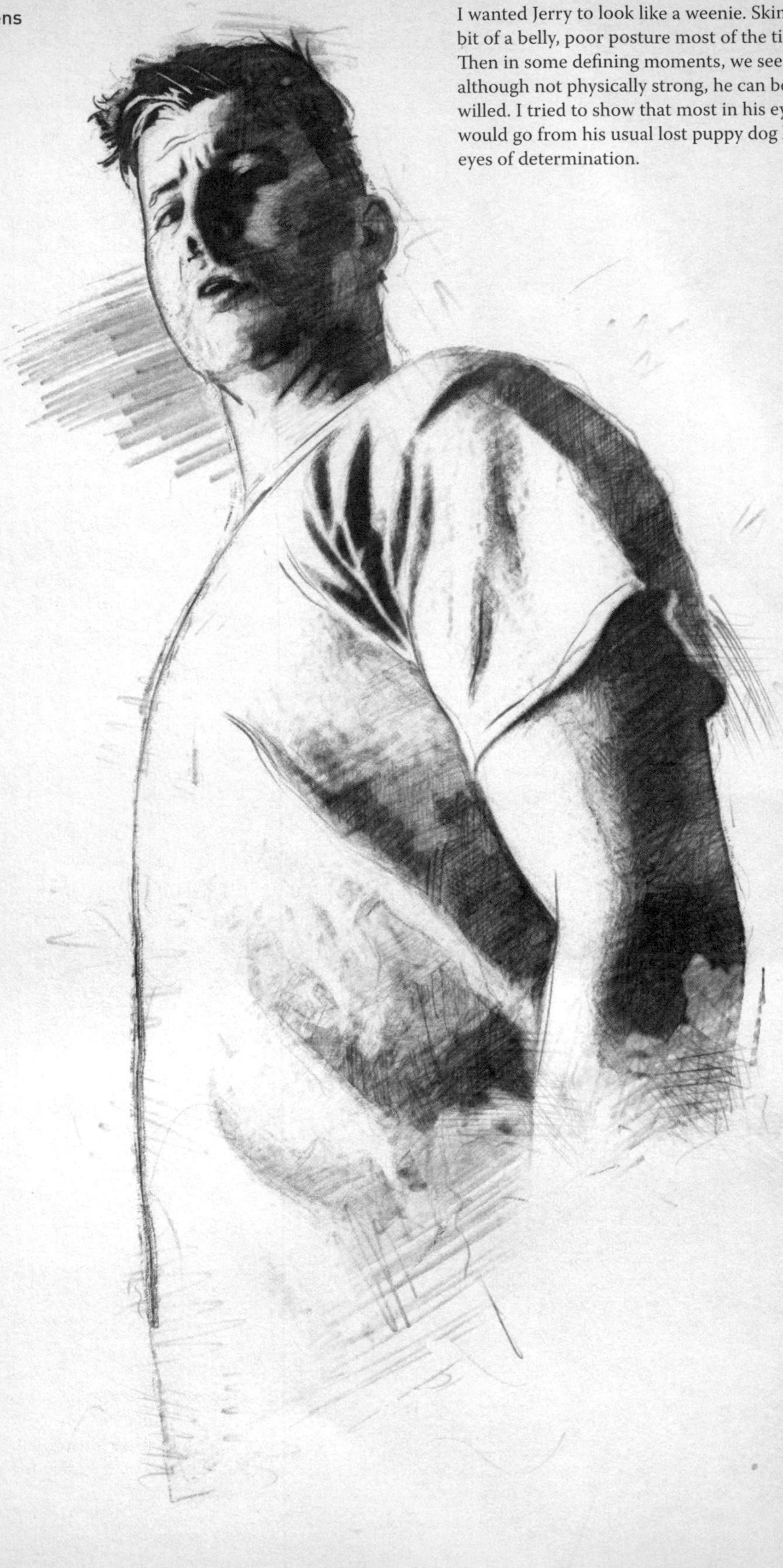

Kim

Peter's description was pretty clear-cut for Kim. However, since much of the time we see these characters in similar clothes to others around them, I felt I needed something to make her stand out. So I added the fun little bang that hangs down.

Agent Sullivan

I pictured Sullivan as a mountain of a man from the get-go. I actually wish I had made him look a bit bigger in some of the earlier issues, ah well. He's the extreme alpha male in contrast to Jerry. Sully, as I started calling him, was probably my favorite character to draw.

Agent McSmith

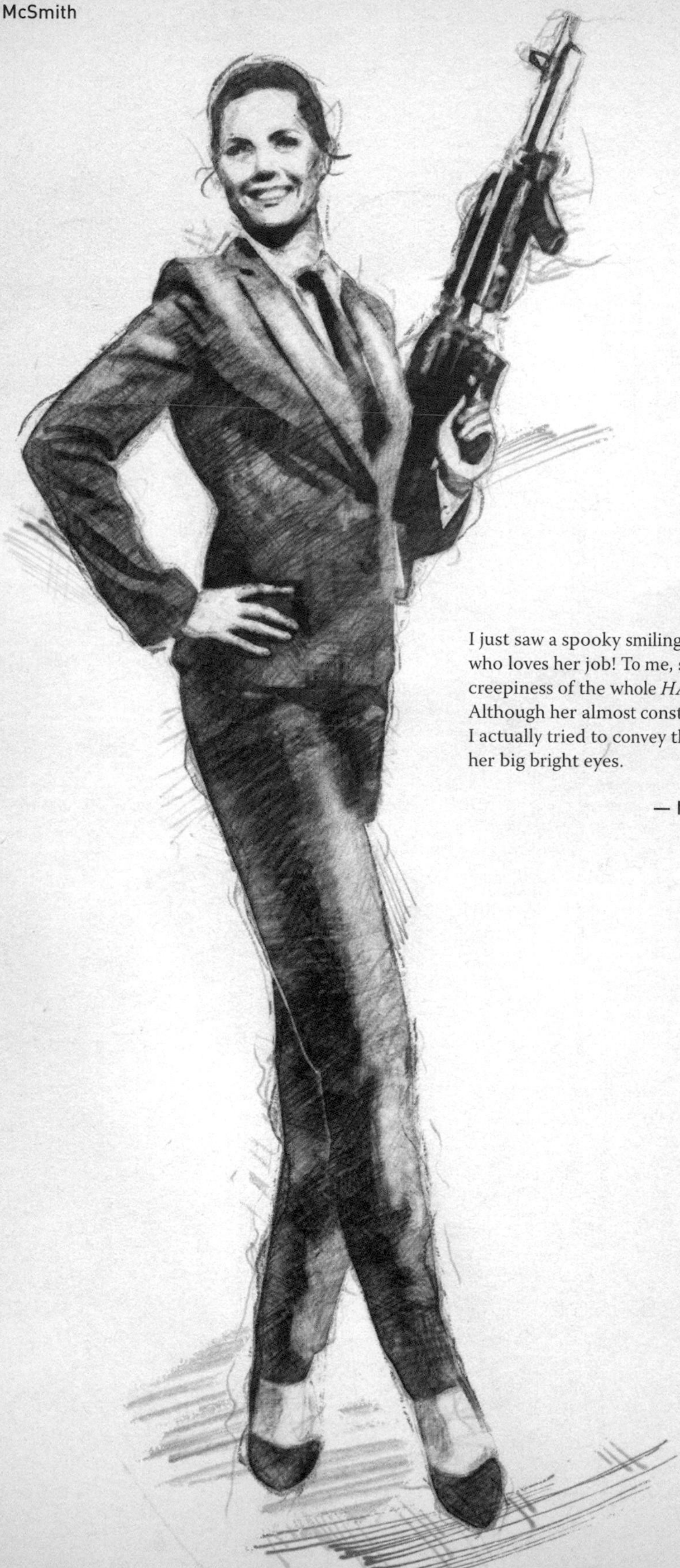

I just saw a spooky smiling cheerleader in a suit who loves her job! To me, she sums up the uber-creepiness of the whole *HAPPY HOUR* concept. Although her almost constant smile is offsetting, I actually tried to convey that creepiness more in her big bright eyes.

— MICHAEL MONTENAT

PPY HOUR #6, PAGE 10, PANEL 4 PENCIL ART by Michael Montenat

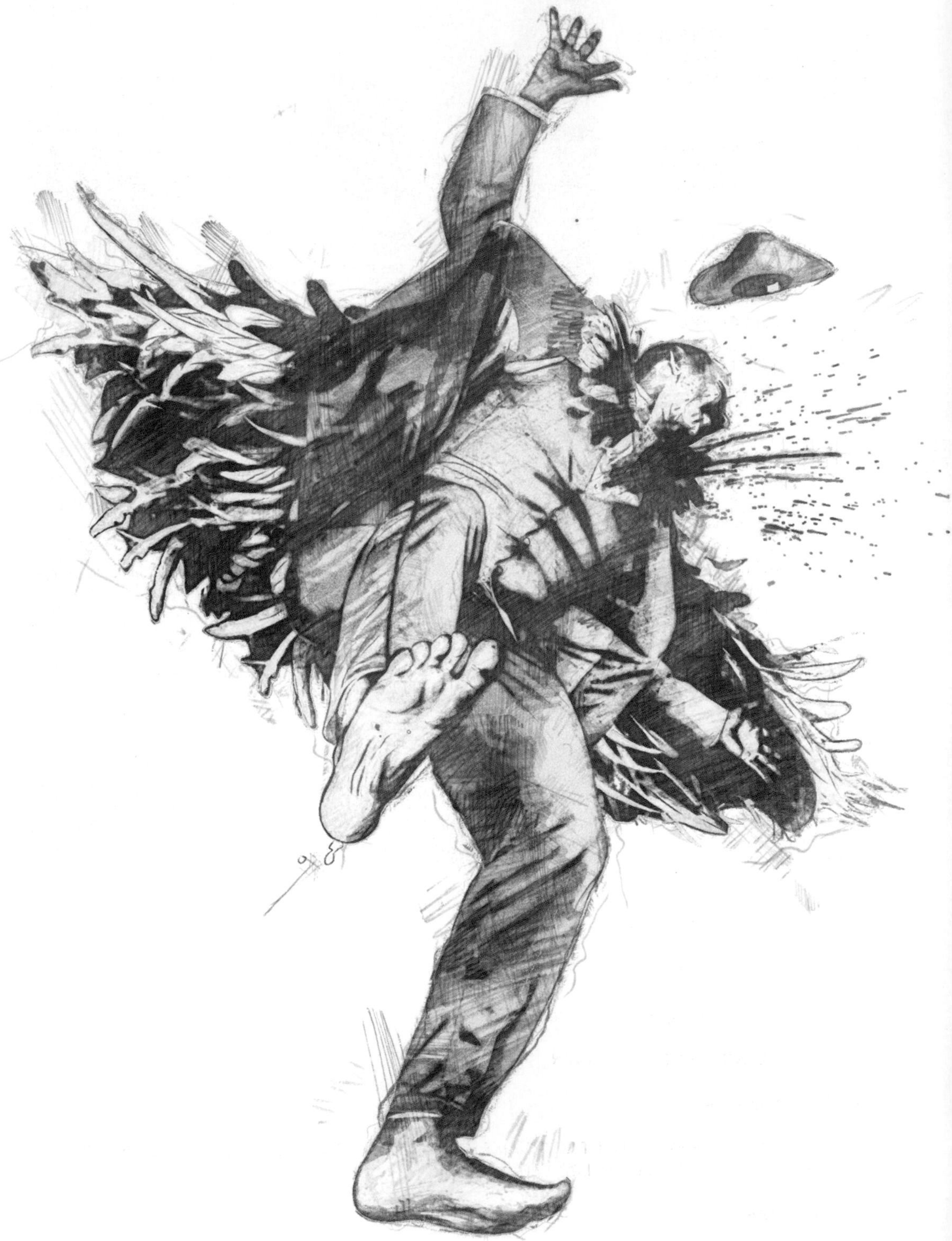

HAPPY HOUR #6

PAGE TEN

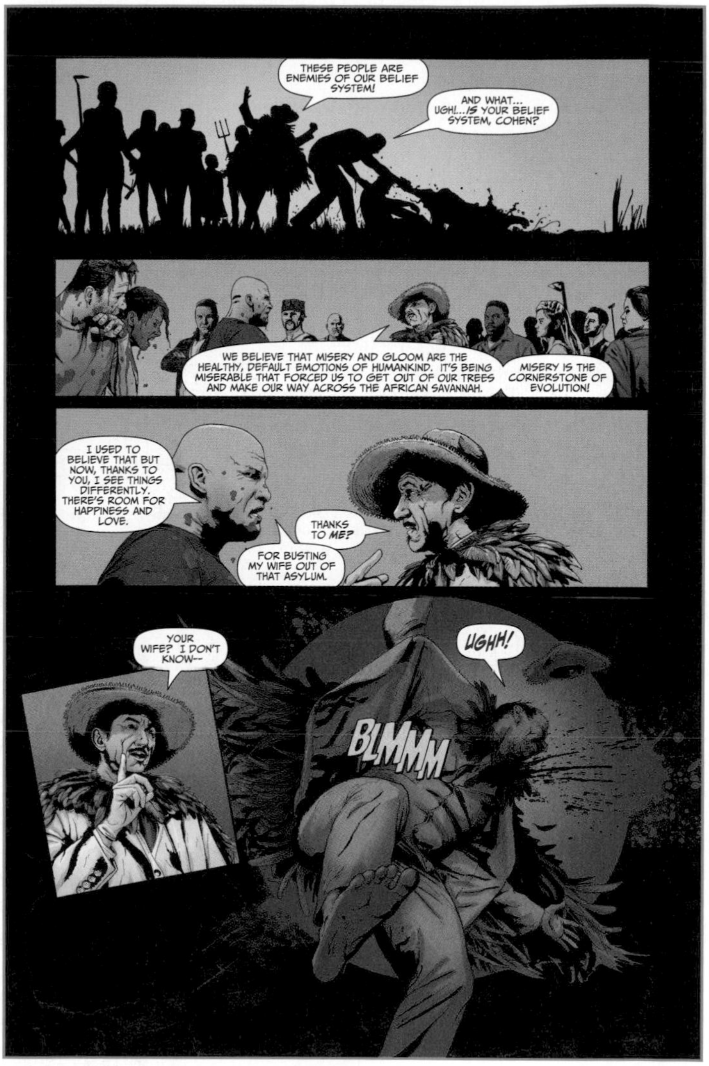
THESE PEOPLE ARE ENEMIES OF OUR BELIEF SYSTEM!
AND WHAT... UGH!...IS YOUR BELIEF SYSTEM, COHEN?
WE BELIEVE THAT MISERY AND GLOOM ARE THE HEALTHY, DEFAULT EMOTIONS OF HUMANKIND. IT'S BEING MISERABLE THAT FORCED US TO GET OUT OF OUR TREES AND MAKE OUR WAY ACROSS THE AFRICAN SAVANNAH.
MISERY IS THE CORNERSTONE OF EVOLUTION!
I USED TO BELIEVE THAT BUT NOW, THANKS TO YOU, I SEE THINGS DIFFERENTLY. THERE'S ROOM FOR HAPPINESS AND LOVE.
THANKS TO ME?
FOR BUSTING MY WIFE OUT OF THAT ASYLUM.
YOUR WIFE? I DON'T KNOW--
UGHH!
BLMMM

PANEL ONE: SULLIVAN PULLS JERRY AND KIM FURTHER OUT OF THE SWAMP. LANDOR IS ANGRY.

LANDOR: These people are enemies of our belief system!

SULLIVAN: And what...ugh!...is your belief system, Cohen?

PANEL TWO: SPLATTERED WITH SWAMP MUD, SULLLIVAN STANDS AND FACES AN ANGRY COHEN.

COHEN: We believe that misery and gloom are the normal, healthy, default emotions of humankind. It's being miserable that forced us to get out of our trees and make our way across the African savannah.

COHEN: Misery is the cornerstone of evolution!

PANEL THREE: THESE TWO ALPHA MALES IN EACH OTHER'S FACES.

SULLIVAN: I used to believe that but now, thanks to you, I see things differently. There is a middle way. There's room for happiness and love.

LANDOR: Thanks to me?

SULLIVAN: For busting my wife out of that Asylum.

PANEL FOUR: LANDOR GOES TO ANSWER.

LANDOR: Your wife--

PANEL FIVE: AND THE NEXT MOMENT, LANDOR IS BLOWN BACK OFF OF HIS FEET. BLOOD SPURTING FROM HIS CHEST WHERE A HIGH-VELOCITY BULLET HAS HIT HIM.

LANDOR: UGHH!

BIOGRAPHIES

One-time Entertainment Weekly Man of the Year ***PETER MILLIGAN*** was at the forefront of the revolution in comics for a more sophisticated, adult audience. *Shade, the Changing Man* for Vertigo offered a skewed look at American culture, while *Enigma*, *Face* and *Rogan Gosh* pushed the boundaries of what comic books could do. The hugely popular *X-Statix* was a radical reworking of the X-Men paradigm that led to controversy when Milligan tried to recruit the late Diana Prince of Wales into his celebrity-obsessed bunch of heroes. While the Princess Diana controversy raged, Milligan was perhaps the most hated man in Britain—at least among *Daily Mail* readers. Milligan was the longest-running writer of the cult horror comic *Hellblazer*, and his take on *Human Target* inspired the TV series. His latest works include the critical hit *Britannia*, about an ancient Roman detective, a retelling of *The Mummy* for Hammer/Titan, and the surreal *Kid Lobotomy* for IDW. Currently he is writing a new take the cult TV series *The Prisoner* for Titan.

MICHAEL MONTENAT is a digital illustrator and nerd whose work always tells a story, whether it be through comics or single illustrations. Montenat's work adds a gritty realism and texture to new characters as well as ones we all know and love. He has illustrated work for clients as varied as IDW, Top Cow, Legendary, Amazon's Jet City, Darby Pop, Boom!, Panel Syndicate and AHOY Comics' ***HAPPY HOUR***. He has also done work for the Dallas Holocaust and Human Rights Museum, country music star Zac Brown, military war veteran and news contributor Johnny Joey Jones, and Universal Studios Japan.

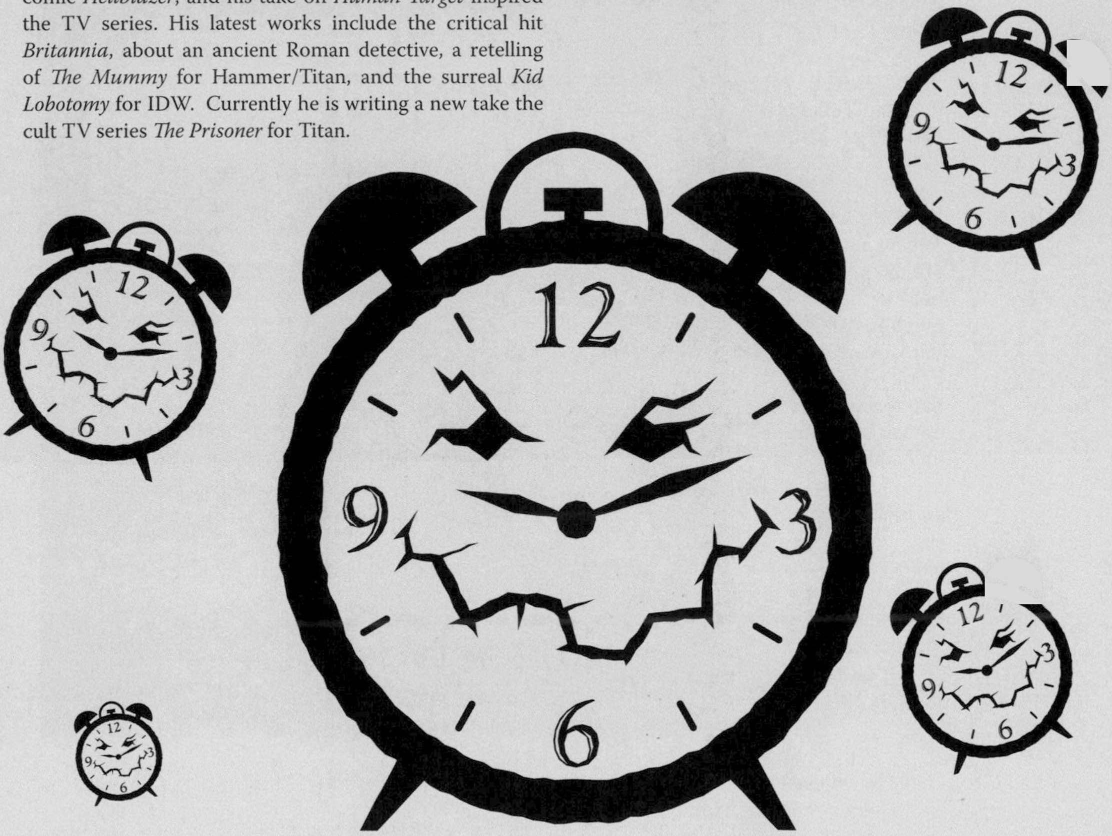

FELIPE SOBREIRO is a Brazilian artist and colorist. He has worked for all major comic book publishers, including Marvel, DC, Image, Dark Horse, IDW, Heavy Metal and others.

ROB STEEN is the illustrator of *Flanimals*, the best-selling series of children's books written by Ricky Gervais, and *Erf*, a children's book written by Garth Ennis.

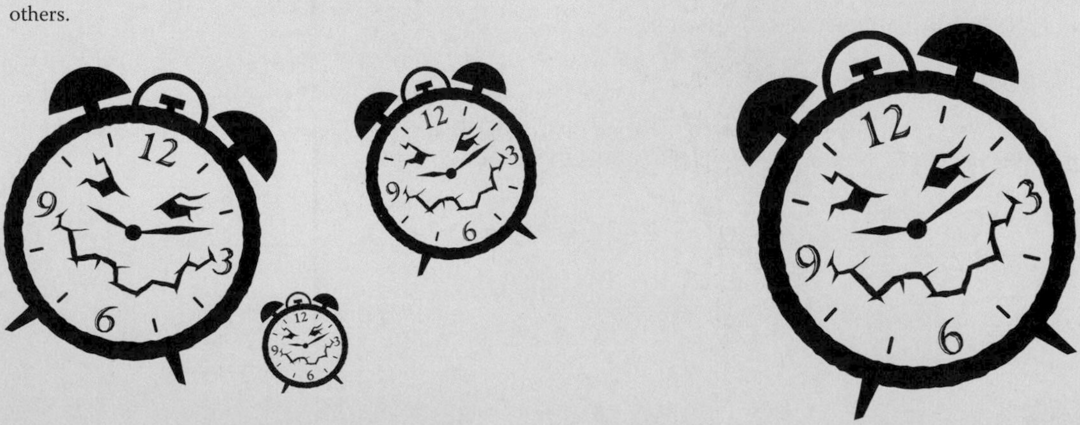